Also by Lu

THE BODY IN THE BACKYARD

LUCY SCORE

Bloom *books*

Published by Bloom Books, an imprint of Sourcebooks
P.O. Box 4410, Naperville, Illinois 60567–4410
(630) 961-3900
sourcebooks.com

Cataloging-in-Publication data is on file with the Library of Congress.

Printed and bound in the United States of America.
LSC 10 9 8 7 6 5 4 3 2 1

To Whitney and Shannon, two of the best neighbor friends a romance novelist could ask for!

1

*T*hey're coming."

The message vibrated with crystal clear intensity.

Trusting her spiritual adviser Gabe to handle the slow-moving roommates, Riley Thorn ran from the office, wiping dog slobber off her hands onto her jeans as she went. She needed to warn Nick, her tattooed, dimpled PI boyfriend, before it was too late. She flung open the front door in time to spy him parking her Jeep nose-to-nose with homicide detective Kellen Weber's police issue SUV across the driveway.

"*Woo-hoo! Finally some action! Lemme at 'em,*" the ghost of Riley's long-dead uncle Jimmy crowed from the Jeep.

Weber was already hunkered down behind the wheel well of his vehicle, wearing a bulletproof vest and loading a rifle with deadly-looking rounds.

"They're coming," she said through cupped hands.

"Get back in the house now, Riley," Nick ordered, hopping out of the driver's seat and rounding the back of the Jeep.

Just then, the distant *pop pop pop* of gunfire exploded, followed by the faraway whine of sirens.

"They're not going to get here in time," she whispered to herself as she was closing the door.

But she didn't do it fast enough. Burt, her burly dog, bolted through her legs, out the door, and off the porch.

"Burt! No!" she cried.

Tires squealed on the street.

Pop. Pop.

Swearing to herself, Riley slammed the door and raced into the yard after her idiot dog.

"Damn it, Thorn!" Nick growled.

She tackled Burt to the cold ground two feet from Nick as tires squealed again before giving way to the crunch and scrape of metal.

In an impressive show of strength, Nick grabbed her and Burt and dragged them behind the Jeep's fender. "Stay down," he ordered.

Burt's tail thumped happily against Riley's leg. "You're in big trouble when this is over," she told the dog.

Nick put a knee to Riley's back, holding her down. From her belly-level view under the Jeep, she watched as Harrisburg's morning news anchor and her regrettable ex-husband Griffin Gentry's snazzy sports car smashed through their gate…again. On his tail was a powder-blue Fiat with guns hanging out of both windows.

"Ready?" Weber yelled.

"Kick ass on one," Nick said. "Three…"

Free of the gate, Griffin's car accelerated, sending gravel flying.

"Two."

Riley watched in horror and braced herself as the car fishtailed before smacking soundly into the driver's-side door of the Jeep.

"One," Nick shouted.

2

1:41 p.m. Thursday, October 31

Riley Thorn's ex-husband hurling himself at her feet and begging for help had *not* been on her bingo card for this sunny Halloween afternoon.

The day had started off nicely enough with champagne, cake, and family for Nick's birthday.

And then about ninety seconds ago, the questionable roof on the crumbling mansion next door had collapsed, sending up a dust cloud that could be seen for blocks. Nick and Riley's historic house wasn't in much better shape, but at least it still had a roof. Which meant the migratory path of their elderly neighbors brought them and their dusty belongings right through Nick and Riley's front door.

But these were things Riley had grown accustomed to dealing with. Problems she could solve, discomfort she could weather.

And then her horrible ex-husband had appeared and ruined what had been, until that point, a salvageable day.

Now, Griffin Gentry, morning news anchor and lousy human being, was wrapped around her legs like an entitled boa constrictor while Riley waved her family off as they pulled out of the driveway. In her experience, fewer things ended a party faster than the sudden appearance of her ex-husband.

"You have to help me! Use your weird psychic mumbo jumbo or whatever you have to do. Just don't let me get murdered," Griffin whined against her thighs. He looked worryingly pale beneath the orange of his spray tan.

"Want me to poke all his pressure points at the same time?" Nick's cousin-in-law, the ferocious Josie Chan, offered from her battle stance next to her husband, Brian, on the front porch.

Riley shoved at Griffin's blond head and got a palm full of pomade for her trouble. "Not yet. Maybe later. Who's going to murder you, Griffin?"

Burt, Riley's pony-sized dog, trotted off the porch to sniff at Griffin's fussy suede boots. Apparently not liking what he smelled, Burt curled his lip in a doggy sneer and pranced off to pee on Griffin's car tire.

"Hey, Riley, I meant to ask, is that mean friend of yours around?" Kellen Weber called as he wandered out of Nick and Riley's front door. He winced, then leaned against one of the porch columns and used one hand to block the sun. The homicide detective was on day three of one hell of a hangover.

"Gentry, if you don't get your grubby child-size hands off my girlfriend in the next point three seconds, I'll be doing the murdering," growled grumpy PI and birthday boy Nick Santiago.

"What's this about murder?" Weber demanded. Even hungover, he was a no-nonsense, rule-following kind of man. Riley had a hunch he'd been the class tattletale in kindergarten.

"The guy's got his badge back for five seconds and instantly turns into the fun police," Josie complained. "I wanted to watch Nick beat the shit out of Griffin."

"Come on, babe. Let's go inside and make out instead," said Josie's husband and Santiago Investigations resident tech genius Brian Kepner. He patted his lap, and she hopped on before he guided his wheelchair around the porch toward the side entrance.

"We don't rent rooms by the hour," Nick yelled after them.

"Excuse me! I said I need your help, and you didn't automatically offer it. Now I'm confused." Griffin's off-air voice was two octaves higher than the one he used on camera, and it grated Riley's nerves like no other sound on earth.

"Point three. Point two. Point one," Nick counted down before shotgunning the rest of his champagne and tossing the glass into a pile of leaves. He grabbed the groveling Griffin by the scruff of the neck and hauled him to his feet.

"Nick, what are you going to do?" Riley asked in exasperation. She wasn't particularly worried for her ex-husband. After all, the man had sued her almost into bankruptcy for breaking his nose after she found him cheating on her in their own bed. But she didn't want Nick committing any crimes in front of an actual cop who would enjoy arresting him.

"I'm just gonna introduce his face to the river until the bubbles stop," Nick said as if it were the most reasonable thing in the world.

"Did you get new shoe lifts, Griffin?" Riley asked, frowning at Griffin, who looked ever so slightly taller. Though it could have been the fact that Nick was holding him on his tiptoes.

Mrs. Penny, followed by the rest of the dust-covered next-door neighbors, trooped out of Riley's house onto the front porch. They were all over the age of seventy-five, all eating birthday cake, and only some of them had managed to wipe the drywall dust from their bifocals.

"Somebody say *murder*?" Mrs. Penny barked. She was eighty years old, had purple hair, and had stopped giving a shit about thirty years ago.

"How about we all calm down?" Riley suggested.

"I won't hesitate to arrest you, Nicky," Weber warned.

"I'd like to see you try," Nick muttered as he grudgingly released the squirming news anchor.

"Darn it! I was hoping for some shirtless wrestling," Lily, the man-crazy octogenarian, lamented. Lily was a good cook, a great bridge partner, and a handsy admirer of the male form.

"Let's go get the rest of our stuff, and then I'll cue up some old WWF reruns for you," her twin brother, Fred, said. His crooked toupee was sloping over his forehead. Little dust bunnies hung from the bangs.

"Gabe, go with these guys and bring back my favorite couch and all my liquor. I need to get to the bottom of this murder business," Mrs. Penny said, gesturing at her aged cohorts.

Gabe was Riley's friend and spiritual guide, who worked with her to hone her psychic gifts. He was tall and muscular with flawless dark skin and a kind, Zen-like attitude that made him unrufflable.

"It will be my pleasure," he assured Mrs. Penny before following Lily and Fred in the direction of their disaster of a house.

"You people can't just walk into a collapsing building," Weber announced, pinching the bridge of his nose.

The neighbors pulled the hard-of-hearing card and made a beeline toward the looming dust cloud despite the official police warning. Weber looked back and forth between the departing pack of fogies and Nick, who still looked like he was about to commit a crime.

"Shit. Do not assault anyone until I get back," Weber ordered before jogging off after the elderly pack.

Sirens sounded in the distance.

Nick sighed and hooked a thumb in the direction of the roofless mansion. "Should I…"

"Oh yeah. Let me check." Riley closed her eyes. It took her more than a few seconds before she could shut out the multitude of external distractions and finally drop into her psychic Cotton Candy World. It was a dreamy, peaceful place that existed…well, somewhere that was definitely not reality. The fluffy pastel clouds served as home to her spirit guides, who passed mostly convoluted messages to her about the living, the dead, and everything in between.

"Hey, spirit guides. Is the house going to collapse on my friends and turn them into walking pancakes?" she asked.

The clouds pulsed a warm, cozy pink in response, and a sense of giddiness swooped through her. Riley guessed this meant a pancaking was not imminent. Suddenly, the clouds transformed into radiant sparkles.

Frowning, she opened one eye. "I don't think there's any danger. I'm feeling happy and seeing sparkles."

"Better not be another damn glitter bomb," Mrs. Penny said. She had icing smeared across her chin.

"You must be seeing this asshole's funeral," Nick quipped, nodding toward Griffin.

"That's really not very nice," Griffin complained.

"I'm not talking to you," Nick said. "Because if I *were* talking to you, I'd remind you that last time you were alone with *my girlfriend*, you asked her to be your mistress. I don't care if you're being hunted down by ISIS. Hell, I'll sell T-shirts that say DING DONG, THE DICK IS DEAD at your crime scene."

"But you *have* to help me! I'll pay you," Griffin squeaked. "How much do you want? A thousand dollars?"

"Pfft. I don't get out of the bathroom for less than twenty K," Mrs. Penny said.

"Fine. Twenty thousand dollars it is," Griffin said, reaching into his suit jacket pocket and producing a checkbook and pen.

"I'll take the case!" Mrs. Penny said, wielding her plastic cake fork in the air.

"The hell you will," Nick barked.

Mrs. Penny tossed her empty paper plate and fork over her shoulder. "Let's step into my office and discuss this primo case."

Nick stomped up to her. "A, you don't have an office here. B, we're not wasting our time on a nonexistent case. And C, no one here cares if this human sack of fertilizer gets whacked."

"Hey!" Griffin said, sounding offended.

Mrs. Penny crossed her arms over her generous bosom beneath her roomy Harrisburg Senators Baseball hoodie. "Bullet point number one, I'll share Riley's office. We'll get those cool partner desks and push them together like in the movies. Bullet point number two—"

"You don't have to say it like that. Pick one. *Bullet point* or *number*. Not both," Nick complained.

"The man said he's got twenty Gs. I don't know about you, but I get off the john for that kind of moola."

Riley quickly did her best to slam her mental psychic doors shut to prevent any accidental sightings of that particular scene.

"Great. Now I'm going to have that picture in my head for the rest of my life," Nick said.

"You're welcome," Mrs. Penny shot back. "Bullet point number three, last time I looked at *my* checkbook, it said you and I were partners, and this partner says we take this human bag of fertilizer's case."

Nick's blue-green eyes landed on Riley.

She shrugged. No one in the history of Mrs. Penny had been able to dissuade her from doing anything. "I don't know. He sounds upset. And it'll give Mrs. Penny something to do. I'll keep an eye on her."

Besides, not only did she not need Nick going to prison for murdering her deserving ex, but he'd promised to clean his office, and she was really, *really* invested in not attracting more vermin.

"Fine. Have at it, *partner*," he said to Mrs. Penny, then turned back to Riley. "I'm gonna go clean my office and pretend none of this mess exists. If this weasel breathes funny in your direction, you let me know. I'll take care of him."

Griffin swallowed audibly and sidestepped to the right until Riley was between him and Nick.

"My hero," she said on a sigh. "Come on, Griffin. Let's go inside."

———

It took a few minutes of vehicle jockeying to get everyone around Griffin's terrible parking job and another five minutes of staring at the roof collapse and police presence next door.

By the time Riley headed inside, Mrs. Penny had Griffin settled on one of the green faux leather chairs in her office and was delivering a glass of water…by sloshing it over the rim every three steps.

Riley's office was an organized room at the front of the house with tall windows, French doors that opened onto the side porch, the aforementioned visitors' chairs, and a utilitarian desk that wasn't so much an antique as it was just old and crappy. As the official office manager for Santiago Investigations, her days were spent scanning and filing paperwork, redirecting the elderly and the stubborn, and studying up on investigative techniques.

"I didn't have sparkling water, so I got it out of the tap and blew bubbles in it through the straw," Mrs. Penny announced, handing over the glass to Griffin.

"Psst."

Nick was peering at Riley through a crack in the door that connected their offices. Burt's nose appeared three feet below Nick's face.

Riley sidled toward the door. "Need a shovel?" she teased. His office had been ground zero for a recent investigation that had involved many late nights and mountains of old takeout containers.

"Might go with the leaf blower."

"Are you sure you don't want to hear what Griffin has to say? I can help you clean later," Riley offered.

"My mess, my responsibility. No one's out to get him. His kind always sails through life without paying for their assholery. Besides, if I listen to one more word that human donkey has to say, I'll end up stuffing his body into a UPS envelope and mailing him home."

"Understood. You deal with your natural disaster. And I'll deal with this one."

He reached over and nudged her chin up. "You do know you have no obligation to waste another second of your life on this idiot, right? I can detach Brian and Josie at the mouth and make them babysit."

"It's fine," she assured him.

"Are you one thousand percent sure you want to deal with this?" Nick asked again, concern lighting his eyes.

"I'm better at wrangling Mrs. Penny. Besides, a small mean part of me likes seeing Griffin freaked out," she admitted.

The double-dimple flash and quick grin from Nick had a swoop of giddiness resurfacing.

"That's my girl. If you need me for anything, especially an extra small UPS envelope, I'm one open door away."

"I appreciate the offer…and you not committing murder in our house. Especially since we just got the smell of the last one out."

A stack of sticky notes hit the back of Riley's head.

"Enough lovey-dovey chitchat! We've got an attempted murder to solve," Mrs. Penny bellowed.

Riley kissed Nick on his stubbly cheek, gave Burt a good scruff of the ears, then returned to take a sentry position behind the elderly woman, who had settled in behind her desk.

"Now what makes you think someone is trying to whack you? Put you in the ground? Turn you into worm food?" Mrs. Penny had to shout the last few terms for getting murdered over the groaning screech of a large piece of furniture being scooted across the floor in Nick's office.

"This!" Griffin reached into his suit jacket and slapped a piece of paper on the desk.

Mrs. Penny snapped her fingers and pointed. Riley bit back a sigh and reached over her to pick it up. "*You'll pay,*" she read aloud. "That's all it says. Where did you find it?"

"I found it after Bella and I finished filming the morning show today. We've been shooting it at home since the studio blew up because we live in a very large and spacious house. A mansion, really," he said, trying and failing to look humble.

"I remember. I used to live there," she said dryly.

"It was stabbed into *my* pillow on the bed. Can you believe that?"

Riley could indeed believe that. Griffin was a selfish jerk who had no qualms about trampling others to get what he wanted. The only thing stopping her from sending him packing right now was the authentic-feeling fear wafting off him like cartoon stink lines. The Griffin she knew was too self-absorbed to be afraid of anything.

"What the hell? I don't remember ordering curry," Nick muttered from the other room.

"Hmm." Mrs. Penny stroked her chin, then, discovering the icing there, licked her fingers. "Read it again. But make it scary this time."

Riley cleared her throat and delivered the line in her best threatening voice. "*You'll pay.*"

"Interesting. Read it again, but with a French accent," Mrs. Penny said.

"I don't think that's necessary," Riley said, putting the note down. She turned her attention to the trembling news anchor in the chair. "As far as threats go, this one seems kinda vague."

Nick walked past the open doorway headed for the front door, carrying a snow shovel and a cordless drill.

"But it's typed in all caps. Everyone knows that's more serious in death threats," Griffin whined.

"Why didn't you go to the police? You had a homicide detective right in front of you a minute ago, and judging from the sound of the sirens, there's a half dozen cars next door," Riley asked.

"The police are bozos. Griffin here wanted professionals, isn't that right?" Mrs. Penny said, scooting her chair forward until her ample bosom rested on top of Riley's desk calendar.

"Actually, I went to the police first. They've never punched me in the face or thrown me in a dumpster."

The man had a point. Nick had done both of those things.

"But *they* didn't take it seriously," Griffin continued. "They said it was probably just a prank."

Mrs. Penny slapped the desk. "They obviously missed the capital letters. Amateurs."

The front door opened again, and Nick backed inside,

holding up his hands. "Look. Can't we talk about this? Isn't there a nice roach motel you could stay at instead?"

In shuffled Mr. Willicott, the last of the next-door neighbors. He was wearing four hats and clutching an ancient accordion. Fred and Lily followed, carrying a hammock between them loaded with pantry supplies. Gabe was behind them, balancing a faded yellow sofa on one shoulder and lugging a crate of liquor bottles under his other arm.

"Put that in the bar," Mrs. Penny told Gabe.

"We don't have a bar," Riley reminded her.

"Then we'll hafta make one, won't we?" The elderly woman snorted and tossed her purple-tinged hair.

"Do *not* go up those stairs, Fred," Nick barked. "You better turn around when you get to the landing. Do *not* go up to the second floor! Damn it! Willicott, do not hang those saddlebags on Burt. Burt, do not carry his shit!"

Riley waved her hands to get Mrs. Penny's and Griffin's attention. "Okay. Let's get this circus back under the big tent. What makes you think this isn't a prank, Griffin? *Besides* the capital letters."

"Because immediately after finding the note, I went to the salon to get my usual, and *this* happened." He started to unbutton his shirt.

"What happened? Is this charades? Is it a movie? *The Exorcist*? *Monty Python and the Holy Grail*? *The Fast and the Furious: Tokyo Drift*?" Mrs. Penny fired off question after question as Griffin frowned down at his monogrammed Oxford.

"I'm unbuttoning my shirt. Expensive buttons are smaller than working-class buttons. It takes longer," Griffin explained.

Riley slouched against the filing cabinets and idly wished that she and Nick lived in a nice hut on a deserted island.

The racket in Nick's office kicked up a notch. She couldn't tell if he was running the vacuum cleaner or a leaf blower.

"You're boring me, Gentry. I don't like boring cases," Mrs. Penny warned.

"Just gimme a minute," he whined. Finally his petite fingers worked the last button free. "Does *this* look nonthreatening to you?"

In the middle of Griffin's chest hair was the letter *G* in hot-pink flesh.

Riley rounded the desk to get a better look.

"Is that your chest hair?" Riley asked.

"Shh!" Griffin pressed a manicured finger to her lips. "I'm a famous celebrity. I'm supposed to be hairless."

"Get your stupid fucking finger off my girl and put your goddamn clothes back on, Gentry, or I'm putting you in this wheelbarrow," Nick snapped from the doorway, where he was indeed pushing a wheelbarrow overflowing with trash bags.

Griffin dropped his finger from Riley's mouth.

"Lemme get a better look at this." Mrs. Penny huffed and puffed her way out of the chair.

"Did someone say *chest hair*?" Lily appeared in the doorway. Her pink housecoat was still covered in a fine layer of dust, and she had several serving spoons in each pocket.

"Take a look at this," Mrs. Penny told her roommate.

Lily motored in and planted her face two inches from Griffin's chest. She raised her glasses and squinted. "Hmm. What an interesting birthmark."

Nick returned through the front door with the now empty wheelbarrow. He glanced their way, shook his head, and stomped off, muttering about how much birthdays sucked.

"I don't understand what I'm looking at," Riley admitted.

"The wax dyed my skin," Griffin lamented. "The esthetician didn't notice until he got to the bottom. He always starts with a *G* for *Griffin*."

"And you think this is related to the note?" Riley clarified.

"Of course it is," Mrs. Penny said, elbowing her way in for a closer look. "Any idiot can see that."

Lily poked Griffin in the belly with her finger.

Riley stepped back and rubbed her temples. "Griffin, I

don't see how these things are connected. They both seem like pranks to me."

"There is nothing funny about defacing my body! Now use that creepy psychic woo-woo or whatever it is to solve this."

Riley had done her best to deny her psychic powers while married to Griffin. Nothing was more important to the man than appearances. She'd put so much effort into pretending to be normal that she'd ended up suppressing her gift until it became uncontrollable.

Now he wanted her to use it...and she wanted to punch him in his pink *G*.

"I'm telling you, this is bullshit," Nick called as he pushed another overflowing wheelbarrow load past the doorway again.

"And *I'm* telling *you,* as long as his check clears, I don't care," Mrs. Penny barked.

"These aren't pranks! Someone *shot* at me," Griffin announced.

"Before or after the capital letters?" Mrs. Penny asked.

Riley's nose twitched. "Oh boy," she muttered. Sometimes the stronger psychic visions came on too quickly to mentally prepare.

Suddenly, she found herself back among the cotton candy clouds. They parted to reveal a worried-looking Griffin behind the wheel with a pink hairless *G* poking out of his unbuttoned shirt. As he swooped his sports car around his circular driveway, a single shot rang out, and a nice neat hole appeared in Griffin's windshield several inches from his head. Riley watched from the clouds as the blood drained from his face. A high-pitched screech emanated from his mouth before his small foot mashed the accelerator.

The car shot across the cul-de-sac, taking out the neighbor's concrete corgi statue next to their mailbox, before he shifted into drive and fishtailed down the street.

Riley's stomach dropped as her body went into free fall. And then just as suddenly, she was back in her office, steadying herself on Lily's sturdy arm.

"Griffin, did you say someone *shot* at you today?" Riley asked.

"Oh yeah. I was very upset about my chest and forgot to mention that part when I got here."

"Nick!"

3

It could have been a small, bullet-size rock," Nick suggested, eyeing the hole in Griffin's windshield.

Of course the little prick had to drive an expensive little prick car. It stood out like a shiny luxury sore thumb in their driveway of weeds and overgrown shrubbery.

It served as an annoying reminder that he, Nick Santiago, had really slacked on his manly yard duties during the last case. Maybe he'd fire up the hedge trimmers in the garage. Shape some bushes. Cut off Griffin's fenders.

"Nick, it's clearly a bullet hole. Besides, I saw it happen in a vision," Riley insisted. His girlfriend had her arms crossed over her chest. She looked adorably not thrilled with this turn of events.

He wrapped his arms around her and brushed his lips over her furrowed brow. "If someone really did take a shot at him, would the world actually be worse off with no Griffin Gentry in it?"

"Nick!"

He grinned at the good-girl indignation that had come just a beat too late. "What? I'm not a cop anymore. I don't have to protect and serve every single body in the county. I became a PI so I could tell assholes they were assholes."

"That's not why you started your own business," she argued. "Besides, twenty thousand dollars is a lot of money. The last few months have been pretty lean."

Nick snorted. "We're fine. The business is fine. We don't need your ex's money. Besides, it's not like he's actually going to write a check and hand it over. The guy thinks he deserves everything for free."

The front door banged open, and Mrs. Penny limped out onto the porch, waving her cane in one hand and a piece of paper in the other. "Quit making out! We got work to do. I got a retainer!"

"Care to amend your statement, birthday boy?" Riley teased.

"What the hell is going on?" Josie asked from around the side of the porch, looking like a deadly bird of prey in head-to-toe black.

"Yeah, I can hear you through my noise-canceling headphones," Brian complained, wheeling himself around the corner behind his wife.

"Just the woman I wanted to see," Mrs. Penny said to Josie, stuffing the check into her bra.

"I'm definitely not depositing a cleavage check," Nick grumbled under his breath.

"I need a bodyguard," Mrs. Penny told Josie.

"Who'd you piss off this time?" Josie asked.

"Not for me. I can handle myself. Hi-yah!" Mrs. Penny kicked her orthopedic shoe three inches off the ground in a show of not-so-athletic prowess. "For our new client. His life is in danger."

"Yeah, from me," Nick said.

Riley gave him a squeeze. "Are you sure you're up for a physically demanding job in your condition, Josie?"

Josie's "condition" was pregnant.

"Yeah, aren't you, like, tired and nauseous?" Nick asked from his extremely limited experience with pregnant women.

Josie narrowed her eyes in a deadly glare. "I am perfectly capable of doing everything I could do before I started growing a human in my abdominal cavity. And if any one of you needs to be reminded of that, I'll be happy to rearrange your face."

Nick would have taken the threat as legitimate if a tear hadn't snaked its way down his cousin-in-law's cheek.

"What the hell is that?" he demanded, pointing at the offending eye water. Normal humans cried. Hell, Nick himself had gotten choked up in the first five minutes of the movie *Up* when his niece had forced him to watch it. But Josie wasn't normal or human.

"You okay, babe?" Brian asked, taking his wife's hand.

"If one more person asks me that, I'm going to…" She trailed off midthreat.

"Back over us with heavy equipment?" Riley suggested.

"Entomb us in the walls of our own attic?" Nick asked.

"Cry like a big dumb baby until your big dumb baby gets here?" Mrs. Penny tried.

Brian grabbed his wife around the waist before Josie could take a swing at the elderly woman.

"Well, this pregnancy is gonna be fun," Riley said out of the corner of her mouth.

"See? That's the fight I need in a bodyguard," Mrs. Penny said, pointing at Josie. "You're hired."

"I already work here." Josie's snarl turned into a sniffle.

"Look, Josie doesn't need to do security because we're not taking the case," Nick interjected.

"Twenty Gs says we are," Mrs. Penny insisted, glancing down at the check in her cleavage. "Well, the first five Gs at least. It's a down payment for services rendered."

"Twenty grand?" Brian repeated.

Josie quit struggling. "I like money."

Nick groaned. "You've got to be kidding me."

Riley cleared her throat.

"Not you too."

She shrugged against him. "Well, I think he *is* in some kind of danger, and wouldn't it be fun to take his money?"

Everyone else nodded in agreement.

"Seriously? Even if his check doesn't bounce, he's a litigious little shit. He'll sue the fuck out of us, and then I'll have to throw him in another dumpster," Nick reminded them.

"I have no problem with that," Mrs. Penny said. "Besides, my nephew or cousin's nephew or whatever is a killer lawyer. He'll sue the petite-cut pants off Gentry."

Everyone nodded and turned to look at Nick.

"Fuck. Fine. Take the case. But don't expect me to take it seriously. And if that tiny toadstool even attempts to make a move on Riley here, I'll be the one threatening his life," Nick warned.

"What could possibly go wrong?" Brian quipped.

A hunk of broken, bullet-ridden soffit fell from the porch ceiling, narrowly missing Mrs. Penny.

"You should fix that," she said, poking it with her cane.

"You're the one who shot it out last night," Nick reminded her through clenched teeth.

"Okay, people. Let's talk suspects," Brian said, computer balanced in his lap.

They had moved their growing investigative team and new client into the living room. Josie had liberated the newly cleaned rolling whiteboard from Nick's office, and Riley was manning the dry erase marker.

Mrs. Penny sat in a throne-like wingback chair while Griffin tried not to sink too far into the squishy sofa cushions. Burt made himself comfy on one of the window seats and was asleep within seconds.

Nick picked a seat on the other side of the room with his laptop so he could catch up on paperwork and heckle his team while they wasted their time.

He consulted his Get Shit Done list.

1. *Pay bills.*
2. *Fix broken windows.*
3. *Evict the elderly.*
4. *Birthday sex with hot girlfriend.*
5. *Take hedge trimmer to landscaping and Gentry's stupid car.*

"Who would want to take you out?" Mrs. Penny asked Griffin.

"No one! Everyone thinks I'm wonderful," Griffin insisted.

"Bullshit," Nick sang.

"Well, almost everyone," Griffin amended.

"You can't think of anyone that you've ever wronged? Anyone at all?" Riley prompted.

He shrugged his elfin shoulders. "No. I'm delightful."

Mrs. Penny popped out of her chair and yanked the shade off the nearest table lamp. She turned it on and shoved the bulb end in Griffin's face. "You better talk fast, buster."

"I–I don't know!" he squeaked.

"Okay, how about Claudia Mendoza, the morning show anchor whose job you took?" Riley suggested quickly before any eyeball–light bulb injuries could occur.

"Pfft. That was years ago. Besides, it wasn't personal. It was just business," he insisted.

"Griffin, you took the woman's job. She was fired because of nepotism," Riley said.

He scoffed, blinking at the light bulb in his face. "It wasn't anything like that. My dad just fired *her* so he could hire *me*."

"That's the definition of nepotism," Josie said dryly.

Riley wrote Claudia's name on the whiteboard.

"What about Bella Goodshine?" Brian suggested.

Riley was already adding the name when Griffin's pea brain sputtered to life. "You think my *fiancée* would ruin my perfectly chiseled chest with hot-pink dye? She loves my chestal region."

"I wouldn't be so sure of that," Nick muttered. He had

unequivocal proof that both the news anchor and his weather girl fiancée were cheating on each other every chance they got.

"You say something, boss?" Josie asked.

"Nope," Nick lied and entered the log-in for his bank. This birthday had gone downhill quickly. Maybe he could salvage it by cooking a nice quiet dinner for Riley and then—

A resounding crash echoed from the kitchen, followed by Lily's trilling, "Oopsie!"

Fuck. The geriatric circus from hell was going to put a cramp in his birthday seduction plans. He should have installed a moat.

"Griffin, sometimes you do things to benefit yourself that hurt other people," Riley continued.

"I have no idea what you're talking about," Griffin insisted.

Nick squashed the urge to hurl his laptop at the man.

"For instance, you cheating on your wife with the new, big-boobed weather girl," Josie said.

Mrs. Penny pointed to Riley. "Put your own name on the board."

"I already broke his nose for revenge. Besides, I have an alibi," she argued.

"We'll see about that," Mrs. Penny said.

Dutifully, Riley added her name to the list of suspects. She glanced in Nick's direction, grinned, then added his name.

Griffin gave a dismissive wave. "That's all water under the bridge. It was nothing personal. I'm Griffin Gentry. Everybody loves me."

"Not me. You suck," Josie said.

"I think you're a dick," Brian agreed.

"I hope you're run down in a crosswalk by a bus full of schoolchildren," Nick chimed in.

"Maybe it wasn't personal to you, but it might be personal to someone else," Riley said to Griffin with the patience of a saint.

Griffin's mouth puckered into a frown. "Are you saying not everyone thinks I'm incredibly handsome and talented and lovable?"

"For fuck's sake," Brian said under his breath.

"I'm saying there are consequences to your actions. You trample people to get what you want and don't give a thought to how it makes them feel," Riley said through clenched teeth.

Griffin was thinking so hard, Nick was surprised smoke wasn't pouring out of his ears. "So when I complained to the country club president about how the large waitress made me lose my appetite and it turned out she was just pregnant but they fired her anyway, you think *she's* mad at me?"

"That's *exactly* what I'm saying," Riley said.

"You're a terrible person," Brian said as he continued to type.

"You got a problem with pregnant people?" Josie held one protective hand to her belly and a gripped knife in the other.

"Let's not stab the new client until after his check clears," Mrs. Penny suggested.

Josie shook her head and looked at Riley. "I gotta ask it. We're all wondering it. What in the hell made you marry this fungal infection of a man?"

All eyes turned to Riley, except for Griffin, who was admiring himself in a compact mirror he'd produced from his pocket.

She blew out a breath. "Honestly, he wasn't always this bad. He didn't turn into this"—she waved a hand in her ex-husband's direction—"until he got his first Dilly."

"What's a Dilly?" Brian asked.

"Only the most prestigious award in local daytime television," Griffin said, snapping his compact closed.

"It was a fundraiser that spoofed awards ceremonies sponsored by Dilly's Sports Bar."

"I won Best Morning News Hair," Griffin said proudly.

"I take it the Dilly went to his head?" Brian guessed.

"Literally. He was standing on a desk chair with wheels trying to put it up on a shelf in his office. He lost his footing and fell off the chair, and the Dilly bonked him on the head. The doctor said it was just a mild concussion, but he was never the same afterward. We separated a few months later," Riley explained.

"That's almost sad," Brian said.

Nick snorted. "The only thing sad about it is now we're stuck with him for the time being."

"Hey, can one of you hold my selfie light? I need to take a picture of me being bravely heroic in the face of danger," Griffin asked, waving a small LED ring light.

Nick tuned out Gentry and his team and scrolled through the business's bank statement with a wince. His bottom line had fallen—make that plummeted—into the basement. Shit.

He pressed his fingers into his eyelids and looked again just to make sure he wasn't seeing things. Unfortunately, clearing his vision didn't distort reality. The bank balance was looking more like the allowance of a ten-year-old, not the cash assets of a business that employed actual people.

He'd shoved his head so far up his own ass that he'd completely neglected Santiago Investigations' financial stability. They were out of the black and into the red. The deep red. The next-week's-paychecks-might-bounce-and-the-electricity-might-get-shut-off red.

This was bad.

They needed a quick influx of cash. Like yesterday. He scrubbed his hands over his face and thought fast. High-stakes poker? Join a car-theft ring? Track down a high-dollar fugitive and collect the bounty? Sell a kidney?

"Maybe the person threatening me is a superfan?" Griffin suggested.

Nick closed his eyes and mentally screamed.

When he opened his eyes, he found Riley staring at him. Of course his psychic girlfriend could hear his inner screams.

He gave her a phony grin, a dumbass's thumbs-up, and pretended to be engrossed in his dwindling bank balance on the screen. Maybe he could sell his old Lego sets or that Kiss guitar pick Gene Simmons had spit on when they performed at City Island? Fuck.

Unfortunately, it looked like the best, most likely option for a quick payday was the orange-tinged Ken doll in his living room.

Maybe he could sell one of Griffin's kidneys?

Nick rubbed a hand over the back of his head. He needed to fix this and fast before anyone else found out. Instantaneously, Riley's gaze was on him. Her nose twitched. Then her eyes widened.

Damn it. Living with a psychic had its downsides. "Thanks a lot, tattletale spirit guides," he muttered under his breath.

"What was her name?" Josie asked Griffin while Riley continued to shoot Nick an embarrassed I-know-that-thing-you-don't-want-me-to-know look.

Griffin blinked. "Whose name?"

Brian groaned. "The server you had fired."

"How should I know? I don't bother learning the names of people who earn less than six figures a year."

The last thing Nick wanted to do was be dependent on Griffin Gentry for a payday. Okay, maybe that was the next-to-last thing. The *last* thing he wanted to do was let Riley down. He'd fucked up by obsessing about a cold case and turning down legitimate business. This was his mess and his responsibility to clean up. Even if it meant doing something so disgusting he could never look at himself in the mirror again.

Nick slammed his laptop shut and got to his feet. "People, let's cut this idiot…I mean *client* a break."

Riley raised an eyebrow and wrote *Unnamed Pregnant Server* on the board while everyone else glared judgmentally in Griffin's direction.

"Knew you'd get on board," Mrs. Penny said as she flopped down in her chair.

"Who else have you gotten shitcanned? Anyone you owe money?" Josie pressed, using the tip of her blade to clean dirt out from under her fingernail.

Griffin took an annoying breath. "Well, there's a jeweler that keeps harassing me, saying I 'stole' something. And then there's the guy whose pickup truck I nudged on the highway because he was going too slow. Oh, and this contractor keeps insisting that I pay her for the work she did to my backyard…"

———

"Oh! Then there's the car dealer president who actually thinks I should be making payments on the Porsche they loaned me. Can you believe that?"

Griffin "Shithead" Gentry had spent the last hour detailing how he'd swindled, blackmailed, and generally fucked over half the population of Harrisburg, Pennsylvania.

Nick had a blinding headache and a double eye twitch. The whiteboard and three pages of legal pad paper were filled with potential suspects. Mrs. Penny was snoring on the thing Riley called a divan, and the house smelled like charbroiled cookies.

"That's really all I can think of from the past two or three months…locally." Griffin looked like he expected a gold star.

Everyone seemed too dazed to break the silence. Well, everyone except for Mrs. Penny, who let out a sinus-rupturing snore.

Riley cleared her throat. "Well, that was…helpful. Thank you, Griffin."

"You're welcome. Now, if you'll just introduce me to my personal security for tonight's masquerade gala, I can be on my way. I have a massage in an hour."

"Masquerade gala?" Josie choked. She was the only one in the room who hated playing dress-up and making small talk more than Nick.

"It's a fundraiser for something about underprivileged children…or plants. I can't remember. Don't forget your masks! They won't let you in without one."

Josie turned a sly, shit-eating grin on Nick. "Gee, I'm real sorry, boss. We can't work tonight. Doctor's appointment." She pointed to her stomach.

"Looks like it's up to you or your partner," Brian said, nodding at the unconscious elderly woman kicking her orthopedic shoe in her sleep.

Nick could only begin to imagine the havoc Mrs. Penny would wreak all over some stuffed-shirt, black-tie shit show.

His birthday officially sucked. But there was no reason he shouldn't make it suck for Griffin.

"Personal security will run you another grand up front in cash," Nick announced. "VIP service for a VIP client."

————

"VIP?" Riley asked as she helped him wheel the whiteboard back into his office. Griffin was on his way to his massage with Josie as his security. Brian was tackling background checks on the first two dozen potential suspects. And Mrs. Penny was still sound asleep. The rest of their roommates were God knows where doing God knows what.

"Vacuous Ignorant Prick," Nick explained.

"Nice. Wow. It doesn't look as horrible in here," Riley noted, scoping out the room. He'd shoveled out most of the actual trash, reorganized his paperwork piles, and pried open the windows to let the fresh fall air overtake the stench of moldy takeout.

"What can I say? I'm a miracle worker," he said as he positioned the whiteboard in front of the windows.

"Soooo, what's with the sudden change of heart on Griffin's case?" she asked innocently.

He sighed and leaned against the desk. "I know you know, so you can quit pretending like you don't know."

"We need money," she said matter-of-factly.

"We're not move-into-a-cardboard-box destitute," he said defensively. "It's more like maybe-we-shouldn't-make-any-medium-size-purchases-or-we'll-have-to-cancel-our-streaming-services inconvenienced."

"Hmm," she said.

"What? No 'I told you so'? You're within your rights. I was a stubborn pain in the ass about finding Weber's sister."

She shrugged one shoulder. "It's not as much fun when you already know I was right. Besides, making you feel worse doesn't help the situation."

Nick tugged her in to stand between his open legs. "You're too good for me. I mean, I want you to know that I know that. But I also have no intention of letting you wander off to find someone more deserving."

Her smile made the knots in his gut loosen.

"How much do we need?" she asked.

"If the check in my pocket doesn't bounce and the cash isn't counterfeit, they'll temporarily stop the hemorrhaging."

Riley slid her arms around his waist. "I'm sorry we have to get dressed up and try to make sure no one kills my crappy ex-husband on your birthday."

"Look at it this way. He's not *your* problem anymore. Now he's *our* problem."

Her smile was soft. "You're a pretty sweet guy, Nick Santiago."

He brushed a kiss over her forehead. "Yeah. Yeah."

"So what are we going to do about outfits for the masquerade ball if we're moderately broke?"

"Leave that to me," he said with confidence.

"I'm not wearing lingerie to a gala," Riley warned.

"Okay fine. I'll come up with a plan B." His hands slid down to cup her ass. He gave her a firm squeeze. "We have some time before we should head out and interview fake suspects for a fake crime. Wanna go upstairs and—"

"Anyone seen my chainsaw?" Mr. Willicott, the best-looking and least lucid of the Bogdanovich mansion tenants, stood in the doorway, still holding his dusty-ass accordion.

"I will lose my mind living with these people again," Nick complained.

"It's only for a little while." Riley patted his chest and then pushed out of his grasp. "No power tools under my roof, Mr. Willicott."

Lily elbowed her way past her roommate. Burt trotted after

27

her, eyes glued to the plate in the elderly woman's hands. Lily shoved the stack of mostly burnt chocolate chip cookies under Nick's nose. "Does the birthday boy want a cookie?"

Nick sighed and picked up a blackened cookie. "Thanks, Lily."

4

G riffin lived on a cul-de-sac on the East Shore, where the houses were ostentatiously big, the yards professionally maintained, and the only people ever seen outside were housekeepers and nannies. His house was an imposing Greek mansion with White House–like columns and concrete urns on the front porch.

Nick parked on the street and scowled up the circular driveway, where Josie and the news anchor were recreating that morning's shooting.

"Do you want to help them?" Riley asked.

"If by 'them' you mean the person who took the shot, yes."

Nick Santiago was still all bantery charm, even when he was mostly serious about committing murder.

"Hehe. Good one. I like this guy."

Riley had inherited the Jeep and, with it, her uncle Jimmy's spirit. He'd passed away fishing on the river after eating one too many double-meat, hold-the-veg hoagies.

"At least Uncle Jimmy thinks you're funny," she said.

"I always liked the ghost of that guy. Let's go knock on some doors and see if anyone saw or heard anything. Maybe we'll get lucky and find the pretend attempted murderer so we can call it a day and go have birthday sex."

"Good plan."

They climbed out of the Jeep and headed for the property to the right of Griffin's.

"Do you know any of the neighbors?" Nick asked.

"I never met any of them beyond waving when they drove by."

An imposing stone wall surrounded the yard, and there was an open gate at the foot of the driveway. Unlike Griffin's golf course–looking lawn, this property was more garden than yard. Huge maples and pines blocked out the late fall sunshine. Beds of ivy, bushes, and boulders ringed the base of tree trunks.

There was a fairy-tale vibe to the place, but Riley wasn't sure if it was more pretty-country-manor-with-an-awesome-library or witch-who-eats-small-children.

"Maybe we should change out our lawn for an overgrown forest. Less mowing," Nick said, eyeing a bed of ferns.

Riley waved to the trio of people in green jumpsuits raking stone around the base of a bubbling fountain in the front yard. "Less mowing might not mean less maintenance. This place looks like it might take an army of landscapers to keep up."

The house was more stone and lots of glass. They followed a path made of slate slabs as it meandered to the portico and front door.

There was no doorbell, only a heavy gold knocker. Nick thumped it against the catch twice. "I feel like we're about to meet Batman," he said.

The woman who opened the door was definitely not Batman. She barely cleared five feet tall. Her brown skin was gracefully lined with age. Her salt-and-pepper hair was fashioned into a bulky bun at her crown, showing off chandelier earrings. A classy knit blazer hung regally from her shoulders.

Nick slid into lady-charmer mode and flashed the woman his dimples. "Hi. I'm Nick Santiago. This is my partner, Riley. We're investigating an incident that happened next door a few hours ago."

The woman rolled her eyes heavenward. "Now what did that Gentry twit do?"

"He experienced a hilarious chest-waxing incident," Nick said.

"And then someone shot at him in his driveway," Riley added, giving Nick a warning glance.

"Allegedly shot at him," Nick corrected.

The woman tilted her head conspiratorially. "Between you and me, I'm surprised it's taken this long. I've never met someone so vapid and self-obsessed. And that's saying something considering I used to live in LA. You might as well come inside. I'm Belinda, by the way."

They followed her across the threshold. The two-story foyer was a dark, cavernous space with huge beams and a chandelier that looked as if it could take out an eight-piece band if it fell. Belinda led them into a library cluttered with books, paintings, and knickknacks. Several shiny awards were tucked onto shelves and side tables.

Riley paused at the framed photo just inside the door. Belinda was on a red carpet posing between two people who looked an awful lot like Harrison Ford and Michael B. Jordan. On second glance, she was almost certain they were the real deals.

Their hostess gestured toward the low leather sofa in front of the marble fireplace. "Please, sit. Would you care for some refreshments?"

Riley was just shaking her head when Nick said, "Well, it *is* my birthday."

Amused, Belinda turned toward the doorway and bellowed, "Thomas, we require treats!" She turned her attention back to Nick and Riley. "Now I suppose you'll want to know if I own any firearms, where I was at the time of the shooting, and whether I have any experience with body waxing. And since you're not a cop, you're hoping I'll still provide you with answers."

"You've either committed a lot of crimes or done your research," Nick said.

Riley's nose twitched, and suddenly she was transported into a room where several people were gathered around the table. A younger-looking Belinda stood at the head of the table, holding what appeared to be a wickedly long blade. "I told you! Carotids are a messy business. It's called arterial *spray* for a reason." She made a slicing motion that had Riley flinching and flying back into her body.

Belinda gestured at an acrylic frame on the coffee table. Inside it was a stack of bound papers titled, *The Man behind the Badge*: "Pilot." Story by Belinda Farnsworth.

"It comes with the territory for the showrunner of a police procedural in the nineties," she said.

"Seriously? I loved that show," Nick said.

"So did I," Belinda said and leaned back in her chair.

Riley relaxed. Just because the woman had shown a bunch of TV writers how to slit a throat didn't mean she was capable of murder in real life.

A man in jeans and a tight-fitting T-shirt appeared in the door carrying a wood tray with mugs, a carafe, and a platter of cookies. "This is my chef, Thomas. He stands between me and too many hot wing deliveries."

"Thanks for the goodies, Thomas," Nick said, diving for the cookies. "So where were you today between twelve thirty and one fifteen p.m.?"

"I was looking disheveled on a conference call here in my study after returning from a trip this morning."

"Coming back from vacation?" he asked, taking another cookie.

"I was addressing a hotel ballroom full of aspiring authors in Philadelphia yesterday and spent the night. The car service delivered me here promptly at noon. Thomas served me a delightful lunch of salmon, wild rice, and mixed greens, which I inhaled with no manners before joining a one p.m. video conference with some producers on the West Coast. That call lasted an hour, and Thomas brought me coffee in the middle of it, so he can confirm my whereabouts."

Nick looked pointedly at Riley and nodded toward Belinda.

Riley sat up straighter. He was letting her take a crack at a witness. "Um. How well do you know Griffin Gentry and Bella Goodshine?"

"Well enough to know they're the kind of neighbors you don't want to have a dispute with over garden statuary and that you're the ex-wife he left for the weather girl."

"Ah. Yes. Well, you didn't live here when I did, so I didn't know...if you knew..." Riley was definitely going to review her interview techniques textbook when they got home.

"What kind of statuary?" Nick asked, smoothly retaking control.

"My next-door neighbor commissioned a twelve-foot-tall statue of himself, which I highly doubt is to scale seeing as it's nude," Belinda reported. "The, shall we say, 'generous' genitalia was pointed at my house, and when I went next door to request they at least point it in a different direction, Griffin explained it was his gift to the world and then tried to hand me a signed headshot."

"Did you think maybe he deserved to get his chest waxed and then possibly be shot at for that?" Nick prompted.

Belinda scoffed. "And give up all this? Of course not. I may write about murder, but I certainly don't try to commit it. If I did, I wouldn't be so sloppy. I simply annoyed his lawyer with my lawyer until they came to an agreement, which took much longer than it should have. But I was motivated to teach the man-child a lesson."

"How long ago was this?" Riley asked.

"It started about a year ago, and it took six months of back-and-forth with his attorney. Griffin ended up not moving the statue since it was important to him to see it when he wakes up every morning. So he had a contractor build a pergola over it. At least now I'm no longer traumatized when I venture into my own backyard."

"You played double-dimple charming boy toy in there," Riley said as they headed back down the driveway. The landscapers were gone, but there was a Summer Daze Pools van parked next to a cleaning service car by the garage.

"Gotta read your suspect and adjust your approach accordingly," Nick explained.

"Do you think she did it?" It was hard for Riley to imagine the seventy-six-year-old scaling her own stone wall to take a shot at a moving vehicle. But it was Harrisburg, Pennsylvania, and it was Griffin Gentry, so anything was possible.

"She stays on the list since she was here—opportunity. She lives in close proximity to Griffin and had a legal dispute with him—motive. She also has the cash to hire someone to do her dirty work—means. But her cookies were good, so I'm inclined to put her lower on the list. Thoughts?" Nick prompted, scanning the yard.

"I got a quick peek at her showing a room full of people how to slit a throat. But I'm pretty sure it was just for a TV show."

"Interesting." Nick took her hand. "You know what else interests me?"

"My boobs."

He gave her a lecherous grin. "Always. Also, traffic flow."

"It's a cul-de-sac. There isn't really much traffic," Riley pointed out.

He shook his head. "I mean the people. Between the gardeners, the chef, and the pool people, that's a lot of coming and going through that gate. This place probably requires constant maintenance."

"Which means she leaves the gate open," she speculated.

"Exactly."

They left the wild garden of Belinda's yard behind them and stepped onto the street. "What kind of a person leaves a threatening note, plays a chest hair prank on someone, and then tries to shoot them?" Riley wondered.

"A weirdo. The world is full of them."

Josie and Griffin were nowhere to be seen, so Riley and Nick headed for the wood and stone mansion across the cul-de-sac.

No one answered the door at that house or the next two, which brought them to the brick Georgian revival on the other side of Griffin's place. It was situated much closer to the property line. An eight-foot-tall privacy fence divided the yards. There was still fresh dirt around the fence posts.

They hiked up the dozen skinny steps to the home's front porch, which was completely barren. No potted plants or rocking chairs or welcome mat.

Nick stabbed the doorbell. It was one of the video ones that lit up when they approached.

"What?" snapped a gruff voice.

"I'm Nick Santiago. I'm a private investigator looking into an incident next door."

There was a pause, then the voice asked, "Is he dead?"

Nick and Riley exchanged a look. "Not yet," Nick said.

"Hold on. I'll be right down."

It took two long minutes, but the front door finally swung open to reveal a disheveled white guy in silk pajamas and a red velvet bathrobe. His blond hair was graying at the temples and stood up in tufts. He had a hard mouth, a soft jaw, and a decent paunch straining the buttons of his pajama top.

"Well? What happened? Was he at least maimed? Horribly disfigured?" he asked, sounding out of breath.

"Sir, can we come inside?" Nick asked.

The man immediately blocked the door with a suede slipper. "No."

"Is there any reason you can think of that someone would want to maim or disfigure Griffin Gentry?"

"I can give you fifty reasons in one breath, starting with that ridiculous fucking farce of a news show filming here five days a week and making enough racket from four a.m. on to drive any normal citizen insane."

Now that he mentioned it, Riley noticed the man's blue eyes were bloodshot. The bags under them looked like they wouldn't fit in a plane's overhead compartment.

"So you're losing sleep because of Gentry," Nick summarized.

"Losing sleep? Losing *sleep*? I'm being driven out of my goddamn mind! It doesn't matter how many sleeping pills I take, I still wake up the second all the car doors start slamming. Slamming! In the middle of the night. Do you know how many doors slam every fucking morning? Seventeen! Then there's the lights. Good God, the lights, man! They aim them through the windows directly into my bedroom! It looks like a thousand suns. How is a man supposed to sleep through that?"

"Have you tried an eye mask?" Nick asked glibly.

"Eye mask? An eye mask?" He stabbed a thick finger into Nick's shoulder. "My life is ruined, and you think an eye mask will help?"

Riley couldn't get a lock on any of his thoughts. It was like standing in the middle of a chaotic windstorm trying to catch a leaf. All she was picking up on was a confusing swirl of rage, exhaustion, and a creepy wired energy.

"Where were you today between noon and one o'clock, sir?" Nick asked coolly.

The man's face was turning beet red. "I'll tell you where I was! I was breaking into my ex-wife's house so I could steal my son's ADHD medicine so I don't sleep all fucking day, because Griffin Gentry is a monster. They called *me* a monster, but I'm a koala bear next to that son of a bitch."

"I think it's just *koala*," Nick said.

Riley cleared her throat delicately in case Nick didn't know he was very close to pushing the guy over the edge.

"What?" the man shrieked.

"Yeah, they're not called *koala bears*. Just *koalas*."

The homeowner shoved his hands into his hair and gripped. "Do I look like I give a damn?"

Riley took a step back just to make sure she was out of the danger zone.

"Actually, you look like you went on a cocaine bender then stuck a fork in an electrical outlet," Nick said.

"First of all, three bumps of coke is *not* a bender. Second, you can tell me what happened to that selfish prick next door—and it better be good. Or you can get the hell off my property before I call the cops."

"I'm afraid I can't discuss an ongoing investigation," Nick said cheerfully. "But you have yourself a nice day, sir. Maybe try getting a little shut-eye?"

"Go fuck yourself!"

The man slammed the door so hard that instead of latching, it bounced back and smacked him in the forehead. "You can fuck yourself too," he shouted at the door; then leaving it open, he stormed off inside.

Riley cocked her head. From the back, he looked a little like Griffin. They had the same rich-guy haircut and color, the same shoulder width. But he had a few inches in height on the news anchor.

"Did you notice that?" Nick said, leading them off the porch and back toward the road.

"That he looks like Griffin from the back?"

"No, that the front room was completely empty. No furniture, no pictures. There was a bunch of men's shoes lined up at the foot of the stairs. Looks like he lives alone."

"Gee, I can't imagine why," Riley quipped. "We didn't even get his name. What do we do now?"

"Brian will track him down through property records and start a deep dive into Mr. Grumpy Pants."

"How did you know he wouldn't punch you for annoying him?"

He slung an arm around her shoulders. "It was a risk I was willing to take."

"So you just provoked our potential bad guy into a murderous rage?"

Nick looked remarkably unperturbed. "If I did, this case will be closed before the end of the day."

"Or Griffin will be dead," she pointed out.

"I won't let him get murdered until he pays up."

"That's comforting."

5

I thought you said we were going shopping for masquerade outfits?" Riley was feeling skeptical as Nick led her and Burt up the steps of the town house with a rainbow welcome mat.

The dog stuck his face in the planter of flowers, his long whiplike tail joyfully whapping Riley across the backs of her thighs.

"Trust me. I've got a guy," Nick said as he rang the doorbell.

"Also, you didn't tell me this was a dress-nice outing," she complained. Her jeans and thermal shirt seemed too casual next to Nick's fitted polo and butt-hugging trousers. A woman on the sidewalk had walked into a trash can when Nick got out of the car.

"Anyone asks—especially the guy who answers this door—I dress like this all the time," he warned.

The slap of flip-flops approached the other side of the door before it opened to reveal a trim white guy with a tidy mustache, short graying hair, and a pair of expensive-looking headphones around his neck.

"Nick Santiago," the man said, putting a hand on one hip. "You're looking delicious."

Nick tugged on the collar of his shirt. "Thanks. I dress like this all the time now." He gave Riley a nudge.

"Uh, yes. I can confirm. He even sleeps in his Dockers."

"Too far. Too far," he muttered from the side of his mouth. "Okay, let's get this over with. Alistair, this is my girlfriend, Riley. Riley, Alistair. We need you to play fairy godfather."

"A fairy godfather request *and* I finally get to meet the infamous girlfriend?" Alistair said with an approving nod at Nick.

"Oh my God! You're *the* Alistair! I'm a huge fan of your makeover work. I used to work with Downer Daryl after his divorce. The whole office was so happy once you got him showering again."

She shook his hand enthusiastically while Nick looked at her as if she'd lost her damn mind.

"My reputation precedes me. Come in, come in. Tell me more about this fairy godfather favor."

Burt let out a low *woof* at a passing bumblebee.

"Is that a medium-size pony?" Alistair asked.

"Oh yeah. This is Burt. He's a dog," Nick said.

"But we also think he's part human. He kind of goes where we go. I can wait outside with him if your house—which I'm assuming is really awesome—is not large-dog friendly," Riley offered.

"Bring him along. Just don't let my husband see him. Danny is Team Pets That Fit in Aquariums."

"Behave yourself, Burt," Nick warned. The dog gave him a baleful look and trotted inside.

"This is so exciting," Riley whispered to Nick as they followed him inside. Alistair's town house was actually two units opening into each other, providing a large living and dining space with a massive kitchen at the back. Everything was designer-magazine perfection.

"You have good timing. I just finished up my last chapter for the day," Alistair said, pulling a pretty glass pitcher of cucumber lemon water from a huge stainless steel refrigerator.

Burt poked his nose into a brass umbrella stand holding a plume of peacock feathers, then sneezed.

"Alistair narrates audiobooks when he's not improving the men of Harrisburg," Nick explained.

"It's not quite as exciting as being a private investigator, but it's an entertaining way to pay the bills." Alistair poured water into three tall, skinny glasses. He topped each one with precise slivers of lemon before distributing them.

Nick sniffed his glass with suspicion while Alistair filled a crystal bowl with tap water and put it on a silk place mat on the floor for Burt.

"Drink it," Riley hissed at Nick.

"I like my water unfancy and unfruited," he complained under his breath.

"We're about to ask *the* Alistair to Cinderella us. Drink the damn water."

Nick took a sip, and his face contorted. Riley stepped on his foot.

"It tastes like a salad."

"Now, what can I do for you…uh, three?" Alistair asked, glancing down at Burt as he slurped and snorted his way to the bottom of the bowl.

"We're doing private security at some adult prom for rich, boring people," Nick said.

"We've been invited to a black-tie masquerade gala tonight," Riley corrected.

"Ah, the masquerade. How exciting to mix and mingle with the elite of Harrisburg," Alistair said.

"Now I wanna go even less," Nick said.

"We don't have anything in our closet that's masquerade appropriate," Riley explained.

Alistair clapped his hands. Burt looked up questioningly from his crystal bowl, water streaming from his jowls. "This is my *favorite* kind of favor."

Riley nudged Nick and tilted her head at the slobber tsunami. He rolled his eyes, then oh so casually swiped what looked like a Burberry tea towel off the oven handle. "Is that a new expensive but cool thing?" he asked, pointing at the built-in bookcase in the dining room.

"What a good eye you have. Danny and I picked that up in Venice last month," Alistair said, turning to admire the twisted black vase on the shelf.

Nick dropped the towel on the floor and swished it through the puddle with his foot.

"And look at this cheeky fellow we found at an estate sale," Alistair said.

They followed him across the room and pretended to admire the miniature cast-iron chimpanzee baring its teeth in a demonic grin.

"Oh! Company, how ni—"

The greeting came from the man Riley presumed to be Alistair's husband, Danny. He was tall and a little bulky with pale freckled skin and salt-and-pepper hair. His sentence was cut short when his Birkenstock hit a puddle.

"Ahhh!" Danny went airborne and landed on his back with an *oof*.

They raced to his aid, but Burt got there first with his tongue lolling and front paws on Danny's chest.

"Al? Why is there a pony in our kitchen?" he demanded.

Burt gave Danny's face a hearty slurp.

"Oh good. You've met Burt," Alistair said.

"You're not taking us to some empty building to get murdered, are you? Because that will piss me off," Nick said as he helped Riley out of the back seat of Alistair's hybrid Lexus. The parking lot of the Krevsky Center, a muraled brick building on Sixth Street, was empty except for a dented minivan with a bumper sticker that read *Sewciopath*. Burt hopped out and immediately jogged off to water a bush.

"I'm creatively solving your problem," Alistair insisted as he led them to the back door of the colorful brick building. He produced a key from the pocket of his gray linen trousers and opened the metal door.

Burt muscled his way inside first.

"Don't go investigating," Riley called after the dog as she followed him into the building. It was dark, and the air had the musty tang of concrete floors and sawdust.

Alistair flipped a light switch, and overhead lights snapped on high above their heads. "Welcome to your VIP backstage tour of Theatre Harrisburg."

Stacks of painted scenery flats and show posters leaned against studded walls. Clothing racks of period costumes were clustered in front of storage rooms constructed from chicken wire and two-by-fours. Along one wall was a trio of makeup vanities. Burt was snuffling his way through a collection of feather boas.

Nick gallantly pulled Riley behind him as he scanned the space for threats. "This place smells weird, like...history," he observed.

Alistair waved toward a door nearly hidden on the black-painted block wall. "Follow me, my little ducklings. This is where you become swans."

At the word *ducklings,* Burt raced to Alistair's side.

"He's definitely going to murder us," Nick decided.

"But hopefully he'll make us look good first," Riley said.

"Robeena, my dear nemesis. I've come to collect on that favor," Alistair called.

"What the fuck is with the lion? We're not staging *The Lion King* until next year," rasped a very pale white woman with heavy eye makeup and a partially shaved head. The hair that hadn't been shaved was swept to one side and dyed a silvery purple. She had a vape pen clamped between her teeth and glasses on a thin chain propped on top of her head. Burt sat at her feet, staring at her expectantly.

Nick ducked behind Riley. "She looks like that sea witch from that fucking mermaid movie."

"Ursula from *The Little Mermaid*?" Riley asked.

She felt a full-body shudder roll through him. "Yeah. My niece made me watch that movie a thousand times, and Ursula scared the shit out of me every time. She *stole* her *voice*."

Riley had a sudden vision of Nick cowering under a unicorn blanket next to his bespectacled niece, Esmeralda, who was absently patting his leg while Ursula belted out her musical number.

"It's okay. Burt and I will protect you," she promised.

This room was even more chaotic than the backstage area. There were more black block walls, more concrete floors. But here were worktables smothered in layers of fabrics and several rolling racks filled with half-finished costumes. A three-way mirror and pedestal were crammed in a corner between two hefty sewing machines and a couple of headless mannequins. There was a half-assed dressing room consisting of plywood walls and a droopy velvet curtain.

"That's Burt. He probably thinks your head looks like a blueberry," Alistair said to Ursula…er, Robeena.

"Bite me, you talentless, Scottish-play-naming imbecile."

"We're sorry to intrude," Riley said, hooking her fingers under Burt's collar and tugging the dog back. "But we're in a bind." Nick gripped her by the hips and kept her between him and the grumpy lady.

"Robeena, meet Nick and Riley. They need a tux, a gown, and two masks for a gala tonight," Alistair announced, picking up a piece of pink tulle and grimacing. "Nick and Riley, meet Robeena, the evil wardrobe mistress of the theatre."

Robeena crossed her arms over her ample bosom. "You came to the wrong place, Alistair. Did you forget that I hate you?"

"How could I forget with you sharpening fabric shears every time I enter a room? But you hating me doesn't negate our deal. You owe me," he said ominously.

"See, babe? Maybe they'll murder each other and forget about us," Riley whispered to Nick.

Robeena glared long and hard. Alistair stroked his mustache and smirked.

"Fine. But this means we're even. No more holding it over my head. No more veiled threats. No more mentioning it ever again."

"Agreed. And for the record, my threats are never veiled. They're just clever," Alistair said.

"Whatever." Robeena hefted herself off the wheeled desk chair and stomped off into the dark with the fearless, tail-wagging Burt trailing her.

Nick loosened his grip on Riley and breathed a sigh of relief.

"If this is going to cause problems for you, we can find another solution," Riley offered to Alistair.

He spun around, wearing a gold and ivory domino mask, and grinned. "Don't mind Robeena. She's just an understudy of a human being. Oh, this is shiny!" he noted, picking up a bolt of silver material.

"You know what? Why don't we just get out of here and forget the whole gala thing?" Nick suggested to Riley.

"Griffin is in real danger," she reminded him.

"We don't know that. He could have shot out his own window," he argued stubbornly.

"And dyed his own chest?"

"I wouldn't put it past him. That jackwagon would do anything for attention."

Nick wasn't wrong. Riley vividly recalled Griffin pushing her into a floral display so the photographer could "get a solo shot" of him in front of their cake on their wedding day.

Robeena and Burt reappeared, and Nick stifled a manly yelp.

"Here. Try these," Robeena announced, shoving two garment bags at Nick.

Riley smothered a laugh as her boyfriend all but levitated out of his boots to get away from the wardrobe mistress, mumbling something that sounded a little bit like "poor unfortunate souls."

"Good luck," Riley called after him as he hightailed it to the safety of the dressing room.

Alistair fluttered his fingertips together and turned his attention on her. "Now, Riley, my dear. Before we choose something for you, tell me—who will be there tonight?"

She frowned. "I don't actually know. We're going as personal security for my ex-husband. He invited us about an hour ago."

"Ex-husband, you say? Was this an amicable split?"

"Only if you call nearly forcing me into bankruptcy after I caught him cheating amicable."

Robeena returned with an armful of gowns. "Here," she said, irritably shoving them at Alistair. "Don't say I never did anything for you."

He ignored the crabby costume maven and tossed aside a lace gown with bell sleeves. "This does *not* say, 'I'm better off without you.'"

Riley chewed on her lower lip. "I'm not really sure that my dress needs to say anything. We're there to work."

"It physically pains me to agree with this delusional fool, but your dress is going to say something whether you want it to or not. Might as well make it a knockout," Robeena said as Alistair discarded two more dresses.

Nick slunk out of the dressing room in his regular clothes. "This one fits," he said, holding up one garment bag without making eye contact with Robeena.

"No fashion show?" Alistair gave a disappointed tut-tut.

Nick's phone rang. Still keeping Robeena at a distance, he cursed and yanked out his phone. "What's up, Bri? Hang on. I'm in a fucking dungeon. Let me see if I can get a better signal far away from here."

"You're welcome," Robeena called after him as he all but sprinted for the exit.

"Thank you," Nick squeaked before slamming the door behind him.

"The theater makes everyone dramatic," Alistair said and shooed Riley toward the dressing room.

The first dress was pink, frothy, and strapless, but it was too itchy, and the sequins gouged the sensitive skin under her arms.

The second dress was a perfectly acceptable navy number in simple satin. However, Alistair insisted it wasn't "main character enough."

The third dress had a singed bustle and was missing a large amount of fabric from the skirt.

"Oops. That was an accident when we were rehearsing *The Arsonists*," Robeena noted.

Riley eyed the fourth and final dress hanging in the dressing room. "No pressure, but it's either you or I go to this thing in yoga pants and a sweatshirt," she said to the sparkly red gown.

She slipped it over her head and contorted herself to mostly zip it up. She was sweating by the time she bothered looking in the mirror.

"Oh boy," she murmured.

"That sounds like a good reaction," Alistair said, yanking back the curtain. "Oh. Boy. If I weren't G-er than the Ice Capades, you in that dress would have me turning Q."

It was Jessica Rabbit red with a sea of tiny blinding sparkles. Strapless with a deep V of beige mesh fabric that swooped almost to her belly button, the dress cinched at the waist with a rhinestone belt. The slit over her left leg went several inches higher on the thigh than she thought necessary.

"Here. Try it with this." Robeena shoved a ruby-red domino mask at her.

Alistair fitted it in place and secured the ribbon. "Now this says, 'I know you still think about me,'" he said with satisfaction.

Robeena harrumphed. "It doesn't say it. It screams it."

"I don't really need to say anything like this to Griffin," Riley hedged. "A few months ago, he begged me to be his mistress. Besides, isn't personal security supposed to blend in?"

Alistair waved away her hesitation. "You're the decoy. Everyone is looking at you while Nick does the blending."

She *did* feel just the tiniest bit spectacular in the dress. And it *would* be nice to show a room full of Griffin's friends that she'd finally come out on top.

"This uncultured swine is wrong ninety-nine percent of the time, but it's possible this is the other percentage point," Robeena said grudgingly.

Alistair placed a hand over his heart. "That's the nicest thing you've ever said to me, Robeena."

"Don't let it go to your head."

"Don't worry. I know any kindness you display is just an attempt to lure in your next victim."

The bickering restarted with an energetic intensity, so Riley headed back into the dressing room. There, she pulled out her phone, snapped a photo of herself in the mirror, then fired off a text.

Riley: Too booby or just booby enough?

An instant later, her phone rang. It was Jasmine.

"There's no such thing as too booby," her best friend announced in lieu of a greeting.

"Not even if you're going to a masquerade gala thing?"

"Oh. My. God. Is Riley Thorn going to the Harrisburg Arts Council Masquerade Gala?"

"It's for work. I'm not suddenly rich and popular," Riley explained, turning around to check out the rear view in the mirror.

"You work for your PI boyfriend. What's going down at the gala? Should I change my RSVP to yes?"

"We're working security…for Griffin."

"Tell me you mean Peter Griffin. Or Kathy Griffin," Jasmine said, enunciating each syllable like it was a threat.

"I wish. It's Griffin Griffin."

Riley held the phone away from her ear as Jasmine shouted a string of colorful oaths. Her friend had not only represented Riley during the divorce, she'd also smashed her car into Griffin's outside the courthouse after the judge had ruled in his favor. Riley took the full sixty seconds of her friend swearing to change back into her regular clothes.

"Are you done?" she asked Jasmine as she zipped up her jeans.

"What would make you *ever* agree to play bodyguard to that lying, cheating, sniveling little troll doll?" Jasmine demanded.

"The business kind of needed the money. Besides, Nick doesn't think Griffin's in any actual danger. So we'll go, we'll eat some shrimp cocktails, stare at some important people, and then we'll go home."

Jasmine blew out an irritated breath. "Definitely wear the dress. I want a full report tomorrow."

"Speaking of full reports, Kellen Weber was over this morning."

"What did that rule-abiding pain in my ass want?" Jasmine asked.

"He was reinstated. And he asked about you."

Jasmine's tone was the epitome of boredom. "And you're telling me this why?"

"I think he was looking for you. Did something happen between you two at the party last night when you were luring him into Nick's office?"

Jasmine scoffed. "Between *me* and *Detective Dick*?"

"You already kissed him," Riley pointed out.

"That was to piss off his horrible mother."

"What about when he was Drunk Kellen and you were digging around in his pants pocket and you found his not-wallet?"

"You're the one who made me reach in there! Just because I kissed him, accidentally pinkie stroked his penis, and played sexy siren to lure him away from a party does *not* mean I'm in any way interested in the man. He's annoying and straitlaced and always looks like he's about to yell at me or handcuff me."

"I know from previous drunken conversations that you're into both of those things."

"Shut up. I have to go. I have a date waiting. Wear the dress. Free the boobs!" Jasmine disconnected the call.

The dressing room curtain twitched, and Burt poked his head inside. He wore a sparkly tulle jester's collar around his neck.

"I see we've been making friends," Riley observed.

She found Alistair and Robeena locked in some kind of staring contest over a tackle box of thread.

"Uh, I'll borrow this one if that's okay," Riley said, holding up the hanger.

"I knew it," Alistair said with a celebratory self-five.

"Remember. This makes us even," Robeena snarled.

"Until next time," Alistair said darkly. He backed out of the room, glaring at Robeena.

"So what was that all about? What kind of favor did she owe you?" Riley asked once they were safely out of earshot.

"I once watered her plants for a week while she and her partner went to Cape May."

"You watered her plants and now you have a feud?"

Alistair opened his arms with a flourish. "What can I say? Theater people are so dramatic."

Riley, Burt, and Alistair found Nick outside in the parking lot, leaning against the brick wall like some sexy rebel waiting for a cause.

"Sorry for bailing." He pushed away from the wall and got in Riley's space to deliver a quick kiss. "She didn't go near your voice box, did she?"

Burt pranced over to show off his Eliza-burt-thian collar.

"What did Brian want?" Riley asked as Nick gave the dog a good scruffing.

He took her garment bag, slung it over his shoulder, then slid his other arm around her waist.

"The asshole next door to Gentry is Lyle Larstein, disgraced executive of one of the biggest health insurance companies in the state. Seems Lyle enjoyed taking cocaine breaks at work and forcing over a dozen of his female employees to admire his not-very-impressive privates. He was sued for sexual harassment. He got canned but with a seven-figure severance. His wife filed for divorce and took the kids."

"Wow. A real-life bad guy next door. This is almost starting to look like a real case, isn't it?" Riley mused.

Nick snorted. "I'll believe it when I see it."

6

They entered the house through the side door into the mudroom.

Nick and Burt both sniffed the air.

"It smells like meat and cheese," Nick noted.

"It sounds like a fight," Riley added as they walked into a kitchen full of chaos.

"You're late," Mrs. Penny announced from the table, where their new roommates were crowded around a mostly empty platter of cheesesteaks. The rest of the room was in shambles. A leaning tower of dirty dishes occupied the sink while the countertops were buried under food and food-making items.

"This was supposed to be your birthday dinner, but we got hungry. You two keep such late hours, don't you?" Lily trilled.

"It's six o'clock. Most people aren't even home from work yet," Nick complained.

"The elderly consume their calories early," Gabe explained over his foot-long cheesesteak.

"We also eat our desserts first since we don't know how much time we have left," Fred said, pointing to the pie plate of mostly crumbs. The man was back in his frosted-tip boy-band toupee.

"Your hair is standing up," Nick told him.

Fred patted his head like a cat. "Had to vacuum the plaster dust out of it. I kind of like it."

Riley turned to Nick, looking like she was on the edge of panic. "I have less than an hour to shower, tweeze, do my hair, and slap on an entire face of makeup."

"Baby, I got this," he assured her. "The zoo is mine." Being a man meant he could be ready to walk out the door in under five minutes...six maybe with the fucking tie.

Relief washed over her pretty face. She grabbed him by the shirt and dragged him down for a fast, hard kiss.

"Barf! Get a room," Mrs. Penny barked.

"Perhaps they cannot since we took so many of their rooms," Gabe wondered.

Nick gave Riley a swat on the ass. "Go. I got this."

She sprinted from the room, garment bag flapping behind her like a cape.

"What've we got here?" Nick asked, sauntering over to his old-new roommates. He picked up a fork and the pie plate. Burt was already under the table, slurping up all the fallen food like a Dyson. "You're all on Burt poop duty tonight. Riley and I have plans," he warned.

"He'll be fine. A little cheesesteak, chips, French onion dip, and pie never hurt anybody," Mrs. Penny said.

"What did the cops have to say about the house collapsing?" Nick asked.

"They said something about the roof and then something about the structure," Lily reported as she sawed her sub in half and offered it to him.

"Very informative," he noted and threw his half in the pie plate.

"The police said the building is not safe and that we should not enter until a structural engineer completes his investigation," Gabe explained.

Nick dropped his fork. "How long is that gonna take?"

"The officer with the nice fanny said it could be a few weeks," Lily filled in.

"Weeks? *Weeks?*" Nick was going to have to develop a drinking problem.

"That's just for the report. The construction will probably take a month or two," Mrs. Penny added.

"And that's if we can get on anyone's calendar. Contractors are booked up, you know," Fred said, pointing at him with a potato chip. "That's why Willicott and I were thinking we should do it ourselves. If it goes well, we could start our own roofing company."

Mr. Willicott needed a lift chair to go up stairs, and Fred had once managed to attach his own toupee to a sheet of plywood with a nail gun.

"Months," Nick whispered to himself and shoved the cheesesteak into his mouth.

"Subject change!" Fred announced. "Figured out how you're going to make up to Riley for everything?"

Nick choked. "Wha?"

Lily patted his knee. "It's okay. You don't have to pretend with us."

"Pretend what?" he demanded.

"What these yahoos here are trying to say is you royally screwed the pooch these last few weeks," Mrs. Penny said.

On cue, Burt's massive head appeared above the table. He had a crumb mustache and part of a hoagie roll hanging out of his mouth like a cigar.

"We're here to help you prove to Riley you're serious about being a better man before she dumps you," Lily explained, looking at him pityingly.

The food lodged in his throat, requiring him to steal Mrs. Penny's water glass. He drank deeply, then choked again. "This is straight gin."

"Gotta stay hydrated," she said.

Nick mopped his face with a napkin. "I already said I was sorry," he said in defense.

"And now you have to show it," Fred said.

Nick dropped the pie plate on the table. "Seriously?"

Mr. Willicott grunted his agreement and then stole Fred's pie.

"I am in agreement," Gabe said. "You have made many embarrassing missteps in your brief relationship."

"You're still new at this whole relationship thing," Lily said, tucking a paper towel into his shirt like a bib. "If you're serious about Riley—which we all hope you are, because she deserves better than Griffin Buttface Gentry—you have to show her how sorry you are."

"That dude sucks," Fred agreed.

Mr. Willicott nodded vehemently.

"His check doesn't suck," Mrs. Penny reminded them. "But the rest of him does."

"I'm better than Gentry in every single way. Riley already knows this," Nick argued.

"I am new to relationships, but it seems to me that there is a possibility your abandonment of Riley in pursuit of your own needs triggered old wounds, reminding her that she has yet to be in a relationship where she comes first for her partner," Gabe said, steepling his fingers in what Nick considered to be annoying superior piety.

Nick pointed a surly finger at Gabe. "I'll have you know I make sure she comes first every time."

"Listen to the wise, muscly hottie Gabe," Mrs. Penny advised. "I don't want you fucking this up and then us having to spend every other weekend with you in some filthy bachelor pad."

"First of all, I'm not getting custody of any of you," Nick began. But the truth behind her words had already caught up with him.

After his obsessive search for Kellen Weber's long-missing sister the past few months, Riley had every right to give him the boot rather than graciously accepting his apology. Was it possible she was still harboring a grudge? He certainly would have.

He rubbed at the throbbing behind his temples. "So an apology isn't enough?"

"Anybody can apologize. According to Blossom, Griffin used to apologize all the time. But he never changed," Fred explained.

Nick was *not* liking this conversation. "Okay. So what the hell am I supposed to do?"

Lily shrugged.

Fred frowned.

Gabe looked at the ceiling.

Mrs. Penny burped.

Mr. Willicott raised a red Solo cup with the name *Steve* written on it. "Feliz Navidad."

"Baby, we gotta go," Nick called from where he was pacing in front of the staircase in a damn tuxedo with a damn tie that felt like it was damn near strangling him. He tugged on his collar and looked at his watch again.

He'd showered and changed in Gabe's bathroom because Riley had barricaded herself in theirs.

"Stop tugging on your tie or Gabe will have to fix it for you again," Lily warned him.

Nick added *Learn to tie a fucking bow tie* to his mental to-do list.

All the unwanted roommates besides Mr. Willicott, who was setting up his bedroom in the bar area, had set up a row of chairs on the marble in the foyer facing the staircase like spectators at a tennis match.

"I'm coming," Riley shouted from the second floor. "Contouring takes a hell of a lot longer than those YouTubers say it does."

She appeared at the top of the stairs, a vision in red, and Nick forgot how to breathe. His cock forgot the fact that he was almost forty years old and should be mostly in control of his baser urges.

"Sorry, sorry, sorry," she said as she hurried down the stairs, fastening long dangly earrings in place. She'd done something to her hair to make it curl. Her eyes were a smoky gold, lips a matte pink. And the dress. The goddamn dress.

Nick barely heard the applause from the roommates behind him.

He'd chanced this. He'd gambled with *this*.

Riley stopped in front of him, cheeks flushed, eyes bright. "What do you think?"

He thought he was the biggest idiot on the fucking planet.

Nick opened his mouth, but nothing coherent came out. There was a lump in his throat. A pain in his chest. He didn't have words. And maybe that was the problem. Santiagos could hurl insults and dishes with ease. But he couldn't just *tell* Riley how he felt, why he loved her, how beautiful she was, or what an unworthy asshole he was.

She did a twirl, and the fabric caught the light like a thousand tiny diamonds.

"Fan-fucking-tastic," Mrs. Penny announced. "Dibs on it for my next date."

"You look like a romance novel cover heroine about to be ravaged," Lily decided.

"I'd romance the heck out of you," Fred said.

Burt plopped his ass on the floor in front of Riley and lifted a paw like a gentleman dog.

"You look like a red lacewing butterfly," Gabe said with a reverence that snapped Nick out of his fog.

Riley grinned. "Thank you, guys." Her eyes skimmed over Nick and his suit. "You look good. Really good."

Everyone was waiting for him to say something. Something good.

Nick swiped a hand over his face. "You have more of that lipstick on you?" he asked finally.

Riley triumphantly held up a tiny, gold clutch. "Lipstick, breath mints, pepper spray, phone, charger, credit card, and Band-Aids."

Nick nodded. "Good." With that, he grabbed her, bent her backward, and kissed the ever-loving hell out of her.

7

Remember, you two have to stay a minimum of ten feet away from me at all times," Griffin said, stopping them just shy of the Hilton Harrisburg's ballroom. Beyond the narrow shoulders of his tuxedo jacket, Riley could see the beautiful and wealthy people of the city gathering in their masks and festive finery.

"Let me get this straight. Not that I would mind watching one of these fancy fuckers exact their revenge on you—hell, it would make this birthday the best one I've ever had. But doesn't that *completely defeat the purpose of personal security, you human toadstool?*" Nick said on a disbelieving snarl.

Riley patted her boyfriend's arm. "What the client wants, right?" she reminded him with a fake smile.

"He could have called a fucking Lyft, and we could be eating birthday tacos naked right now," Nick complained.

"We'll get birthday tacos on the way home," Riley promised.

"I can't have you two encroaching on me." Griffin's gaze fastened on Riley's dress. "You're too...colorful."

"He means your boobs look amazing," Nick said.

Griffin pointed at Nick. "And you're too...imposing."

"He means you're tall," Riley filled in for Nick. "He doesn't want us overshadowing him and taking attention away from him. Which means we look good. So thanks for the compliments, Griffin."

"We *do* look good, and I hope someone tries to murder you just for ruining my birthday. We'll be by the shrimp fountain or whatever the hell they feed you people," Nick said, towing Riley in the direction of the food.

The ballroom was a cavernous space with a grand staircase perfect for posing on and a candlelit upper-level balcony that, judging by the number of couples on the stairs, was the perfect spot for canoodling. A string quartet played classical versions of pop songs on a skirted riser in front of the dance floor.

"Wow. Is that an actual vat of caviar?" she asked when she spotted the food tables.

"You got me," Nick said, realigning the eye holes of his matte black mask and surveying the room. "Does it feel weird to be hobnobbing with all the Richie Riches you used to hang with when you were married?"

"We weren't married long enough for me to hobnob. I doubt anyone remembers me, and even if they do, I'm wearing a mask. I can pretend to be anyone I want."

"A mask and one hell of a dress."

"See? Ursula isn't so bad," Riley teased.

Nick shuddered.

"Why didn't Bella come tonight?" she asked as they approached the first food table. Appetizers were staged on tiered acrylic displays above artfully rumpled gold table linens.

Nick picked up a tiny glass plate and frowned at it. "Short and Orangey said something about weather girl continuing education, which I'm pretty sure is code for Bella is boning someone on the side."

"Suspicious," Riley said. "Always look at the spouse…or the weather girl in this case." After recently losing her powers and not knowing when or if they'd return, she'd decided it was important to bone up on her nonpsychic investigative studies.

"Yeah, when an actual crime has been committed."

"You still don't believe someone's threatening him?" she asked, crossing her arms as Nick loaded the surface area of his little plate with food.

"Like I said, the twerp is looking for some attention. And even if someone is out to get him, I'm having trouble getting worked up over the idea that one of the hundreds of people he's screwed over decided to get some revenge."

"You do realize we only get the rest of the money after we solve the case, right?" she pointed out.

"Technically, we get paid for performing a service, not for solving the case. I figure we spend a week pretending to care, and then I'll skip off to the bank with a big fat check like I'm a pack of schoolgirls on the playground."

"They have mobile deposit now. But I still would like to see the skipping."

Nick scowled down at the tiny plate in his hand. "How are you supposed to fit any food on this? Here," he said, thrusting the plate at her and getting a second one.

Riley turned away from the food to scan the crowd. There were a lot of beautiful masked people circulating everywhere. She rolled her eyes behind her mask when she spotted Griffin in the center of a circle of fawning middle-aged women.

She took a breath and mentally lifted her psychic garage doors. Other people's thoughts glided into her consciousness like parade floats.

"Why the hell can't these events serve real food? I don't want raw squid compote. I want a fucking cheeseburger."

"I can't believe Nancy is here showing her face after that humiliating loss in the last election. I think I'll go remind her she lost."

"Look at that hideous Dexter with his new facelift and his twenty-two-year-old wife. Does she have to tuck him in before she goes out with her friends for the night?"

"Did Griffin Gentry get taller?"

"It's my fucking birthday, and I have to spend it with Booster Seat. But damn is it worth it just to see Riley in that dress. I wonder if I can talk her into taking a naked tour of a janitorial closet?"

"Here. I brought you some shrimp and whatever this stuff is. Maybe some kind of seafood dip? There was a crab leg sticking out of it," Nick said as he pushed a second appetizer plate at her.

"No," Riley said.

"You don't want any food?"

"I don't want to have sex in a janitorial closet. At least not until we're off the clock."

Both dimples winked into existence. "How did a guy like me get lucky enough to land a girl like you, Thorn?"

His tone was teasing, but she could feel something else behind it.

"Are you okay?" she asked, abandoning her assessment of the crowd.

Nick popped a shrimp into her mouth. "Baby, with you, I'm better than okay."

"Did you hit your head getting out of the car again?"

"No. But that dress knocked me out."

"Champagne?" The offer came from a young cocktail waiter behind them.

"Sorry, man," Nick said. "We're on the job, making sure no one tries to murder one of these rich pains in your ass."

A gentleman with silvery hair and a *Phantom of the Opera* mask who had just reached for one of the glasses changed his mind and swept away into the crowd. Riley craned her neck but lost him when he disappeared behind two men resembling refrigerators in their white dinner jackets.

"If it's Ing Theodoric, I'll give you this entire tray of champagne if you look the other way when it happens," the waiter grumbled.

Riley juggled her appetizer plates to elbow Nick. Ingram Theodoric was on their list of suspects.

"Ow. What was that for? Do you want more shrimp?" Nick asked, rubbing his arm.

"Ingram Theodoric sounds like a *bad guy*," Riley said pointedly.

"Very subtle, Thorn," Nick said with a wink.

"He just made my boyfriend get on his hands and knees and mop up the scotch he didn't spill on the asshole's wingtips," the waiter said, drawing Riley's attention again. He was a gangly white twentysomething with a head full of shockingly blond curls. His dinner jacket was a few sizes too big, his pants were too short, and his bow tie was crooked. He winced. "Sorry. I'm not supposed to say stuff like that. Please don't tell my boss. I don't wanna get fired again."

"Tell you what"—Nick leaned in to read the waiter's name tag—"Garvey. You point us in the direction of this Theodoric guy, and I'll be sure to spill this cocktail sauce all over him."

Garvey's eyes lit up. "Deal. I'll save you a bottle of champagne to go if you get some up his nose."

"Consider it done."

Riley took a preemptive bite of shrimp just in case they were about to get thrown out by security. It was never a dull moment with Nick Santiago on the loose.

Garvey pointed across the ballroom. "Standing over there by that urn of flowers. He's the tall dude with the gold mask and the comb-over who looks like he's got an ice sculpture shoved up his butt."

Nick popped a crostini in his mouth and straightened his shoulders. "Let's get to work."

"Are you sure dumping cocktail sauce on someone is the best way to get them to talk?" she asked nervously as she trailed him across the ballroom.

"Gotta read the situation and adapt. Sometimes you need to throw a punch or hurl some condiments to get someone to open up."

"Listen, I remember Ingram Theodoric the Third from a fundraiser at Fort Hunter. He's a bank vice president and colossal jackass," she warned.

"Then this will be even more fun," he insisted.

"He makes underlings cry on a daily basis at the bank.

According to the suspect list, Griffin says Ing screamed at him on the court after a pickleball match."

"What the hell is pickleball?" Nick asked. "Never mind. Tell me later."

"All I'm saying is if you dump cocktail sauce all over him, he's not going to stand around and answer questions."

Nick glanced back at her, his grin wicked. "Baby. This isn't amateur hour. Play along. It'll be fun. Oh, and don't be afraid to whip out those psychic abilities. The faster I can prove no one is out to get Gentry, the better."

"Spirit guides, prepare for…anything," Riley muttered under her breath as he led her directly into the path of Ingram Theodoric.

Nick froze midstep. "A-a-choo!"

His fake sneeze had him bobbling his appetizer plate. He dramatically pulled a dinner napkin out of his jacket and blew his nose noisily. "Ugh. Darling," he said with a suddenly posh British accent. "When will event planners stop insisting on using chrysanthemums? For the last time, if it's in season, it's too cheap."

"Uh, you're so right, dear," Riley said, struggling to keep a straight face.

"I've said the same thing a thousand times of these ridiculous dinners," Ingram announced with the slightest slur to his words. The glass of scotch in his hand was almost empty.

Nick tucked the napkin back into his suit jacket like it was a handkerchief. "And *shrimp* cocktail?" He gestured with his plate of shrimp tails and sauce. "How gauche."

Riley hadn't been aware that Nick knew the word *gauche*, let alone how to pronounce it.

Ingram polished off the rest of his drink with a noisy slurp. "Next thing you know, they'll be feeding us SpaghettiOs and expecting us to say thank you. By the by, I'm Ingram Theodoric the Third. I'm sure you've heard of me."

"I'm Poindexter Flopper the First," Nick said. "And this is my wife, Gilligan. Say, old man, you don't know that tiny tosser over there with the unforgivable spray tan?"

Riley didn't miss the subtle tightening of Ingram's jaw

beneath his garish mask. "That's Griffin Gentry. He's on the morning news," he said. He snapped his fingers at the nearest waiter. "Scotch. Double. Now. And don't get your fingerprints all over the glass this time."

Nick snorted. "I don't care if he's on *The Price Is Right*; the man's a colossal prick. He insulted me on the pickleball field."

"Court," Riley muttered.

"Right. Court, of course. I was thinking of rugby," Nick continued in his ridiculous accent.

"You're not the first person Gentry has rubbed the wrong way," Ingram said stiffly.

Riley's nose twitched. Nick gave her hand a squeeze, and then she found herself swooping along through clouds of baby blue and candy pink. The clouds parted, and there was Griffin in an all-white tennis outfit, standing on a pickleball court. His sweatband was stained orange from his fake tan. Ingram stormed the court just before a serve and began hurling plastic balls and paddles at the news anchor.

She couldn't hear what Ingram was shouting. The sound was muffled like it was coming from underwater, but she was fairly certain some of the words were "you son of a bitch."

Griffin did his best to dodge the onslaught by hiding behind his doubles partner, a young man of possibly Asian heritage with messy hair, glasses, and a resigned look on his face.

"These pickleball folks sure take their sports seriously," Riley observed to her spirit guides.

But the scene was gone as quickly as it appeared, changing and shifting into something else. The clink of cocktail glasses and a sudden explosion of laughter in the ballroom threatened to pull her out. Riley clung tighter to the wisps of a new scene.

Focus focus focus, she ordered herself.

Griffin—hands stacked under his head, expression smug—lounged naked on a king-size bed with an imposing wrought-iron canopy.

"Is this view really necessary?" Riley asked her spirit guides as she tried not to dry heave.

The woman partially draped in a sheet next to Griffin was not Bella. She was too blurry to make out more than a leggy brunette with pouty lips and long fingernails. "That was it?" the brunette asked, sounding flummoxed.

"That was it," Griffin said with pride. "You can give me a back rub now."

The scene spun, and Riley found herself zooming in on the shelves on the wall opposite the bed. Closer, closer, closer until she realized she was looking at an oil painting of a scowling man in a suit. Ingram Theodoric III.

Was this Ingram's bedroom? Did that mean the woman was his girlfriend? His wife? His daughter?

The band played an orchestral riff, and the gala attendees began to applaud, which popped Riley's little psychic bubble.

"Oh boy," she muttered, lurching sideways into the strong, solid heat of Nick's body. She really needed to ask Gabe if they could practice more dignified exits from Cotton Candy World.

"You all right there, love?" Nick asked.

Ingram was staring at her, but judging from the tilt of his head, it wasn't her face that had caught his attention.

"I'm fine," she said brightly. "I just caught my heel on the carpet."

Ingram scoffed in the general direction of her chest. "The cleaning staff probably separated the carpet seams by vacuuming the wrong way. I swear these uneducated buffoons should be paying *us* for putting up with their ineptitude."

"What an *interesting* opinion," she said and covertly elbowed Nick.

"I must say. That's a lovely dress, my dear," Ingram said, openly leering at Riley now. "You're a lucky man, Poindexter."

"Don't I know it," Nick agreed. "Achoo!"

This time, Nick's comical fake sneeze registered on the Richter scale. His entire body spasmed outward, sending his plate of shrimp tails and cocktail sauce flying directly into Ingram's masked face.

Silence reigned as every mask within twenty feet turned in their direction.

"Oh, dear. I told you to see a doctor about those allergies," Riley chided, patting Nick on the arm.

He produced the dinner napkin again and dramatically blew his nose as sauce dripped from Ingram's face onto the pristine white shirt. His mouth hung open, and he had a shrimp tail in his hair.

"Terribly sorry, old chap," Nick said, handing the immobile Ingram his used napkin. "Come on, Gilligan. I think it's time to get off this island."

Garvey the waiter flashed them a covert thumbs-up as they hurried away from the snarling Ingram.

"That was..." Riley searched for the right word.

"Awesome?" Nick filled in.

"I was going to say *ridiculous*, but *awesome* works too. Nice accent, by the way. Do you think it'll help when security hauls us out of here?"

"Are you kidding me, Thorn?" He took her hand and twirled her in a circle as they crossed the dance floor. "We're Poindexter and Gilligan, filthy rich assholes. We do what we want."

She yelped as he dipped her low. "I'm concerned that fifteen minutes of hobnobbing with the upper class is rubbing off on you."

"You should be more concerned that we're rubbing off on them." He returned her to her feet and led them to a quiet table on the opposite side of the ballroom. "Now spill it. What did that twitchy little nose of yours tell you?"

Riley glanced over her shoulder to where Griffin was now slow dancing a little too close to a tall woman in a feathered mask. "Ingram attacked Griffin on the pickleball court all right. But it wasn't over a match. I can't be sure, but I think it was because Griffin slept with his wife or daughter. It's hard to tell with these kinds of age gaps."

"Nice work, Thorn. I'll text Brian and tell him Ingram gets

bumped to the top of the fake motive list," Nick said. "Is there anyone else we should dump cocktail sauce on, or can I go get another tiny plate of tiny food?"

8

Y ou know, before I met you, I used to think PI work was glamorous," Riley said on a yawn. The cash bar hadn't deterred the gala's attendees from overindulging. Many of Harrisburg's wealthiest couldn't seem to hold the liquor they'd paid for. There had already been a slap fight at the chocolate fountain, and Griffin was currently dirty dancing with a state senator and the daughter of a district magistrate.

"You say that sitting here in a gown made for Jessica Rabbit after eating two plates of fancy-ass finger food and eavesdropping on the thoughts of Harrisburg's one percent," Nick pointed out, forking up a bite of cake as the string quartet switched to a classical version of Taylor Swift's "Anti-Hero."

"Yeah, but I'm boooored. It's been an hour since you assaulted anyone with a condiment," Riley teased. "Hey. Where did you get cake? The only dessert I saw was the fourteen-carat-gold trifle."

"Garvey's boyfriend," Nick said with his mouth full. "Said it's for a wedding this weekend."

"You're eating someone's *wedding cake*?"

He held out a bite to her. "Hey, it's not like *I* cut it."

She was about to explain to him that it wasn't in his best

karmic interests to eat someone else's wedding cake before the actual wedding when she spotted a familiar-looking woman in a silver mask and a chic bohemian gown hovering near the bar. It was hard to tell with the mask, but it looked as if she were staring straight at Griffin as he sucked up all the attention on the dance floor.

"Hey, I think that's Claudia Mendoza," she whispered, craning her neck when two large men in white jackets and matching masquerade masks lumbered by and headed for the stairs.

"Why are we whispering?" Nick asked.

"She's one of the suspects. She's the anchor Griffin's dad fired. I recognize the tattoo on her shoulder."

"Why don't you go interview her?" he said.

"Me?" Riley squeaked.

"Yeah, you. You've met her before, right?"

"Yes, but—"

"You're a badass psychic who's learning how to investigate shit, right?"

She nodded. "Also yes. Again *but*."

"Then go on over there and ask her a couple of questions."

Riley bit her lower lip. "What if I screw it up?"

"Then I'll come over and throw shrimp tails in her hair," he said, his dimples appearing beneath his mask. "Think of it as practice. You and Gabe practice the psychic stuff all the time. This is the same except you're just trying to figure out if she was in town this morning."

She pouted. "You're just making me do it because you want to sit here and eat your cake."

"It's really good cake."

She slapped his thigh. "Nick!"

He laughed. "You've got this, Thorn. You're the queen of polite. You're a damn genius when it comes to getting people to open up. And that's even without your secret mind-reading weapon."

Riley straightened her shoulders. He was right. She *could*

do this. Or at least she should be able to do this. She blew out a breath. "Okay. Fine. But try not to steal anyone else's celebratory desserts while I'm gone."

She left Nick and his cake at the table and gave herself a pep talk on the way to the bar. She was a badass investigator in training. She could talk to people about stuff.

The woman was definitely giving Griffin the death glare. She had thick dark hair that curled around her shoulders, partially camouflaging the tattoo of a lotus blossom.

"Excuse me. Are you Claudia Mendoza?"

The woman in question turned her back on the view of the dance floor and gave Riley a hair-to-shoes once-over. "Yes?"

"I'm Riley Thorn. We met briefly at the broadcasting brunch a few years ago. I thought I'd come reintroduce myself."

Claudia's red lips pursed. "Hmm, Riley Thorn. Why do I know that name?" She spoke as if she were narrating a traffic jam on Route 83.

Riley didn't have to feign her grimace. "I've been in the news once or twice in the past few months."

Claudia's brown eyes sharpened. "Ah, yes. The psychic who survived the trigger-happy mayor and saved everyone from the bomb at Channel 50."

"I used to work there."

Claudia toyed with the stack of bracelets she wore on her wrist. "Yes, well. So did I once upon a time."

The mask made it hard for Riley to judge the woman's facial expressions, but there was no mistaking the bitterness emanating from her. It was an experience worth bonding over, Riley decided.

"I got fired from Channel 50…by my ex-husband, Griffin Gentry."

An elegant eyebrow arched over Claudia's mask. "Is that so?"

"Well, I couldn't really keep working there anyway after he decided to leave me for the weather girl."

Claudia's smile was feline as she slipped an arm around Riley's shoulders. "Let's have a drink and chat, shall we?"

Riley ordered a glass of white wine and followed her quarry to a cocktail table where they could observe the rich and fabulous around them.

"That man has quite the track record, doesn't he?" Claudia asked as they watched Griffin kiss the knuckles of one woman while making awkward bedroom eyes at her friend. "And he's never once paid the price for his sins."

"I keep hoping someone will hold him accountable eventually," Riley said as she once again mentally rolled up her spiritual garage doors. She drew the psychic ethics line at forcing herself into people's heads unless it was a life-or-death situation. But if she happened to catch snatches of thoughts that they broadcast…well, that was slightly less icky.

"Yes, well. I've turned all my revenge fantasies over to karma. She'll take care of him…eventually."

"Any tips on how to forgive and forget? Because every time I see his face, I just want to throw something," Riley admitted.

"Here's a page out of my playbook," Claudia offered. "First I let the bitterness simmer for a few years. Then I continued to let it eat away at me while I used it as fuel to achieve. Every rung of the ladder I've climbed has been so I could one day stand over him and rub his little pig nose in my success. I'm the highest-paid anchor on Channel 49. I won four Dillys. And I bought my parents a condo in Sarasota."

She paused and took a delicate sip of her champagne, still watching Griffin. Then she put the glass down and deliberately turned her back on the man.

"And then I realized I was still miserable. I woke up one day and discovered that making choices to spite someone doesn't lead to happiness. So off I went on a self-healing journey." She plucked absently at one of the threads on the embroidered wrap she wore draped over her elbows.

"What did that entail?" Riley asked.

"Oh, I tried therapy for the helplessness. I took up boxing for the rage. Then I went to a tarot card reader and asked to see Griffin's downfall. Instead, she showed me a journey. So I packed my things, took a sabbatical, and booked a flight."

The kerfuffle around the chocolate fountain had reignited, this time spilling over to the dessert table. Insults and plates of tiny desserts were hurled back and forth. Griffin didn't seem to be involved, but a bowl of pudding landed rather close to him.

"Where did you go?" Riley asked, trying to stay focused on the conversation at hand while signaling Nick to stay focused on Griffin.

Claudia seemed oblivious to the drama erupting around them. "First I went to visit my parents in Colombia. Then I went to an ashram in India and meditated for forty-five days, the first thirty of which I meditated on all the ways I wanted Griffin's life to implode. And then on day thirty-one, all that hatred, all that frustration was just…gone."

Riley's nose twitched, and she was treated to a sudden flash of Claudia in wrinkled off-white linen on a meditation cushion in a stuffy, windowless room surrounded by more than a dozen other sweaty people desperate for enlightenment. It didn't smell good.

"Wow," she said, not sure what else she could say.

"Yeah, it was a real eat-meditate-forgive kind of experience." Claudia tapped a manicured finger to her chin. "I might write a book about it."

"And now you're fine being in the same room with him?" Riley pressed.

"Of course. I've evolved. I've found inner peace. Every year, I go away to a spa in upstate New York for a silent meditation retreat and juice fast. I come back feeling even healthier and more at peace. I just got back yesterday afternoon."

Knowing what was required, Riley gasped theatrically. "I wondered why your skin was glowing."

Claudia gave her thick hair a shake. "It's all the broccoli sprouts I eat," she said conspiratorially.

"I'll keep that in mind for my healing journey."

―――――

"Lay it on me," Nick said when Riley returned to the table.

"Well, I learned that broccoli sprouts make your skin glow."

"Gross."

"And that Claudia claims she's given up her animosity toward Griffin after years of working on herself."

"Hence the broccoli sprouts."

"Exactly. She also just got back into town yesterday from a spa retreat."

"Did your spidey senses tell you anything?"

"She isn't lying about all the self-work she's been doing. But she also stood at the bar glaring eyeball daggers at Griffin for a good five minutes before I interrupted her. I remember her doing a special report years ago from a gun range where she shot up a target with what looked like expert precision. I think she stays on the list."

"God, you're sexy when you get all investigate-y."

"Are you sure it isn't just the dress?"

Nick rose from his chair and held out a hand to her. "It's the whole package, baby. Come on."

"Where are we going?" she asked as he led her away from the table.

"It's my birthday. I'm gonna dance with my girl."

Nick twirled her once on the dance floor, then drew her into his arms just as the cellos and violins eased into an instrumental version of "Love Me Like You Do."

"Birthday boy's got moves," Riley observed.

"Just wait until I get out of this straitjacket. Then I'll show you some moves that'll make your eyes roll back in your head."

"And people say romance is dead," she teased. "Where did you learn to dance?"

"My aunt Nancy was an amateur ballroom dance competitor who was always between partners. By the time she moved on to her next hobby of real estate mogul, all of us cousins knew how to bust the right moves."

"How many cousins do you have?"

"It feels like hundreds. Let's not talk about my screwy family. Let's talk about us. You know how much I like working for myself? Not answering to anybody? Setting my own schedule?" he asked.

"I am aware."

"You make it all ten times better."

Her feet faltered, but Nick didn't let her miss a step. "I don't know what to do when you get all sneaky sweet on me like that," she admitted.

"Maybe you should try getting used to it," he suggested, spinning her out only to reel her back in.

"I'll take that under consideration," she said, appreciating the warmth of his body against hers. She was the lucky one, she realized as Nick dipped her low, holding her effortlessly. Just a few short years ago, she'd been in a very different position.

Her eyes were drawn to a movement over his shoulder. "Oh, hell. Griffin!"

"I realize I'm wearing a mask, but I thought the height and general charm would have tipped you off, Thorn. I'm Nick," he said, still holding her in the dip.

"No! Griffin!" she said, pointing.

He pulled her back to her feet and spun them around. "Crap," he muttered.

Their client was balanced precariously on the top step of the grand staircase, waving at the gathering like he were some sort of benevolent despot. The shadows behind him seemed to be moving. There was a flash of white, and warning bells rang in Riley's head. Someone was standing behind Griffin.

Nick was already on the move, fighting his way through the crowd. Riley picked up the skirt of her dress and jogged after him just as Griffin pitched forward down the stairs.

9

C an I have a glass of warm milk?" Griffin asked pitifully from his eight-thousand-thread-count bed linens.

He had a satin eye mask perched on top of his head. His cheek was bruised, he had a bandage on his jaw, his right arm was in a sling, and the doctor at urgent care had handed over an inflatable doughnut for the next week's worth of sitting.

Riley almost felt sorry for him.

Nick had no such feelings.

"No, you can't have a fucking glass of warm milk. What are you? Three years old?" he snapped, double-checking the locks on the bedroom windows. "Holy fucking shit. What is that?"

"That's a statue of me," Griffin said, sounding cheerier. "Isn't it amazing?"

Riley joined Nick at the window and shuddered. Under a large wooden lean-to, there was indeed a twelve-foot stone statue of a buck-naked, erect Griffin Gentry in the yard. It had up lights shining from the ground, so even in the dark, the thick veined erection could be seen.

"How's the scale on that?" Nick asked Riley.

"You know how all of Griffin's 'life-size' cardboard cutouts are six inches taller than he is?"

"Yeah?"

"The sculptor could have saved himself a foot and a half of cement on that."

She turned away from the eye-searing view.

The bedroom hadn't changed too much since Riley had called it home. The four-poster bed was the same. The carpet was the same mint-green pattern because Griffin wanted to feel like he was walking on money every morning. The art on the walls was the same boring abstract slashes of beige and khaki chosen by Griffin's boring beige mother. And there was still a huge black-and-white portrait of Griffin hanging on the wall in a frame worthy of some European royal dynasty.

But there were a few notable differences. Riley's former nightstand was now cluttered with nail polishes, a laser facial device, a phone tripod, and clumps of jewelry. The stately lamp had been changed out for one with a bedazzled body and pink shade with fur trim. Above the lamp was an oversize photo of Bella blowing a kiss to the camera.

It was autographed to Bella from Bella.

Riley shook her head. "I'll get you a glass of water," she offered Griffin.

"Okay," he said morosely.

She plucked the pink crystal tumbler off Bella's nightstand and headed into the bathroom to fill it. It was a spacious room with marble walls and high-end fixtures, and it looked like an active war zone. His and hers cosmetics crowded the counters. Not one but two makeup vanities were crammed up against the glass-block wall of the shower, both buried under more beauty products.

Five robes of varying lengths and materials hung on hooks next to dueling towel warmers. A doorway opened into a walk-in closet that was twice the size it had been when Riley had hung her clothes in it.

Reaching around skin creams, lip masks, and bottles of perfume, she filled the glass out of the tap and sighed. It looked like it took a lot of work to be high-maintenance.

She returned to the bedroom to find Nick standing over Griffin and clutching a pillow in both hands. Griffin was obliviously rambling on about the importance of a nighttime skincare routine.

"Put the pillow down, Nick," she ordered, rounding the bed and setting the glass down on Griffin's nightstand.

Grumbling, he tossed the pillow back on the fainting couch by the windows.

"Think of the money," she reminded him.

He grunted. "Fine. I'll go check the rest of the windows on this floor. Don't let him try to drag you into bed with him."

"I think I can take him," Riley said, giving him a shove toward the door.

"Is this tap water? From the *bathroom*?" Griffin's face was contorted.

"It's water from the plumbing in your home."

"I didn't know you could drink water from the tap," he said, sniffing the glass with suspicion.

"Seriously? Don't you use tap water to brush your teeth?"

"I keep San Pellegrino in the bathroom refrigerator for that. I could drink that."

"You're all out," she lied.

He grumbled and held up his phone to his face. "Staff, it's an emergency. I need you to come over right now to restock the bathroom refrigerator with San Pellegrino."

Riley snatched the phone away from him and deleted the voice message. "Someone just pushed you down a flight of stairs. No one is coming over after we leave."

He flashed her that cagey look that had taken her way too long to learn to mistrust.

"No," she said firmly.

"But, but what if I get *lonely*?"

"Then call someone."

"Can I call you?"

"Why don't you call Bella? Your fiancée. I'm sure you two have a lot of wedding plans to discuss," she said pointedly.

"Oh right. Her."

Riley could hear Nick moving through the rest of the second floor muttering to himself, "Who the hell needs a fireplace in their closet?"

She took a seat on the fainting couch. "Are you sure you don't remember seeing anyone behind you on the stairs tonight?"

True to narcissistic form, Griffin had proved to be an unreliable witness to the crime. He had once wandered right through a gas station robbery to buy a local paper that featured an interview with him.

"No. I was getting ready to offer a toast and make a little speech about what a good person I am for supporting under-privileged plants. I thought it would be nice of me to make sure everyone could see me, so I went upstairs."

"And when you went up there, you didn't notice anyone around you?"

"I didn't see anyone. There was a mirror hanging on the wall, and I wanted to make sure I looked my best, so I did a few poses and practiced a few sincere facial expressions."

If there was a mirror anywhere in his vicinity, Griffin couldn't take his eyes off it.

"What about any hotel employees? Did you notice any catering staff? Any cleaners?"

"I never notice people like that," he answered with a yawn. "I just remember waving to my fans and holding up my champagne. And then something hit me from behind, and I remembered to cover my moneymaker. If my face gets broken, I can't have an on-camera career, you know."

Annoyed and exhausted, Riley got up and snagged the remote off his nightstand to dim the lights. "On that note, go to sleep and try to wake up a better person."

She hit the button. But instead of the room lights dimming, they turned purple and started flashing. Loud, thumpy club music poured forth from hidden speakers under the bed, and the crystal ceiling fixture began to spin like a disco ball.

Griffin triumphantly rose to his knees on the mattress. "I knew you still wanted me! I accept your advances!"

He stretched his good arm toward Riley. She stepped back, frantically pushing remote buttons.

"What the hell is going on?" Nick demanded, racing into the room.

Griffin reached for Riley and missed, pitching forward off the side of the bed.

"I hit the wrong button," Riley yelled over the mood music.

Nick stepped on Griffin's prone form and snatched the remote from her. The music stopped, and the lights went back to normal.

"Owie," Griffin moaned from the floor.

"That's what you get for being a dick," Nick said.

"I'm starting to believe he really can't help himself," Riley said. "Come on. Let's get him up."

"I got him," Nick insisted. "I'm afraid of what he'll do if you willingly touch him. Then I'll have to kill him myself, and I didn't bring any spare crime scene clothes." He hauled Griffin to his feet and all but tossed him back on the mattress. "Josie will be by in the morning to play security. Go the fuck to sleep."

"We'll be back to talk to Bella after the morning show," Riley told Griffin.

"Wait! Did you check under the bed for bad guys?" Griffin asked, hugging a pillow to his chest with his good arm.

"Your bed sits so low no one could fit under it," Nick said.

"What about the closet? It's very large. There could be a whole bunch of bad guys hiding in there."

"Nick will check," Riley volunteered.

"Seriously, babe? I just want to go home and close out my birthday with you naked."

"The sooner you check the closet for bad guys, the sooner we can go home and I can give you your *birthday present*," she said out of the side of her mouth.

Nick stomped out of the bedroom, through the bathroom, and into the closet. Lights came on automatically, and an automated voice said, "Hello, Griffin. You are looking handsome today."

"There's no bad guys in here. Just a delusional robot."

"That's my automated wardrobe assistant," Griffin called. "Isn't that neat?"

Nick reappeared. "Swell. Try not to get murdered overnight."

"Help yourself to the gummy trophies on your way out. A special fan sends me a bag every month."

"Bye, Griffin," Riley said as Nick took her hand and marched her out the door.

She arrested their forward momentum by the entryway table at the front door. Next to the stack of signed headshots was a fancy dish filled with packets of gummy candies.

"I'll get you real food if you let us leave right now," Nick promised.

She picked up one of the packets and smothered a laugh. "These aren't trophies. These are gummy penises."

"You're telling me someone's been sending Gentry a bag of dicks every month and he thinks they're trophies?"

"Look! They're even personalized."

"I'm suddenly feeling less enraged," he said, helping himself to a handful of the packets.

"I'm thinking about selling a kidney," Nick said as he perused the touch-screen menu at Sheetz. The convenience store was crowded with late-night munchie customers. No one gave their elegant evening attire a second glance, because after midnight, everyone was equally weird at Sheetz.

"Which kidney? Ooh, get an order of fries too," Riley said, peering over his shoulder.

"Whichever one doesn't require us to see that walking cheese doodle again."

"You have to admit, someone is definitely after him," she pointed out.

He grunted and snatched the receipt from the printer's teeth. "You're not cheering me up."

"I'm just pointing out that this is a legitimate way to earn the money we need to keep the business afloat. Plus, you get to be the hero while Griffin plays the pathetic, whiny victim."

He guided her toward the register manned by an expressionless kid with bloodshot eyes and a sideways visor. "Yeah, and now in order to get that money, we have to comb through a list of suspects longer than Statue Griffin's cock, find the bad guy, take them down, knock down Gentry's I-deserve-everything-for-free-because-I'm-a-fucking-Muppet entitlement, and pry open his checkbook for him."

Riley frowned. "When you put it that way, this sucks."

———

They tiptoed into the darkened kitchen with their haul of gas station food.

"No Burt?" Nick noted when the big dog didn't lumber out of the shadows.

"I wonder whose bed he's sharing," Riley said.

"Probably Penny's. She snacks in bed," he guessed, setting the bag on the counter. "I'll get some plates."

While he was occupied, Riley unlocked the pantry. It didn't store as much food as it did power tools they'd confiscated from Fred and Mr. Willicott, and Lily's recorder when she'd briefly taken music lessons from her grandson.

She liberated the wrapped package from a dented metal bread box labeled *Screws & Stuff*.

Nick glanced up from the plates he was piling high with nachos, tacos, and French fries.

"So I got you something," she said, suddenly feeling self-conscious. While most of their relationship had moved at warp speed, this was the first birthday they'd celebrated together. There were expectations attached to these kinds of things, and she didn't want to mess it up.

"Gimme." He snatched the gift out of her hands and tore at the wrapping paper like a toddler on Christmas morning.

"Whoa. Okay. So you're into presents. I didn't see that coming."

"What's not to like about stuff other people buy you?" He held up the box and examined it. "*The Thin Man* box set?"

"It's Blu-rays of these black-and-white movies about a private investigator and his wife, Nick and Nora Charles, and their dog, Asta. They drink a lot and solve mysteries."

He looked up at her and grinned. "Sounds like it's right up my alley. Good gift."

"Yeah?"

His eyes went lusty. "Yeah. Why don't you come over here and let me tell you to your face?"

"My face or my boobs?" she teased, sidling closer.

"Why not both?"

His strong, warm hands settled on her hips. His lips were closing the distance from hers. Her pulse kicked into overdrive.

It was right about then that two things happened simultaneously. Something cold and wet grazed her leg, and the kitchen lights snapped on.

Riley yelped and jumped backward, falling ass over feet over Burt's back.

"I told you I smelled nacho cheese," Mrs. Penny announced from the doorway. She was wearing a hockey jersey and men's boxers. Lily appeared behind her in a pink robe embroidered with kittens.

"Ooooh! Are we having a party?"

"We were," the birthday boy snarled.

10

Nick woke fully hard from a dream about Riley in that red dress. He could hear the rain as it pattered against the windows. With his eyes still closed, he snuggled closer to Riley, relishing the feel of her warm body against his.

"Mmmph," she said.

"Morning, beautiful." He pressed his lips to her nape.

"We need to find jobs that let us sleep more," she grumbled into her pillow.

"What if I find a creative way to wake you?" He'd already run through sixteen morning sex scenarios in his mind and had narrowed it down to five.

"Be my guest," she said, burrowing deeper into the pillow.

"Challenge accepted." Nick rolled her over.

She was grinning up at him, and he was feeling like the king of fucking Harrisburg when their doorknob rattled.

"This the bathroom?" Mr. Willicott called.

"Go the hell away, Willicott!" Nick yelled.

But Riley was already sliding for the edge of the bed. "How did he get upstairs? We don't have a lift chair." She reached for a robe.

"He's a grown man. He'll figure it out," Nick said, patting the mattress. "Stay here with me so I can debauch you."

She looked up at him as she stuffed her feet into slippers. "A man with mobility issues and what is probably some kind of dementia thinks this is the bathroom. I do not want to clean that up."

On a few colorful four-letter words, Nick vaulted out of bed, yanked on a pair of sweats, and flung the door open.

Mr. Willicott was wearing Riley's missing pink gym shorts and a flannel pajama top.

"In there," Nick said, pointing at the connecting bathroom. "But don't make this a habit. Your bathroom is downstairs."

"Not my fault the cheesesteak is fighting its way out." Mr. Willicott tucked a magazine under his arm and marched into the bathroom.

"Oh God," Riley groaned.

"We're not sticking around for this." Nick grabbed his slippers and a sweatshirt.

"Whatever's happening downstairs can't be worse than this," she agreed.

They hit the stairs, and Nick was relieved to discover no new disasters or messes in the foyer. Breakfast smells wafted through the house, and the sounds of companionable conversation came from the kitchen.

Burt bounded into the foyer, his paws slapping at the marble. He gave a cheerful bark and danced in a circle at the foot of the stairs.

"Hi, handsome," Riley greeted the dog. "Did you have a sleepover?"

Nick gave Burt a thump on the side. Orange dust puffed out of his fur and into the air. "What the—"

The dog had orange handprints down his back. His snoot and jowls were also covered in a fine orange dust.

"We should have moved far, far away," Nick lamented.

Burt, sensing someone was about to be in trouble, made a mad dash for the kitchen. They followed him through the swinging door.

"What did you do to my dog?" Riley demanded.

"Good morning, lovebirds! I made you heart-shaped pancakes for breakfast," Lily announced from the stove.

"It's just a little cheese doodle dust," Mrs. Penny said, pulling her head out of the sink. Fred's torso and legs stuck out of the cabinet beneath. "Me and Burt stayed up late snacking and gaming."

"What's the number one rule about Burt?" Riley said.

"Get out of his way when he's excited or he might break our hips?" Lily offered.

"Avoid his tail because it leaves whiplashes?" Fred suggested.

"Don't feed him people food," Riley reminded them.

"Fred, what are you doing to my sink?" Nick asked.

The elderly man slid out of the cabinet. He was holding a wrench and wearing a Phish T-shirt and track pants. "Just helping out. Mrs. Penny dumped an entire box of denture cleaning tablets down the garbage disposal."

"Why would you do that, Penny?"

"To see if the fizzing would dislodge the strip of condoms that fell down there first."

"How…? Why…?" It didn't really matter. These people who had invaded his home were capable of anything. "Never mind. I don't want to know."

Riley retrieved a damp dish towel from the counter and hid it behind her back as she sauntered casually in Burt's direction.

"So what's on the PI agenda today? We dragging in a few suspects and interrogating them?" Mrs. Penny asked. "I packed my ski masks, just in case."

A bolt of inspirational lightning struck Nick. "You can't interrogate suspects today. You'll be too busy going undercover."

The old woman perked up. "I will?"

"Yeah, Penny. Whoever is after Griffin is going to catch on fast that he's got security, especially with Josie lurking around playing with her knife collection. I need you to go undercover as his grandma. Don't leave his side all day."

The plan he thought of ten seconds ago was sounding better and better. Griffin was going to be laid up from last night's injuries. Mrs. Penny could babysit him from the couch. Meanwhile, he and Riley could start digging into actual suspects.

Mrs. Penny rubbed her hands together. "Oh boy. Do I get to carry a gun?"

He thought fast. "You need to sell this grandma thing. The only weapons you can take are knitting needles."

"No problemo! I can still do a lot of damage with those," she said cheerfully.

"Who wants a nice pancake?" Riley crooned, dangling one in front of Burt's suspicious face. "Just come a *little* closer, and you can have this."

"I thought you said no people food," Lily said.

"I'm just trying to get him to come close enough that I can wipe off all the cheese doodle dust before he goes and rolls on someone's bed."

Several loud whacks rang out from under the sink, and a geyser of water erupted. The noise startled Burt, who backed into a chair, knocking it over.

Riley dove for him as he streaked past. Lily squealed as dog and human barreled by. The plate of pancakes went flying.

"Fred!" Nick yelled.

The soggy senior slopped his way out from under the sink. "Yeah?" he gurgled.

"Turn off the fucking water!"

Burt was distracted by the screaming and the flying breakfast food. Riley used it to her advantage and tackled him to the floor. But not before he hoovered up three of the pancakes.

The door swung open.

"Good morning," Gabe said. His dark skin glistened with a coating of sweat. "May I be of some assistance?"

"You." Nick pointed at Fred.

They were lined up in the living room in their soggy clothes. All except for Willicott, who had missed out on the chaos because he'd been too busy clogging the toilet upstairs.

Fred pointed to himself. "Me?"

Nick ripped a piece of paper off the top of the notepad and slapped it to the muscly senior's chest. "This is your honey-do list for the day. You're in charge of mopping up the kitchen, calling my plumber cousin, and reminding him he owes me big. Then you're boarding up the broken windows from the party and Mrs. Penny's breaking and entering. You will use plywood, a hammer, and nails. No power tools."

Fred saluted. "Aye, aye, captain!"

Nick moved down the line and handed Lily her own sheet of paper. "You are going to call these three contractors about your roof and ask for a quote and a timeline. Hire the one with the shortest timeline. I don't care if they replace your roof with thatched grass and bee colonies. Get it done."

She hugged the list to her chest. "I just love it when you play drill sergeant."

Nick stopped in front of Mr. Willicott and handed the man a roll of dog doody baggies. "Since you're so well versed in bowel movements, you are going to walk Burt until every single cheese doodle has been evacuated." He looked down at Burt. The dog's tail swished back and forth across the floor with vigor. "And *you* are going to make sure *he* finds his way back."

Mrs. Penny was next in line.

"You already have your assignment. Riley and I will drive you over to Gentry's. Don't blow it. Don't let him out of your sight. If anyone suspicious shows up, I wanna know. If he talks to someone on the phone, I want you eavesdropping."

"Penny PI is on the case," she squawked.

Gabe was next. "Okay, you muscly walrus in a muscle tank, you are in charge of everyone when Riley and I aren't here. You will keep everyone alive and intact and will prevent all future plumbing and construction disasters until we get back. This is not a job for the faint of heart."

Gabe nodded gravely. "I understand, and I will not let you down."

Nick moved to Riley. "Thorn. You're with me."

Assignments delivered, everyone sloshed and squished their way out of the room. Riley followed Nick into his office. He kicked off his slippers and wrung them out over the trash can.

"Are you sure it's a good idea to let Mrs. Penny be Griffin's personal security?"

"Nope. But it'll annoy Gentry, and she's batty enough to scare off most people with any sense of self-preservation. Plus, with someone else babysitting him, Josie can help Brian whittle down the phone book of suspects we're looking at."

"Do they still make phone books?" she wondered.

"Are you calling me old?"

"Well, you *did* just have a birthday."

He caught the tie of her robe and used it to reel her in. "You know, this is not how I planned to start our morning."

"I believe I caught your drift before we were interrupted."

"Maybe after we interview BlaBla Nosewhine, we can find a quiet place for some midmorning delight."

She smirked. "Do you mean Bella Goodshine?"

A door slammed somewhere on the second floor, voices rose as a squabble broke out, and Burt barked excitedly.

Nick groaned and lowered his forehead to Riley's. "We need a secret sex room. With a fridge and a TV and a very good lock."

"Hi! I'm Bella Goodshine!"

Riley jolted and looked at the TV, only to discover that Nick's office TV was tuned in to Channel 50's morning show.

"Everything is looking a little bit dampy wampy out here today in Central PA." Bella pouted prettily for the camera under a sunny yellow umbrella that somehow made her skin look even more luminous. She was in the backyard. The Griffin statue was fuzzed out behind her for the broadcast. "Watch out for those puddles! Now, back to my handsome soon-to-be hubby!"

She blew a kiss to the camera, and the show cut back to Griffin in their living room studio, catching the kiss and putting it in his pocket. The bruises on his face had been hidden under a thick layer of spackle.

"Thank you, Bella. I will now bravely continue the show despite my grave injuries."

"I'd like to dig a grave and injure him," Nick muttered at the TV.

11

"A re you sure you want to do this?" Nick asked Riley when they pulled into Griffin's driveway next to Josie's car. The windshield wipers screeched across the glass.

There were several thousand things Riley would rather be doing right now, but part of being an adult meant doing frustrating, painful things you didn't want to do. She opened her mouth to answer Nick, but their back-seat passenger beat her to it.

"I was born for this," Mrs. Penny announced, leaning between the seats.

"Not you. I meant Riley," Nick said, releasing his seat belt.

Mrs. Penny snorted. "What the hell does Riley have to worry about?"

"Gee, I don't know. Maybe it's weird to come back to the house she used to live in to interview the woman her husband cheated on her with," Nick snapped.

"Huh. I guess that would suck," Mrs. Penny agreed.

"Thanks, guys. Bringing up all that horrible emotional baggage is definitely the way to get off on a good foot," Riley said dryly as she got out of the vehicle and stared up at Griffin's house. It *was* weird, and it *did* suck. But she was an adult with a job to do.

"I was going for empathy," Nick called after her as she jogged through the rain.

The front door swung open before they made it through the puddles to the porch. Josie, in motorcycle pants and a black leather jacket, stormed out, looking lethal and not at all like a delicate mom-to-be. Riley winced as she caught a whiff of Josie's level of annoyance.

"How did it go this morning?" Nick asked.

"They're both vapid narcissists who are barely aware the other one exists. The morning show sucks. And if it weren't for the money we apparently so desperately need, I would have superglued their faces together and burned down the set to save Harrisburg from getting dumber just by tuning in."

"Okaaaaaay," he drawled. "I meant, were there any security issues?"

"Oh." Josie looked nonplussed and slammed the door behind her. "No. But there's freaking people freaking everywhere during the show. This place is like that place with the trains that's really busy?"

"Grand Central Station?" Riley filled in, hoping to be helpful.

Josie pointed at her. "Yeah. That. Despite being surrounded by a few dozen potential murderers, Griffin just whined constantly about his injuries, and Bella spent the last three hours baby talking to that stuffed animal she calls a dog. And now I'm leaving before I commit a crime."

"Bye, Josie," Riley called as the woman stomped past them. Even Mrs. Penny wisely gave her wide berth.

Nick waited until Josie got into her car and backed down the driveway. "Those pregnancy hormones seem to be coming along nicely," he observed.

The car came to a sudden halt at the foot of the driveway, and Josie glared through the windshield at them. She revved the engine once.

Riley held up her hands in surrender. "He's sorry. He didn't mean it," she yelled.

With another long glare, Josie shifted into reverse again and backed into the street. She blew her horn at the glossy black SUV idling in front of the house across the cul-de-sac. The startled driver took off, tires squealing with Josie aggressively tailgating.

"I didn't know pregnancy hearing was a thing," Nick said, rubbing a hand over his chest.

"Are we sure she isn't part vampire?" Riley asked.

"Come on, people! Quit your dillydallying. Gam Gam Gentry needs to see her grandson," Mrs. Penny barked from the walkway, where she batted away raindrops with her cane.

"She really does look like a Gam Gam," Riley observed as they watched her huff and puff her way up to the porch.

Mrs. Penny had dressed the part in lilac elastic-waist pants hiked up to the underboobs. Her pastel flower cardigan looked like it was made from a few dozen potholders sewn together. She'd fluffed her purple hair at the crown, smeared on a pearly pink lipstick, and stuffed half a box of tissues up her sleeve.

She strutted right on up to the porch and stabbed the doorbell with her cane.

"I will not punch the turd in the face. I will not punch the turd in the face," Nick repeated to himself as he took Riley's hand.

The door opened, and they found themselves face-to-face with a young guy with thick dark hair and glasses.

If Riley wasn't mistaken, she was looking at Griffin's pickleball partner and human shield from last night's vision of Ingram Theodoric. He wore a neatly pressed polo shirt with the word STAFF embroidered on the chest.

"I'm sorry, folks. Mr. Gentry and Ms. Goodshine aren't accepting visitors at this time. If you have any gifts, I'll be happy to make sure they receive them. Feel free to take a signed headshot of Mr. Gentry," he said with a gesture to the stack on the table next to him.

"Outta my way, sonny." Mrs. Penny prodded him with her cane. "I'm here to see my grandson."

"Who is it, Staff? Adoring admirers? Do you have my autograph pen?" Griffin limped into view with the inflatable doughnut pillow looped over one arm and a goblet of orange juice in hand. He still wore his on-camera makeup.

"It's us," Nick said, making it sound like a threat.

"Oh. Well, I'm still happy to autograph something for you," Griffin said.

"Should I let them in, Mr. Gentry?" the door guy asked.

Taking matters into her own hands, Mrs. Penny strutted over the threshold and pinched Griffin's cheeks. "There's my special boy."

"Ow! My face," Griffin howled.

"Gam Gam wanted to spend some quality time with you," Nick said pointedly.

Griffin's confusion was obvious.

"I'm happy to get some refreshments for your guests, Mr. Gentry," the guy offered.

"I'll take a coffee, black, and a side of bacon. Oh, and a couple of breakfast tacos if you have any handy," Mrs. Penny said.

"And I'd like some fresh pineapple cut up and stacked like onion rings. Then I need you to schedule a massage for my legs and wear my new driving moccasins around the house to break them in, Staff," Griffin added.

"Of course," the employee said. "Anything for you two?"

"Uh, Nick and I are fine," Riley told him.

"I'm Staff, Mr. Gentry's personal assistant. If you change your mind, just yell obscenities or insults and I'll appear," he said before heading for the kitchen. The back of his shirt had an even bigger STAFF across the shoulders.

Left alone with Griffin, Riley noticed he was staring strangely at Mrs. Penny. "Gam Gam? I thought you were dead," he whispered.

"Oh boy," Riley muttered under her breath.

"For fuck's sake," Mrs. Penny groaned.

"No, you lobotomized puppet," Nick snapped. "Mrs.

Penny is going undercover as your grandmother. She's your security today."

Understanding dawned slowly. Very slowly. "Ohhhh. Thank goodness, because Gam Gam used to hit me with a ruler, and I didn't care for that *at all*."

"It's safer for you if other people don't know you have security with you. It'll make it easier for us to catch them if they don't know who we are," Riley explained.

"Ohhh, okay. But I can tell Staff, right?"

"Do you trust him?" Nick asked through clenched teeth. The vein in his forehead looked a little throbby.

Griffin placed a hand over his heart. "I trust him with my dry cleaning," he whispered earnestly.

"Maybe let's keep this between us for now," Riley suggested.

"If you think that's best," Griffin agreed. He frowned. "You don't think my dry cleaning is in danger, do you?"

"Jesus, Gentry. Go sit on your doughnut with Gam Gam. We have a few questions for your fiancée," Nick said.

Mrs. Penny produced a ruler from her oversize GRANDMAS GIVE THE BEST HUGS tote bag and rapped Griffin's wrist with it.

"Ow! Gam Gam!"

"I'm a method investigator," she said.

———

They found Bella Goodshine, perky weather girl and soon-to-be bride, on her back in a compromising position with a female personal trainer.

"Do you feel that?" the trainer asked as she used her body weight to press Bella's bent knee into Bella's waxed armpit.

Riley had to give Nick credit. He wasn't staring at the semi-erotic stretching happening on the mat. No, his appreciative gaze was fixed on the huge flat-screen TV mounted to the wall. Dance music thumped from a speaker in the corner. There was a small scruffy dog wearing a purple scrunchie curled on a fluffy matching pillow next to a mini fridge filled with expensive bottled water and fresh pressed juices. Rain pattered against the basement windows high up on the wall.

"I do. I really feel it," Bella chirped as she admired her own reflection in the wall of mirrors.

"I get the feeling she has to say that line a lot," Nick muttered to Riley under his breath.

"Am I crazy, or does that mirror have a filter on it?" Riley asked, turning her head from side to side. "Look how dewy my skin is."

"Focus, Thorn." He crossed to the speaker and hit the power button. "Okay, ladies. Sorry to break up whatever the hell it is that you're doing, but we need to ask Ms. Goodshine some questions."

The trainer jumped to her feet with catlike grace. She reached down and hauled Bella up.

Bella was dressed in bubble-gum pink spandex that showcased her monumental chest. Her perky blond ponytail swung jauntily above a white sweatband.

The trainer had long thick hair that exploded out from under a sleek ball cap, ruby-red fingernails long enough to gouge out an eyeball, and an enviable set of shoulders. Sweat glistened on her tan skin. She was looking at Nick and Riley like she was assessing their fitness. Feeling self-conscious, Riley stood straighter. She'd been meaning to go to the gym but kept getting distracted by dead bodies.

"I remember you," Bella said to Nick. She had the kind of voice that was usually reserved for talking to newborn lambs. Sweet and breathy. She turned to Riley and extended her hand. "Hi, I'm Bella."

Riley blew out a sigh through her teeth. "We've met. On several occasions. I'm Riley."

There was no glimmer of recognition in Bella's wide, cartoonlike eyes.

"Riley Thorn. The psychic. You came to my house for a

séance? I made sure you didn't get blown up at Channel 50 this summer? You slept with my ex-husband while we were still married?"

Bella's lashes fluttered, and she tapped a finger to her chin. "Hmm, nope. Not ringing a bell. But don't worry. I'm sure we'll be good friends in no time."

"Bella has female face blindness," the trainer explained.

"That's not a thing," Riley said.

"Chupy, be a dear and whip up one of those protein and placenta smoothies for me before you go," Bella said.

"Sure thing," the trainer said.

"Hang on. Your name is what?" Nick asked.

"Chupacabra Jones," she said, pointing to the name tag clipped to her tank top. "I'm a mixed martial artist. It's my fighting name."

Nick nodded and rubbed a hand over his stubbly chin. "Uh-huh. Uh-huh. Please allow me to confer with my colleague," he said before leaning in to Riley. "If we have kids someday, I think we should name one Chupacabra."

The vision flashed into her mind before she could stop it. Nick with a cherubic little girl balanced on his hip. Their dimples matched.

It was gone as quickly as it had come. Riley shook her head to clear it.

"Focus, Santiago," she whispered, then turned back to the women. "Do you train together often?"

"Chupy trains me four days a week," Bella explained.

Great. Yet another person who had access to the house on an almost daily basis.

"Were you here yesterday?" Nick asked.

Chupacabra picked up a plastic bottle of pink liquid and squeezed a stream into her mouth. "Yeah. After the show wrapped. Leg day." She eyed Riley. "You ever lift?"

Food to face? Yes. Weights? No.

"I'm more of a yoga person," Riley said.

"You should give lifting a try. Get those biceps poppin'."

"I'll keep that in mind," she said.

"I'll leave the smoothie in the fridge for you," Chupacabra said to Bella, who had picked up the little dog and was making loud smoochy noises.

"Thank you! Say buh-bye, La La," she said, waving the little dog's paw. Its nails were painted purple.

Chupacabra slung a duffel bag over her muscled shoulder, threw them a salute, and jogged out of the room.

"You're here about my Griffy Wiffy, aren't you?" Bella pouted, still snuggling the dog. "Someone tried to hurt Daddy, didn't they?"

"I can't tell if she's talking to us or the dog," Nick said.

"Bella, do you know of anyone who would want to hurt Griffin?" Riley asked, cutting to the chase. She was starting to feel claustrophobic…and exceedingly annoyed.

Bella's eyes were wide and guileless. "No, of course not. Everyone loves us."

"Do cartoon birds help you get dressed in the morning?" Nick asked.

Bella batted her spider-leg eyelashes. "Huh?"

"Someone left a threatening note, shot at, and then pushed Griffin down the stairs," Riley said. "Not everyone loves him."

Bella lifted her shoulders in a dainty shrug. "It must be jealousy. Not everyone can be as wonderful as we are."

"Yeah, sure. Everyone's jealous. Who pays Chupacabra and your Staff guy?" Nick asked.

"Griffy takes care of all those pesky bills."

"Pretty sweet setup. Big house. Fancy clothes. Personal trainer. You don't seem too concerned about someone trying to take out your meal ticket," Nick pointed out.

Bella gasped. "Are you insinuating that *I* had something to do with poor Griffy's troubles?"

"Nothing personal. Rule number one: always look at the spouse," Nick said.

Bella's face went cagey for a split second before smoothing

back into youthful innocence. "We're not married yet. If I'm after Griffin's money, why would I throw it all away before I'm officially Mrs. Gentry?" she asked haughtily.

Riley's nose twitched. Something was incoming from her spirit guides.

"Maybe the prenup's not favorable? Or maybe he just chews his Cornish hen too fucking loud in the mornings. People try to kill people for a whole lot of crazy reasons."

"We don't eat Cornish hen for breakfast, silly," Bella said.

The pink and blue clouds were rising up in Riley's head. She took a steadying breath and let it happen. She could see Bella in a spectacular wedding dress. Pieces of paper flitted in front of the image. A legal document of some kind. Phrases popped out at her. *Infidelity. Financial penalty.* Bella was back, smiling smugly and pointing at a weather map of the state of Florida. The dog panted happily off camera in a Louis Vuitton tote.

"Just level with us, Bella. Do you know who's after Griffin?" Nick's words brought Riley back into her body.

"No." Bella's expression darkened, and she pointed a very sharp fingernail at them. "But I want you to find them and make them pay. *No one* is going to stop our wedding."

"I assume what you meant to say is no one is going to hurt your fiancé," he said pointedly.

She immediately transformed back into her bubbly weather girl self. "Of course, silly! That's the most important thing."

12

"Chupacabra Jones has got to be the coolest name ever," Brian said as he reviewed his copy of the list of suspects.

"I know, right?" Nick agreed, frowning down at his phone. Riley sensed testosterone-fueled enthusiasm and wondered what he was up to.

"We're *not* naming the baby Chupacabra," Josie said.

"Let's at least put it on the maybe list," Brian insisted.

"Speaking of lists, we need to narrow down these suspects," Riley announced. She was sitting on the couch in Nick's office with Burt's heavy head in her lap. He was snoring against her belly.

"The focus is on the breath and the flow. We are present in the moment." Gabe's mellow voice came from the foyer, where he was teaching Fred, Lily, and Mr. Willicott tai chi.

Nick put his phone down and picked up his copy of the suspect list.

It was four single-spaced, two-columned pages that included everyone Griffin had mentioned who might have a problem with him, all the staffers affiliated with Channel 50's morning show, and anyone with regular access to Griffin or his house. After signing the affidavit Mrs. Penny had prepared for her, swearing she had nothing to do with the threat on Griffin's life, Riley had taken her own name off the list to save space.

"I started background checks on the first dozen or so names yesterday," Brian said, scrolling through a document on his laptop. "The neighbor Belinda came up clean. She's mostly retired from Hollywood but still does some consulting. Enough in cash and investments to be considered rich by anyone's standards. No priors. No bad press. However, the neighbor on the other side of Gentry is a different story."

Riley shivered, remembering the rage-fueled confrontation.

"Lyle Larstein is a bad dude," Brian continued. "He was a top executive for Blue Banner Health, pulling down seven figures in bonuses alone every year. Second home in Cabo. Garage full of exotic sports cars. The wife and kids left him and took pretty much everything not nailed down after it went public that Larstein had a long history of sexual harassment and firing those who didn't submit to his advances."

"If that isn't bad enough," Josie added, "the shitbag decided seven figures a year wasn't enough and got caught embezzling from Blue Banner's nonprofit arm. He literally stole money from sick babies."

Riley wasn't surprised.

"He goes to the top. Theodoric stays up there too," Nick said. "Gentry slept with his girlfriend/daughter. I wouldn't put it past him to take a shot at someone who embarrassed him like that."

Burt's tail tapped happily in his sleep.

"Claudia Mendoza claims she's over Griffin getting her fired, but she's still carrying a grudge," Riley said. "She was also in town when he was shot at yesterday."

"What did you get from Goodshine this morning? Besides a blinding headache?" Nick asked her. "Her nails are too long to hold a gun, let alone shoot one, but she's the one who lives with the annoying asshat. That could drive anyone to attempted murder."

"I'm pretty sure she's planning to marry Griffin, catch him

cheating, and collect a big fat payout from the infidelity clause in the prenup before moving to Florida where the weather is easier to report." She tapped her highlighter against the page. "As much as I would love the karma of it, I don't think she's our bad guy."

"It's so fucking cool to have a psychic on the team," Brian said.

"I hate to bring this up," Josie said, flipping through her copy of the suspects. "But what if it's someone who didn't make the list?"

"Then we pin it on one of the bad guys we did find, collect our check, and go out for a steak dinner," Nick quipped.

Riley was only half-sure he was kidding.

"I'll keep digging into the list and see if anyone else has any priors or if they're spouting off threats on social media," Brian said.

"What do you want me to do, boss?" Josie asked.

"Something you're not going to like, but you're the only person I trust to get the job done."

"I'm listening."

"We need to deploy the elderly."

Burt rolled over onto his back with a hefty yawn, and his paws shot up in the air, bopping Riley in the chin. "Deploy the elderly for what?" she asked.

"Too many suspects and not enough time. I need the fogies to start surveillance of our most likely baddies."

This wasn't the first time Nick had employed their roommates. He'd once hired Mrs. Penny to follow Riley around in disguise. She still had dreams about being chased by an elderly mime.

"Noooooooooo," Josie moaned, then scraped her hands over her face. "You know how I feel about old people."

"Look, I need someone who can keep them in line and out of trouble. Brian can bust out some of our toys, and you two can monitor them from the van," Nick said.

"Are you sure that's a good idea?" Riley pressed, dodging

Burt's tongue. There were a million ways this could go horribly wrong.

"No one looks twice at an old guy feeding the birds on a bench. Besides, it'll keep them from destroying our house," he insisted.

As if on cue, there was a resounding crash from the foyer. "Whoopsie!" Lily called.

"I hate everything about this," Josie said.

Brian patted his wife's leg. "Look at it this way, Jos. It'll be good practice for parenting. We just gotta keep a couple of tall toddlers alive for a few days."

"That's the spirit," Nick said. "Tell them we'll pay them in shingles vaccines or whatever they're into."

The meeting broke up, and everyone dispersed. Burt rolled off Riley's lap onto the floor for a big stretch before trotting out of the room.

"What time do you want to leave?" she asked Nick, checking her watch.

"I've got a few things I want to take care of here first. How about we head out in an hour? We'll grab lunch and fuel up before interrogating half of Harrisburg."

"Sounds good. In the meantime, I think I'll confiscate Gabe and see if we can psychically narrow down the list."

"I'll be eternally and sexually grateful," Nick said with a wicked, dimpled grin.

"I'll pass that along to Gabe."

"So how do we do this?" Riley asked her spiritual adviser.

She and Gabe were sitting cross-legged facing each other on the dusty wood floor of the attic. It wasn't the most comfortable space, but none of their other roommates had the endurance to make it up the extra flight of stairs, so it was a distraction-free zone.

Gabe peered down at the list. "I fear you may be opening yourself up to too much information if we seek answers to questions that are too general."

"Meaning?"

"Griffin Gentry is not a nice human."

"No, really?" she said dryly.

Her lovable hunk of a spiritual guide cocked his head. "Do you not agree?"

"Of course I do. I was just being sarcastic."

Gabe looked at her blankly.

"It means you use words that say the opposite of what you mean. But it kind of only works when it's obvious. Griffin is obviously a terrible person," she explained.

"Ah. I believe I understand now."

Happy to be the instructor for once, Riley grinned. "Here, let's practice. Gee, Gabe, November sure is chilly."

"I find the month to be quite invigorating."

"Okaaaay. Not quite. How about this one? Do you like ice cream?"

He blinked, then a slow smile spread across his handsome face. "I do not care for ice cream."

"That's better. But to make the sarcasm more obvious, you can exaggerate it. Like 'Nooo. I *hate* ice cream,'" she said. "Sometimes an eye roll helps convey the message."

"But is it unkind to use words that mask your truth?" he pressed.

"I like to think of sarcasm as a humor tool. Words can tell the truth, but you can also have fun with them and tell the truth at the same time."

"Then I will *not* practice this sarcasm," he deadpanned.

Riley laughed. "I think you're getting the hang of it. Now back to our list of suspects. How do we narrow it down?"

"If you ask your spirit guides who wishes him harm, the answer may be overwhelming," he warned.

"So I should be more specific, like, 'Who shot at Griffin?'"

"I believe that will be the most effective approach." Gabe produced an elegant crystal pendant on a long silver chain from under his tank top. "We shall work together."

"What's that for?" she asked.

"This is a pendulum for divination. While you discuss the situation with your spirit guides, I will see if this crystal stops above any names on the list." He laid out the pages side-by-side between them.

"Okay. Here goes nothing," she said, closing her eyes. Together they breathed in the dusty air. "Hey, spirit guides. It's me. I've got a job for you."

Cotton candy–colored clouds were just beginning to drift into the edges of her vision when someone began blasting a big band playlist on the second floor.

It was immediately followed by distant shouting.

"Maybe we should have done this anywhere but here," Riley said through clenched teeth.

"Distractions are everywhere. It is best to learn to work through them rather than only away from them."

She squeezed her eyes shut and covered her ears with her hands. "I need to know who tried to shoot Griffin Gentry yesterday morning."

Everything behind her eyelids wavered for a moment. The clouds peeked through again, only more muted this time. She doubled down on her focus, grasping for the vision. Finally, the murky clouds began to part.

"What is it that you see?" Gabe asked.

"I'm seeing someone's legs. Ew. I'm seeing Griffin's legs. His calves. The trainer said yesterday was leg day. Does that mean it's Chupacabra Jones?"

The floor under her butt trembled when a door slammed beneath her. The vision legs disappeared.

"Crap," she muttered.

"Find your focus," Gabe directed.

"Any tips on how?" she grumbled irritably. "Wait. I'm seeing something else now. Glitter. Or sparkles?" A wave of elation rushed through her. "It's bright and…happy. The sparkle makes me feel happy."

"The pendulum is moving," Gabe reported.

Riley could hear the thud of a fist on a door followed by bits of a muffled conversation beneath her.

The sparkles wavered, and a bead of sweat slid down her back as she fought to keep them.

The music shut off abruptly, and the sparkles vanished.

"Damn it," she said.

"The pendulum appears to like a name."

"Who?" Riley asked, still trying to focus. But the feelings were starting to spin out of control. "Uh-oh."

"What is wrong?" Gabe asked.

Happy, scared, surprised. The visions followed in blurred chaos. Griffin's legs. Sparkle. Someone was shouting. Was that Ingram Theodoric or one of their roommates? She couldn't focus. Suddenly she found herself zoomed in on Gabe. And Riley's sister Wander. Oh shit, they were naked. She'd accidentally fallen into Gabe's head.

Pull up! Pull up!

The naked couple disappeared behind a frantic blur of clouds. She caught a glimpse of a room. There were too many people in the room, all of them scowling at Griffin. Then Nick. *Bang!*

Riley's eyes flew open. "Whoa," she said. And then she keeled over.

———

Gabe helped her down the stairs with a chivalrous and muscly arm around her waist.

"What the hell, Gigantor?" Nick demanded, jogging to meet them. "What did you do to my girl?"

"I'm fine," Riley assured him as Gabe transferred her to Nick. "My spirit guides were frisky today. That's all." They weren't the only ones feeling frisky. Either she'd stumbled on Gabe's fantasy world, or he and her sister had finally gotten it on.

Did Gabe know she'd slipped into his head? Should she confess and apologize? Should she pretend it hadn't happened and just never make eye contact with him again? She wasn't sure what the proper psychic etiquette was in this situation.

"Uh, Gabe?" she began tentatively as they resumed their journey down the stairs.

"Yes. Wander and I did take our relationship to another level," he said.

"Oh boy." Riley looked at her feet. Her face felt like it was a million degrees.

"Please say you're talking about organizing her holiday decor in a basement or an attic," Nick complained, tightening his hold on her.

"It was…ethereal," Gabe said. It sounded like he was smiling, but Riley was still staring at her feet, willing away the images that floated into her mind like a parade of naked Gabes and Wanders.

"Let's talk about something else. Anything at all. Who has an opinion on sports, politics, or religion?" Riley begged.

"I am sensing discomfort. Is this accurate, or are you providing another example of sarcasm?" Gabe asked.

"Don't teach him sarcasm, Thorn. It's more fun when he doesn't know I'm busting on him," Nick said as he helped her down the last few steps.

"Soon I will bust you with my sarcastic prowess," Gabe promised.

The bickering was better than picturing Gabe and her sister naked, so she allowed it.

Nick helped her into a tall wingback chair with wooden arms in the foyer. "You're not supposed to push yourself so hard. Or do you not remember losing your powers this week?"

"I wasn't pushing. I just wasn't controlling the volume of information shooting into my brain."

He crouched down in front of her and rubbed his hands up her thighs. "Do you need a snack?"

"Always."

"I will make you this snack and bring you some water," Gabe offered gallantly.

"Thanks, Gabe."

They watched him all but float to the kitchen door, a dreamy smile on his face.

"I accidentally slipped into Gabe's head while we were working with my spirit guides and saw things I shouldn't have seen. Naked things. They looked like something Michelangelo would have painted if he was into super sexy erotic paintings," she told Nick.

"Listen. The only naked bodies I care about are yours and mine. Especially considering we're way better at sex than those two."

"Has anyone ever told you you're the tiniest bit way too competitive?" Riley asked.

"You should see game night in the Santiago house. It's not over until someone cries and someone else is bleeding. Back to this accidentally slipping into people's heads. Aren't you always reading minds?"

She grimaced. "People are always broadcasting their thoughts. I just make an effort to block them out. It's like when the neighbor's dog has been barking for six years. You kind of learn to not hear it anymore. This time, I was already open to the visions from my spirit guides, and Gabe was feeling...let's say *pleased* with his recent experiences. So I got an accidental front row seat to his memory reel."

"So how the hell am I ever supposed to surprise you with something?"

Riley shrugged. "Good luck with that. I've known what every Christmas present was before it even made it under the tree."

"Challenge accepted," he said.

She slapped her palm to her forehead. "I was so distracted by Sexy Time Gabe I almost forgot. Wilfred Peabody."

"Gesundheit," he said.

"Har har. Wilfred Peabody. He's the jeweler on the list. Griffin said Wilfred's been harassing him over some piece of jewelry or something. I kept seeing sparkles in my vision."

"So it's not another glitter bomb?"

"I think we're safe. Gabe confirmed it by doing some other psychic stuff."

"Thank God. I'm still finding glitter in my underwear," Nick said.

"I also kept seeing Griffin's legs."

"That's a straight up nightmare."

"I know, right? Do you think we should take a closer look at the personal trainer?" she asked.

"I'll bump her up on Brian's list and see what he can dig up," he promised.

The doorbell rang, and he jumped to his feet.

"Are you expecting someone?" Riley called after him as he practically sprinted for the door.

He yanked it open and disappeared onto the front porch.

"Your snack," Gabe said, returning from the kitchen with Burt on his heels. He held out a plate with a picture-perfect peanut butter and jelly sandwich cut diagonally with precision.

"Hey, Schwarzenegger 2.0, get your biceps out here," Nick called from the porch.

"I think he means you," Riley said, taking a bite of her sandwich. Burt sat in front of her, staring hard at the food and drooling. "Don't even think about it, buddy. Mr. Willicott said your poop looked like Orange Julius."

Nick and Gabe returned, carrying a large flat box between them.

"Just set it down against the table," Nick said through gritted teeth. They maneuvered the box into position.

"What is that?" Riley asked, the words muffled by peanut butter.

"That is an eighty-five-inch TV." Nick patted the box with affection.

The sandwich lodged in her throat. "Nick! I thought you said no medium-size purchases?"

"That was before I saw the TV in Gentry's gym. And before I got Mom and Dad's birthday check in the mail. Besides, now you and I can watch those movies you got me upstairs in our *locked* bedroom."

Mr. Willicott shuffled past in his bathrobe, chugging a bottle of Diet Pepsi. He paused in the middle of the foyer and released a dragon-worthy belch.

"I know I'm supposed to be the voice of reason, but I'm not hating this idea," she admitted.

"This television appears to be quite small," Gabe said.

"He's being sarcastic," Riley explained.

13

Peabody Jewelry was sandwiched between a vape shop and a vegan restaurant in one of Camp Hill's mini strip malls. Nick eyed the classy gold lettering on the shop window as he put Riley's Jeep in park, then noted the handwritten *Going Out of Business* signs.

Riley snickered in the passenger seat. "Uncle Jimmy is offended by the vegan place. He says he doesn't trust anyone who doesn't eat fish."

"Don't worry, Uncle Jimmy. We're going fishing for a bad guy."

"Wilfred Peabody doesn't look like much of a bad guy to me," Riley said, turning her phone screen to face him.

It was an article from the local paper about Peabody donating a paw print necklace to a local animal shelter's charity auction. He was a small man with graying hair and a hook nose above a tidy little mustache.

Nick rubbed a finger over his upper lip. He wondered if he could pull off a mustache. Like one of the *Top Gun* ones.

"I can see it," Riley said.

"You bouncing around in my brain again?" he teased.

"It's not my fault you broadcasted mustache thoughts loud enough that I could hear them."

"Facial hair considerations aside, how do you feel about having a little fun in there?" he asked, nodding toward the jewelry store.

"Why do you think I dressed in disguise?" She gestured at her outfit.

She was wearing a faux leather jacket over a tight Harley Davidson T-shirt with a deep V-neck and even tighter jeans. Nick hadn't gotten past approving of the fit to notice it wasn't her usual style. Being dazzled by female curves wasn't exactly a smart move for a private investigator.

"You didn't even notice I was in disguise, did you?" she asked with a smirk.

"I'm a simple man. You show off cleavage like that, and I'm bound to get a little distracted."

"I'll keep that in mind," she said. She pulled an eye shadow palette out of her purse and flipped down the sun visor to get at the mirror.

A few quick swipes of a brush, the application of one of those little claw hair clips, and he found himself staring at a completely different woman.

"Two can play at that game," he said, reaching into the back seat and producing a worn NASCAR ball cap. "Let's go see what our jeweler suspect is up to."

———

The bell above the door tinkled when they walked in. The walls were papered in understated gold and decorated with framed black-and-white photos of happy bridal couples with big-ass rings. Waist-height glass display cases ringed the perimeter of the store. At the back was a cash register on what looked like a classy bar.

A chubby tabby cat exited its bed and dug its nails into the thick cream carpet.

"Welcome, welcome!" The greeting came not from the cat but from the man who bustled out of the back room in a navy pin-striped suit. He wore spectacles perched on his hawklike nose and had a polka-dotted pocket square. Wilfred Peabody in the flesh clocked in at somewhere around five feet six inches and one hundred forty pounds.

"Hi there. I'm Toby and this here's my fiancée, LuEllen," Nick said in a twangy southern accent. "I just asked this little lady to be my bride."

"And I said only if the ring is nice enough," Riley piped up as a chipper, flirtatious LuEllen. "I can't control the fact that Toby here leaves toothpaste smeared all over the sink like he was using it to ice cupcakes. But I *can* make sure that I get a pretty little something for my trouble."

Nick was impressed. He gave her an approving wink before turning back to Wilfred and leaning an arm on a case of watches. "Whaddaya say, jewelry man? Help a fella out?"

"It would be my pleasure. Please call me Wilfred."

"Wilfred, in your expert opinion, do you think this little ol' finger would look better with a princess cut or a cushion cut?" Riley asked.

"Well, why don't we see what your ring finger has to say," the jeweler said with enthusiasm.

The cat twined itself around Nick's legs while Riley and Wilfred oohed and aahed over a velvet rectangle display of diamond rings.

"What do you think, Toby?" Riley asked, holding up her hand to show off a ring. Not just a ring. *The* ring.

Nick blinked and took her hand to get a better look.

"It's a classic cushion-cut stone with a baguette halo set in platinum," Wilfred explained.

"It's, uh, nice," Nick rasped. It was more than nice. It was fucking awesome.

Why was he suddenly sweating? Why was the ring so sparkly? Was there some kind of spotlight shining down on the ring like it was Taylor Swift onstage?

Get a hold of yourself, dipshit.

He was just having a blood sugar crash. Or a panic attack. Or a small mental break. He was not staring at a diamond ring on Riley's finger and wanting to actually put it there.

Still in character, Riley cocked her head and pouted. "Hmm. I think it's a little *too* classy. Don't you, Toby? I think I need a ring that says, 'Sometimes makes bad decisions but has a damn good time making them.'"

"I've got just the thing," Wilfred promised gleefully.

Riley and Wilfred moved down to the next case. Nick knelt to pet the cat and catch his breath.

He wanted to put a ring on Riley Thorn's finger. Before her, he'd never even considered things like getting engaged or married or, you know, the future.

They'd only known each other for four months. There was mozzarella in the cheese drawer older than their relationship. Sweat ran in rivulets down his back.

They owned a home together. They worked together. They had a dog together. This wasn't just another new relationship. This was *the* relationship. This was it. *She* was it.

But how the hell was he supposed to pop the question when he'd just blown all his spare cash on a TV? Hell, Griffin had managed to buy her a ring. A real one. Not some diamond chip purchased from the trunk of someone's shady cousin's car.

His head felt heavy and woozy. The cat was giving him a what-the-hell-is-wrong-with-you look. Nick wasn't sure what was wrong. But little pinpricks of light danced before his eyes. Darkness rolled in like the tide, and he decided the carpet looked like an awfully nice place to hyperventilate.

"Toby, honey? You okay?" Riley asked, her voice strained.

"Perhaps try slapping him?" Wilfred suggested.

"No slap," Nick murmured. He managed to pry his eyelids open and found Riley hovering over him. She was fucking beautiful. And she had what looked like fifteen carats of diamonds on her fingers.

"I'll call 911," a worried-looking Wilfred volunteered.

"I'm fine," Nick grumbled, working his way into a seated position.

"What happened?" Riley asked.

"You know how I get when I don't get a bag of Sour Patch Kids every few hours," he said, regaining his feet and his character.

"May I ask how you heard about my store?" Wilfred asked, glancing down at Riley's diamond-clad finger nervously.

Nick decided to take a gamble. "Griffin Gentry."

Wilfred jumped like someone had just announced the floor was lava. "You will kindly hand over the jewelry and leave immediately."

"Now hang on a second," Nick said, dropping the accent.

"You're not southern. Is your name even Toby?" Wilfred squeaked and scampered behind the register. With shaking hands, he pulled out a pearl-handled Colt revolver and aimed it at the ceiling. "I am done being victimized by that man."

Nick stepped in front of Riley, hands in the air. "Let's take it easy, Wilfred. We're not here for that. My girl here is going to carefully take off the rings and put them back on the case, and you're going to keep that six-shooter pointed at the ceiling."

"Okay," Wilfred said in a whisper. Sweat dotted his forehead. His mustache twitched.

With Nick as her human shield, Riley slowly removed all four rings and placed them in a neat row back on the blue velvet cloth.

"We're not here to hurt you or steal anything. We're here to help," she said, raising her hands in the air.

"No one affiliated with Griffin Gentry is out for anyone but themselves."

"He's my ex-husband. We got divorced because he slept with a coworker; then he fired me and sued me for breaking his nose," she explained. "I almost went broke because of him."

Wilfred wavered.

Riley tried to inch past Nick's shoulders, but he blocked her. "We think he took something from you that's very important, and I'd like to talk about how we can help you get it back," she continued.

"How am I supposed to trust you?"

"That's a good question. How about we start with the fact that your grandfather's gun isn't loaded because the firing pin stopped working in the seventies and you don't even own bullets for it. But we're still standing here with our hands up because we just want to talk."

Wilfred dropped the gun. "How did you know that?"

"It's a long story," Riley said, sagging against Nick's back.

"Man, I don't know about you guys, but I could go for a drink," Nick said, dropping his hands.

————

"So you *are* working for Griffin?" Wilfred clarified as he stared morosely into his Long Island iced tea.

They were sitting at the bar of a divey restaurant. The cat—Elizabeth Taylor—purred happily on the bar in her carrier.

"Technically in the sense that he hired us to find out who's been threatening him, yes," Nick said, then took a swig of his beer.

"But we're not happy about it," Riley assured the jeweler as the bartender plopped a beer down in front of her.

Wilfred put his head in his hands. "I never should have made those cuff links."

"What cuff links?" Nick asked.

The jeweler sighed. "A few months ago, Griffin came into my shop and told me he wanted to design a pair of custom cuff links. He was going to wear them at some local daytime TV awards ceremony. I was ecstatic. I thought it would be great exposure for the store. We've been struggling since the rent went up at the beginning of the year. We were falling behind. I just needed to hold on until our December trunk show, which always brings in three months' worth of revenue in one weekend, but it was becoming apparent that we might not make it until then."

"So you agreed to make the cuff links," Riley filled in sympathetically.

Wilfred nodded. "It was a $25,000 job. I set aside all other paying jobs and worked night and day to get them done." He reached into his suit jacket and pulled out his phone. "They were perfect." He thumbed through his photos and turned the screen their way.

They were something all right, Nick noted. Ridiculously over the top, ostentatious. They didn't whisper "I'm wealthy." They screamed it.

"They're art deco emerald-cut canary diamonds. Some of my best work," Wilfred said. "And I'll never see them again because Griffin Gentry is a crook."

Riley paused midsip. "What happened to the cuff links?"

"He showed up the day of the event to collect them. When I took him to the register to ring him out, he said that he was running late and would settle up with me later. He left the store with the cuff links, and he's avoided me ever since. After several phone calls and letters, I finally received a letter from his attorney saying that the cuff links were a gift from me and that any further attempt to collect payment would be met with legal action. Legal action I can't afford."

Elizabeth Taylor let out a mournful meow in her carrier.

"Is that why you're closing your store?" Riley asked.

"I have no other choice. I had to let my staff go. There just isn't enough revenue coming in. And even if some miracle occurred and he returned them, it's not like I could find someone else willing to spend $25,000 on a set of cuff links." Wilfred took a morose sip of his drink. "Three generations of my family have run this store, and now I'm the one to drive it into the ground."

Riley met Nick's eyes over his head with a can-we-please-help-this-guy look on her face.

"Let's get this part out of the way," Nick said. "You pulled a gun on us. What's to say you wouldn't do the same to Griffin... even though he deserves it?"

Wilfred sighed. "It's my grandfather's gun. My parents kept it in the shop as a deterrent. I kept it for nostalgia. Like

LuEllen…er, Riley said, there are no bullets because the firing pin is broken. The best I could do would be to throw it at a robber."

"Okay. Easy enough to verify. Now, let's talk about where you were yesterday between noon and one thirty."

"My mother watched the store for me while I went to a twelve o'clock Pilates class with my friends. Afterward, we went out for crepes." Wilfred took off his glasses and rubbed his eyes.

"Do you have any reason to do harm to Griffin Gentry?" Nick asked.

"What would I gain from that? He already won. He can afford better lawyers than I can. Besides, with my luck, if he gets himself murdered, he'll probably be buried with my cuff links."

———

"I feel awful," Riley groaned when they got back in the Jeep.

"It's not your fault Gentry is a selfish, entitled shit," Nick pointed out. "I didn't catch any nose twitches. Nothing from the spirit guides?"

She shook her head. "I didn't pick up on any homicidal tendencies. Just an overwhelming sense of despondency, which seems to have seeped into my brain, and now I'm sad and I want ice cream."

"My girl wants sad ice cream, she gets sad ice cream," he said, patting her knee.

He'd just reversed out of the parking spot when his phone rang. He answered it on speaker phone. "What's up, Gam Gam?"

"You better get over here. We've got a Code Cold Burrito," Mrs. Penny barked. It sounded like women were screaming in the background.

Nick thumped his head against the driver's seat. "I don't care about your leftovers."

"I'm not talking about leftovers. I'm talking about a Code Cold Burrito. Don't you read the memos I leave on your desk?"

"I haven't seen the top of my desk in weeks. Just tell me what a Cold Burrito is so I can regret knowing."

He glanced Riley's way just in time to catch her nose twitch.

"Uh-oh," she murmured.

"There's a stiff in the shrubbery at Gentry's. A Cold Burrito. I suggest you get here before the cops."

"Christ. Who did you murder?" Nick said, accelerating out of the lot.

"I can't hear you over the dipshit twins trying to out-scream each other. People act like they've never seen a stiff before." With that, Mrs. Penny hung up.

14

Griffin's assistant was ghostly pale when he opened the front door. His hair was messier than usual, and his staff shirt had fresh stains down the front. Riley had a feeling it was barf. He managed to point a trembling finger toward the backyard, but it wasn't necessary considering they could just follow the sound of the screaming.

"You know how quiet my life was before I met you?" Nick said to her as he took the lead.

"I could say the same, except for my roommate situation."

They walked straight through the house, out the open French doors, and onto the patio. Riley could hear the far-off wail of a siren. It was becoming the soundtrack of her life.

They found the source of the screaming on the back patio. "OhmyGodohmyGodohmyGod!" Griffin screeched with his hands on his face, *Home Alone*–style, as he ran in tiny circles. Bella was howling while shaking her hands like she was trying to dry her nails.

"Christ," Nick said, staring up at the twelve-foot-tall aroused Griffin statue.

"Focus, Santiago." Riley pointed to Mrs. Penny, who was

in a flower bed next to a bushy rhododendron and a pair of legs wearing men's loafers.

"Yo!" Mrs. Penny called, waving her cane in the air.

They stepped off the patio and headed in her direction.

Bella's dog sniffed the dead guy's shoe, then resumed barking. Mrs. Penny poked the facedown body with the tip of her cane. "Yep. He's definitely dead."

Bella's screaming went up an octave, and Riley plugged her ears with her fingers.

"Stop poking the body," Nick ordered. "Thorn, take care of these two. Duct-tape their mouths shut if you have to."

Riley picked up the dog and returned to the screaming couple.

"Hey, guys. Let's go sit down for a minute," she shouted over the noise, pointing toward the seating area next to the hideous statue.

Still screaming, Griffin abruptly changed direction and ran face-first into the statue's erection. He fell backward to the grass, dazed and blinking.

"That's gonna leave another mark," Riley guessed.

Bella took the dog from Riley's arms and continued howling as she jogged toward the patio furniture.

"Bella, you have to save your voice for TV, right?" Riley asked.

"TV?" Griffin repeated dazedly, still staring up at the statue's penis.

Bella hiccupped. "Oh my goodness! I was so upset I forgot I was on TV."

"You have the morning show, and someone's probably going to want to interview you about this, so that's even more screen time," Riley said. The siren was getting closer. "You two stay here and try not to scream," she told them.

Riley returned to Nick and tried not to look at the body.

"Do we know who he is?" she asked.

"How the hell should I know?" Mrs. Penny said, whacking the rhododendron out of the way with the cane.

"Can you stop fucking up the crime scene, Penny?" Nick said. He was crouched down a few feet from the legs. There was a wooden block in the grass and a long pair of bolt cutters in the mulch.

"What exactly happened, Mrs. Penny?" Riley asked.

"We were inside watching *The Price Is Right* reruns, and Griffin wouldn't shut up about how much better a host he'd be when *bam!* The power went out. These yahoos didn't know what to do, so I came out here to investigate and *bam!* Dead guy."

The electrical meter mounted on the wall above the corpse was still intact, but the tubing around the wires had been cut.

"Who puked?" Nick asked, eyeing a chunky-looking puddle of fluid.

"The assistant. Everyone acts like they've never seen a dead body before," Mrs. Penny complained.

The siren blared into the cul-de-sac.

"I'll go find Griffin's assistant and let the cops in," Riley volunteered.

"Thanks."

She found the assistant rocking back and forth on the kitchen floor. "You okay?" she asked tentatively.

There was no response.

She walked up to him and clapped her hands in his face. "Staff!"

He fell over on the tile and curled in a ball. "I don't want to die!"

"I'm not here to kill you. We just need to let the cops in," Riley explained.

On cue, there was a pounding at the front door. "Harrisburg PD. Open up."

Detective Kellen Weber and Sergeant Mabel Jones marched through the door when Riley opened it. To his credit, Weber barely bothered to roll his eyes when he saw her. "I should have known," he muttered.

"Hey, girl," Mabel said. "I take it Santiago's here too?"

"He's out back," Riley said. "Follow me."

She led them through the house and out onto the patio. Weber approached Griffin, who was still lying like a starfish on the ground.

"What in the ever-loving hell is that?" Mabel asked, wide-eyed as she took in the scene.

"That's not the dead guy," Riley told them. "Griffin's just stunned. He ran into his statue's erection. The body's over there."

———

Riley watched from the kitchen as a uniformed cop unspooled the yellow crime scene tape in the backyard and the coroner's gurney wheeled into view.

"I was just saying how I would be an excellent game show host because I'm so handsome and charming when the power went out," Griffin explained to the officer. He and Bella were sitting at the glass and chrome kitchen table. He held an ice pack to his forehead, and Bella was delicately sipping on one of her creepy placenta smoothies.

"And I was doing my facial exercises so I don't get wrinkles," Bella added, demonstrating by scrunching her face like a prune.

"Okaaaaay," Mabel said.

"Here we are again. You, me, and another dead body. I'm starting to think we're cursed," Riley whispered to Nick as he helped himself to a cup of coffee.

"Are you kidding? Thorn, if that DB turns out to be who I think it is, we just scored. Big time."

She frowned. "Who is it?"

"I can't be sure, but the back of his head looks a hell of a lot like Gentry."

Riley instinctively looked out the window toward the fence. "Lyle Larstein?"

"Looks to me like the neighborhood sleep-deprived weirdo was cutting the power and managed to electrocute himself."

"Hence the block of wood and the bolt cutter thingies," Riley said.

"Exactly. He was at the top of our list of suspects, and he just did us the favor of taking himself out. This is what we call an open-and-shut case. You and I are gonna celebrate by hooking up that TV tonight, installing a dead bolt on our bedroom door, having sex, and then watching movies."

"That sounds perfect. Maybe we could add paying some bills in there somewhere?" Riley suggested.

Weber stepped inside from the backyard, his no-nonsense footsteps echoing on the tile. He removed his latex gloves and pointed at them. "You two, with me," he ordered.

"You two, with me," Nick mimicked under his breath.

"Play nice," Riley hissed.

"I don't know how."

They followed the detective out the glass doors and onto the patio.

"Why do I keep finding you at my crime scenes, Santiago?" Weber demanded, gesturing for them to sit down at the slate-topped table.

"If you were better at your job, maybe I wouldn't get there first every time," Nick shot back, pulling out a chair for Riley.

"Hey, maybe we could save the habitual pissing contest for later," she suggested as she sat.

Nick took the chair next to her.

Weber took a look around them at the manicured lawn, the stone patio, and the unmissable twelve-foot-tall Griffin. Someone had taken the initiative to drape a blue tarp over the statue's nether regions. He shook his head and pulled out a third chair.

"All right, you two. How do you just so happen to be on the scene of another unattended death?"

"Just lucky I guess," Nick said.

"Do you want me to haul you down to an interrogation room?"

"Mrs. Penny was here with Griffin. She called us," Riley said.

"What was an eighty-year-old troublemaker doing here, and why did she call you?"

"Don't blame us for doing our jobs," Nick snarled. "Gentry went to the cops first, and your boys in blue dismissed the threats."

"The threat at the time was"—Weber paused to consult his notes—"a 'mean note' in his bedroom and a chest-waxing accident."

"Well, maybe if you had taken it seriously, we wouldn't be standing over a dead fucking body," Nick said.

"*I* didn't take the report. I'm homicide."

"Right, because what's the fun in preventing murders when you can investigate them?"

They both came halfway out of their chairs. Riley waved her hands between them. "I really can't tell how much of this is actual animosity and how much is old habit. But we're in the middle of a crime scene, so let's at least pretend to be professionals."

"Who the hell is the DB?" Weber demanded.

Riley opened her mouth, but Nick beat her to it. "How the hell should we know? That's your job."

"Did you disturb the body or the scene in any way?"

"I stopped four feet away and didn't touch anything. You'll find my size thirteen prints next to the block of wood. The orthopedic size eights and cane prints in the mulch are Penny. Who the hell knows what Gentry and his girlfriend did before we got here? They were running around like headless fucking poultry when we arrived. Thorn got them under control and corralled them away from the scene. The puke is from the assistant who came outside before we got here. I don't have a gun on me. I didn't witness anything except the aftermath. Now get the fuck out of my face before I decide to throw caution to the wind and rearrange yours for you."

"Fuck off, Nicky," Weber shot back after Nick's recitation of mostly the facts.

"You two about done? We'd like to roll the body," the coroner called from the flower bed.

Weber glared at Nick. "Don't leave town."

"'Don't leave town,'" Nick mimicked.

"We'll just get out of your way, Kellen," Riley said, grabbing Nick by the arm. "Come on. Let's go get Mrs. Penny a snack. You know how hungry she gets at crime scenes."

"Have fun playing detective," Nick called over his shoulder as Riley towed him toward the door.

"Okay. Why aren't we telling Kellen we might know who the dead guy is?" she asked under her breath.

"We're not gonna do his job for him. Besides, if we tell him we think we know him, he'll want to know how we know him, which will involve a much longer interview, and we have a TV to hang and an old lady to feed."

"You sure you aren't just being unhelpful to see if Kellen comes to the same conclusion or gets it wrong?"

"That too, Thorn. That too," he said, slinging his arm around her.

They found Griffin, Bella, and Mrs. Penny in the kitchen. Griffin and Bella were gargling what smelled like a concoction of hot vinegar and honey. Mrs. Penny was drinking bourbon straight from the bottle.

"Well? What happened? Who is it?" Mrs. Penny asked and wiped her mouth on her sleeve.

"Was it the bad guy?" Griffin demanded in a whisper.

"Why are you whispering?" Nick asked. "He's dead."

"The nice lady in the backyard told us we should save our voices," Bella squeaked.

"That was me. I was the nice lady," Riley said.

Bella cocked her head. "Hmm, you don't look familiar."

"I honestly don't know why I bother," Riley muttered.

"Look, Griffin. In my professional opinion, the threat has been mitigated," Nick said.

"Mimigated?" Griffin repeated in a whisper.

"Threat go bye-bye. No more bad guy," Nick said. "So I'll take that check now."

Griffin got that cagey look in his eyes. "Check? What check?"

"The one you owe me for hiring Santiago Investigations."

"Ohhhh, that check. I just assumed that you would enjoy working for me so much you wouldn't need to be paid."

"You assumed wrong. I regret every second I spend with you, and if you don't cough up the cash—"

"We'll get you an invoice and an itemized receipt," Mrs. Penny interrupted, hefting herself out of the kitchen chair with an audible fart.

"I'll be back tomorrow for the money," Nick said.

"We might be busy tomorrow with national news interviews about our harrowing experience," Bella warned.

"Let's go. I need some prime rib," Mrs. Penny announced.

They headed for the front door. In the study, the uniformed officer was interviewing Griffin's assistant. "Okay, Staff, what's your full name? Stafford? Staffington?"

The nervous assistant looked like he was about to puke again. "I can't take it anymore. I confess."

Riley, Nick, and Mrs. Penny stopped in their tracks.

"My name isn't Staff. It's Henry. Henry Wu. Does that count as an alias? Am I in trouble?"

Riley rolled her eyes. Nick snorted.

"Last time you'll ever have to see the inside of this house," Nick said.

"Let's go celebrate being twenty Gs richer," Mrs. Penny suggested.

As Riley followed them out, something tickled at the back of her subconscious, and once again, she saw a fuzzy vision of Griffin's bare legs.

Mrs. Penny tripped over one of the porch urns. The urn toppled off the porch, shattering on a landscaping boulder below. Nick caught Mrs. Penny by the elastic waistband and pulled her back from the edge.

"That thing came out of nowhere," she barked, stomping over the carnage on the steps.

Riley gripped her purple-haired roommate's arm and brushed away the tickle in her head. Nick was right. Griffin was no longer her problem. She had a life of her own now. With a TV to hang and an old lady to feed.

15

Nick helped extricate Mrs. Penny from the back seat of the Jeep. Her cane smacked him smartly in the jaw as she landed on the garage floor with a burp.

"Ow," he said dryly, wondering if he was destined to forever regret making the elderly woman his business partner.

"It looks like Fred got to work on his to-do list," Riley observed as they exited the garage and headed for the house. The mudroom window had been boarded up with plywood and spray-painted with a rudimentary drawing of a window lest they forget what had been there before.

"Let's hope Lily started dialing contractors today. The sooner we can get rid of the geriatric circus, the better," Nick said, admiring the way Riley's jeans accentuated her ass as they traipsed across the leaf-strewn driveway toward the house.

Maybe he'd have enough cash left over after paying bills and buying Riley that engagement ring to hire a lawn service.

Mrs. Penny snorted. "It's no picnic for us either. I'm sharing a room with Lily, who talks in her sleep about all the erotic dreams she's having."

"I didn't need to know that," Nick said.

"Hmm. It's eerily quiet," Riley noted. "And it doesn't smell like anything is burning."

"Everyone is out on surveillance today. I called it off after my prime rib snack," Mrs. Penny said. "The mean one said she and her nerdy hubby would round everyone up."

As if on cue, Brian's van made the turn into the driveway and pulled up to the front of the house. The side door slid open, and senior citizens in a variety of disguises clambered out. Mr. Willicott was dressed like what Nick could only assume was a 1920s paperboy with a newsboy cap and tweed shorts that came to his knees. He had a huge film camera hanging from his neck. The muscular Fred had donned his "sporty" toupee and was wearing embarrassingly short shorts and running shoes. Lily had clearly misunderstood the assignment and emerged in a lumpy taffeta bridesmaid's dress.

They were all eating candy bars.

Gabe and Burt bounded down the van's ramp. Gabe wore a T-shirt with handwritten letters that spelled out DOG WALKER. He was munching on hummus and pretzel chips.

Burt gamboled over to Riley to show off the new chew bone clamped between his teeth.

"Look at you with a special doggy treat and not people food. Good job, buddy," Riley said, giving the dog a series of enthusiastic pats.

Josie stomped out of the van, looking pissed off despite the fact that she had a bag of chips, a protein chocolate milk, and four candy bars in her arms. Brian appeared last and wheeled his way across the driveway to them.

"They all wanted snacks," he said. "Do you know how hard it is to get them all out of a convenience store at the same time?"

"I'm having second thoughts about this whole parenting thing," Josie grumbled.

"Babies are way easier than wrangling the elderly," Nick assured them. "Babies can't move. You put them down, and they stay there. These guys are all on the move, and each one has a different agenda. Just don't have five toddlers at the same time and you'll be fine."

"I need a nap," Josie grumbled.

"You can sleep during Nicky's debriefing," Brian promised.

Nick cupped his hands and yelled, "Everybody in the living room for a meeting."

Fred was just unlocking the front door with a key Nick didn't remember giving him when a white panel van whipped into the driveway. It came to a halt behind Brian's van, Guns N' Roses tunes pouring through the open windows.

"Who is that?" Riley asked as the driver's door opened.

"My cousin the asshole," Nick said.

"Also known as Carlo the plumber," Brian explained.

Carlo strutted around the van like a five-feet five-inch-tall rooster. He wore cowboy boots, jeans, and a hoodie that read CARLO'S PLUMBING: I'LL PLUG YOUR LEAK. He hooked his thumbs in the belt loops of his jeans and glared at Nick. "Nice digs for an asshole."

"Does your cousin hate you?" Riley asked.

"Yeah. It probably has something to do with me arresting him a few years back," Nick said to her before facing his cousin. "Carlo, always nice to see you this side of the prison bars."

"Fuck you. Where's the leak?"

"It's a leak *and* a clog," Lily trilled, shoving Nick out of the way. "I'd be happy to personally show you all my plumbing problems."

"Lead the way, pretty lady," Carlo said.

Lily's eyes went wide behind her thick lenses, and she began to emit a high-pitched squealing noise. Whimpering, Burt took his chew bone and ran into the yard.

Carlo jogged up the porch steps and came nose to sternum with Nick. "This makes us even, Nicky."

"Yeah, yeah. Go snake a drain," Nick agreed.

Carlo spun on the balls of his feet and gave Riley the eyes. "You the girlfriend?" he asked.

"I am."

He gave her a once-over. "You're hot."

Nick slapped Carlo upside the head. "Stop hitting on my girl."

Carlo slapped him back. "Fish's gotta swim."

"Go swim your ass through my pipes."

"You ever get tired of this guy, you give ol' Carlo a call," Nick's cousin said to Riley.

"I'll be sure to do that," Riley promised.

Carlo swaggered his way through the front door after Lily, who was still squealing.

"So you arrested your cousin, and he still owes you a favor?" Riley asked.

Nick shrugged. "I told his mom he was in Guatemala digging wells for orphans for six months while he was in prison."

"Isn't it nice that our families are equally weird?" she said as their elderly roommates filed past them into the house.

"I need booze," Mrs. Penny barked.

———

While Carlo swore at the pipes in the kitchen, Nick found himself in the sunroom, which had been converted into Mr. Willicott's bedroom and a makeshift bar. At some point, his new roommates had managed to confiscate furniture from all over the house to create a mismatched lounge of sorts.

Mrs. Penny was mixing drinks behind the bar while Frank Sinatra sang about doing things his way from a Bluetooth speaker. Josie was sound asleep on a small wicker couch next to the wall of windows. Mr. Willicott and Fred were playing a game of chess. Nick was ninety percent sure neither of them knew what they were doing.

Riley, with a fresh gin and tonic in hand, was in conversation with Brian, Gabe, and Lily at Nick's poker table.

"Now, *this* is how you do a meeting," Mrs. Penny said with satisfaction as she topped off her bourbon.

"This isn't a meeting. This is a happy hour," Nick complained.

"Quit your whining and drink up. We're celebrating," Mrs. Penny insisted.

Burt appeared on the patio and pressed his nose against the glass. Nick crossed the tile floor and let the dog in.

"Come on, coz. Give us all the gory details," Brian encouraged.

Josie woke with a start. "Someone say *gory*?" she asked woozily.

"Yeah, spill the beans. I was getting some good intel on my mark," Lily said.

"Me too. What's the deal?" Fred asked, looking up from the game. "That ChooChoo Cabernet Jones hit a PR on the bench press at the gym. I love a fit lady."

"Horseface guy to napkin," Mr. Willicott said and moved his knight to Fred's cocktail napkin.

"Good news. You're all retired again." Nick took the seat next to Riley, who was solicitously holding Burt's bone for him while he chewed it.

"But I already had tomorrow's outfit picked out. I was going to be Scarlett O'Hara," Lily complained.

"Just talking to these people gives me a migraine," Nick complained to Riley as he scrubbed his hands over his face.

She took pity on him. "While Mrs. Penny was guarding Griffin, a man we believe to be the stalker cut the power to Griffin's house and may have electrocuted himself," she said.

"Who was it?" Lily asked.

"We weren't there for the official identification," Riley hedged, her gaze flicking to Nick. Their cohorts weren't exactly known for their ability to keep their mouths shut.

"He was Gentry's sexually harassing, money-embezzling asshat of a next-door neighbor," he announced.

A collective *Ooooooh!* rose up from the room's occupants.

"Why'd he do it?" Josie asked before biting into both Twix bars at the same time.

"He was pissed and sleep-deprived because Channel 50 was shooting the morning show at Gentry's house."

"That's a dumb reason," Josie said with her mouth full.

"People have attempted dumber murders for dumber reasons," Nick pointed out.

"Does this mean I will no longer have to spend my time ensuring the safety of unnecessarily annoying people?" Gabe asked hopefully.

Mrs. Penny attempted to prop her sneakered feet on a small occasional table. Instead, she managed to kick it over, sending a dusty vase that had survived the roof collapse next door crashing to the floor. "Oops."

"I wouldn't say you're completely off the hook in that area," Riley said to Gabe.

"What this means is payday comes tomorrow," Nick announced.

"Damn it. I should have gotten a Payday at the gas station," Josie grumbled, looking down at the remains of her candy bars.

"Babe, I've got you," Brian said and produced a Payday from his pocket.

"You've never been sexier to me. Let's make more babies," she said.

"Let's celebrate with more alcohol." Mrs. Penny headed for the bar again, crunching over the remains of the vase.

"I believe I shall send a text message to Wander since I am now free for the evening," Gabe said with the kind of glow only a man with imminent plans of getting naked would have.

Nick gave Riley's thigh a squeeze. "I'm gonna go hang a TV so we can have naked movie night." He could see it now—some energetic, celebratory sex followed by naked cuddle time while basking in the eighty-five-inch 4K glow.

"You've never been sexier to me," Riley teased, fluttering her lashes.

He gave her his best smolder. "Just wait until tonight." Burt chose that moment to give Nick's hand an affectionate slurp. "After I shower off the dog slobber."

She smiled, but it didn't quite go all the way to those brown eyes he was so fond of.

"What's wrong?" he demanded.

"I'm not sure. Probably nothing," she said. "Ignore me. Everything's fine."

"Riley," he prompted.

She winced. "I just get a sense that this Griffin thing isn't over yet."

Fuck. "What do the spirit guides have to say?" he asked.

"I haven't had a chance to ask them."

"Maybe it'll feel over when we have the check in hand?" he suggested.

"Maybe. Mrs. Penny! Don't climb on the furniture!"

Their lavender-haired roommate was balanced precariously on a footstool, trying to reach the highest shelf behind the bar. "How the hell else am I supposed to get to the top-shelf bourbon?"

Riley rolled her eyes at Nick.

"Gabe!" they yelled in unison.

———

Whistling, Nick headed into the kitchen, where his cousin was still swearing colorfully from under the sink. He grabbed his tool bag from the pantry and a beer from the fridge, then returned to the foyer and came to an abrupt halt.

The TV box was missing.

"Where the hell…?" He performed a quick search of Riley's office, his office, and the living room. The powder room under the stairs was also TV-less.

"Where's my TV?" His bellow echoed around the two-story foyer.

"What TV?" Mrs. Penny yelled back as she, Fred, and Riley marched out of the bar.

"The TV I had delivered today!" Nick snarled.

"Oh. That TV. I had Gabe install it in my room for my gaming," Mrs. Penny said, wiggling her thumbs like she was holding a controller.

"You…what…? Why?" Nick couldn't quite form a sentence. "That was *my* TV."

"I apologize," Gabe said, looking chagrined. "Mrs. Penny told me it belonged to her."

"What do you want me to do? A gamer's gotta game. It keeps me sharp."

Nick clenched his hands into fists at his sides so he wouldn't be tempted to strangle Mrs. Penny. "Sharp? You're duller than a plastic butter knife."

She hefted her elastic waistband pants. "Need I remind you that I'm the one who brought in the Gentry money?"

"I don't care! You stole my TV!"

"I didn't steal it. I *borrowed* it."

"Then unborrow it."

Mrs. Penny waved a dismissive hand in his direction. "Trust me. You don't want it back. We knocked out a few hundred pixels when it fell off the wall onto Lily's erotic fireplace poker collection."

"Thorn?" Nick breathed. If his nostrils flared any wider, he was afraid they would split open.

"Yep. On it," Riley said, gripping the back of his shirt. "Mrs. Penny, order Nick a new TV."

"And a full-motion bracket," he added.

"And whatever a full-motion bracket is," she repeated.

"Fine. Sheesh. Everybody's so damn sensitive about their damn electronics," Mrs. Penny muttered as she stomped back to the happy hour.

Riley released Nick's shirt and patted his chest. "Are you ready for more good news?"

He growled.

"My mom just texted. We're invited to dinner at my parents' house. She says she has something exciting to show us."

"It better not be more nude self-portrait pottery," he said.

"I think she's done with that class until spring."

16

W"ait till you see my surprise," Blossom sang by way of a greeting when she flung open the front door of Riley's childhood home. Not much had changed since she'd lived at 69 Dogwood Street. Her mom still wore hippie outfits and gardened barefoot. Her father still lived to annoy the next-door neighbor. The brick two-story still butted up against the sidewalk, and the neon PSYCHIC READINGS sign in the front window still lit up on Mondays, Wednesdays, and Saturdays.

It was chilly edging toward cold as the November evening fell. Riley was tired. Finding dead bodies took a lot out of a person.

A low moo sounded from the fenced backyard. Burt answered his four-legged bovine friend with a cheerful bark and barreled past Blossom into the house.

That was the main difference, Riley supposed. Instead of raising children, now her parents had a backyard cow named Daisy. Her father was more enthusiastic about the addition than her mother.

"Thanks for the invite, Blossom," Nick said.

Riley signaled to him that he had a spot of ketchup in one

dimple. As was their Thorn family dinner tradition, they'd stopped at a drive-thru for predinner dinner on their way. Her mother was a bit too much of an adventurous cook when it came to her family's digestive systems.

Nick surreptitiously swiped his forearm over his face before dropping a kiss to Blossom's cheek.

Riley used the sleeve of her jacket to erase all evidence of Gabe's milkshake mustache.

"Come in! Come in," Blossom said, all but dragging them across the threshold.

"I literally can't wait to see what the surprise is," Nick whispered to Riley.

Giggles and cheers erupted from the kitchen. "Mr. Gabe!" Riley's nieces exclaimed in unison.

River smiled up from her crayon drawing. Rain and Janet abandoned the carrots they'd been sword fighting with and raced to hug Gabe around his tree trunk legs.

Riley's sister, Wander, looked up from a pot of something that smelled horrendous on the stove and beamed like a lighthouse at the man she'd recently seen naked.

"Something...uh...smells," Riley said.

"It's a lentil and mung bean soup. I sprouted my own mung beans," Blossom announced proudly as she ruffled River's hair.

"You hear that, Rye Bread? Your mother *sprouted her own mung beans*," Roger said, enunciating each word.

"I did indeed hear that. Very impressive," Riley said and patted the pocket of her jacket.

"Hey, Bloss, didn't you want to get that thing out of the basement?" Roger asked.

Blossom frowned. "What thing?"

"You know. The thing that you talked about. It sounded important. Maybe if you go down there, you'll remember," he prompted.

"Oh, all right. But then I'm showing everyone my surprise," she said.

The second Blossom disappeared down the basement

stairs, Riley produced the cheeseburger she'd hidden in her coat pocket and handed it over to her father.

"You're my favorite," Roger whispered before making a mad dash into the TV room. She was fairly certain he was talking to the burger, not her.

Wander floated over and gave Riley an incense- and aloe-scented hug.

"We have a lot to catch up on, don't we?" Riley teased.

Wander's smile was like looking directly into oncoming LED high beams. "Maybe. Speaking of, would you and Nick mind watching the girls Sunday evening?"

"I don't know about Nick, but count me in," Riley said.

Nick wrapped his arms around her waist from behind. "I'm an awesome babysitter," he insisted.

"Really?" Wander and Riley said in unison.

"Just because I'm not a seven-foot-tall human jungle gym doesn't mean I don't know how to entertain kids. My niece, Esmeralda, used to spend every other Friday night at my place until my sister found out about our ice cream dinners."

"As long as it's sustainably sourced, dairy-free ice cream, I have no problem with that," Wander said quickly.

"Hear that, kids? Ice cream dinner with us Sunday," Nick said.

Riley's nieces abandoned Gabe and threw themselves at their favorite aunt and uncle. "Yay, ice cream dinner! Thanks, Uncle Nick," Rain said, hurling herself at Nick's knees.

He picked the six-year-old up and held her aloft. "Uncle Nick. That's better than *Mr.* Gabe," he said pointedly.

"Why must everything be a competition?" Gabe asked.

"Nothing's a competition because I win everything," Nick insisted, tossing Rain over his shoulder and catching four-year-old Janet with his other arm as she jumped at him from the kitchen chair.

At eight, River was more dignified than her sisters and hastily added another smiling stick figure to her crayon drawing and labeled it *Uncle Nick*. She frowned at it for a beat and then added three red slashes to his face. Riley cocked her head over her niece's shoulder, but before she could ask any questions, Burt drew her attention with an excited yip.

Her dog was already planted at the sliding door, nose to the glass, hot doggy breath fogging it up.

The basement door flew open, and Blossom returned to the kitchen. "Well, I went down there and stared at the BowFlex for a full two minutes and still couldn't remember for the life of me what I was supposed to be down there for. I swear it happens at least once a week. And when I come back, it always smells like red meat. It's the darndest thing," she said, putting her hands on her hips.

Roger, who had just stuck his head into the kitchen from the den, slunk guiltily back into the shadows licking his fingers.

"So what's this surprise, Mom?" Riley asked.

Blossom clapped her hands. "Okay, everyone unhand Uncle Nick so Hesty can show off her surprise." Hestia, Greek goddess of hearth and home, was the name Blossom had chosen instead of Grandma. However, her granddaughters had shortened it to Hesty.

Nick shed Riley's nieces at the table next to their sister.

"I drew this for you, Uncle Nick," River announced, holding up her drawing. It was a series of crayon-drawn diamond shapes encircling two stick figures. "It's you and Aunt Riley. I couldn't get the pretty glitters the right color, so I went with orange."

"Wow, Riv. That's a cool drawing. It would be even better if the artist signed it for me," he said. Over River's bowed head, he pointed at the drawing. "I got a drawing, Mr. Gabe. What did *you* get?"

"We wove him matching drink coasters," Rain announced.

"Yes. I received handmade gifts from the heart," Gabe said with just a hint of smugness.

"You annoy me on so many levels," Nick said.

Blossom clapped her hands like a kindergarten teacher. "Save the testosterone-fueled grudge match for dinner, and move your rear ends to the backyard."

"Is it another cow?" Riley asked her sister out of the side of her mouth.

"Oh, it's worse," Wander whispered cheerfully.

Blossom wrestled open the door, and Burt shot out like a bullet. "Be careful with my babies, Burtie boy," she called after him.

"What the—" Nick's sentence was abruptly cut off by a white feathery thing that bounced off his head. With lightning-quick reflexes, Gabe snatched the flying object out of the air.

A head emerged from the ball of fluff, then bobbed. Dull, emotionless eyes blinked at Riley.

"Oh boy."

It was a fat feathery chicken.

"Why did you hit me in the face with a chicken?" Nick demanded, rubbing his stubbled cheek.

"I did not hit you in the face with a chicken," Gabe insisted. "I saved you from being further attacked."

"You didn't save me. You intervened before I could react," Nick complained.

"If your reactions were not so slow, I would not have had to intervene," Gabe pointed out.

"They're just a little wound up," Blossom insisted, wringing her hands like a nervous mother.

"They?" Riley repeated and glanced around the backyard.

"Well, you can't expect me to get just one. She'd be lonely," her mother explained.

The squawking bird in Gabe's huge hands was not the only fowl in the backyard. Daisy the cow morosely munched on a patch of grass while a clucking chicken clung to her back and pecked at her haunches. Burt galloped around the swing set, barking joyfully at the pair of brown birds squatting obliviously atop the sliding board. A small banty rooster strutted out of the remains of Blossom's vegetable garden. He gave them all a dead-eyed stare and crapped on the grass.

"That's Mr. Feathers," Blossom said, gesturing to the rooster.

"Wow. That's a lot of…poop," Riley noted.

"Apparently chickens shit all day every day," came her father's disgruntled commentary from inside the house.

She didn't need to be psychic to know her dad wasn't pleased with the new additions to the family.

"A coodle doodle do," Mr. Feathers warbled.

"Is there something wrong with that rooster?" Riley asked.

"I'm just saying, I was stunned by beak and feathers. I would have handled it myself," Nick insisted to Gabe.

"Of course. You have the reflexes of a panther," Gabe said. There wasn't a hint of smugness on his handsome face when he released the chicken from his grasp.

It immediately flew at Nick's face again. "Goddamn it," he yelled, swinging wildly as the chicken flopped around his head and shoulders.

"Aww! I think KFC likes you," Blossom said. "Your father named her."

Nick ducked behind Riley's mother, and Blossom gently captured the flapping fowl, cradling it in her arms like a newborn.

"Ursula the sea witch and poultry. Who knew?" Riley said. It was kind of nice seeing her usually cocky, fearless boyfriend show a little bit of vulnerability…even if it was over a small, feathered barnyard animal.

"Who the fuck throws a chicken?" Nick groused.

"Once again, I did not throw the chicken. I merely released it. I cannot help that it finds your face peckable or that your reflexes are slow and full of panic," Gabe insisted.

Nick spit a feather out of his mouth. "I'm not panicked. You're panicked."

"Coo coo ca-cha," the rooster said.

"Aren't roosters supposed to crow?" Riley asked.

"Mr. Feathers fell off a truck on the highway. I think he might have a tiny little traumatic brain injury," Blossom explained. She lifted the chicken in her hands, and Nick nervously dodged out of the way. "The one playing with Daisy is Summer Solstice. Those two are Toni Morrison and Yolanda," she said pointing at the two birds on the swing set.

Upon hearing her name, Yolanda hurled herself to the ground in front of Burt in a feathery, clucky flutter. Burt let out a nervous whimper. Toni Morrison landed next to her bird sister with a cackle that had the dog slinking backward. The chickens advanced on him with a dead-eyed agenda of mayhem.

"Burt, come here before you get your eyes pecked out," Nick called.

The lion-size dog gave his humans and the safety of the deck the side-eye. Riley could practically hear him calculating whether he could make it.

"Come on, buddy," she encouraged, slapping her hands to her thighs.

Burt backed toward them one paw at a time, not taking his eyes off the potential enemy. But it was all for naught. Without warning, both birds pounced. Burt yelped. Feathers flew. Chickens squawked. And suddenly they were off, Burt in the lead, galloping around the yard, ducking under Daisy's belly as the chickens gave chase.

The chicken in Blossom's arms flopped to the ground and joined in. "Aren't they just the cutest things?" Blossom said to no one in particular.

Daisy let out a plaintive moo as the chicken strutted up her back, pecking as it went.

Roger charged out onto the deck. "See?" he said, gesturing wildly at his beloved cow. "They're torturing my sweet Daisy. I told you she wouldn't like 'em."

"They're just getting used to each other," Blossom insisted, watching her new feathery progeny with maternal delight. "You know, I was watching homesteading videos on the YouTube, and some people let their chickens in the house."

Roger stomped off the deck to shoo the chicken away from Daisy. "No freaking way, Bloss. If Daisy can't come inside to watch football with me, your demon brood ain't allowed to crap all over the carpet."

"It smells like Burt's cabbage aftermath in here," Nick observed as they returned to the kitchen, leaving Riley's parents outside to argue. The emotionally scarred Burt belly-crawled under the table and whimpered until Janet deigned to join him and pick the feathers of his enemies from his fur.

"I see you met KFC," Wander observed. The girls were all drawing at the table now. River had added several pairs of stick figure legs to Nick's drawing.

"Nick was ruthlessly attacked and barely survived," Gabe said. "I, however, did not receive injury."

"He threw a chicken at me," Nick complained.

Riley dampened a fresh hand towel and pressed it to the trio of scratches on Nick's face. "Poor baby."

"Am I gonna end up with bird rabies or something?" he asked.

"Probably," she teased. "Let's go bandage you up." She ushered him into the tiny powder room crammed under the stairs and opened the vanity.

He sat down on the toilet lid. "What the hell is that?" he demanded as she unscrewed the lid of a jar filled with green goop. "It smells almost as bad as dinner."

"Mom's first aid balm. If you're a brave boy, I'll give you a lollipop after."

His hands settled on her hips. "I love you."

Riley paused her ministrations and met those gorgeous blue-green eyes. "Where did that come from?"

He shrugged. "Probably my near-death-by-poultry experience."

Her lips curved. "I love you too."

"Yeah, but enough to stick with me even though you now know I'm maybe slightly concerned about cartoon sea witches and backyard chickens?"

"Maybe even more."

"What dumb shit are you afraid of?" he asked as she smoothed a layer of the goop over his abraded cheek.

"Hmm. Definitely gorillas. Mrs. Penny. And I guess not mattering."

"Gorillas are scary as shit, and Mrs. Penny is goddamn terrifying," he said, reaching up to grasp her wrist. "And you really fucking matter to me, Riley."

Her heart did that awkward flip-flop it always did when Nick Santiago got sneaky sweet on her. "Wow. That near-death experience must have really rattled you," she said lightly as she tore open a bandage.

"Chickens are stupid," Nick muttered.

"You were very heroic fighting off poultry like that."

"We're stopping on the way home, and I'm getting two hundred nuggets."

17

Nick pulled his SUV into the garage and handed Gabe the hemp tote full of leftover mung bean stew.

"Do me a favor, Chicken Thrower. Bury this in the garbage, and take Burt inside. Thorn and I have some important yard maintenance to take care of," he said.

"It will be my pleasure," Gabe agreed. He climbed out of the vehicle with the dog bounding after him.

Riley undid her seat belt and reached for the fast-food bag of chicken nuggets, but Nick closed a hand over her thigh.

"Sit tight, Thorn. I've got a plan."

He watched Gabe and Burt exit the garage in the rearview mirror and then stabbed the button on the remote. The door slid closed behind them.

"Yard maintenance in a dark garage?" she teased.

Nick waggled his eyebrows at her in the glow of the dome light. "I've got a plan. I've had thirty-seven plans since you walked down the stairs in that outfit."

Riley glanced down at the plain rust-colored V-neck sweater and jeans. The nice thing about Nick was that he would find her attractive in a paper bag.

"You want to have sex out here? But it's cold."

His wolfish grin was lightning quick. "I'll keep you warm, baby."

With that, he hooked her under the arms and dragged her across the console to his lap. His mouth was on hers immediately. She could taste his hunger, his hurry, his need.

"Remind me to wear this sweater more often," she said against his hard lips.

"Take off your pants," he ordered.

"Need more room," she groaned.

Nick obliged, opening his door and climbing out with her still in his arms.

"Four months," he said, giving her just enough room to shuck her shoes and pants before dragging her into the back seat.

Riley pulled back. "What?"

"We've been doing this for four months, and every fucking morning, I can't wait to wake up and do it all over again with you," he rasped.

Grumpy Nick, Hot-to-Trot Nick, and Nick Doing Something He Didn't Want to Do But Doing It Anyway Because She Wanted To were some of her favorite Nick Santiagos. But Romantic You're the One For Me Nick was on a level all his own.

"Come here, Riley," he said, his voice husky.

She didn't bother playing coy. Instead she launched herself at him, straddling his thighs and bumping her head on the ceiling in the process. They kissed through the pain as Nick magically made her underwear disappear. She wondered distantly if that counted as a superpower.

"Condom?" Riley whispered.

Nick reached behind her into the seatback pocket and produced a variety pack of condoms.

"Good job," she praised.

"Oh, baby. I'm just getting started," he said, sliding his hands under her sweater to cup her breasts.

He brought his face to her cleavage. She wasn't sure if

he used his fingers or his tongue to release the front closure but decided it didn't really matter because his hot mouth was skimming its way over her bare skin, and his hands were everywhere at once.

His erection pulsed against her, and Riley responded with a slow roll of her hips. They knew each other's bodies, desires, needs. And it just kept getting better. Her nipples pebbled under his attentive mouth, and her brain finally, finally went quiet.

"You drive me wild, Thorn. Every day. I can't get enough," he confessed to her boobs.

"Uh-huh," she breathed.

And then he was lifting her higher, shifting under her, and then they were one.

His growl of possession made her tremble from toes to hair roots.

"Better every time," he murmured against her neck.

"Yeah, this doesn't suck." She let out a sharp gasp at his upthrust. Her body responded to his with an eagerness that would have been embarrassing if it didn't feel so damn good.

Nick raked his fingers through her short hair and gripped. "Shut up and ride, baby."

She slapped a hand to the foggy window and did exactly that, rising and sinking onto him with a growing fever. Riley rocked against him, onto him, and wondered how she didn't just disintegrate with pleasure.

"I fucking love you, Thorn."

That was all it took. One gravelly profession and a violent orgasm detonated in her body.

"Nick!" she cried.

He groaned under her as he gripped her hips and pumped mercilessly into her. Just when she thought she couldn't take any more, a second climax hit her. Nick went rigid, his teeth closing over her clavicle as he joined her in release.

Sweaty and breathless, she collapsed on top of him. The tension slowly seeped out of his body. Still panting, he stroked a hand over her hair and down her back. "See, baby? I told you we were good at this."

"Feel free to prove it to me whenever convenient," she teased, her face buried in the crook of his neck.

Nick's arms tensed around her. "Ow! Ow! Ow!"

She sat up. "What's wrong?"

"Charley horse. Hamstring," he wheezed.

They entered the house disheveled and sleepy to find Burt slurping water from his bowl in the disaster zone of the kitchen.

Nick tested the sink faucet and grunted when a biblical flood didn't flow forth from the cabinet. "Fucking Carlo," he said in what Riley guessed was approval.

"What happened in here?" she wondered, taking in the half dozen open bags of chips, the greasy pizza boxes, and the mountain of dirty dishes.

"Looks like happy hour turned into snacky hour," he guessed.

"Where is everybody, Burt?" she asked.

The dog, with water still streaming from his mouth, jogged to the swinging door.

"Did Mrs. Penny fall in a well again?" Nick quipped.

The foyer was dark, but there was a strange sound coming from the sunroom. Like the faint grind of a buzz saw or crunch of a wood chipper.

"This feels like a horror movie and we're about to get chopped up by a deranged serial killer," Riley observed.

Nick took her hand. "Don't worry. I'll protect you."

"What if it's a room full of chickens?"

"Then I'll use you as a human shield."

They tiptoed to the doorway, and Nick stealthily reached inside to snap on the lights. "I think I'd rather face a serial killer," he noted as they took in the scene.

Happy hour had definitely taken a turn.

Empty glasses and bottles of open booze littered every flat

surface. More snacks had been massacred in this room. There were two baking sheets dotted with crumbs on the bar and the remains of an exploded foot-long sub on the poker table. Their geriatric roommates were passed out cold.

Mrs. Penny snored on the divan with one arm thrown over her head and one foot on the floor.

Fred, who appeared to be mostly naked, was curled up snoozing peacefully under the poker table, using his toupee as a pillow. Mr. Willicott slept sitting up in an armchair with a cowboy hat perched on his head. Haunted house noises escaped from his open mouth.

Lily was on the couch, wearing a gingham housecoat, a green face mask, and curlers in her hair. Some of the curlers had french fries stuck to them.

Nick looped his hand through Burt's collar. "No way, buddy. That room is a digestive war zone."

"I don't have the energy to get them all to bed," Riley confessed.

"They're technically all adults. Let them wake up hungover and sore as hell. Maybe it'll teach them a lesson," he said.

Mrs. Penny let out a throat-abrading snore.

"Cute butt," Lily whispered in her sleep.

"Eeeeeeeeeeeeeeeee," Mr. Willicott wheezed.

Fred rolled over, his toupee stuck to the side of his face like a gigantic hairy spider.

"Let's go upstairs and pretend we live alone," Nick said.

"Good call."

They trooped up to the second floor with Burt. Riley could hear Gabe's deep timbre coming from his room. "No. You must be the first to hang up... No, you... I am sorry, Wander, but I cannot disconnect our call without suffering physical pain."

"At least they're not having phone sex," Nick said, leading the way to their room on the opposite side of the house.

"What a day," Riley said as she opened the bedroom door. "From a dead body to attack chickens to mung bean stew."

"To hot sex in the back seat of a car." Nick closed the door behind him and leaned against it.

"It's amazing how a couple of orgasms will put the rest of the day into perspective."

"What do you say we keep the fun going?" he asked with a suggestive eyebrow wiggle. "I dug up one of Brian's old laptops. We could watch one of those *Thin Man* movies and eat nuggets in bed."

"You get me. You really get me."

18

Nick woke up feeling amorous. Which is to say he woke up feeling like he normally did.

They'd stayed up late watching *The Thin Man* on an ancient laptop with a CD drive. Riley had been right, as usual. He'd loved the black-and-white private investigator with his fancy mustache and snarky banter with his wife. He definitely needed to grow a mustache. It was a sign from the universe.

Nick's plan for the perfect day came together as Riley snuggled closer to him in her sleep. They would enjoy a little morning delight, fall back to sleep for another hour or so, then he'd collect their check from Griffin and go buy that new TV again so they could watch the next movie.

It would be the perfect day...as long as he didn't think too hard about the fact that they shared a roof with several unhinged over-the-hill individuals who had trashed the house with an aggressive happy hour.

He was just putting step one of his plan into motion by waking Riley up with sexy neck nuzzles when the bedroom door flew open and bounced off the wall.

"What in the fucking fuck?" he demanded, yanking the covers over his naked lower half. No matter how many times he went to bed wearing shorts or underwear or pajamas, he always woke up naked. His sleep stripping had been a source of teasing in junior high during sleepovers, but as an adult, Nick found sleeping naked saved time.

Lily smiled serenely at them, a tray laden with breakfast foods clutched in her hands.

"Come back and murder us tomorrow," Riley said sleepily.

Burt lifted his head with a grumbly yawn.

"I made you two breakfast in bed," Lily said, tottering into the room and sloshing orange juice everywhere.

Nick face-planted on his pillow. "Riley, will you please explain to Lily that she can't just barge into people's bedrooms even if she does have food?"

"Lily, you can't just barge—is that bacon?" Riley asked, sitting up.

"A moat. I should have dug a moat," Nick complained, even though the bacon *did* smell good.

Riley patted his sheet-covered ass. "What's with the hotel-style service?" she asked Lily with a yawn.

"Oh, I'm the distraction while everyone else cleans up so you don't realize what a mess we left after happy hour," she explained.

"Too late. We already saw it. You're all getting evicted," Nick said.

"Is there anything more delectable than a grumpy, naked man in the morning?" Lily asked.

"I can think of several things. One of which I was about to do before you kicked our door in," he complained.

"This bacon is good, Lily," Riley said.

"I know! I nibbled on two slices on the way up. Scootch over," their elderly room service attendant ordered.

Riley wriggled into the center of the bed, and Lily hopped in next to her, propping herself up on pillows. "Ahh. Isn't this nice?"

The mattress dipped again as Burt belly-crawled onto the bed, wriggling his way toward the breakfast tray. The king-size bed was getting stupidly crowded.

151

Nick gathered the comforter around him with an irritable flourish and got out of bed. "I'm gonna hit the gym so I don't hit anything else," he said, looking pointedly at Lily.

"You guys should have a TV in here," Lily said.

He growled and slammed the bathroom door.

———

Ignoring the roar of the vacuum cleaner and the clink of glass bottles coming from the sunroom turned rave, Nick stalked into the kitchen, muttering about roommates and boundaries.

Gabe stood at the sink, serenely washing the dishes.

"Hey," he said, slapping a hand to Gabe's shoulder. Turning, the man mountain gripped Nick's forearm with one slippery bear paw, twisted, and efficiently tossed him to the floor.

Nick landed with an *oof.*

"What was that for, you hairless Chewbacca?" he wheezed, fighting to get the air back in his lungs.

"Oh dear. I seem to have misunderstood. I thought you wanted me to demonstrate an effective self-defense move," Gabe said innocently.

"Why in the hell would you think that? I just wanted to talk to you," Nick rasped.

"Because you were so easily defeated by tiny birds last night. Do you not remember? Perhaps the trauma is affecting your short-term memory."

"Shit. You're being sarcastic, aren't you?"

"Riley said sarcasm is a tool for humor. I am being amusing," Gabe explained.

"Fuckin' hilarious." Nick accepted the gigantic hand Gabe offered and let the man pull him to his feet.

"I agree. I am only sorry I did not have an audience to appreciate my humor. What is it you wished to discuss?"

Nick cracked his neck on his way to the coffeepot. "I have a question on a hypothetical situation. No sarcasm required."

"Please share your hypothetical situation."

He reached for a mug. "Say someone has a psychic in their life, and they need to keep something from her."

"If we are discussing my very good friend Riley, I do not like this conversation."

"Relax, hot-air balloon," Nick said, pouring himself a cup of coffee.

"I do not understand that particular reference."

"I don't know. Balloons are big. You're big. I just woke up. Gimme a break."

"Ah. I see. Please continue with the topic I am not enjoying."

"Say I want to surprise Riley with something. How does a mere mortal go about surprising a psychic?"

"Is this a good surprise?" Gabe asked with suspicion.

"It better be. I want to do something completely out of character."

"You wish to become well-mannered and charming?"

Gabe's insult game was strong in the morning. Nick didn't care for it.

"A, I'm charming as fuck. B, I'm sure as hell not going to tell you since you basically broadcast the NC-17 version of your date with her sister to Riley yesterday."

"I did not mean to share my intimate memories with Riley. But my joy made it difficult for me to concentrate."

"Yeah, well, maybe I'm feeling pretty damn joyful myself, and I want to surprise her."

"Riley is my friend. I merely tolerate you. If this is something that could hurt my friend, I will stop tolerating you."

It was as close to a threat as Gabe got, and Nick appreciated him for it.

"Understood. This is a good surprise. I hope. I mean, it should be. I think. But the important thing is I have to figure out how to keep it a surprise."

Gabe crossed his arms over his chest. His forearms looked like bulging pythons. "I would like to consider your request," he decided finally. "I do not want to do anything that would make me disloyal to Riley."

"Fine. But think fast, because otherwise I'll just do it, make a mess of it, ruin everything, and then blame you."

"That does sound like something you would do."

Nick sighed through clenched teeth. "Look. I appreciate and respect your loyalty to Riley. It's something we have in common. So you might as well hurry the fuck up and get on board, because I'm not going anywhere. Riley's it for me. Now, if you'll excuse me, I have to go relieve her ex-husband of a large sum of money."

With that, he took his coffee and left.

———

Since it was still early, Nick hit the gym first and ran through a workout on autopilot. All through weight training, he thought about Riley and how she was too good for him and how he needed to make sure she forgot about that fact. When he hit the treadmill, he thought about private detective Nick Charles and was in the middle of wondering whether he should grow a mustache first and then buy a fedora, or vice versa, when his cousin wheeled up next to the treadmill.

"You look confused and pissed off like you're back in trigonometry class," Brian observed.

Nick smacked the Stop button on the treadmill and bent at the waist to catch his breath. "Thinking about hats," he panted.

"You're a weird dude, you know that, coz?"

"So I've been told." Nick swiped his sweat towel over his face. "Hey. Totally innocent question here. How did you convince Josie you were the one?" His cousin had sowed his wild oats all over the damn place until he'd fallen for Josie.

Brian shrugged. "After I figured out she was the one, I just kept her too distracted to think about what a long shot I was on paper."

"Did anyone try to convince her she could do better?"

"Literally everyone. Including my own mother."

"Classic Aunt Nancy."

"Your actions speak louder than other people's words. Gotta make 'em count."

Nick was aware that his actions in recent weeks had spoken up too loud against him.

"Why? You fuck up again already?" Brian asked.

"No, I didn't fuck up again, asshole." Unless getting flopped by a chicken counted. "I'm just looking to up my relationship game."

"Ah, you're looking to dazzle Riley into forgetting your flaws."

"Yeah. That."

Brian pulled a water bottle out of the bag on the back of his chair. "Anytime I'm a dumbass, I just buy Josie a cool new weapon for her collection."

Nick threw the towel over his shoulder. "You're really unhelpful, you know that?"

"See, if you were Josie and you just said that, I'd be on the phone with my weapons guy and I'd be out of the doghouse by noon."

"Men are idiots," Nick mused.

"Hell yeah, we are," Brian agreed.

"Hey, do you think I could pull off a fedora?"

"Absolutely not."

———

"I'm here to see your boss's checkbook," a freshly showered Nick said when assistant to the asshole Henry opened Griffin's front door. Bella's tiny dog wore a crystal-encrusted collar and yapped at his ankles.

The assistant winced. "I'm afraid Mr. Gentry isn't here."

"Yesterday, I told him to be here. Half an hour ago, I texted him to be here. Where is he?"

"I–I'm not sure. He was looking at his phone, and then said he had an important meeting. He left in a hurry."

"An important meeting on a Saturday morning that he didn't need his assistant to attend." Nick strolled across the threshold into the foyer. "Sounds suspicious to me. Especially if he left immediately after I texted him to tell him I was coming to collect."

The dog pranced over and sniffed his boots before resuming her yaps.

Nick scooped up the piece of fluff and cradled her to his chest. "You know what? I think I'll just wait here for your boss."

Henry's eyes widened. "Look, I know Mr. Gentry is really good at avoiding paying people, and he can be kind of a horrible tool, but that's no reason to hurt a dog."

"What?" The dog slurped Nick's chin with an enthusiastic kiss. "I'm not going to hurt a dog."

"Oh, so you're going to hold her for ransom. Makes sense. I should have thought of that."

"First of all, if I was going to intimidate Gentry into paying me, I wouldn't ransom his fiancée's dog. I'd throw him in another dumpster or pick him up by the lapels so his tiny feet were dangling off the floor. Second, Gentry's not paying you either?"

"Technically, I'm just an intern, which apparently means he's free to abuse me as he sees fit," Henry explained.

"Here's a thought: Why don't you just quit?"

"My parents said if I stuck out an internship until the end of the year, they'd front me the money to take my punk band on tour."

Nick eyed Henry's thick nerd glasses and his pristine shirt.

"I know. I look more likely to fix your printer network settings than front a punk band."

"It's the glasses," Nick told him. "I wonder if your parents would still honor the deal if something unfortunate happened to your employer?"

"I don't know. I guess I could check with them."

Just then, Bella swept into the room in a pink robe with feathers at the cuffs and hem. "There's my little sweetie weetie! Mommy needs her kisses before she goes to the spa." She plucked the dog from Nick's arms and placed several loud kisses on its head, adding fresh lipstick stains to the white fur.

"I'll just go be...uh...somewhere else," Henry said and scurried away.

"Your fiancé owes me money. I've come to collect," Nick said.

"Griffin's not here," Bella said with wide guileless eyes. She looked like an anime character.

"I don't care if the check has his signature or yours on it."

"Oh, I can't write checks out of Griffin's accounts. Not until I'm officially Mrs. Gentry. Speaking of, do you have any opinions on napkin rings? I had decided on these beautiful brushed gold ones, but Griffin said they made his hands look too small."

Nick pinched the bridge of his nose. "Bella, where did Griffin go?"

"Gosh. I don't know. He was gone when I got up. I take my beauty rest very seriously."

"That's great. I care so much about what you're saying," Nick said dryly. "Can you just call him and tell him to get his ass home?"

Bella cocked her head to the side. The dog did the same. Both stared at him with blank eyes.

"Hmm, I never thought of that. I guess I could call him," she said finally.

Nick massaged his temples. "That would be great."

She handed the dog back to Nick and produced a bejeweled phone from the pocket of her robe.

"Griffin Gentry, central Pennsylvania's favorite newscaster, speaking," Griffin's assholey voice sang from the speaker of Bella's phone.

"Griffy, Nick Santiago is here. He says he's waiting for a check."

"Tell him I'm very busy and important. And if he won't leave, make something up about me winning a Nobel Prize for handsomeness. I swear, poor people have nothing better to do than ask rich people for handouts."

Nick's blood pressure spiked into head-exploding territory.

Bella turned to him and smiled. "Griffin said—"

"I heard what Griffin said," Nick said, snatching the phone

from her hand. "Now you listen to me, Gentry. First of all, paying for services rendered is not a handout. It's how the fucking world works. Just because you were born with a trust fund shoved up your ass doesn't mean you get every damn thing for free. Second, if there were Nobel Prizes for handsomeness, I'd be a hell of a lot higher on the list than you. Now drive your pint-size ass back here, and blow the cobwebs off your checkbook, you cheap, narcissistic bastard."

"You can't talk to me like that," Griffin squeaked.

"I'll do more than talk to you like that if I don't have a check with your name on it in my hand by the end of the day."

"What do you think of my new bustier, darling? Do you like the leather?" a throaty, feminine voice asked on the other end of the call.

"I'm being called into an urgent meeting for very important, successful people," Griffin announced. "Bye!"

Nick handed the phone back to Bella, who showed no reaction to her husband admiring another woman's lingerie. "Your husband-to-be is a dick."

Bella waved a dismissive hand. "He's just entitled, silly. It's not poor Griffin's fault that he's always been given everything he ever wanted or that people do nice things for him for free."

Nick was tired of the Griffin Gentrys of the world getting away with their bullshit. This time, he wasn't going to get away with it.

He handed the dog back to Bella. "Here. Take this. I need to use your restroom."

"Of course. The powder room is over there through the trophy room. That's for guests. There's another bathroom off the kitchen, and that's for the help. You can take your pick."

"Due to mysterious religious and political beliefs, I can only use restrooms on the second floor," Nick announced. He didn't wait for a response and jogged up the staircase, taking the stairs two at a time.

"Staffy! La La needs her yum-yums, and I need my spa flip-flops," Bella called behind him.

Nick veered off into the primary bedroom suite and headed through the bathroom into the closet to Griffin's accessories bureau, an entire dresser full of belts, watches, ascots, and...

"Bingo," he said when the next drawer he opened revealed a velvet jewelry tray.

The hideously huge cuff links winked at him from an open Peabody Jewelry box. Tucked in the drawer under the box were several past due notices from Wilfred's jewelry store.

"Asshole," Nick muttered, pocketing the cuff links. He was just getting ready to close the drawer when something else caught his eye. Griffin Gentry's passport. He flipped it open and rolled his eyes. Even the man's passport photo was airbrushed.

Curiosity got the best of him, and he flipped through a couple of pages. Lots of Caribbean travel. He also found several stamps for Brazil and a recent one for Colombia.

The stop-doing-stupid-things voice in his head that sounded a lot like Riley was getting louder, so Nick replaced the passport and closed the drawer.

He was almost out of the bathroom when Griffin's gold-plated electric toothbrush caught his eye from the vanity. Whistling, he plucked it out of the holder and swirled it around the toilet bowl twice. Feeling a little more cheerful, Nick jogged back downstairs where he found Bella hand-feeding the dog what looked like clumps of granola.

"I'm going to go," Nick said as he opened the front door. "But don't think for one second that means I'm giving up. Gentry will pay up if I have to rip the money out of his spray-tanned skin."

"Okay, bye!" Bella said, waving with the dog's paw.

Nick turned to exit but found the way barred by none other than Kellen Pain-in-the-Ass Weber.

"Sergeant Jones, make note that Nick Santiago was witnessed harassing the fiancée of the intended victim and verbally threatening the intended victim."

"Noted," Mabel Jones said wearily.

"What do you mean 'intended victim'?" Nick demanded.

"We're investigating yesterday's incident as a homicide, Santiago. And you just bumped yourself up the suspect list."

19

Riley had done her best to clear the decks. She'd walked Burt, started a load of laundry, and made sure that everyone else in the house was occupied and entertained. The power tools and other contraband were locked in the kitchen pantry. And everyone was under strict instructions not to bother her or let any strangers through the front door unless it was a contractor who could fix the roof next door.

She couldn't shake the feeling that something was off with the whole Griffin thing, so she was going to close her eyes and concentrate until she figured out what it was...or until she fell asleep. The late-night movie watching had taken its toll, and she was already planning a nap.

With Burt snoring peacefully in his dog bed and a relaxing playlist in her ears, she settled on the cushion on her office floor and closed her eyes.

Her brain was a blur of thoughts, images, and to-do lists. Life was chaotic enough under normal circumstances, but throw in an ex-husband that wouldn't go away, a dead body, and five new roommates, and Riley felt like she was on an out-of-control merry-go-round.

She needed to go to the grocery store, or they were going to end up ordering out again. Or worse, Lily and Fred would use every dish in the kitchen on some other complex dish that had a fifty-fifty chance of going horribly wrong.

That reminded her, she needed to find a reasonably priced new set of baking sheets since Lily's burnt-on cookie goop wasn't coming off theirs.

Ugh. Burt needed his toenails trimmed. But he was such a baby about it. Maybe she could send him to one of those doggy day spas and make it someone else's problem? But if Griffin didn't pay them like she was almost certain he wouldn't, there would be no cash for doggy day spas and bakeware.

Ugh. She needed a nap. And maybe a snack. But her roommates had decimated the snack population in the house, which brought her full circle to her grocery list.

Oh my God. Focus, she told herself.

She needed to concentrate on the thing that made her sit down in the first place: Griffin Gentry.

An involuntary shudder rolled up her spine, but Riley persisted. She brought an image of him to her mind's eye. The expensive suit, the shellacked hair, the lifts in his shoes. She frowned as her mental image of Griffin seemed to stretch and grow taller.

The front door burst open. Even through noise-canceling headphones and her rain flute playlist, she would know Nick's agitated stomp anywhere.

"How did it go?" Riley asked him. She cracked open one eye, then jolted. "Ah!"

Mrs. Penny was sitting in front of her, trying to fold her legs into a semblance of crisscross applesauce.

"Where did you come from? I thought you were napping!" Riley said.

"Naps are for old people. Did ya get the money?" Mrs. Penny demanded as Nick stormed into the room.

"No. Where's my TV, Penny?"

"Back ordered. Where's my money?"

"*Our* money is in the tiny, freaky doll hands of that

cheapskate weasel Gentry." Nick flopped down on the floor and put his head in Riley's lap.

"Don't get your boxers in a twist. I've got a plan—" Mrs. Penny began, but Nick steamrolled on.

"He's hiding from me so he doesn't have to pay up. And when I reminded his dingbat girlfriend what will happen if he doesn't cough up the cash, Detective By the Book overheard and spent an hour questioning me."

"Why?" Riley asked.

"Because apparently Lyle Larstein didn't electrocute himself. He got his ass murdered."

"The stiff in the shrubs was murdered?" Mrs. Penny asked.

Nick scrubbed a hand over his face. "Yeah. Only Weber won't say what evidence they have. But Jonesy was there, and all I could get out of her without getting thrown behind bars was that they got something while reviewing Larstein's home security footage."

Riley stroked a hand through his short hair. "You're not an actual suspect, are you?"

"Of course not. Weber was just being a dick about me being a dick."

"You know, you two might get more accomplished if you stopped antagonizing each other and worked together," she pointed out.

"I would rather gargle dish soap and eat those leftovers your mom sent home with us."

"So that's a no then?"

"Weber's probably going to show up here later to question both of you since you were on the scene," he said.

Mrs. Penny rubbed her hands together. "It's been a while since I got to outfox the five-oh."

"Yeah, well, it gets worse. We still have to solve this case if we want a snowball's chance in Costa Rica of getting paid. If Gentry was the intended victim and he ends up dead, his corpse sure as hell won't be shelling out any cash."

"To the whiteboard!" Mrs. Penny said, pointing a finger in the air.

Nick got to his feet and pulled Riley up.

Mrs. Penny scrambled her legs around on the floor and grunted, reaching for her cane.

"Need a hand?" Riley asked.

It took her, Nick, and two farts to get the eighty-year-old on her feet.

Mrs. Penny brushed them off and jogged out of the room, waving her cane. "We've got a Code Cold Burrito, people!" she yelled.

"Brian, I need you to get into Larstein's security system and see if you can pull up whatever footage the cops got their hands on," Nick said, pointing a stick of beef jerky at the whiteboard that was covered in photos and his spidery scrawl.

An all-hands-on-deck meeting called for snacks, according to Mrs. Penny.

"On it. I'll park the van out front and see if I can slip through the Wi-Fi," Brian said before shoveling a handful of sunflower seeds into his mouth.

"Is it really that easy?" Riley asked.

"Sure. As long as this guy never changed the Wi-Fi password from the ISP and he's broadcasting his SSID with no encryption," Brian said.

"Uh-huh. Yeah. That's what I was going to say," Mrs. Penny said, squinting at her iPad through bifocals thicker than encyclopedias.

"Sure you were," Nick said before continuing. "I also need a background check on this Henry personal assistant guy. He was on scene but out of the room when Larstein got dead. He's got access to Gentry's house, and he hates working for the miniature pain in the ass."

Brian gave a thumbs-up.

Nick slapped the beef stick to the next name and photo on the list. "Gabe, I need surveillance on Chupacabra Jones. Again, she's got access to the house and seems to genuinely like both Gentry and Goodshine, which makes her suspicious. Josie, you're on Claudia Mendoza. I want to know if she even breathes in Gentry's direction."

Josie was eating cereal doused with chocolate milk out of a glass mixing bowl. "You got it, boss," she said with an enthusiastic crunch.

Nick circled a long list of names with the jerky. "The rest of you will divvy up these suspects and take turns following them. You will immediately report any and all suspicious activity as it relates to this case. Do not be suspicious. Do not get caught. If you do get caught, do not admit that you were following anyone. Do not utter my name. Do not tell the nice police officer or building security that you're working for a PI or that you *are* a PI."

He looked pointedly at Mrs. Penny, who was too busy examining the screen of her tablet to notice.

"What's my assignment?" Riley asked.

"I'm glad you asked, Thorn. Since your readings seem to get more accurate the closer you are to someone, you're going to be getting up close and personal with our top suspects."

Riley perked up. Usually Nick was too protective to let her get too involved in the investigations. Now, not only was he embracing the whole my-girlfriend-is-a-psychic thing, he was giving her an honest-to-goodness, real-deal, I-respect-your-value-to-this-business assignment.

"I will, of course, be going with you everywhere," he added.

Whatever. It still felt like a win.

"Okay," she agreed, trying not to sound too excited.

"Now, if I can get that little tangerine turd to call me back, we'll also be stepping up our personal security on Gentry. One of us needs to be with him at all times. And by 'us,' I mean me, Josie, or Gabe."

Gabe tipped his head regally. "I am honored my sarcastic self-defense demonstration has convinced you of my prowess."

"Uh, what sarcastic self-defense demonstration?" Riley asked.

"Don't worry about it," Nick said.

"I hurled your boyfriend to the kitchen floor for my own amusement," Gabe explained.

"Did you do it shirtless?" Lily wondered.

"We were fully clothed, and I was minding my own business. He took advantage of me," Nick said.

The doorbell rang, and Riley excused herself, confident that it would take at least five or ten minutes to get Lily back on track and forget about shirtless men.

She opened the door, then stifled a sigh when she spotted yet another complication. Weber stood on the welcome mat, hands on hips, badge and Glock on display. He looked like a man who wasn't having a very good day.

"Riley."

"Kellen. Tough day?"

"I wasted an hour of my life interrogating your boyfriend because he can't share his toys."

"Did you come to take another crack at him? Because I don't think it'll go any better than the first round," she warned.

"I'm here to follow up with you and your purple-haired anarchist roommate. And you two had better be more forthcoming than Nicky, or else I'm going to get pissed off enough to haul someone downtown."

Riley had always felt that she wouldn't fare well in jail. Mrs. Penny on the other hand would probably end up running a profitable, illegal goods–based business behind bars.

"You know, now isn't a great time," she hedged.

"It's never a great time to get murdered, but that's exactly what happened to Lyle Larstein, and if you and your friend don't give me ten minutes of your time here, I'll drag both of you into an interrogation room."

Interrogation rooms were small, and Mrs. Penny was a gassy woman.

"Fine. Come in, *Detective Weber*. You can wait in the *kitchen* while I *get Mrs. Penny*," she said in a near shout, hoping someone in Nick's office would hear the warning.

"Very casual, Riley," Weber said dryly. "I think I'll come with you to get your friend."

Freaking great.

Riley made a production of stomping her way slowly toward Nick's office. "Can I get you anything to drink, *Detective Weber?*" she shouted.

Behind her, he muttered something that sounded a lot like "I hate my job."

Riley entered the room and found everyone still staring raptly at Nick and his whiteboard. Only instead of being covered with suspect names and photos, it was a mathematical equation with arrows and complex shapes.

"And that's how quantum physics works," Nick said, capping his marker.

"Ahhh," the roommates said in unison, nodding their heads.

"Oh look, it's my favorite ex-partner and current pain in my ass, Detective Weber," Nick said, acknowledging their guest.

"That was sarcasm. I am laughing," Gabe said with enthusiasm.

"Mrs. Penny," Riley said.

"Present!" the woman barked.

"Detective Weber would like to have a word with us."

Mrs. Penny heaved herself off the couch and straightened to her full five feet, two inches. "Lawyer."

"You're not under arrest. Yet," Weber added.

"*Lawyer,*" she repeated with unnecessary enunciation. "Me and my pal Riley here won't talk without a lawyer present. Fortunately for you, mine is already on his way."

"He is?" Weber, Riley, and Nick all said together.

"Yeah, so you can either shut your trap and have a cup of coffee or cuff me, copper," Mrs. Penny said.

"Honestly, it's probably just easier if you go for the coffee," Riley said out of the corner of her mouth.

"Fine. Whatever," Weber said wearily.

Riley led him into the kitchen and programmed a cup

of coffee in a JASMINE PATEL ATTORNEY AT LAW mug. "Still hungover?" she asked, sliding the mug in front of him.

"It's like I got six cases of the flu at the same time. Everything still hurts, and I don't remember what normal feels like," he complained.

She was just beginning to feel sorry for him when Mrs. Penny strutted through the swinging door with a young man in an ill-fitting suit and a dinosaur tie. On closer inspection, he wasn't just young. He was a teenager.

Nick brought up the rear, looking smug.

"I don't get paid nearly enough for this," Weber muttered into his coffee.

"Meet my attorney, Billy," Mrs. Penny said. "Billy, meet the five-oh trying to trample my civil rights."

"Detective Weber, is it?" Billy asked, holding out a hand that was nearly covered by the sleeve of his suit jacket.

"Is this some kind of joke?" Weber asked. "You're twelve."

"Actually, I'm seventeen. I just have a young face," Billy said.

"He's one of them there genius prodigy kids. Graduated high school at nine. College at eleven. And law school at fifteen," Mrs. Penny said proudly.

"I took a gap year and went to med school for a little while," Billy said humbly.

"And he's about to lawyer your ass," Mrs. Penny said gleefully.

Weber looked at Nick, who shrugged and grinned. "I'm just here to make a sandwich."

"Fine. Whatever. Why should any of you care about a murder?"

"Kind of hard to care when the victim spent his life terrorizing others," Nick pointed out. "But again, I'm just here to make a sandwich."

"Let's just get this over with," Weber said. "Everybody sit down."

"So to clarify, you didn't see or hear anything besides *The Price Is Right?*" Weber repeated, sounding as if he'd be willing to give up his pension if someone told him he could just go home.

Mrs. Penny had just gone on an eight-minute tangent about the price of toaster ovens. Nick had eaten his sandwich and was now noisily crunching his way through one of the bags of chips that had survived the happy hour snack massacre. Burt sat at his feet, patiently waiting for the first casualty of gravity.

"It's kinda hard to hear someone get murdered in the backyard when that Drew Carey is such a hottie," Mrs. Penny said.

"My client is not saying she ignored a crime in progress. She is saying she had no knowledge of the crime being committed," Billy interjected.

"Your client is giving me a migraine. Why the runaround, Mrs. Penny? Are you protecting someone? You recently became a partner in Santiago Investigations, which I can only assume makes you privy to case information," Weber said.

"I'm more than privy, bucko!" Mrs. Penny said, pounding the kitchen table with her fist. "I run this place. I have my hands in every investigation—"

"What Great-Aunt Jocelyn means is she is only a financial backer for this business endeavor. She is a retired eighty-year-old woman who doesn't have the time or the inclination to involve herself in private investigations," Billy said.

"Your name is Jocelyn?" Nick asked.

"Didn't you know that?" Riley asked him.

He shrugged. "I just assumed she was hiding her first name from everyone like you do with your middle name. Wait a second. Is there a Mr. Penny somewhere out there?"

It was Weber's turn to hit the table. "Isn't it true that Nick Santiago and Riley Thorn visited the victim the day before he was murdered?"

It took two tries, but Mrs. Penny came halfway out of her seat to lean menacingly over the table. "You can't handle the truth!"

Burt let out a concerned *woof*.

"Oh, for Pete's sake, I have too much on my plate to deal with this," Riley said. "Yes, Nick and I knocked on the victim's door the day before his murder. Which, if you have access to Larstein's security footage, you already know. We were knocking on doors asking neighbors if they saw or heard anything related to the shot fired at Griffin Gentry."

"Yeah. Remember the guy the Harrisburg PD sent packing, telling him it was all just harmless pranks?" Nick interjected.

"Don't start with me, Nicky."

"Don't continue with me, Weber."

Billy was starting to look nervous.

"Okay, boys. Let's keep it civil. You're scaring the prodigy," Riley cut in.

"You withheld information relating to an investigation," Weber said.

"Yeah, well, back at you, pal," Nick said. "You think I want to be working for Griffin Fucking Gentry? Fuck no. You have information that could help me protect this asshole and get me paid, but noooooo. You've got the law shoved so far up your a—"

Riley's phone buzzed on the table with an incoming call.

"It's Griffin," she said.

Nick rounded the island as Riley answered the call. "Hello?"

"Riley?" Griffin sounded far away and scared.

"Gimme the phone," Nick said.

"What's wrong, Griffin? Where are you?" Riley asked.

Nick reached for the phone, but Weber batted him away.

"I'm in my car. I just left…uh…an important meeting, and they're chasing me."

"Who's chasing you?" Riley asked. She heard the squeal of tires through the phone. Nick lunged again, but Weber grappled him to the table.

With a roll of her eyes, she hit the speaker button.

"It's one of those really small cars that the airport makes you rent when they say they're out of SUVs."

"Listen here, you little weasel. Where's my money?" Nick barked as he planted his hand against Weber's face and pushed.

"How do you know they're chasing you?" Riley asked.

"A very large man leaned out of the passenger window and shot off my side mirror!"

"Are you sure you didn't just hit something? You're not a very good driver," Riley said.

"Oooh! Wrestling! I'll make some popcorn," Lily chirped from the kitchen door.

There was another noise on the line that sounded a lot like gunfire to Riley's untrained ear. She couldn't concentrate on the call or the images she felt bubbling to the surface of her mind with Nick and Weber wrestling on the table like children.

She picked up her water glass and dumped it on them.

"Whoa," the lawyer said.

Sputtering, Nick and Weber broke apart and frowned at her.

"You are adults. Act like it! Griffin, where are you?" she snapped.

"I'm heading down…street."

"You're cutting out. I didn't catch that. Are you near a police station?"

"…front…house."

A vision finally surfaced. Griffin speeding into their driveway with the bad guys on his heels.

"Uh-oh," Riley said.

"What?" Weber demanded.

"He's coming here."

Nick snatched the phone from her. "If you bring your shit to my house after refusing to pay up, you'll have more to worry about than a shooter in a smart car. Hello? Hello?"

But the call had already dropped.

20

Get everyone upstairs or hidden," Weber said tersely. He was already dialing his phone as he stormed out of the kitchen.

"Keep everybody to the back of the house," Nick ordered Riley, following Weber out and looking just as steely.

"You heard them," Riley said, helping Mrs. Penny out of her chair. "Billy, help Mrs. Penny and Lily. I'll warn the rest."

She could see bits and pieces of it play out in her mind. Two cars sending gravel flying as they careened up the driveway. A sense of urgency permeated the candy pink clouds. Griffin was bringing danger right to their doorstep.

"They didn't teach us about this in law school," Billy said, looking a little green around the gills.

"You're a smart kid. I have faith in you," Riley called as she hurried out of the room.

She ran into a grim-looking Nick coming out of his office loading his gun. Weber was pocketing extra magazines for his sidearm. "We need to set up—"

"A barricade," Nick finished for Weber. "You get the—"

"Gate," Weber said.

"Meet you out front." Nick turned to her. "Stay inside and

stay down, Thorn." Then he grabbed her by the front of the shirt and hauled her in for a short, hard kiss.

"Don't do anything stupid," they said in unison.

Nick's dimples winked to life. "See you in a few, baby."

The rest of the occupants of Nick's office seemed to be taking the situation too much in stride. "Hey! Everybody needs to vacate immediately," Riley ordered, clapping her hands.

Burt woke up with a snort and looked around, dazed. Mr. Willicott continued to snore with vigor.

Riley shook him by the shoulder.

"Huh? Wha? I don't wanna go to school today," he mumbled.

"Wake up, Mr. Willicott!" she shouted.

"Try this," Fred offered from his lotus pose on the floor. "Who wants action on the Denver Broncos?"

Mr. Willicott woke mid-snore. "I'll take fifty on the Broncos."

"We'll take the front windows," Josie said, yanking up her pant leg to reveal an ankle holster and small handgun.

Brian rifled through his backpack and produced a much larger gun with a silencer. "Let's go have some fun," he said.

"It's baby's first gunfight," Josie said with more enthusiasm than Riley had ever seen from her.

"Gabe, I need you to get these guys moving," Riley said, pointing at the cross-legged Fred and the groggy Mr. Willicott. "Follow Mrs. Penny and Lily, and keep everyone quiet. Burt, go with Gabe."

The dog, looking nervous, loped over to her and took her hand in his mouth. He tugged gently.

"Sorry, buddy. I can't go with you," she said, giving him several loving pats with her free hand. "It'll all be over soon."

They're coming.

The message vibrated with crystal clear intensity.

Trusting Gabe to handle the roommates, she ran from the office, wiping the dog slobber on her jeans as she went. She needed to warn Nick before it was too late. She flung open the front door in time to spy him parking her Jeep nose-to-nose with Weber's police issue SUV across the driveway.

"*Woo-hoo! Finally some action! Lemme at 'em,*" the ghost of Riley's long-dead uncle Jimmy crowed from the Jeep.

Weber was already hunkered down behind the wheel well of his vehicle, wearing a bulletproof vest and loading a rifle with deadly-looking rounds.

"They're coming," she said through cupped hands.

"Get back in the house now, Riley," Nick ordered, hopping out of the driver's seat and rounding the back of the Jeep.

Just then, the distant *pop pop pop* of gunfire exploded, followed by the faraway whine of sirens.

"They're not going to get here in time," she whispered to herself as she was closing the door.

But she didn't do it fast enough. Burt bolted through her legs, out the door, and off the porch.

"Burt! No!" she cried.

Tires squealed on the street.

Pop. Pop.

Swearing to herself, Riley slammed the door and raced into the yard after her idiot dog.

"Damn it, Thorn!" Nick growled.

She tackled Burt to the cold ground two feet from Nick as tires squealed again before giving way to the crunch and scrape of metal.

In an impressive show of strength, Nick grabbed her and Burt and dragged them behind the Jeep's fender. "Stay down," he ordered.

Burt's tail thumped happily against Riley's leg. "You're in big trouble when this is over," she told the dog.

Nick put a knee to Riley's back, holding her down. From her belly-level view under the Jeep, she watched as her ex-husband smashed his snazzy sports car through their gate...again. On his tail was a powder-blue Fiat with guns hanging out of both windows.

"Ready?" Weber yelled.

"Kick ass on one," Nick said. "Three…"

Free of the gate, Griffin's car accelerated, sending gravel flying.

"Two."

Riley watched in horror and braced herself as the car fishtailed before smacking soundly into the driver's-side door of the Jeep.

"One," Nick shouted.

Both men jumped to their feet and opened fire on the Fiat. Riley closed her eyes and covered Burt's ears with her hands as he whimpered under her. Gunfire was seriously loud, she thought as hot shells rained down on her.

The Fiat zigged into the yard through an overgrown flower bed encircling a tall oak. The *pop* and *pow* of Nick's and Weber's weapons was interrupted by a terrific *boom* that came from behind her.

Riley whipped her head around and spotted Mrs. Penny balanced precariously on the porch roof. She had a bandana tied around her head and a gleaming handgun in her grip.

"You've got to be kidding me," Riley muttered.

The oak tree above the Fiat shuddered, then gave a mighty *crack*. A huge branch dropped, crushing the roof of the vehicle.

Riley glanced back at the roof in time to spy Mrs. Penny's feet and cane disappearing through the bedroom window.

"Hold fire," Weber barked.

She chanced a glance under the belly of the Jeep and saw something white—maybe a fast-food napkin—waving out of what was left of the passenger window.

On the street, an expensive-looking Lincoln Escalade came to a halt, stopping the southbound traffic to lookie-loo at the active crime scene.

"Come out with your hands up," Weber yelled, his voice crackling with authority.

Behind them, the front door opened, and Josie stalked out, gun trained on the Fiat. Brian wheeled around from the side of the porch and took up position on the corner.

Horns blared on the street, and traffic began to move again.

The Fiat's doors creaked open, and two sets of hands appeared. The car rocked back and forth violently as if a sumo wrestling match were taking place inside.

"What the hell are they doing?" Nick demanded, dragging off his ear protection.

"What?" Weber asked without taking his eyes off the tiny car.

"I think they're stuck," Riley said.

Just then, the passenger, a burly guy in a shiny gray pin-striped suit and snakeskin cowboy boots, fell out of the car onto a clump of chrysanthemums. He had a mop of fiery red hair. Beneath his freckles, his skin was the shade of pale that required SPF 100 or higher.

The driver's exit was no more graceful. The afternoon sun gleamed off the top of his tan shaved head as he tilted sideways until his large frame popped free and he tumbled onto the ground. He wore head-to-toe black from his combat boots to the knit turtleneck that looked as if its seams were straining over an excessive amount of muscle.

"Hands where I can see them," Nick and Weber shouted together.

Riley had to admit, the two ex-partners certainly had a rhythm together when they weren't too busy bickering. She doubted that either man would take it as a compliment.

"Jesus. These guys are the size of linebackers who retired and became lumberjacks," Josie called from the porch.

She wasn't wrong. Both men looked as if they shopped exclusively in the Big and Tall section.

"Am I dead?" Griffin's head popped up on the other side of the Jeep, drawing Nick's and Weber's aim.

The news anchor yelped and collapsed to the ground.

"We should be so lucky," Nick muttered.

"Facedown, on the ground, hands behind your back," Weber shouted to the two men from the Fiat.

Riley smirked into Burt's fur when Griffin complied too.

"I'll take the one dressed like a night prowler. You take Lizard Boots," Nick said to Weber.

"What?" Weber barked, shaking his head. "I can't hear shit."

"Maybe you should have thought to put on your fucking *ear protection*, dummy."

"Don't fuck with me, Nicky. I'm still hungover,"

"Get the guy on the right," Nick yelled. Together they rounded opposite ends of the vehicles, guns trained on the men on the ground.

Riley felt an entirely inappropriate pitter-pat of female appreciation as she watched her muscly, tattooed boyfriend slap zip ties on a bad guy. Griffin was still shivering on the ground, whining about the gravel damaging his sensitive skin.

Lizard Boots started muttering as Weber reached for his cuffs. But Night Prowler hissed at his partner. "Remember, keep your mouth fucking shut," he said in what sounded like it could be an Austrian accent.

"I'm so sick of you telling me what to do," Lizard Boots growled.

Nick nudged Lizard Boots in the hip with his foot. "Hey, ol' buddy, ol' pal. We're all friends here. Go ahead and confess to Uncle Nick and Detective Pain-in-the-Ass why you shot up my goddamn yard."

Both shooters looked at him, their faces going carefully blank.

"What are you saying?" Weber demanded several decibels louder than necessary.

"None of us like your suit," Nick quipped, tightening the zip ties on a very unhappy-looking Night Prowler.

The sirens were ear-piercing now. Burt let out a pathetic whimper under her, and Riley rolled off him. The dog gave her face a grateful slurp before galloping onto the porch and through the front door.

"You're welcome," she called after him.

She got up, dusted herself off, and rounded the vehicles.

Nick and Weber were busy going through the shooters' pockets and making a pile of the weapons they found. The men from the Fiat didn't look very happy about their predicament. Both of them were aiming death glares at Griffin, who was still lying facedown and whining pathetically.

Riley sighed. Griffin had managed to T-bone her Jeep dead center, though it did look as though his car took the brunt of the impact. The front end was smashed in to the dashboard. Her Jeep bore a large dent on the driver's-side door and a spray of new bullet holes in the windshield.

"Sorry, Uncle Jimmy," Riley said, patting the rear fender.

"*That was the most excitement I've had since I caught a sand shark in Ocean City,*" Uncle Jimmy's spirit said, cackling.

She reached down and hauled Griffin to his feet. "Are you okay?" she asked.

"No, I'm not okay! My suit is wrinkled, I have dirt in my mouth, and this ugly Jeep destroyed my cute little car," he whined.

Riley exhaled through her teeth. "I meant did you get shot?"

"Oh. No. I don't think so. Just great! Grass stains. Those will never come out," he complained, wiping at the knees of his trousers.

She narrowed her eyes when he straightened. "Did you get new lifts for your shoes? You look taller."

The first police cruiser charged through the broken gate into the driveway, followed immediately by a second and third.

Happy to leave the boring cleanup to the cops, Nick holstered his weapon and crossed to Riley. "You okay?"

"No! I have grass stains everywhere," Griffin wailed. "Who's going to pay for my dry cleaning?"

Nick planted his hand on Griffin's chest and shoved him over backward into a bush.

"I was talking to you," Nick said to Riley.

"I'm fine."

He hooked a hand around the back of her neck and pulled

her in until they were forehead to forehead. "Good. Don't ever fucking do that again. You took ten years off my life. And we could have a lot of sex in ten years."

She winced. "I'm sorry. I just couldn't leave Burt out here."

"I know," he said. "Still mad though."

"I know," she said with a sigh.

They stood that way for a long moment, breathing each other in while Griffin flailed his way out of the holly and Harrisburg cops swarmed their front yard.

"You know, usually I just leave my Jeep at crime scenes. This time, it *is* a crime scene," she said, trying to lighten the tension.

"You're a hell of a girl, Riley Thorn. Now go inside and check on the others while I deal with this mess," he said.

"Okay," she agreed. But when he moved to pull away, Riley gripped him by the front of his shirt. "That was really hot, by the way."

"What was?"

"You being all defend-y and authoritative and stuff."

His grin was lightning quick. Both dimples appeared and did funny things to her stomach. Once again, she caught the shimmer of something sparkly in her head. Giddiness swept over her, and she couldn't help but giggle.

Nick rolled his eyes. "Go on," he said, turning her toward the house and smacking her on the ass. "Oh, and tell Penny she better hide that fucking gun."

"How did you know?" she demanded.

"I know the sound of a fifty caliber, and I know there's only one person stupid enough to fire it from our porch roof."

"Handsome *and* smart," she said on another sigh. "How did I get so lucky?"

"We'll talk about getting lucky later," he promised.

Riley left him to deal with cops in the driveway and jogged up the porch steps. "Let's go check on everyone," she said to Josie and Brian.

They followed Brian around to the ramp to his office

entrance. It was a skinny room that contained a counter-top, a half dozen monitors, and a lot of expensive computer equipment.

"I can't believe I didn't get to shoot anyone," Josie complained as they poked their heads into the empty kitchen, bar, and dining room.

"Next time, babe," Brian promised.

"Where is everyone?" Riley wondered. "Did they all make it upstairs?"

They found Burt sitting in front of the built-in hutch outside the dining room. His tail thumped a staccato beat as he stared at the glass doors.

"Achoo!"

"Bless you," Riley, Josie, and Brian said.

Riley rolled her eyes, then knocked on the carved molding surrounding the hutch.

"Who is it?" Lily called sweetly from within the wall.

"Pipe down! We're supposed to be hiding, remember? It could be the bad guys knocking," Fred said loudly.

"Right! I forgot. Nobody's here but us house ghosts," Lily said. "Woooooooooooo."

"Buncha amateurs," Mrs. Penny muttered.

"Please remain calm…and much quieter," Gabe said.

Riley sighed and swung the hutch open to reveal the secret staircase.

Lily, Fred, and Mr. Willicott were playing cards on the stairs using potato chips for money. Gabe was eating the rest of the chips that hadn't become currency. Billy the prodigy lawyer had loosened his dinosaur tie and was drinking a Dr Pepper with shaking hands.

Mrs. Penny took a slurp of the bourbon in her glass. "I was here the whole time," she announced.

———

"What in the name of all fuckery is going on here?" Jasmine demanded, shoving aside the crime scene tape and holding a hand in the face of the cop who dared to stand in her way. "Not today, junior."

Riley excused herself from the officer who was trying to take a statement from all her roommates at the same time and hugged her best friend.

"What the hell happened here?" Jasmine demanded, returning the tight squeeze before releasing her.

"Oh, you know, the usual. Griffin was being chased by two men with guns, so of course he drove straight here, endangering everyone and crashing his car into my Jeep. Then Nick and Kellen returned fire until a tree branch mysteriously crushed the bad guys' car and they were forced to surrender."

"Mrs. Penny shoot down the branch?" Jasmine guessed.

"Yep. But we're pretending it was Mother Nature. You look good," Riley observed.

Jasmine wore a red pantsuit with a lacy white tank and beige stilettos that looked as if they could be used as weapons. Her bangs were ruler-straight and as glossy as the rest of her jet-black hair.

"I had to take a deposition today. Some dirtbag son tried to bleed his parents' estate dry while keeping them locked up in a basement in-law suite. If the trial goes anything like today, I'll have him crying on the stand in less than five minutes."

"I believe in you," Riley said. Making men cry in fear was a specialty of Jasmine's.

"This is an active crime scene, not Sunday brunch. You need to leave," Weber announced, stomping over to them.

"Don't even start with me, Detective Dick," Jasmine challenged. "I already eviscerated one man today. I wouldn't add myself to that list if I were you."

"I'm a homicide detective. Pain-in-the-ass attorneys don't scare me."

Jasmine stepped closer until the pointy tips of her shoes were touching Weber's boots. "Oh yeah?"

"Yeah," he growled.

"It's so nice to see you two getting along," Riley said.

21

Nick navigated his way around the cops still littering his front yard in search of Riley. Other than a few bleeding scrapes from broken glass that still stung, he'd survived the shootout remarkably unscathed.

A wrecker added its flashing lights to the chaos, squeezing into the driveway between cruisers and SUVs. Radios squawked. Neighbors gawked along the property line, probably gossiping about how they always knew there was something funny about the couple that lived in that house. Cars on Front Street eased by to rubberneck.

He spotted Sergeant Mabel Jones muscling one of the shooters into the back seat of an SUV with a hand on top of his shaved head. There was something nagging him, and he hoped to hell he was wrong about it.

"They say anything yet?" Nick asked when she shut the door.

"Not a word. They just keep doing this creepy, smug smiling thing that makes me want to punch them," she said.

Night Prowler was indeed smirking through the rear window at Nick.

Nick held up a closed fist and made a cranking motion,

with his other hand raising his middle finger at the man. The smirk turned to a glare.

"Very mature, Santiago," Mabel said.

Nick turned his back on the SUV. "Weber and I didn't find any IDs on them, but it shouldn't be hard to track them through the rental car." He nodded toward the crushed, bullet-ridden Fiat.

"These two goons fit in that little Matchbox car?"

"Barely."

"Any idea why they were after Gentry?" she asked, jerking her chin to where a blanket-wearing Griffin was being examined by an EMT.

"I got grass stains on my pants. I need them dry-cleaned immediately," Griffin whined.

Nick rolled his eyes. "I can give you a thousand reasons why someone would want that miniature moron dead." Though there was only one reason he could think of that two idiots with no identities and guns with no serial numbers would go after Gentry. "I'd appreciate it if you kept me in the loop on this one," he said to Mabel.

"You know I can't do that, Santiago."

"Think of it as professional courtesy."

"You're not a cop anymore," she pointed out.

"No, but apparently I'm still protecting and serving. Besides, technically I'm a victim in this case."

She gave a rueful shake of her head. "Yeah, you look like a victim."

He grinned. "Appreciate it, Jonesy. I gotta go check in with my girl."

He was just working his way around Gentry's stupid smashed-up car when his phone buzzed in his pocket.

Mom.

He sighed and answered the call. "Hello, Mother."

"Why am I hearing from your aunt Nancy that there was some sort of *gunfight at your house*?" his mother demanded.

"Because Aunt Nancy has a gigantic mouth?"

"Nicholas." Dr. Marie Santiago had a way of packing a whole shitload of condescension into one word.

He dodged around two uniformed officers who looked like they were working on a pair of migraines while trying to question Lily and Fred. "Everything is fine. No one was hurt."

"This is all because of that girlfriend of yours, isn't it? Mark my words, trouble follows her. Why can't you date a nice normal girl? I know a single pharmacist named Felicity on the research committee at work. She makes six figures a year and plays the harp."

"Riley *is* nice, I don't want normal, and I hate harps, Ma. The sooner you get it through your snobby thick head, the better."

"I am not a snob just because your father and I want you to date a respectable woman with an actual profession."

"Oh really? What does it make you?"

"A mother."

He finally spotted Riley running interference between a fiery Jasmine and a pissed-off Weber near the front porch. Relief coursed through him.

"Yeah, well, get used to Riley, Ma. If I have my way, she's going to be sticking around for a long, long time."

"If you'd just let me introduce you to Felicity—"

"Goodbye, Ma."

Nick disconnected and made his way over to his girlfriend.

"You have a stick shoved so far up your ass—"

"Hey, Jasmine," Nick said, interrupting her insult.

"Oh, hi, Nick. You doing okay? No stray bullets take a bite out of you?"

"All good," he promised.

"You didn't ask if I was okay," Weber pointed out like a petulant child.

Jasmine narrowed deadly brown eyes on him. "That's because I don't care if you're alive or not."

"Really? Because kissing me on my mother's doorstep seems like caring."

"They've been at this off and on for almost thirty minutes. I think it's their love language," Riley reported to Nick.

"Love language?" Jasmine and Weber scoffed in unison.

"I need you for a second," Nick said, taking Riley by the hand.

"Have you guys ever heard of enemies to lovers?" Riley asked Jasmine and Weber as he dragged her away.

"I wouldn't sleep with him if he needed an orgasm to live," Jasmine said, pretending to dry heave.

"I don't even find you attractive," Weber shot back.

Jasmine's gasp followed them as Nick led Riley into another overgrown flower bed next to the police cruiser with Lizard Boots in the back seat.

"Why do you look like you want to punch someone?" Riley asked.

"Because it's not freaking over."

"What do you mean it's not over?" she demanded. "The guys with guns are in custody. They were clearly trying to kill Griffin." She gestured at Lizard Boots through the window.

The arrestee winked at her and puckered his lips.

"Barf," she said.

"Stop flirting with my girl, asshole," Nick snarled, slapping the window.

"Okay, let's go waaay over here and talk." Riley dragged him toward the relative quiet of the garage. She pulled him inside and stabbed the button to close the garage door. "Why is this not over?"

"Because those two dumbasses are pros…ish," he amended. "Stupid, bad-at-their-job pros. They're hired guns. Which means someone did the hiring. Someone who didn't want to get their hands dirty. Someone—"

"Who's still out there," she said with a groan.

"Exactly."

"Damn it. What do we do?"

"We figure out who's at the top, take them down, and force Griffin to cough up the cash…after we raise our rates of course."

"Of course," she said with a teasing eye roll.

"We'll get started as soon as I get back," Nick said as the SUV hauling Lizard Boots pulled onto Front Street.

"Where are you going?" Riley asked.

———

Nick strolled into the Harrisburg PD's bullpen like he belonged there. He had once, back in his young idealistic days.

The smell was the same, old coffee and industrial tile cleaner. The desks were the same battered commercial furniture some chief had squeezed out of the budget in the eighties. However, with a few exceptions, most of the faces were different. It was either a sign that he was getting older as this chapter of his past got more distant in the rearview mirror…or it was that cop work sucked and burnout was inevitable.

He was leaning toward the latter, but to be fair, working in the private sector hadn't been a walk in the park recently thanks to Griffin Fucking Gentry.

Nick's stomach grumbled, reminding him that he'd missed lunch, so he veered off in the direction of the break room. There were two rookies in uniform sitting at the same shitty table with wobbly legs he'd eaten at. They were arguing about who ran a faster mile pace at the police academy.

Nick strolled to the refrigerator and opened it. There on the top shelf, all the way to the left where it had always been, was an old black lunch bag with WEBER stitched across the top.

"How's it going?" he asked the rookies as he rummaged through the bag.

"Who are you?" the one on the left asked.

The other one kicked the first under the table. "That's Nick Santiago, dummy."

"Oh. Shit."

Nick was pleased to note his reputation was still part of departmental lore.

He pulled out the Lebanon bologna sandwich inside, took a big bite, and frowned. Weber never used enough mayonnaise.

Something about his lame-ass arteries. Nick took two more bites just to make sure he'd ruin Weber's day before shoving the remains of the sandwich back in the bag.

"Have a good one," he said, tossing a salute at the rookies on his way out the door.

"Did he just eat Weber's lunch?"

"Shit. Let's get out of here before we get blamed for it."

Nick's phone buzzed in his pocket. It was a call from his cousin.

"What's up, Bri?"

"Man, people really need to secure their home security components better. I got the footage from Larstein's cameras. Our two friends from today were the ones who jumped the fence in gardener getup and broke Larstein's unlucky neck," Brian said.

"Nice work. Where's Gentry?" Nick asked.

"He and Gabe are in Gentry's house. He was whining about wanting new pants, so I figured I'd swing by the neighbor's and poke around his network while he changed."

"I really hate that guy," Nick muttered.

Brian took a slurp of something on his end. "You and me both, coz. Get this. Mrs. Penny upped the fee to thirty grand. Still don't see how she's going to make him cough it up, but she said something along the lines of 'Mind your business and get me a pizza.'"

"He'll pay if I have to rip out his pancreas and sell it on the street corner," Nick said, nodding to the cop holding the coffeepot.

"That's the spirit."

A crowd had gathered in the hallway outside the interrogation rooms. "I gotta go. Let me know if anyone finds anything."

"Will do. Try not to get arrested."

"I'll do my best," Nick promised and headed into the clump of cops. "What have we got, boys and girls?"

There was a collective groan as well as a few grins of recognition. "Who let you in here, Santiago?" asked a grizzled robbery detective Nick remembered for his devotion to his grandchildren and his extended bouts of heartburn.

"What? Can't a guy say hi to his old coworkers?"

"Not when that guy is you," Mabel said pointedly.

"Come on. We can help each other out. You scratch my back, I send you all pizza for lunch tomorrow," Nick cajoled.

"What kind of pizza?" the hefty desk sergeant demanded.

"Niko's. Just tell me if Weber cracked either one of them yet."

"Damn it. I love their primavera pizza," a uniform muttered.

"Come on, guys. These assholes tried to shoot up my house with my girl in it," Nick pressed.

"Neither one of those burly fuckers has said a damn word yet," the detective said. "And I want a whole grandma pizza to myself."

"Done," Nick agreed.

The debate about who was getting what pizza raged until the interrogation room door opened and the captain and Weber stepped into the hall. Cops scattered like chickens.

"Let me guess. You got big fat nothing out of them," Nick predicted.

Weber stuck his finger in his ear. "This investigation is none of your business, Nicky," he said in a near shout.

The captain rolled his eyes ceilingward as if praying for patience. "Both of you shut up before I lock you in a cell. I don't care who did what." He pointed at Weber. "You, find out who these assholes are. And you, Santiello, get out of my precinct."

One of the captain's more endearing traits was that he liked to call people by the wrong names to keep them from feeling important in his presence.

"Come on, Captain. I was just offering my expertise—"

Nick's bullshitting was interrupted by the throat clearing of a tall bald man in tortoiseshell glasses and a tailored suit that screamed, *I make $900 an hour*. "I'm Bradford Carpendale, attorney at law. Can any of you gentlemen point me in the direction of my clients?" he asked in that polite way that felt like a disguise for a haughty *fuck you*.

"You'll have to be more specific," the captain said.

Nick and Weber shared a dark look. This wasn't good.

"I believe they were arrested about two hours ago after accidentally trespassing on private property and getting shot at by the homeowner. I need to confer with them immediately," the attorney said, opening a leather-bound folio and showing the contents to the captain.

Nick remembered how the captain's jaw always did that tightening thing when he was pissed and wondered if the man's dentist had ever commented on the state of his molars.

"Detective Weber, please show Mr. Crapathon to his clients," the captain said.

"It's Carpendale," the lawyer said.

"I don't care," the captain said before walking away.

Weber jerked his head at Nick, which meant *stay here and don't fucking talk to anybody.* Nick took it as an invitation to camp out at Weber's desk and snoop through case files until a couple of rookies swung by and asked him about some of his more colorful exploits while with the department.

"I heard that you jumped off a three-story building into a dumpster to beat a perp on the fire escape to the ground."

"That's how I got this scar," Nick said, pointing to his neck, where there was no scar because it had been the roof of a ranch house and he'd tackled the suspect on a half-inflated bounce house.

"Are you telling them about the time you got stuck in the elevator of a suspect's building and cried until the fire marshal carried you out like a baby?" Weber asked, elbowing his way through the crowd that had gathered.

The rookies dispersed.

"I'll have you know lots of people don't like small enclosed spaces," Nick pointed out.

"Chief Jennifer told that story at her retirement," Weber said.

Nick sighed at the memory. "I never felt safer than I did nestled between her bulging biceps." He took his feet off

Weber's desk. "What's Million Dollar Suit Baby doing here? Did the perps make a call?"

Weber shot a dark look in the direction of interrogation. "They did not."

"Maybe their lawyer's psychic?"

"A psychic who got on a private plane in Dulles and arrived at Harrisburg International Airport half an hour ago."

"Who's the plane belong to?" Nick asked.

"A holding company based in Grand Cayman."

"That's helpful," Nick said dryly.

"It gets better. The lawyer came armed with extradition papers," Weber said.

"Seriously?"

"It seems our gun-toting, compact-car-loving friends are getting a free ride back to Colombia, where they're wanted for murder and extortion."

"Columbia, Maryland?" Nick asked hopefully.

"Colombia, South America. Do you want me to draw you a map?"

"I've played Pictionary with you before. Your South America would look like a three-legged horse wearing a bucket on its head."

Weber ignored the justifiable jab at his artistic skills. "You know what this means, don't you?"

"That I was right and they're hired guns who work for someone with private plane money."

"Someone with private plane money who wants Griffin Gentry dead," Weber said.

They stared at each other stonily for a few long seconds. Weber gave a subtle nod at the two detectives who were obviously eavesdropping. Nick lifted his chin in acknowledgment.

"I guess we'll see who bags the bad guy first," Weber snapped loudly.

"Yeah. I guess we will," Nick shot back. "Spoiler alert. It won't be you."

"Get the hell out of my chair, Nicky."

"Gladly. Oh, and enjoy your lunch," Nick said, getting up and heading for the exit.

"What did you do to my sandwich?" Weber demanded.

Nick answered with a middle finger over his shoulder. He was still smirking when his phone vibrated in his pocket. It was a call from Riley.

"What's up, beautiful? Miss me already?"

"Hi. We, uh, have a small problem. Actually two problems, and I can only handle one at a time."

22

W hat's the plan?" Josie asked, poking her head up between the front seats of Jasmine's car when Riley disconnected her call with Nick.

Burt squeezed his head in next to Josie's.

"Nick's going to handle Fred and Claudia Mendoza's building security. Which means we're going after Mrs. Penny and Mr. Willicott," Riley said.

She was making an executive decision. Nick could handle the underpaid security guard who had detained Fred after he couldn't produce a building key card, but his PI license couldn't handle a potential breaking and entering that would be required to save two under-the-table employees from a trespassing situation that would likely end in a Code Cold Burrito.

"Where does suspect number two live?" Jasmine asked from behind the wheel.

"Mechanicsburg," Riley said, reaching for Jasmine's phone to program Ingram Theodoric III's address into the GPS.

Jasmine slid on a supercool pair of sunglasses that made her look like a spy, then shifted into drive and stomped on the accelerator. The sporty tires chirped, then bit as they flew out of the drugstore parking lot.

"Woo-hoo!" Josie cheered from the back seat.

Burt braced himself by flopping down in Josie's lap.

Gripping the handle above the door, Riley tried to plot how not to get arrested.

For a day that had begun with a shootout, the Saturday afternoon weather was shaping up quite nicely with sunny skies and temperatures in the fifties.

"So what's the situation?" Jasmine asked as she careened into the left lane, barely eking past the back end of a city bus as it chugged along.

Riley pumped the imaginary brake beneath her foot. "Mrs. Penny and Mr. Willicott went rogue, and instead of watching Theodoric's house, they wandered inside when the housekeeper took out the trash. Why would they do that when we explicitly told them not to do anything illegal or suspicious? Great question. We'll have to ask them when we're all crammed in the back seat of a police cruiser heading to jail." She was winded by the time she hit the end of her explanation.

"This is why you don't work with amateurs," Josie commented.

"Offended," Jasmine said, punching the gas.

"Getaway driver excluded," Josie conceded.

"Yeah, well, when the list of suspects is longer than Santa's naughty list, you use whatever resources you have available," Riley said.

"We need better resources," Josie muttered.

Riley's phone buzzed.

Mrs. Penny: Code Cold Burrito update. Continuing surveillance from inside kitchen pantry. Suspect does not have any good snacks.

"I hate to say it, but can you drive faster, Jas? They're eating their way through Theodoric's pantry," Riley reported.

Ingram Theodoric III lived in a sprawling development where the five-acre lawns were manicured and the houses were the size of high schools.

Mrs. Penny's minivan was parked in front of a clump of fancy-looking evergreens at the foot of the winding driveway. The house was an imposing dark stone and stucco home with steep rooflines and a wrought-iron balcony over the front door. A pair of concrete lions flanked the porch stairs between ruthlessly trimmed topiaries.

"How are we supposed to sneak up on them with all this stupid open space?" Josie complained, eyeing the expanse of front yard.

"Mrs. Penny figured out a way," Riley pointed out. She wiped her palms on the thighs of her jeans. "Okay. Let me think."

"Why don't we just ring the bell and say we're looking for two confused elderly people?" Jasmine asked. "It's at least partly true."

Riley sighed. "Because Mrs. Penny said it's ageist and an offensive stereotype."

"Three days ago, she pretended she couldn't remember where she was when the deli guy caught her ripping open containers of roast beef because she goes by smell, not expiration dates," Josie said.

"Apparently it's different when the elder in question uses it as an excuse," Riley explained.

"So what do we do? Break in? Drive over the mailbox? Set fire to the lawn?" Jasmine asked.

"No more fires. Remember what happened last time? As in last week?" Riley said. What should have been a simple surveillance had turned into arson. Granted, the "victims" were terrible people, and the neighborhood was still celebrating the arrest of their horrible son. But still.

"The fire part wasn't our fault," Jasmine insisted.

Riley glanced into the back seat. Burt's tail thumped against the leather. "I think I have an idea."

"You know what to do, buddy?" Riley asked, unhooking Burt's leash from his collar.

He danced in a circle, lifting his huge feet like a show pony.

"Good boy! Go get in position!"

Burt let out a happy bark and raced up Theodoric's driveway.

"You know I love Burt like I would a fake human nephew," Jasmine began. "But how do you know he's going to do what you want him to do?"

"He's my soulmate. We speak the same language...except when it comes to people food," Riley said, looping the leash around her neck and pulling out her phone.

Riley: We're here and we have a plan. Get ready to run when the diversion happens.

Mrs. Penny: Speaking of the runs, hurry the hell up because these seaweed snacks aren't sitting well with my intestines.

Riley rolled her eyes. "We better get up there. Mrs. Penny got into the seaweed snacks."

"Are you sure she's not Burt's soulmate?" Josie quipped as they started the hike up the driveway.

"Keep an eye out for security cameras," Riley ordered. "Try to look unsuspicious."

"That means put the knife away," Jasmine translated for Josie.

"How's a girl supposed to be prepared to stab someone or cut up some charcuterie if she doesn't have a blade handy?"

"You will be doing neither of those things because stabbing is illegal and charcuterie is off-limits while you're pregnant," Riley reminded her.

"Damn it," Josie muttered.

"The goal is to get Mrs. Penny and Mr. Willicott out of here without getting arrested," Riley said.

"Fine, but didn't you meet this guy before? What if he recognizes you?" Josie asked.

"I was wearing a mask and showing a lot more cleavage then."

"Well, just in case," Jasmine said, fumbling around in the slim backpack she was carrying. "Here." She handed Riley a ball cap and a pair of oversize sunglasses.

"Thanks," she said, putting the items on.

As they approached the house, Riley gave the nod, and they began to pan the yard. "Quick. Give me a fake dog name."

"Pork Rind," Josie offered.

Riley didn't want to waste time thinking of a better one, so she went with it. "Pork Rind! Here, boy!" she called.

"Why are you calling him Pork Rind?" Jasmine asked out of the corner of her mouth.

"Because I don't want him to actually come running," Riley responded from the corner of hers.

"Oh, right."

Josie whistled, and Jasmine clapped her hands.

They made their way up the imposing stone steps to the heavy oak front door. The doorbell, when pressed, set off an impressive symphony of gongs inside.

"Somebody thinks he's fancy," Jasmine noted.

"You know what they say. Loud doorbell, small penis," Josie said. "On the bright side, there's no cameras out here."

"Help a girl out, spirit guides," Riley murmured under her breath. Mentally, she rolled up her psychic garage doors to welcome in any messages from the beyond. A warm shiver rolled up her spine, and she felt reasonably sure her spirit guides were ready to help should the need arise.

The door opened to reveal a short roundish woman in a drab gray maid's uniform. She had brassy red hair and held a mop in one hand. "Yes?" she asked, sounding both bored and inconvenienced as she peered down her perky nose at them.

"Uh, hi. We're looking for a…um…missing dog," Riley announced quickly. She remembered the leash on her shoulder and held it up as proof. Riley heard Josie's groan at her lackluster performance.

"There are no dogs here," the maid said with a sniff over the distinct sound of barking. A dachshund and a dog that looked like a mini Ewok trotted into the hallway on the gleaming Italian tile. They stopped halfway, turned around, and, still barking, disappeared into a room.

"I told you to quit barking at the pantry. You're not getting early treats," the housekeeper yelled after the dogs.

"What are those?" Josie asked, pointing at the tiny yapping welcome committee.

"Those are what's commonly referred to as none of your business," the housekeeper said, making a move to slam the heavy front door in their faces.

Riley decided to borrow from the ol' Santiago school of charm. "We're really *so* sorry to bother you. But it's an emergency. Pork Rind is the sweetest dog. He belongs to my aunt who lives just down the road."

"She's kind of a horrible snob. You know, one of those vaguely racist old ladies. But she's on her death bed, so we walk her dog for her," Jasmine cut in.

"Uh, yes. My aunt is terrible and dying," Riley agreed. "Anyway, we were playing fetch with him in the yard—"

"And then explosive gunfire scared him," Josie added.

"Gunfire?" the housekeeper repeated.

"It was probably just a lawn mower backfiring," Riley said, elbowing Josie. "It looked like he ran this way. He has to have his dewclaw medicine in the next twenty minutes, or he could get seriously sick."

"Well, I don't know what you want *me* to do about it," the housekeeper huffed.

"We just want your permission to look around the yard. We didn't want to go traipsing around uninvited. You could come with us." Riley gave the woman her best puppy dog eyes.

The housekeeper harrumphed and put down the mop. "Fine. But only to make sure you don't steal anything."

"Great. Thanks. Also, would you mind if I used the restroom?" Riley said, trying to look full of urine.

"Yes, I would mind. I just cleaned the powder rooms. You'll just have to hold it," the housekeeper snapped. She stepped out on the porch and shut the door behind her. "Let's get this over with."

Josie and Jasmine sent Riley pointed looks.

"Okay," Riley said with a fake smile. "Jasmine and I'll go this way, and you two go that way. We'll meet in the backyard."

"Hurry up. I haven't got all day," the housekeeper said, stomping off the porch. Josie trailed after her.

Riley and Jasmine pretended to head in the opposite direction, but as soon as the housekeeper was out of sight, Riley raced back to the front door. "Damn it! It must be one of those automatic locks," she said, trying the knob.

"Want me to break a window?" Jasmine offered.

Riley turned and found her best friend hefting a decorative rock from the flower bed.

"Let's hang on to that as plan B. We'll find another way in."

They jogged off the porch and around the opposite side of the house.

"This place is huge," Riley said, fighting her way through a thorny bush to test one of the first-floor windows. It was locked.

"Ouch! This tree just pulled my hair," Jasmine complained, batting at a prickly blue spruce.

"How do we keep ending up in landscaping together?" Riley wondered out loud.

"Some friends do spa days. We do breaking and entering."

"I wouldn't say no to a nice manicure next time," Riley panted as they fought their way along the stone wall.

"Look! A patio," Jasmine said, pushing her way through a holly bush and pointing at the stone terrace jutting out from the side of the house.

Riley took a branch to the face. "Ow."

"Oh shit. Duck!" Jasmine hissed, turning around and tackling Riley to the ground just as the glass patio door opened.

Just beyond a row of squat dwarf spruces, Ingram Theodoric stepped out onto the stone. With his phone sandwiched between his ear and shoulder, he held a lit cigar in one hand and a glass of booze in the other.

Puffing clouds of smelly smoke into the overcast November air, he strolled to the edge of the patio, a rich guy surveying his kingdom.

"*Go*," Riley's spirit guides whispered.

Riley signaled for Jasmine to stay hidden, took a deep breath, and crawled on her hands and knees between the spruce and the wall.

"Don't bore me with your foreclosure guilt," Ingram slurred into the phone. "People shouldn't borrow more than they can afford to pay back once the balloon payment comes due. I have more important things to worry about."

Riley eased onto the patio and tiptoed toward the door, keeping one eye on Ingram. He ended the call with an aggressive stab of his pointer finger.

"Things like ruining Griffin Gentry," he said to the smoky air.

She froze when she heard Griffin's name, but her spirit guides were insistent. "*Go. Go. Go.*"

Her sneakers slipped on the wet stone as she ran as quietly as she could through the open door, leaving Ingram laughing diabolically behind her. She found herself in a stately office full of leather furniture, carved wood, and old books she bet no one had read. There was a lion head midroar mounted above the fireplace. A taxidermied polar bear stood proudly in the corner. Behind it, a cabinet held more than a dozen rifles.

Riley jogged through the set of double doors and found herself in a long hallway. "Shit. Why is this house so big? Okay, spirit guides. Which way to the kitchen?"

She felt a nudge toward the back of the house and headed in that direction. It guided her through a moody sitting room with the kind of furniture that looked as if it had never hosted a single butt. On the other side was another hallway wallpapered in linen with framed photos of Ingram hunting, Ingram accepting awards, Ingram shaking hands with a safari guide, both holding aggressive-looking automatic weapons and a nauseating pile of zebra carcasses at their feet.

Riley heard a loud yipping noise. It grew louder the closer to the back of the house she went. She followed the noise through a swinging door and found a kitchen the size of a city block. It smelled divinely of meat from the juicy roast resting on the counter beside triple wall ovens.

Lily would have had a field day checking out every single cabinet and appliance. But Riley only had time to zero in on the frosted glass door with the word PANTRY painted across it.

In front of the door sat the two little dogs, still yapping incessantly.

A quick scan of the cavernous space told Riley there was no team of chefs ready to jump out at her with knives. But there was a pot simmering on the stove and a cutting board of half-chopped herbs on one of the three islands.

"Sorry, doggies. I need you to scoot out of the way," Riley said, nudging them out of her path and flinging the pantry door open.

Mrs. Penny was perched on a step stool with her hand in a bag of gluten-free pretzels. Mr. Willicott had his shirt pulled up over his nose and was brushing granulated sugar off his pants.

"About damn time," Mrs. Penny announced.

"This woman smells like the inside of a septic tank," Mr. Willicott complained.

"It's because my intestines are hungry," Mrs. Penny explained.

The dogs raced inside to bark at the intruders.

Riley spied the glass container labeled DOG TREATS and dumped the contents on the floor.

Her phone buzzed with a text.

Jasmine: He's back in the house. Go out the front if you can.

"We have to go. Now," Riley insisted.

Mrs. Penny threw the pretzels over her shoulder and hopped to her feet. "Let's go get us some evidence."

"Forget the evidence. We need to get out of here without being arrested."

Riley led the way out of the pantry, leaving the door open in hopes that it would look as if the dogs were somehow responsible for the mess.

"Duck."

She just managed to drag Mrs. Penny and Mr. Willicott to the floor when Josie and the grumpy housekeeper appeared just outside the window above the second sink. Josie spotted them inside, rolled her eyes, then pointed dramatically in the opposite direction, drawing the housekeeper's attention.

"Let's go," Riley hissed and began to crawl for the door to the hallway.

Mrs. Penny followed in a surprisingly flexible duck walk.

Mr. Willicott, who had never gotten around well to Riley's knowledge, speed crawled around Mrs. Penny's gas emissions and joined Riley in the mad dash for the door.

Somewhere in the kitchen, a door opened and closed, then a cheerful whistling started. Riley chanced a peek over the marble counter and saw a guy in an apron and chef's hat turning the water on in the third sink. The dogs were still barking, and the pantry door was wide open. It was only a matter of time before he looked up.

"Go!" she mouthed, pushing her two charges through the swinging door as silently as she could.

They miraculously made it through the door without being spotted and started down the hallway, limping and jogging toward what Riley hoped was the foyer and the freedom of the front door.

"Let's split up and see if we can find some evidence," Mrs. Penny said.

"I told you damn dogs to shut the hell up. I refused to give you back to your mother to teach her a lesson, but that

201

doesn't mean I won't take you on my next hunting trip. You wouldn't make it back alive," Ingram shouted drunkenly from somewhere. The echoing off the walls made it sound like his voice could be coming from anywhere.

But Riley's spirit guides knew he was close.

"Hide."

"In a hallway? Seriously?" she muttered.

Panicked, she pushed Mr. Willicott behind a tapestry of a bloody hunting scene. His shoes stuck out, but there wasn't really anything that could be done about that. "Stay there. Don't move. Don't talk," she ordered.

Mrs. Penny snatched a short club off the display of primitive weapons.

"What are you doing?" Riley hissed, grabbing her arm.

"Hide. Now."

"If we have to fight our way out, I want to be prepared," Mrs. Penny said.

"Hide. Hide. Hide."

"Oh my God. We're not fighting. We're hiding." Riley dragged Mrs. Penny to the closest door as footsteps drew nearer. She flung it open, stuffed Mrs. Penny inside, and then followed. She was just pulling the door shut behind her as Ingram stormed into the hall.

It was pitch-black inside. A closet of some sort, she guessed.

"Quiet. Quiet. Quiet."

Riley held her breath and slapped a hand over Mrs. Penny's mouth as the footsteps came closer and closer.

"Damn woman can't even be bothered to close a door. They're all the same. Useless," he muttered as he came into view through the open crack. An ugly, angry vibe pushed at Riley's consciousness.

Damn it. Was this how it was all going to end? Nick was going to be royally pissed if she ended up as a Cold Burrito.

Mrs. Penny wiggled against her grip, but Riley held firm.

Suddenly, there was a cacophony of shouting and then a crash. A deep *woof* echoed through the house, followed immediately by an excited chorus of yips.

Swearing under his breath, Ingram changed course and stormed off in the direction of the kitchen. "Wash going on in here, and where's my scotch?" he bellowed.

"*Go.*"

Riley let out the breath she'd been holding and dragged Mrs. Penny back into the hallway.

"I got a vacuum cleaner up the butt in there," the woman complained.

"I'll take you to a proctologist if we can get out of here alive," Riley said, yanking Mr. Willicott out from behind the tapestry.

She pulled both of them into the foyer and out the front door.

It slammed behind them, but judging from the noise level inside, no one would have heard.

"Come on," she said to her coconspirators. "Let's go this way." They'd just pretend they'd been looking on this side of the house for Burt, she decided. Totally innocent. Definitely not breaking or entering.

They jogged off the front porch and around the side of the house, sticking to the grass this time. Mrs. Penny was huffing and puffing and falling behind. Mr. Willicott gave up and slowed to a walk.

Riley had just cleared Ingram's office patio when Burt bolted past with what looked like the roast clutched in his jaws. The two tiny yappers raced after him. Josie, Jasmine, the chef, and the disgruntled housekeeper appeared, looking slack-jawed.

"Is that your dog?" the housekeeper demanded as Burt zigged, then zagged into the neighbor's yard.

"Uh, no," Riley said wisely. "Pork Rind is smaller and doesn't break and enter."

Ingram appeared behind her on the patio of his office with one of the long rifles clutched in his hands. "I'm gonna shoot those dogs and all you intruders, and then I'm firing everyone else," he shouted.

"Here we go again," the chef muttered, plugging his ears.

Ingram shouldered the gun and took aim.

The housekeeper covered her eyes.

"Noooo!" Riley, Josie, and Jasmine screamed. They were all in motion with Riley leading the way in a dead sprint toward the man with the gun.

Burt ducked into a copse of trees on the property line a split second before the rifle fired. Ingram was already crumpling to the ground when Riley reached him.

Mrs. Penny appeared behind him, holding the club she'd stolen off the wall. "Told you this would come in handy," she said, tapping it against her palm.

The housekeeper nudged Ingram with her foot.

"Shit. Is he dead?" the chef asked, lighting a cigarette and looking remarkably not concerned enough given the situation.

"Nope. Knocked out," the housekeeper reported.

Movement from the trees had Riley sagging with relief. Burt pranced unscathed out of the shadows and spit the roast on the grass. The little dogs joyfully pounced on the meat.

"Oh, thank God. He didn't shoot them," Riley breathed.

"He can't. We replaced all his ammo with blanks after he got drunk and shot out the windshield of the Pritchetts' golf cart this summer," the chef said, hooking the unconscious Ingram under the armpits.

The housekeeper grabbed his ankles.

"How can you two stand working for him?" Jasmine asked, looking aghast.

"He's a drunk. Last year, he told us he was cutting our pay. Turns out he was wasted and accidentally added a zero to both our salaries. The guy's so rich he never even noticed," the chef said as they carried Ingram to one of the chairs on the patio.

The housekeeper shrugged and wiped her hands on her apron. "For half a million dollars each, we don't mind cleaning up after the drunk asshole. At least not for a few more months when I can afford to retire to Italy and Chef here can open his own place at the beach." The chef held up a hand, and the housekeeper high-fived him. She turned back to Riley and her crew. "Now I'm assuming it would be better for all of you if Mr. Theodoric didn't remember you when he wakes up."

Riley bit her lip. "Um, maybe?"

"Yeah, I thought so. Game recognizes game," the housekeeper prompted.

The chef ducked into Theodoric's office.

"Okay, yes," Riley admitted. "It would be great if no one ever mentioned we'd been here."

"We won't bother telling him about whatever this was," she said, gesturing at Riley and her cohorts. "As long as you never encourage him to review his payroll."

The chef reappeared with a tumbler full of liquor. He splashed most of it on Ingram's chest and sleeve, then positioned the glass in the unconscious man's grip.

"We were never here," Riley agreed.

"Are there any security cameras that we need to worry about?" Josie asked.

The chef shook his head. "Mr. Theodoric prefers not to have his indiscretions recorded."

"Thank fuck for us," Josie muttered.

The housekeeper frowned at Mrs. Penny, who was now spinning the club like a baton, and Mr. Willicott, who had taken his shoes off and was walking through the mulch barefoot. "Who are they?" she asked.

"It's probably better if you don't know," Riley said, taking the club from Mrs. Penny and handing it back to the housekeeper.

"We'll just be getting out of your hair," Jasmine said.

"Hang on," Riley said. "I can't in good conscience leave those dogs here with him."

"Take 'em with you," the housekeeper said and shrugged. "They've been yapping their little brains out since Mr. Ingram threw his ex out a month ago. They're her dogs."

"We'll tell him he passed out with the door open and they got out," the chef said.

"Thanks. And good luck with retirement and your restaurant," Riley said.

"What do you say, Chef? Let's order some surf and turf DoorDash on Mr. Ingram's account and call it a day?" the housekeeper asked as Riley and company headed for the front of the house.

23

"G o potty in the yard right now," Riley ordered when they returned home and exited Jasmine's car.

Burt looked up at her with soulful doggy eyes and a muzzle saturated in a red wine reduction.

"Don't give me that look. You ate an entire roast. I don't want your rear end anywhere near the furniture when that bill comes due," she insisted.

With a grumble, Burt trotted off into the trees, taking his two new four-legged friends—who hadn't stopped yapping the entire car ride—with him.

"Nicky is going to flip when he finds out you stole two more dogs," Josie predicted before shoving a saltine in her mouth.

"I didn't *steal* them. I temporarily took possession of them so we could return them to their rightful owner," Riley said. "And I didn't steal Burt either. I liberated him and then he refused to get out of my car."

"Besides, Nick's not allowed to flip out over anything for a while. He incurred a hell of a lot of relationship debt tracking down Kellen's sister, Beth," Jasmine said as they crunched through the fallen leaves.

The cops were gone, leaving behind tire ruts, crime scene tape, and trampled landscaping.

Riley wrinkled her nose. "I don't think we do that score-keeping thing."

"Seriously? How else do you know who's winning?" Jasmine asked.

"I'm starting to get why you're so hot and yet so single," Josie observed.

Mrs. Penny's minivan rolled into the driveway with Lil Nas X blasting from the open windows. The van came to an abrupt stop, and the purple-haired problem causer and her confused compadre exited the vehicle, each holding greasy fast-food bags.

"I thought I told you to come straight home," Riley said.

"Can't expect us to narrowly avoid death and not stop for a midafternoon snack," Mrs. Penny said.

"Let's maybe keep it down about the whole 'narrowly avoiding death' thing," Riley suggested. She wanted Nick to trust her in the field, and kicking off her debut performance by confronting a crazed, drunken maniac with a rifle wasn't exactly the A-plus she'd been going for.

"Are you asking me to keep something from my business partner?" Mrs. Penny demanded, looking stern behind her thick glasses.

"You always keep things from Nick," Riley pointed out.

"Only for dramatic flair purposes. It's all about timing, see?"

Riley wasn't given any time to see anything because Mrs. Penny was already shoving her way into the house. Burt and the other two dogs, still yapping, raced inside after her. Mr. Willicott wandered off into the backyard.

"Crap," Riley muttered.

"Come on. Let's get this over with," Josie said, nudging her toward the door.

"Why do I have to go first?" Riley hedged.

"I'm pregnant."

"Come on, you big babies. I'll protect you from Scary Nick," Jasmine said, leading the way.

———

Mrs. Penny perched on a barstool and rained french fries on the floor while she recounted their afternoon to Nick, who listened with eyes closed and fingers massaging his temples. Lily was relaxing in a kitchen chair and thumbing through an ancient recipe book. Fred, dressed in incredibly inappropriate yoga attire, was sitting cross-legged on the table, listening with rapt attention.

"Remind me to disinfect the table," Riley said to no one in particular.

"So then the guy's pointing this old-ass rifle at Burt, and Riley's all 'Don't shoot my dog' and running at him," Mrs. Penny continued as the dogs slurped up her floor fries.

Nick's eyes came open and pinned Riley with "the look."

"Uh-oh," Josie muttered and shuffled away from the death glare.

"So I run up behind him like one of those superfast ninjas, and I bonk him on the head with a club I stole off his wall," Mrs. Penny said.

"Thorn," Nick said, his voice deadly calm as the dachshund scrabbled her little paws at his legs.

"Um. Yes. Present," Riley said, trying to look both alive and competent.

"He's gonna blow like my elementary school science fair volcano," Josie said in a stage whisper.

The kitchen door swung open, and Griffin trotted inside, holding a plate with a sandwich on it. Gabe was behind him.

"Excuse me," Griffin sang. "I believe I ordered my sandwich with truffle mayonnaise. This tastes like regular mayonnaise."

Nick was still staring at Riley, his left eye twitching.

"This ain't no diner, bub," Mrs. Penny said to Griffin. "You want truffle mayo, you gotta cough up the cash for it."

209

Griffin sighed and pulled out his money clip. "Fine. How much does mayonnaise cost? Forty dollars?"

Mrs. Penny snatched the twenties out of his hand and pocketed them. "Who wants to go on a grocery store run?"

"I'll go," Lily volunteered. "That cutie with the booty stocks shelves on Saturdays."

Gabe's hand shot into the air. "I would very much like to attend the grocery store outing and leave Mr. Gentry's personal security to someone else."

Riley sensed a teensy bit of desperation coming from her spiritual adviser. She couldn't blame him. Griffin was hard to take in even the smallest doses.

"Not it," Josie said, putting her finger on her nose.

"I'll take over," Riley volunteered.

"The hell you will. I have yelling to do," Nick snapped.

"Don't you tell my friend what to do." Jasmine stepped in front of Riley and crossed her arms. Jasmine's idea of conflict resolution was to throw as much gasoline on the fire as possible until everything exploded.

"Don't criticize *my* feelings about my girlfriend *putting herself in the literal line of fire!*"

"Don't *you* tell *me* what to do!"

"Wow. She really has no sense of self-preservation at all," Josie said, hopping up on the kitchen island to get a better view of the argument.

"I forgot to tell you the best part," Mrs. Penny said over the shouting. "So the guy pulls the trigger right as I'm knocking him out…"

"I also requested sparkling water for my afternoon snack, not tap water," Griffin yelled over the commotion.

"Fred, your balls are on the table," Josie noted.

He peered down at his short shorts. "Oops!"

"What the hell is going on in here?" Brian wheeled into the kitchen and paused. "Why do we have extra dogs?"

Nick tried to peer around the seething Jasmine. "Riley Middle Name Thorn, you better have a good explanation for why you would willingly run toward an armed man, steal two dogs—"

"Don't forget the breaking and entering," Mrs. Penny piped up.

"You did the breaking and entering first," Riley argued. "I was just coming to rescue you!"

"Pfft, I would have had us out of there in no time," Mrs. Penny argued.

"Yeah, with a body count," Josie shot back.

"And another thing! You don't get to get mad at Riley when you're the one who spent the last however many weeks obsessing about another woman," Jasmine yelled at Nick.

Nick was still trying to dodge his way around her best friend to get to Riley. "If you don't get out of my way, Patel, I will physically remove you from it!"

All the dogs were barking, and everyone was yelling at once.

"I also don't care for this plate made of paper! I feel like I'm eating off a napkin," Griffin announced over the shouting.

"Everybody shut the hell up!" a voice of authority snapped.

Everyone looked toward the kitchen door, where Weber was standing looking almost as pissed off as Nick.

"Who let you in?" Nick demanded.

"The Denzel Washington look-alike," Weber answered.

"How much did you hear, copper? You have to tell us. It's the law," Mrs. Penny said, brandishing a french fry.

"Hey! I'm not done with you, Santiago." Jasmine drilled a finger into Nick's chest.

"And I haven't even gotten started yelling in concern at Riley," Nick said. "If you don't step aside right now, Patel, I'll cut your bangs."

All the women in the room gasped together.

Weber was suddenly standing between Nick and Jasmine. "Back off, Nicky," he growled.

"I can take care of myself," Jasmine snarled at the cop's back.

"Oh really? Because from what I heard, so far today, it's

been breaking and entering, abducting dogs, and encountering a shooter."

Great. Riley was definitely going to jail.

"We were running lines for a play," Nick lied.

"What play? *How to Fuck Up Your Life and Everyone Else's* by Nicky Santiago?" Weber said.

"Why didn't I get an audition? I'm leading man material," Griffin whined.

The yelling started again, this time accompanied with wild gestures and some french fry throwing. Mr. Willicott walked into the room, clapped his hands to his cheeks, screamed, and then disappeared again.

"Did he just *Home Alone* us?" Riley asked Fred, who had thankfully tucked his balls back into his shorts.

"He didn't want to feel left out."

Mrs. Penny's french fry supply had run out, and Burt began to howl. The other two dogs joined in.

Emotions were running high, and Riley's psychic sensor was on overload. She looked at Gabe in desperation. "Uh. Help?"

He bowed his head, closed his eyes, and folded his hands at the center of his chest.

Immediately Riley felt a peaceful wave of well-being wash over her. The tension left her shoulders, her nervous system calmed, and each breath felt like a massage. Her brain finally quieted, and she felt fully present in the moment.

The fight seemed to leave everyone else at the same time. Mrs. Penny was happily licking the salt off her fingers. Still on the table, Fred leaned back on his elbows with a dreamy smile. Jasmine and Weber stood there blinking at each other. Burt and his new dog friends curled up in a puppy pile and went to sleep.

"Want. To. Stay. Mad," Nick gritted out between his teeth. His hands were balled into white-knuckled fists at his sides.

Riley felt an extra punch of peace from Gabe's direction, then watched as Nick sagged against the island.

"Damn it. What the hell was that?" he demanded.

"Does it really matter?" she asked.

"It will later, when I remember how to be mad," he said. He pointed at Weber. "You stay here and keep this mayonnaise-eating moron alive." He looked at Riley. "My office. Now."

She fervently hoped Gabe's psychic reach would extend to the other side of the house as she followed Nick out of the room.

"I know it looks and sounds bad. Like really bad. And honestly it was. I thought we were either going to get murdered or end up in prison. I screwed up, and I understand if you want to fire me." Riley blurted the words out in a rush.

He dropped down on the squeaky couch and surprised her by pulling her into his lap.

This was way better than getting yelled at. She wondered if Gabe could teach her the emotional cloud trick.

"I'm not firing you. I'm just struggling with the fact that I love you and you keep ending up in danger," Nick said.

"It does appear to be a reoccurring theme in our relationship," she agreed. "What are you going to do? Stop loving me?"

He ran a thumb over her lower lip. "No, dummy. I'm going to train the hell out of you and turn you into a self-defense expert."

She perked up, shifting in his lap. "Really?"

"Really," Nick said, giving her a gentle squeeze. "Besides, since whoever wants Griffin whacked is still out there, it's the best way I can think of to keep you alive."

"And you're definitely sure about that?" she asked.

"My gut is. Those two idiots this morning were just that, idiots. Someone hired them to do a job, and that someone isn't going to stop just because their pawns got sacrificed."

She felt the same thing. That fog of uncertainty was still clinging to her. "Is your gut usually right?"

"It was right about you."

"Aw."

Another chorus of barks erupted from the kitchen, making Nick groan.

"I swear to you I'll track down their owner tonight and return the dogs. She's Theodoric's ex, so she might have information we could use about him."

"Are you sure you won't get shot at or kidnapped?"

"I'll leave Mrs. Penny here to even the odds."

He gave her another affectionate squeeze. "I'm going to swing by the jewelry store tonight. I have something to return to Peabody."

"You didn't buy anything," she pointed out.

"No, but I did steal something out of Griffin's closet that didn't belong to him."

"You big softy, out there righting the world's wrongs."

"Keep it down. I don't want to damage my reputation as a careless badass."

She leaned in and kissed him. "I love you, Nick Santiago, you careless badass."

"I love you back, Riley Thorn. Which is why self-defense boot camp starts bright and early tomorrow morning," he said with a stinging slap to her butt.

"*How* bright and early?"

"I hate to ruin this make-out session, but we've got a problem," Weber announced as he entered the room.

"I got my hand stuck in a pickle jar," Griffin said, holding up the jar in question and raining pickle juice all over the floor.

"How…? Why…?" Riley began.

"I didn't know you were supposed to use a fork. My pickles always arrive on my plate with my truffle mayonnaise. Not to be a jerk, but poor people mayonnaise is terrible. I fed the sandwich to the dog that looks like a lion."

"Christ," Nick muttered.

"Trust me, after this afternoon, a sandwich is the least of our worries," Riley said.

"And so is an idiot with a pickle jar stuck on his hand," Weber said.

Griffin held up the jar and banged it experimentally off a filing cabinet.

Nick and Weber both rolled their eyes.

"Why don't you go ask Lily if she has any of her organic lube handy," Riley said, climbing off Nick's lap and giving her ex-husband a push out of the room.

"Let's cut to the chase. Which one of us are you here to arrest, Weber?" Nick demanded when she returned.

"I'm not here to arrest anyone…for once. I'm here to casually mention that the two shooters from this morning are on a plane back to Colombia with a couple of U.S. marshals and their fancy-ass lawyer," Weber said.

Nick drummed his fingers on the arm of the couch. "Fuck."

"That seems fast," Riley asked.

"Light speed. Extradition usually takes weeks. Which isn't necessarily a bad thing when it gives local law enforcement time to interview the suspects," Weber explained.

"I take it you didn't get that time," she guessed.

"We had them in the box for barely an hour before some lawyer from DC showed up with all the right paperwork," he said. "The official department line is the persons responsible for this morning's shootout have been brought to justice."

Nick nodded at the quantum physics side of his white-board. "So, you in?"

"I'm not out."

"What's happening here?" Riley asked.

"Weber here is gonna help us keep that vapid bowl of butterscotch pudding alive," Nick announced.

"That's great. Now, I hate to be that girl, but is there any way we can negotiate a you-won't-arrest-any-of-us-during-the-investigation deal?" she asked Weber.

It looked as if it physically pained him to answer. "As long as everyone stays on their best behavior and doesn't break any laws, I'll stay focused on the investigation."

"Yeah, that's not gonna happen," Nick said.

"Fine. As long as no one does anything worse than whoever the hell we're looking for, I'll try to maybe look the other way. Within reason. Final offer."

Riley and Nick exchanged a look. She nodded. It was as good as they were going to get.

"Deal," Nick said. "Brian! Get your ass in here."

The sound of glass shattering and dogs barking rang out from the kitchen. "I'll go fix whatever that was," Riley volunteered.

She left the men and headed back to the kitchen, where she found Lily and Fred sweeping up shards of pickle jar. Mrs. Penny had her feet propped up on the table and was reading over a fat legal document.

"My hand smells like pickles," Griffin complained.

"I hope you get run over by a fleet of golf carts at your next charity function," Jasmine said.

"I'm a great golfer. Everyone says so," Griffin said.

Jasmine frowned at him and stepped into his personal space. "Did you get slightly taller?"

Nick poked his head into the kitchen. "Hey, Gentry. You ever been to Colombia?"

"Never heard of it," Griffin chirped.

Riley got the distinct feeling that her ex-husband was lying, and the gleam in Nick's eye told her he was reading it that way too. But before she could dig in any further, Burt whimpered dramatically from the mudroom.

"Gabe, do you have a minute? I need to ask you something," she said, tilting her head toward the door.

"It would be my pleasure to leave this room as quickly as possible," Gabe said.

They shrugged into coats, and Riley opened the door to the chilly November afternoon. The dogs bolted out in front of them, the little ones yapping like their lives depended on it.

"What you did back in the kitchen," Riley began.

"I like to think of it as a calming ether," Gabe said.

"Yeah, that. Is that something I can do? I mean at least to myself?" she added quickly. Though it would be handy to have that in her arsenal to deploy on Nick when he got too worked up or her grandmother whenever she opened her judgmental mouth.

"Why do you ask?"

"I don't know. I guess I've spent the last few days running around from distraction to distraction until I'm too exhausted to function. And when I do try to convene with my spirit guides, I'm either yanked right back out by some emergency or I can't stop thinking about all the other things that I should be doing. It's like my brain is too busy to be psychic right now."

"One must always be able to find peace in chaos," Gabe said.

"Yeah, but *how*? It seems like chaos is everywhere and peace is—hey! Dog number two, no chasing squirrels," Riley said, clapping her hands. The dachshund ignored her and continued to race around the trunk of the hemlock tree. Its partner in crime, the wiry one, was barking furiously at the front tire of Mrs. Penny's minivan.

There was a shout and another crash from inside the house that had all three dogs racing to the door in a chorus of frantic barks.

"Perhaps you are only looking at the chaos?" Gabe suggested.

"What if that's all there is to see? And are you Zen riddling me right now?" she asked.

He gave her a beguiling smile and bent to pick something up off the ground. It was a perfect scarlet maple leaf. He handed it to her. "Nooooo."

She smiled, twirling the stem between her fingers, making the leaf spin. "Now you're being sarcastic."

"Only in jest. Look at the leaf," he suggested.

Riley held it up and examined the paper-thin skin, the delicate, symmetrical veining, the precise curves of each edge. It was a perfect piece of nature just existing no matter how many other leaves fell or dogs barked or squirrels raced. It was just there, waiting to be discovered, appreciated.

She felt it then. The quieting. The gradual release of tension she hadn't been aware she was holding.

"You're a very good teacher," Riley told him.

Gabe winced. "I have a confession to make. I am not a good teacher or a good person. It was I who suggested Mr. Gentry insert his hand into the jar."

She patted him on his muscled forearm. "You're not a terrible person. You're just human. Griffin has the ability to bring out the absolute worst in everyone. And if your worst only involves a pickle jar prank, I think you're still pretty wonderful."

"I have never wished ill will upon someone before. However, I cannot help but hope chronic constipation will haunt him for the rest of his life," he confessed.

"Me too, big guy. Me too."

"Hey! Tall, Dark, and Biceps," Mrs. Penny yelled from the door. "I'm making a grocery run for dumbass's truffle mayo. Still wanna go and help me get crap off the top shelf?"

"It would be my pleasure," Gabe rumbled. "Would you care to join us, Riley?"

"I think I'll stay here and look at this leaf for a few minutes."

There was a horrible clattering of pots and pans in the kitchen.

"I'm okay," Lily yelled.

Riley winced. "Maybe a few hours."

24

Nick opened the door to Peabody Jewelry.

"I'm afraid we're closing, probably permanently," Wilfred said defeated without looking up from the cash register.

"I come bearing good tidings," Nick said, waving the rest of his party inside. Gabe, Weber, and Griffin filed inside. They were all moving a little slowly after Lily and Fred's early-bird meatloaf-with-four-kinds-of-potatoes dinner.

"Nicholas, how nice to see"—Wilfred's eyes narrowed when he spotted Griffin—"*you.*"

"This place looks vaguely familiar," Griffin said, pausing to admire himself in a mirror above a nearly empty display of earrings.

"Ignore him," Nick insisted. He pointed at Griffin. "You, go sit in the corner over there, and don't say anything. If you're good, we'll get you a fucking ice cream cone on the way home."

"I do not wish to have this man in my store," Wilfred said. His mustache twitched indignantly.

Weber wandered over to the watch case and began a perusal of the paltry selection.

"Do not be concerned. Mr. Gentry has that effect on most people," Gabe said amicably as he sank to the floor to pet Elizabeth Taylor the cat.

"Did someone say they want my autograph?" Griffin piped up from the chair in the corner.

"No!" they all snapped.

"As I was saying, I've got something for you you're going to want," Nick said, reaching into his jacket pocket.

"Unless it's a winning lottery ticket, I'm not interested," Wilfred said morosely.

Nick tossed the cuff links on the counter like they were dice. "How about now?"

"My cuff links! How did you…?"

Nick chanced a glance at Weber. "It's probably best if you don't know. I hope this helps you out and irons out any grudges you may be carrying."

Wilfred went back to looking morose. "Thank you for returning these. It means the world to me. It really does. But unless I can find a buyer in the next three days, I'll still have to close."

"Funny you say that, because I happen to know someone with questionable taste and a credit limit higher than the Empire State Building," Nick said, sliding a phone number across the counter. "I made a call and sent some pictures. My friend Beth wants the cuff links to surprise her husband with before they start shooting their reality show this week. You'll be credited in the show as the jewelry designer."

"My sister? Seriously, Nicky?" Weber muttered.

"Zip it," Nick told him before turning back to Wilfred. "She also said she's interested in a bunch of other stuff, but I stopped listening, so that's on you now."

"Hey! Those look like my cuff links," Griffin noted, craning his neck from his chair. "I had a jeweler design them, and then he didn't make me pay for them. Isn't that great?"

"What did I say about ice cream?" Nick snarled.

"Oops. Sorry! I forgot," Griffin said. He took out his phone, opened the camera app, and began entertaining himself with selfies.

"I–I can't thank you enough," Wilfred said. "This is an

answer to our prayers, isn't it, Elizabeth Taylor? Goodness. I might need to sit down."

"Mind if we take a look around?" Nick asked with his eye on a case of sparkle.

"Mind? You can play beer pong on top of the Rolexes," Wilfred said, sounding dazed.

Nick sidled over to the case and eyeballed the engagement rings. The ring was still there. His fingers itched to handle it.

"You can't be serious, Nicky," Weber said, looking over Nick's shoulder.

"Serious about what?"

"You're looking at engagement rings. Are you actually thinking about proposing?"

"I would be, but my girlfriend is a psychic, and Muscle Milk over there refuses to tell me how to hide it from her."

Gabe joined them at the case. "This is what you wished to hide? I naturally assumed it was a gambling debt or a bed-wetting problem."

"You know, the more time you spend with us, the meaner you get. And the meaner you get, the less I hate you," Nick said.

"I believe you just complimented me," Gabe said.

"Maybe I'll be more complimentary if you help me figure out how to surprise Riley."

"It would be my great honor," Gabe said.

"What makes you think she'll say yes? You're not exactly an easy sell," Weber pointed out.

"I was thinking about asking her during sex. You know, when she's more inclined to say yes a dozen times in a row. Hey, Wilfred. What the hell is a karat?"

Wilfred's response was cut off by the crash of the glass door flying open and hitting an empty sunglasses display. Three men wearing ski masks and carrying guns stormed inside.

"You've got to be kidding me," Weber muttered.

"Hands up!" shouted the first guy. He was wearing a buttercup-yellow ski mask that looked like he'd gotten it in the children's section. Nick was ninety percent sure the gun in his gloved hand was a toy with the orange tip painted black.

"Everybody on the ground," insisted the second, who waved a definitely real twelve-gauge shotgun with cobwebs on the barrel at them. A neck tattoo of a spider peeked out of the neckline of his sweatshirt.

The third was a head shorter than his buddies. He and his Ruger semiautomatic with the safety still on hung back closer to the door.

Amateurs.

"Hey, mustache man. Open that register," the one with the toy gun said to Wilfred.

"Make up your mind, boys. Hands up, on the ground, or open the cash drawer," Nick said, gauging the distance between the gunmen and Griffin, who was cowering in his chair behind a jewelry insurance brochure.

"I don't think they're here for him, Nicky," Weber said quietly as he put his hands in the air and stepped behind Nick, probably to hide the shiny badge on his belt.

Nick agreed. It was just his luck that buying an engagement ring would be interrupted by a couple of local boys who probably got tuned up at the fire hall and decided it was a nice night for an armed robbery.

The first gunman sneered through the mouth hole of his too-tight ski mask. "I told you to let me do the talking, DeWayne."

"And I told you not to use my name, Virgil!" the rifle guy said.

"Both of you shut the fuck up. We want the cash and diamonds and a couple of them there fancy watches in this here bag," the third guy said, tossing a paper shopping bag at Wilfred, who was clutching the feline Elizabeth Taylor in his hands over his head. Gabe was still sitting on the floor in lotus position with his hands up.

The door jingled open, and a man sporting a deep tan, a goatee, and fedora took one step inside. All the gun barrels in the store swiveled in the newcomer's direction.

"I like your hat. Get out," Nick said over the din.

The man took a sweeping glance around the store, then pulled his hands out of his pockets and held them aloft. "I'll just come back...never," he said, flashing a nervous smile in Griffin's direction before backing out the way he'd come.

"Gentlemen, let's talk this out," Weber said, drawing the attention of the bad guys.

"These guns speak for themselves. Put the shinies—startin' with them earrings or cuff links or whatever the hell they are—in the bag or Imma start puttin' holes in big dude over there," the third guy said, pointing his Ruger at Gabe.

"Hey, Gabe, you remember that hilarious joke you made in the kitchen?" Nick said, holding his hands at ear level and inching toward the third gun.

"I do," Gabe said solemnly.

"Great. Practice makes perfect," Nick said.

"Enough talking! Get on the goddamn floor," the shotgun-wielding guy bellowed at Nick.

"Weber, you remember that time in that bar on Second Street?" Nick said, chancing another step forward.

"With the bachelorette party or the motorcycle club?"

"Motorcycle club."

The third guy had had enough. He stepped forward and pressed the barrel of the Ruger against Nick's sternum.

Nick grinned. "Now!"

With his left hand, he swept the gun to the floor while his right hand plowed into the man's face, snapping his head back.

Gabe flowed to his feet, grabbed the yellow ski mask guy's arm, and tossed him over his shoulder, sending him flying behind the counter before anyone could blink. Weber stepped into shotgun guy's personal space with a spinning elbow that caught the bad guy square in the jaw.

Nick's guy recovered first and charged. He was wiry but quick with his hands *and* feet, Nick realized with an oath when he caught the toe of a cowboy boot to the midthigh.

Gabe's quarry crawled out from behind the jewelry case

and started throwing office supplies at Gabe, who batted them away.

Weber was wrestling shotgun guy on the floor, their limbs flailing. Wilfred was frantically pawing under the register. It took him a minute, but he stood back up, holding his nonfunctioning revolver in shaking hands.

"Everybody, freeze," he squeaked. But no one paid him any attention.

"I don't like this," Griffin wailed from his hiding place behind the brochure.

Wiry Guy got a lucky punch past Nick's defenses, which only served to infuriate him. "You don't. Get. To steal. Shit. From other. People," Nick said, punctuating his sage advice with swift punches.

Gabe dodged the chest of a mannequin wearing a heavy necklace and grabbed his guy by the front of his shirt. "You will stop misbehaving now," Gabe said, giving him a shake. The man's feet dangled helplessly six inches off the ground.

The door burst open again, and a bleached-blonde woman with a too-dark tan and a Lynyrd Skynyrd T-shirt that had seen one too many decades stomped inside. She was smoking a cigarette and waving a cowboy-style six-shooter. "What in the hell is takin' so damn long? You morons told me five minutes! I got the El Camino parked at the curb, drawin' attention."

Griffin, startled by the woman's sudden appearance, flinched in his chair. She tripped over his feet and went sprawling.

Wilfred hurled the gun at the woman, hitting her in the crispy hair. "Ow! You son of a bitch!"

Taking advantage of the distraction, Weber jumped to his feet and drew his weapon. Nick yanked his Sig Sauer out of the back of his jeans and kicked both revolvers away from the woman on the floor.

"Harrisburg PD. Get on the floor! Hands behind your head!" Weber barked.

"A dang cop? Ah, shit. Why didn't you say so?" Virgil grumbled.

"Hang on. This here is Lemoyne. Yer outta yer jurisdiction. You can't do jack shit to us," insisted Gabe's still-dangling opponent.

"I suggest you find a new source for legal advice," Weber said. "Wilfred, call 911."

"Anybody got any zip ties?" Nick asked.

"Is it over? Did I save the day?" Griffin asked, peeking out between his fingers.

25

"A hem."

The headphones she'd donned to block out the pile of dogs snoring at her feet weren't quite powerful enough to handle insistent throat clearing.

"AHEM!"

On a sigh, Riley took off her headphones and looked up. "Yes, Mrs. Penny?"

Somehow between nearly getting arrested and shot for breaking and entering, and early-bird meat-loaf dinner that day, Mrs. Penny had made good on her threat to turn Riley's office into a coworking space. She'd pushed a folding table against the front of Riley's desk, then added a few of her old gaming monitors and her BarcaLounger office chair.

Now whenever Riley looked up, it was at Mrs. Penny's expectant face. It gave her a jolt every time.

"What do you think the boys are up to?" her new office partner asked.

Riley had a sudden glimpse of sparkle that shifted into a dangerous metallic gleam. A queasy feeling spread through her intestines. "Uh. I don't know."

She picked up her phone, scrolled to the tracking app, and

zoomed in on Nick's location. He was at the jewelry store. That at least explained the sparkle.

"Why aren't *we* out running down clues and chasing bad guys?" Mrs. Penny asked, swinging her feet up on her makeshift desk with a meaty thump.

"Because we're in here running down the identity of Ingram's ex-girlfriend so we can return her dogs and ask her if she thinks her ex is capable of hiring hit men to murder someone who embarrassed him," Riley explained for the third time.

"Why don't you just ask Gentry what her name is?"

"I did. He didn't remember. So I'm tracking her down the old-fashioned internet stalking way."

"Boring! I'm gonna go make a drinky drink," Mrs. Penny grumbled.

"Hang on," Riley said, clicking on a photo to enlarge it. "I think I've got something."

"Lemme see." Mrs. Penny pried her feet off the desk and toddled around to Riley's side.

"This is from the local paper about a fundraising dinner for an animal rescue last spring. It's Ingram and his date, Laurel Shellen."

"She looks like she's thirty years younger than him," Mrs. Penny said, squinting through her bifocals.

Riley typed Laurel's name into the social media search engine. "Aha! Here she is. She lives in Harrisburg, and look at her profile picture."

"Huh. Girl's got some big teeth," Mrs. Penny noted.

"Not her perfectly normal-size teeth. Her *dogs*," Riley said, tapping her screen.

Mrs. Penny studied the picture, then examined the puddle of dogs under the desk. "Well, I'll be damned! Let's go interrogate a witness!"

"We're not interrogating—"

The doorbell rang, and a tidal wave of barking dogs shoved Riley and her chair back from the desk.

"You gonna get that?" Mrs. Penny asked.

Rubbing her abused shins, Riley followed the dogs to the front door and opened it. "Mom?"

Riley's mother and sister were standing on the front porch. Blossom had that unnaturally shiny, perky look on her face that meant she was upset about something.

"Hi, sweetie! Your sister and I were just in the neighborhood," Blossom said, bustling into the foyer. "We thought we'd come over and see if you needed any help organizing your kitchen or maybe mulching your flower beds for winter. Oooh! Or we could watch a movie. Who's up for *Bridges of Madison County*?"

Wander glided inside after their mother. *Fighting,* she mouthed to Riley.

"Ah."

When Riley's parents had their one big blowup fight every three or four years, Blossom pretended everything was wonderful while coolly ignoring Roger. She would show up on a daughter's doorstep with a demand for quality time, and if that daughter didn't immediately comply, she'd drop the Blossom Basil-Thorn guilt trip.

"Of course, I'll understand if you're too busy to spend time with your discarded old crone of a mother." Blossom sank to the floor to greet the dogs that scrabbled at her wide-legged corduroy pants. "At least *you* love your grandma, don't you, Burtie boy? And who are your friends?"

"You have more dogs than usual," Wander observed as she trailed Riley a few feet away for a whispered sister conference.

"I'm about to return them to their rightful owner. What are they fighting about this time?" Riley asked. The last fight had been over GPS directions. Blossom had moved in with Wander for almost a week.

"From what I could discern when I dropped the girls off with Dad, it's the chickens. One of them pecked Daisy too aggressively according to Dad."

Riley had a lightning-quick vision of her father standing

between his cow and the advancing chickens, yelling, "Beak-faced bullies!"

"Oh boy."

"I hate to do this to you when you already have a full house of characters, but not it," Wander said, bringing her finger to her nose. "I can't survive Mom staying with me for another week of pretend quality time. We just kicked off Gratitude Month at the yoga studio, River has basketball, Rain is hosting her Ruth Bader Ginsberg Dissent Club dinner this week, and Janet has three birthday parties."

Wander took a deep breath, then winced. Riley guessed it was probably the lingering psychic scent of murder victim tickling at her nostrils.

This was as panicked as her yogic breathing sister got.

"I bet *you* three like chickens, don't you?" Blossom cooed, squishing Burt's face between her hands.

The two little dogs yapped excitedly.

Riley sighed. At this point, she and Nick were practically running a fifty-five-plus community for the unhinged. What was one more? "Say no more. It's my turn for any overnights."

"Maybe we can put things back together tonight before we start moving her in," Wander offered.

"I just had the best idea," Blossom announced. "Girls' trip to the commune! We'll can applesauce and take that yarn dyeing class we've always talked about."

None of them had ever mentioned a yarn dyeing class.

"Actually, I was wondering if you and Wander wanted to come do some exciting investigative work with me tonight?" Riley asked with the feigned brightness inherited directly from her mother.

———

"Laurel's not here," announced the roommate dressed in a hot-pink onesie. She was wearing a green face mask and had a bowl of ice cream in one hand.

Riley, Blossom, and Wander stood on the front porch of a

three-story town house in one of those developments that was laid out like a miniature town. Three dog faces poked out of the passenger window of Wander's minivan at the curb.

By the time they were ready to leave, Mrs. Penny had—thankfully—fallen asleep in her desk chair, allowing Riley to make the executive decision to leave her behind. After all, they weren't running down leads. They were just handing over some dogs and confirming from another source that Ingram Theodoric III was a terrible person.

"Well, this was fun. Who wants to make our own organic hair dye and color our hair? I've always wanted to go pink," Blossom said.

"Do you know where Laurel went or when she'll be back?" Riley asked, ignoring her mother.

The roommate shrugged. "She's at her support group. They meet in the Wegmans café. Dunno when she'll be back. I gotta go. If I leave this face mask on for too long, it turns my skin green."

The door shut in their faces.

"Everybody back in the van," Riley said, ushering her mother and sister off the stoop.

"Don't you think it's a little unethical to crash a support group meeting?" Wander asked.

"I don't think. I *know* it is. But maybe we can just wait outside for her," Riley said. "Unless you want pink hair."

"Let's go invade a woman's privacy," Wander said and hit the unlock button on her key fob.

———

Waiting in the grocery store parking lot turned out not to be a viable option. Apparently everyone in Silver Spring Township did their Wegmans shopping on Saturday night. Laurel's dogs' incessant yapping was the final nail in the coffin.

"Okay. We're going inside. This is who we're looking for," Riley said, passing her phone up to the front seat to show her mother and sister a photo of Laurel.

"She's a cutie. Do you think I could pull off bangs like that?" Blossom wondered.

"Focus, Mom," Riley said. "She's part of an active investigation. She just doesn't know it yet, so I don't want to scare her off."

"Is she dangerous?" Blossom asked hopefully.

"Just her taste in men. She dated one of our suspects and slept with Griffin."

"I don't know what women see in that little weasel," Blossom said. "No offense, sweetie."

The terrier launched itself at Riley and licked her face between migraine-inducing yaps. "None taken. Let's go."

Wegmans was known for their café and alcohol sections. A hungry shopper could come in for milk and eggs and leave with freshly made sushi, hot chicken parm, and a six-pack of blueberry lager. Riley led the way past the hot food buffets and beer coolers to the cavernous community room full of tables.

"Did you hear about the jewelry store robbery?" Riley heard a cashier ask her shopper. Something inside her pinged.

The shopper with a toddler and a twelve-pack of spiked seltzers gasped. "No! What happened?"

"I heard three hot guys—"

"Look! I got us a snack," Blossom said, holding up a to-go container of vegetable korma.

"Mom, we don't have time for snacks," Riley said as she pawed through her bag for her phone.

"Isn't that Laurel?" Wander pointed toward a group of women standing around a pink balloon arch with an easel sign that said GGS Support Group.

"Let me get a closer look," Blossom said and scooted toward the far end of the room.

"Damn it," Riley muttered. Fishing her phone free, she opened the tracker app and saw Nick was still at the jewelry store in Lemoyne, which should have closed almost an hour ago.

Riley: Everything okay? You didn't get involved with some kind of robbery, did you?

"Are you all right?" Wander asked her.

"Fine. I just hope Nick and Gabe are—"

"I lost sight of her," Blossom announced, returning with a fork stuck in the open container of korma.

Riley's phone buzzed.

Nick: Long story. All good. I'm totally heroic. Call you when I can.

That was definitely not a *no*.

Brow furrowed, Wander held up her phone so Riley could see the screen.

Gabriel: We have just thwarted an armed robbery. Nick is taking us for ice cream after the police finish questioning us.

"Well, at least it sounds like they're all alive," Riley said. "Come on. Let's go find Laurel."

They had just made it under the balloon arch when a woman in leather pants and one of those short haircuts only someone with great cheekbones could pull off clapped her hands. "Ladies, thank you so much for joining us tonight. The GGS Support Group has meant so much to so many over the years, and I'm delighted but also saddened to see so many new faces. Please, have a seat, and we'll get started."

She gestured at a long dining table. Riley spotted Laurel taking a seat near the head and motored off in that direction. Laurel sat between two women who were both beautiful and on the youngish side. In fact, everyone at the table was gorgeous.

The organizer gestured for Riley to take the chair across from Laurel. Riley sat and watched her mother and sister take places toward the opposite end of the table.

"Thank you for joining us," the organizer said, standing at the head. "I'm Kiki."

"Hi, Kiki," the women around the table echoed.

"Five years ago, I had my GGS experience. Like so many of you, I felt so alone. But now, looking at all your faces, I know that together, none of us are alone," Kiki continued.

Riley was wondering if she was going to have to sit through the entire meeting for this mystery ailment before she got a chance to talk to Laurel when she felt a nudge of the psychic variety. She locked eyes with Wander down the table.

Her sister held up her cocktail napkin with a mix of uneasiness and amusement sparkling in her eyes.

Riley glanced down at her own. *Griffin Gentry Sucks.*

Well, shit.

"Who would like to begin?" Kiki asked.

A curvy woman with jet-black hair and cat's-eye glasses raised her hand. "I'm Li-Mei."

"Hi, Li-Mei," everyone said.

The woman took a shaky breath. "I met Griffin six months ago at a spa. He was charming and attentive. Handsome. I didn't realize how short he was until the esthetician called my name and he stood up to walk me to the door like a gentleman."

It took every ounce of willpower Riley had not to roll her eyes.

"I knew he was seeing Bella Goodshine. I even asked him about her," Li-Mei continued. "But he insisted it was just for ratings. They weren't actually together." She looked around the table, her eyes teary. "Normally I wouldn't fall for that. I have a master's degree. I'm not an idiot. But I guess understanding seventeenth-century English literature doesn't protect you from being taken advantage of."

The women gathered around the table all nodded over shared experiences.

"We had been dating for a month when he canceled our dinner plans. He said he was sick. He sounded so sincere, so sorry. I believed him. I thought I was being nice when I made a pot of chicken soup and took it over to his house to surprise him."

Riley winced in secondhand embarrassment, knowing what came next.

"He wasn't sick. He was naked. In the hot tub. And it wasn't with Bella either. It was with another woman." Li-Mei burst into tears.

A stunning young woman with waist-length blond hair shot to her feet. "It was me. I was in the hot tub," she said with what to Riley's untrained ear sounded like a Russian accent. "I met him at a remote broadcast from a car dealer earlier that week." Her jaw jutted forward.

"We were both yelling at him when Bella came home. He made both of us hide from her in the bushes," Li-Mei pressed on. A tear slid down her cheek. "I was humiliated."

"I was mad. I did a poop in his driveway when I left," the blond announced proudly.

The woman next to the blond jumped to her feet. She was scowling. "My name is Rose, and I didn't sleep with Griffin Gentry, but he still screwed me. I'm an interior designer, and he hired me to decorate his office at Channel 50. It was some of my best work. I spent months on it, and then the asshole refused to pay. I got lawyers involved until it got too expensive. Then the studio blew up, and now I'm out twenty thousand dollars in design fees plus another ten grand in legal fees. I wish he would have blown up with that custom leather ottoman," she snarled.

"Okay, well, thank you all for sharing," Kiki said. "What do we say to our sisters?"

"We're sorry Griffin Gentry sucks," everyone said in unison.

"Thank you," Li-Mei whispered.

The blond high-fived Rose.

"Ohhhhhh! Griffin Gentry sucks. Now I get it. I'm up to speed," Blossom said a few chairs down.

"A new member, how lovely," Kiki said. "We'd love it if you would share your Griffin Gentry story."

Riley sank lower in her chair. "Oh no."

"Well, it's not really my story so much as my daughter's," Blossom said, rising from her chair and waving her hand in Riley's direction. "That's her. My daughter Riley."

"Hi, Riley," everyone around the table said.

Riley managed a weak wave and wished she had an armed robbery to thwart right now.

"That's my other daughter, Wander. And I'm Blossom."

"Hi, Wander. Hi, Blossom."

"Hello. Hi. So nice to be here," Blossom said, preening under the attention.

"What brings you and your daughters to our group tonight?" Kiki asked magnanimously.

"Oh, well, Riley was married to Griffin a few years back," Blossom began. The collective gasp egged her on. "I know, right? I mean, I'm sorry, sweetie, but what were you thinking? Actually, what were any of us thinking? I mean who decided the construct of marriage was a good idea? You're just going to pick a stranger, decide to start a life and maybe a family with them, then before you know it, you're arguing over whose farm animals are more problematic."

Wander hid her face in her hands.

———

"The cards say you're going to be just fine, Laurel," Blossom said as she gathered up her tarot deck. "You just need to remember, self-worth comes from within, not without. Now who's next?"

"Laurel, right?" Riley asked when the teary-eyed brunette got up from the table. She looked like a fitness influencer in her mulberry workout tights and matching cropped sweatshirt. Her long hair was slicked back from her face in a low ponytail.

"Yeah. Your mom is amazing," she said, digging a tissue out of her bag and dabbing at her eyes. "I've just been in such a dark place the past few months. I have the worst taste in men, and it cost me my dogs."

"About that…" Riley began.

"How did it go?" Wander asked when Riley returned from the parking lot. Her sister had procured a matcha latte from the coffee stand and was watching from a safe distance while Blossom finished up a tarot reading for a pair of sisters who both had the misfortune of falling under Griffin's spell.

"Good. The yappers are—thank you, universe—back with their mom, who was so grateful, she confirmed that there's nothing Theodoric wouldn't do to get revenge for a wrong. She said in high school, he ran his own cousin off the road after he scored higher on his SATs than Theodoric did."

Riley believed her. From what she was able to read through Laurel, Ingram was exactly the kind of person who would do something like hire a contract killer.

Wander grimaced. "He sounds like a challenging personality."

A throat cleared gently behind them. They turned to find Kiki holding a pink balloon. "Riley, is it?"

"Uh, yes. That's me."

"Here. New members get a balloon on their first visit," Kiki said and thrust the balloon at her.

"Thanks."

"I'm going to go check on Mom," Wander said, wisely reading the situation and floating off.

"So you were actually married to Griffin Gentry?" Kiki asked with a sympathetic smile.

"Unfortunately, yes," Riley admitted.

"I bet you have your share of stories," Kiki ventured.

"I guess we all do." Riley gestured around at the women still gathered.

"I just want you to know that I'm here for you. If you ever need someone to listen, someone to show up with a tarp, a shovel, and no questions, or *anything* in between, you can count on me," Kiki offered. "We're a full-service support group, if you know what I mean."

Oh boy. "Um, thanks?"

Kiki grinned. "I'm totally joking." Then she shook her head and mouthed, *No, I'm not,* before waving at another one of the group members. "Joy! Wait up. I have an update for you." With a wink at Riley, she disappeared into the crowd.

Riley found her way back to her mother and sister. Blossom was packing up her tarot deck.

"This couldn't have been an easy evening for you," Wander predicted.

Riley shrugged. "I've been through worse." For instance, that time she'd gotten shot by the murderous mayor during a foot race through downtown Harrisburg...or that time she married Griffin. The evening had made her feel both better about herself for not being the only one to fall for the slippery eel of a man and sad that Griffin was still causing pain everywhere he went.

"You know, after listening to all those women's stories, it made me think that maybe your father isn't a complete jerk with no empathy whatsoever," Blossom admitted.

"Let's go get a drink. And not some spiked homemade kombucha," Riley said before her mother could suggest it.

Blossom slung her arms over both daughters' shoulders and pulled them in. "Yay! Girls' night with my girls."

26

"Come on, Riley. Squeeze those beautiful thighs," Nick ordered.

"I. Hate. You," she said through gritted teeth as she powered through the last three reps. Her quads were quaking. Her hamstrings were trembling. Whatever the musculature of her outer hips was called, it was screaming at her. She was red-faced and bathed in sweat. Worst of all, she was still half-asleep.

At this ungodly hour, Nick's gym was full of glistening, awake people who were tackling free weights and machines with a grim determination.

"That's my girl," he said, holding up a hand for a high five that she ignored. "Hey, you're the one who insists on being put in danger on a weekly basis. This is how you get in fighting shape."

Riley rolled off the machine and slumped to the floor, hiding her face under an already-damp sweat towel.

"All right. Fine. You win. I don't want to be in danger. You can lock me in a closet. I surrender," she muttered.

Nick tugged the towel off her face and gave her the full Santiago dimple charm. "Too late for that. We've already established that closets aren't safe. So until we have a cool sex room accessible only via retinal scanner, you're in danger boot camp."

"What did you do to Riley?" Weber asked, peering down at her.

"I made her get out of bed," Nick said and hauled her to her feet.

"What are you doing here?" she grumbled at the chipper homicide detective.

Weber hefted a chunky grayish smoothie and leaned against the machine. "Hangover finally broke. And this is the best way for us to meet without anyone on my end getting suspicious. What have you got for me?"

Nick mopped Riley's face with a fresh towel. "Well, my girl here just IDed a dozen or so new suspects last night while we were fighting bad guys."

Riley was still just the teensiest bit jealous that she missed out on thwarting an armed robbery.

"Lay it on me," Weber said.

"I hate how awake and alive you both are," she complained.

"Boot camp's going well, I see," Weber said with a smirk.

Riley limped over to a weight bench just so she could sit down. "My mom and sister and I accidentally stumbled into a Griffin Gentry Sucks Support Group for women who have been wronged by him."

"Like, an actual support group?" Weber asked.

"They had balloons and an easel sign and these," Riley said, pulling the crumpled, sweat-soaked cocktail napkin out of the pocket of her tights.

Grimacing at the napkin's saturation level, Weber unfurled it. "Realistically, how many of these women are probable suspects?"

"I don't know. They're all hurt and angry. Some more angry than others. The organizer, Kiki, said something to me afterward that rang a little bell. She offered to show up with a tarp and a shovel if I ever needed help."

"I assume she was joking," Weber said.

Riley shrugged. "I got the feeling she was fishing for something. Maybe feeling me out to see if I wanted to do more than just talk about how Griffin was a shitty husband?"

"Did you get a last name for this Kiki?" Kellen asked.

"Knappenberger," Nick said. "I had Brian do a dive this morning. She wasn't too hard to find. She owns a fancy clothing store in Lemoyne and conveniently lives about half a mile from Gentry."

"Also, Theodoric should stay at the top of the list. His ex-girlfriend confirmed he's murder-for-hire material after I returned her dogs," Riley said.

Something caught Nick's attention, and he quickly handed Riley two dumbbells. "Hit the deck, Weber," he ordered quietly. "Let's bang out another set of seated shoulder presses," he said louder.

"Huh?" Riley said as Weber dropped to the floor and started doing push-ups.

Nick nodded to the right. Chupacabra Jones was loading a bar with fifty-pound plates just a few feet from them.

"Oooh," Riley said. So her boyfriend wasn't just torturing her with a wicked morning workout and meeting with Weber on neutral ground. Nick was also doing surveillance.

"Don't blow our cover, Thorn. Be a good girl and work those shoulders," he said under his breath.

"Crap. Fine. Which one is the shoulder press again?" she asked.

Nick circled the weight bench and straddled it behind her. He adjusted her arms into the correct position and then trailed a sneaky, sexy finger across both shoulders. "You should feel it through here."

He smirked at her in the mirror when she nearly bobbled the weights. Her boyfriend was too sexy for her own good.

"Jerk," she muttered as she heaved the weights over her head.

"You want to get big and strong to fight suspects, don't you?" he teased.

"I fail to see how shoulder presses are going to turn me into a lean, mean, bad guy–fighting machine," Riley said as her trapezius muscles began to spasm.

"First rule of danger boot camp: don't question danger boot camp," he said.

In the mirror, she watched Chupacabra shoulder the bar and drop into a low squat as if the weights were made of tissue paper. "I hope you're not expecting me to do that," she said to Nick.

"Baby, I don't think *I* can do that. And stop stalling. Next set."

"Your mom's next set," she puffed.

"Nice try. We'll add trash-talking to the danger boot camp syllabus."

"Can't. Wait."

She sweated her way through four more reps while Chupacabra breezed through another set of ten.

"Gah! Fifty." Weber collapsed to the floor, sweating and panting. "Is she still looking?"

"You did not just do fifty push-ups," Nick argued.

"Fuck. You. Nicky," Weber wheezed.

"Why don't you show Kellen how it's done?" she prompted through her teeth as she fought against the pull of gravity to raise the dumbbells again.

Nick scoffed. "I don't need to prove myself in a push-up contest."

"Because you know you'd lose," Weber pointed out, flopping onto his back.

"She just saw us," Riley said without moving her mouth.

"Good. Wake up those spirit guides of yours." Nick swapped weights, handing over a lighter set. "Time for triceps," he said louder.

A fit and muscly shadow fell over Riley. "Hey. You guys are the investigators, right?" Chupacabra asked, tossing a bone-dry sweat towel over her shoulder.

"That's us," Nick said. "Chupacabra, right?"

"Good memory," she noted.

"Hard to forget the best name ever. This is my friend Yan." Nick gestured at Weber. "He's visiting from Sweden. He makes clocks for dollhouses."

"Nice to meet you, Yan," Chupacabra said, offering her hand to Weber.

"Yah. Is pleasant to meet you as well," Weber said in a reasonable-sounding Swedish accent while shaking her hand.

"A clockmaker?" she asked.

Weber bobbed his head. "Yah. I makes the teeny tiny clocks. And you? You make clocks?"

"No, I don't make tiny clocks. I make big muscles," Chupacabra explained, tapping her biceps. "I'm a personal trainer."

Weber frowned in confusion and looked at Nick.

Nick gestured at Chupacabra. "Hon slår pingviner som Arnold Schwarzenegger."

Riley wasn't sure if her boyfriend was speaking gibberish or actual Swedish because he did it with such confidence.

Weber bobbed his head. "Åh! Ja. Du bär damunderkläder."

"Cool," Chupacabra said.

"So how are things going with the Gentrys? Do you have them ready for an amateur bodybuilding show yet?" Nick asked.

She might have been half-dead from her workout, but Riley still caught the distinct flash of something that emanated from Chupacabra at the mention of the Gentrys.

"Great," she said with a smile that was almost believable. "Those two are getting in better shape by the day. Bella finally convinced Griffin to work out a couple of days a week now too. Almost can't believe he was on medical leave just a couple of months ago. It's practically a miracle."

The way Chupacabra said *miracle* sounded less impressed and more...irked. Like when you found out your high school nemesis had just bought a beach house.

Riley felt the nudge from her spirit guides. "When was that?" she asked.

"May," Chupacabra said. She glanced down as her phone screen lit up. There was a picture of a guy in a Harrisburg Senators ball cap on the screen below the name Pete.

Riley sensed twin pulls of annoyance and affection from the trainer.

"Excuse me, I have to take this. Nice to see you guys again. If you ever want to train, give me a call. I'm the only Chupacabra in the phone book." All three of them admired her muscled back as the trainer hustled in the direction of the locker room.

"I hate when you do that to me, Nicky," Weber complained.

Nick snapped him with Riley's sweat towel. "But you handle it so well."

"Yeah? Well, I get dibs on the next introduction. You'll be a retired gigolo from the south of France."

"Uh, so where did you two learn Swedish?" Riley asked.

"We didn't. My asshole cousin's family hosted a high school exchange student from Sweden when we were in junior high," Nick explained.

"Astrid." Weber sighed. "She was seventeen and gorgeous to two scrawny fourteen-year-olds."

"Yeah. So my cousin the asshole—"

"Brian or Carlo the plumber?" Riley clarified.

"Different asshole cousin. The then cheerleader, now physical therapist who lives in Baltimore. She told us she'd teach us some Swedish phrases to impress Astrid," Nick continued.

"Oh boy," she said, getting a glimpse of teenage Nick and Weber—gawky in braces and pubescent bodies—eagerly memorizing phrases written in a notebook.

"Yeah. Needless to say, we weren't actually saying, 'You're the hottest girl ever,' and 'I'm mature for my age,'" Nick said, clapping a hand to her shoulder. It slid right off as if she'd rubbed herself down with bacon grease. He wiped his hand on his shorts. "Now, my beautiful, talented, sweaty girlfriend. It's time for you to do something that this tiny clockmaker and I can't."

Curiosity had her looking up from her towel. "What's that?"

"Follow the suspect into the women's locker room and eavesdrop on her phone call."

Riley jumped to her feet. "On it!" She limped off, grateful for the temporary reprieve from physical fitness.

The locker room was as utilitarian as the gym itself, with concrete floors and rows of mint-green metal lockers that looked as if they'd been repurposed from an old high school.

Chupacabra was sitting on a long wooden bench between two rows of lockers, still talking on the phone as she untied her sneakers.

Riley held her towel over her face and eased into the next row of lockers to eavesdrop over the sound of a shower...and the woman in it singing Mariah Carey. She closed her eyes and did her best to hit the mute button on the Mariah wannabe so she could focus on Chupacabra's voice.

"Pete, I *told* you I'm working on it," Chupacabra said in exasperation. "I know...I know. Justice takes time, but think how sweet it'll be when that little orange fool *finally* pays."

She was definitely talking about Griffin. But what did she want to make him pay for? A past due invoice? Or was she talking about revenge? The woman in the shower shifted into a really not great version of an a cappella solo from the soundtrack for *Pitch Perfect*.

Come on, spirit guides. Show me something, Riley begged.

There was a flash of something...a car. Someone was behind the wheel. Someone else was reaching for it. She sensed rather than saw the struggle. Heard the crash. Felt the grit of broken glass.

Oopsie.

She fought for more, clinging to her senses, but the shower warbler was distracting, and another woman had just turned the corner to open a locker a few feet from Riley.

"Don't be like that, Pete. I can't make the cards fall into place any faster, and we can't afford for them to get suspicious,"

Chupacabra said, yanking Riley out of the vision. "And *I* told *you*, this is the best way forward. Damn it. You just made me dump my bag." She wasn't bothering to keep her voice low.

There was a beat of silence filled only by the amateur a cappella solo of "Party in the U.S.A."

"Goddamn it, Pete." The sentiment was followed by the rattling thud of metal. Riley was just easing her way to the end of the row when Chupacabra shouldered her gym bag and stormed out the door, muttering, "Men are fucking idiots."

Rather than following the muscular trainer, Riley decided it was safer to snoop around in the locker room. She headed up the row Chupacabra had occupied and stopped in front of the locker with the fist-size dent in the door. Opening it, she found it empty except for a scrap of paper wedged against the metal plates of the shelf and side of the locker.

The paper was a heavy-weight textured card stock that took a good tug for the locker to release it. It appeared to be the corner of a business card, but the only thing visible on it was a maroon triangle framed in gold and four digits.

————

When she returned to the gym, Nick and Weber were in side-by-side squat racks in what was clearly a macho contest. Riley noted neither of them had nearly as much weight on the bar as Chupacabra had.

Nick dumped the bar into the cradles and bent at the waist. "Jesus. My spleen," he complained.

"That's not where your spleen is, idiot. Did you ever even take an anatomy class?" Weber huffed as he tried to catch his breath.

"I know where all the important stuff is," Nick insisted, panting. He spotted her in the mirror and straightened, pretending not to be winded. "Hey, babe. I beat Weber in squats. What did you find out?"

"Your gym shorts are on fire," Weber retorted.

"Chupacabra has a temper and a reason to want Griffin to

pay. It involves a guy named Pete and possibly a car accident. Also, I found this in her locker after she punched it," she handed over the sliver of business card.

"Nicely done. Now, get that sexy ass of yours on the treadmill," Nick said and gave her sweaty rear end a slap.

She balked. "Shouldn't we go run down this lead? Or get some doughnuts? Or take shower naps?"

"There's no time-outs in danger boot camp for doughnuts and shower sex," her mean boyfriend insisted.

"I said shower nap, not sex," she grumbled.

"Treadmill. Now."

"For what it's worth, I'd take you for doughnuts," Weber called after her as she trudged toward her cardio fate. His sentence was cut off by a grunt of pain, which Riley guessed meant Nick had elbowed him in the stomach.

She glanced behind her and found the big strong, danger-taunting men locked in what appeared to be a stand-up wrestling match. An aggravated employee with tattoos down both arms stomped over with a spray bottle and squirted them both in the face.

"Damn it, Sheila!" Nick sputtered.

"Don't make me arrest you for assaulting an officer," Weber threatened, using the hem of his T-shirt to dry his face. The man had a six-pack as impressive as Nick's. Riley made a mental note to relay that information to Jasmine.

"You remember what happened last time you dumbasses got into a tickle fight? You knocked over the water cooler, turned this place into an aquacise class, and got banned for six months."

Nick and Weber broke apart.

"Sorry, Sheila," they grumbled.

She gave them each one last squirt in the face, then turned to Riley. "Here. Hang on to this. You might need it," she said, handing over the bottle. It was labeled *Testosterone Antidote*.

"What's in it?" Riley asked.

"Rose-scented facial toner. Makes dudes less fighty and improves their skin texture."

Sheila left, and Riley climbed aboard the closest treadmill.

Nick and Weber took the machines on either side of her, sandwiching her between them.

"So what now?" she asked, stabbing the Start button and wondering how long Nick would allow her to walk at a 1.0.

"You start moving faster than a glacier," Nick said.

Not long then.

"I mean in the case," she said, cautiously bumping the belt to a 1.5.

Her jerk of a boyfriend took matters into his own hands and bumped up her belt speed to a slow jog.

"I'll run background on the personal trainer," Weber volunteered as he smoothly shifted into a run.

"I'll get Brian digging into this Pete guy and the business card," Nick said, increasing his own pace to match Weber's. "Gabe is keeping an eye on Gentry at our place for the day. And Thorn and I are going to pay Bella another visit. She's been pretty quiet for someone whose fiancé almost got shot yesterday."

"I get the feeling those two don't have a traditional relationship," Weber said while his long legs effortlessly ate up the speed.

"If you call getting married for the adultery clause payout in the prenup nontraditional," Nick said.

"How'd you dig that up?" Weber asked.

Nick hooked his thumb in Riley's direction. "Hot psychic girlfriend."

"Speaking of things we're doing after I die on this treadmill. Don't forget we're babysitting tonight," Riley reminded him on a wheeze. She was already out of breath, and her feet were hitting the belt like they were encased in Gene Simmons's platform stage boots.

Weber snorted. "Someone's trusting Nick with their child?"

"Three childs, dickhead. I'm Uncle Nick. I'm the favorite."

"He's in a competition with Gabe for my nieces' affection," Riley explained on a wheeze.

"Of course he is. Who else do you have eyes on?" Weber asked.

She couldn't believe the guys were carrying on a normal conversation *while running*.

"Nice try. I gave you the tit. Where's my tat?" Nick said.

Weber grimaced. "Don't ever say that again."

"You know what I mean."

"I told you, as far as the PD is concerned, the case is closed. I can't exactly pull in witnesses for questioning. The shooters were extradited back to Colombia. Their lawyer went with them."

"Come on, Weber. Even your rule book isn't shoved that far up your ass. I'm sure there are other threads you can pull on," Nick said.

Riley tried to ignore the cramp in her left side, but it was sharp enough that she wondered if her appendix had migrated and was about to burst.

"Fine. Maybe I stopped by the FBO at the airport on my way home last night," Weber admitted.

"That's more like it. An FBO is a fixed base operator for private flights," Nick explained to Riley.

"Uh-huh," she rasped.

"What did you find?" Nick asked.

"That the private plane the lawyer flew in on is still sitting on the tarmac, and that when he arrived yesterday, he was in the middle of a heated phone call with someone who sounded like a very unhappy boss. Unfortunately, without the department behind me on this, I can't get a warrant for flight records."

Riley was doing her best to listen and keep her feet moving, but her migrating appendix and newly asthmatic breathing were demanding more and more of her attention.

"I'll put Brian on it. So we've got a bad guy—or girl—with private-plane-and-hit-man money out there who wants Griffin Gentry dead, and all we know now is the plane their lawyer flew in on is still here," Nick recapped. "Maybe it's the lawyer."

"Could be, but then why did he fly back commercial

and leave a perfectly good airplane behind?" Weber reminded Nick.

Nick shrugged. "Maybe he likes those shitty bags of pretzels? Or maybe he wanted to make sure his guys kept their mouths shut?"

Riley liked this scenario where all the bad guys had left the country.

"Might be time to consider taking Gentry underground at least for a few days," Weber warned. "You already thwarted one murder attempt. If this boss gets word that you're also sheltering Gentry, he might decide to retaliate."

Riley's heart rate—which was already dangerously high thanks to the jogging—kicked up another notch. "We have…a lot of…kind of innocent…people in that house."

Nick shook his head. "My gut tells me those clown car idiots from yesterday were probably the only henchmen on the ground. Until we know we're being watched, I don't think we need to pack up our village of idiots and move them."

Riley nervously glanced behind her to see if anyone sinister was lurking in the shadows and immediately stumbled. Nick and Weber both grabbed her by the soaking wet tank top and righted her without breaking stride.

"Don't worry your pretty little sweaty face, Thorn. I'm working on a contingency plan," Nick assured her.

"Don't even think about bringing them to my condo," Weber said.

"Mrs. Penny would drink you out of house and home in under twenty minutes," Nick predicted.

He was keeping things light, but Riley caught a distinct whiff of *"this is going to suck"* from her sweaty, sprinting boyfriend.

Nick peered over her to sneak a look at Weber's treadmill display, then bumped his speed up another notch.

"It's not a race, Santiago."

"It's always a race."

27

Why do you keep sniffing your armpits?" Nick asked as Riley did exactly that for the third time as they crossed the parking lot toward the spa entrance under the cheery green awning.

The Hotel Hershey was a huge Mediterranean-style building perched on a grassy hill that overlooked the sugar-fueled chaos of Hersheypark. On one side of the highway, kids screamed and vomited their way through roller coasters and amusement park rides. On the opposite side, adults enjoyed fine dining and chocolate-scented spa services.

"I've never been here before. It looks fancy, and you just made me sweat myself half to death," Riley complained.

"We're questioning a suspect, not shoving our armpits in people's faces," Nick reminded her. Bella Goodshine had evaded his calls, which meant if he wanted to talk to her, they were going to have to crash her spa day.

"You're the one who told me it's important to blend in," Riley argued.

"Baby, you've got that 'just worked out' dewy glow. No one's going to know that it's not from shoving your head under a goop fountain or whatever the hell they do here," he said with confidence.

"You've never been to a spa, have you?" she guessed as he took her hand and led her through the door.

"It never landed on my list of things to do." The idea of putting on a bathrobe and letting a complete stranger rub weird concoctions all over you held little to no appeal to him.

"Well, I've always wanted to come here as a legitimate guest, so I'd appreciate it if you didn't get us kicked out."

"You didn't come here when you were married?" he asked.

Riley shook her head. "Griffin always preferred to travel for his spa stuff. He likes those med spas where you can get cosmetic procedures done. Everyone sits around in bathrobes, drinking cucumber water with their lasered faces and their new noses bandaged up. I just want a good massage that makes me feel like cooked spaghetti."

The fleur-de-lis carpet was thick underfoot, and the wallpaper under the spa's directional sign whispered *old money*. They followed the arrow to the carpeted staircase and started up the stairs.

Riley groaned. "My thighs are on fire."

"You'll get used to the burn."

A woman in her midfifties, wearing a white skirt and carrying a tennis racket, jogged down the stairs toward them.

"Excuse me," Nick said, turning on the charm. "You're Sabrina Van Der Woodsen, aren't you? It's me, Bojack Flintstone, class of 2002."

The woman blinked, then frowned. "Sorry. You've got the wrong gal. I'm Matty West, and I wish I were class of 2002."

"Sorry." He feigned chagrin. "You look just like her."

She continued on down the hall.

"What was that about?" Riley asked.

"That was just in case. Game face, Thorn," Nick said as he reached for the door handle to the spa entrance.

"Wait. What's the plan?" Riley demanded.

He winked. "Part of danger boot camp. Learning to adapt to unpredictable situations."

"Nick!" she hissed, but he was already pulling her into

the room. There were two employees manning the front desk, both female. Women with shiny faces and thick robes orbited around the space, admiring spa accessories and looking blissful. Weird instrumental music with flutes and drums seeped softly from invisible speakers.

"How can I help you?" one of the women at the desk asked with a serene smile.

Nick wondered if working in a spa was relaxing or if the employees got in their cars at the end of the day and blasted death metal music.

"My wife and I are staying here and were wondering if we could get a tour. We just moved to the area and are particular about our spas," Nick said with a friendly smile as he helped himself to the dish of Hershey Kisses next to the card reader. "Isn't that right, sweetheart?"

Riley pasted what Nick could only assume was a spa fan girl smile on her pretty face. "Yah! I'm from Sweden. Ve invented Swedish massage."

He gave his beautiful psychic girlfriend a subtle impressed nod. Riley Thorn had come to play.

"Of course. We're always happy to introduce new couples to our facility. What's your room number?" the woman said, showing no signs of not believing Riley's accent.

Nick blanched. "Shoot. I can't remember. That workout in your gym wiped my brain clean. We're the Wests if that helps. I'm Matty, and this is Helga."

"Certainly, Mr. and Mrs. West. If you'll wait over there, I'll have a hostess show you around."

They sidled off and pretended to admire a display of chocolate-flavored lip balms. "You invented Swedish massage?"

Riley shrugged smugly as she picked up a tube of some kind of cocoa-scented face goop. "What? I wanted you to feel like you were finally getting your shot with the hot foreign exchange student."

He shook his head. "One of a kind, Thorn. One of a kind."

"That's Helga to you. So how are we going to question

Bella if we have a spa tour guide tagging along?" Riley asked in a hushed tone as a man and woman with matching robes and shiny, blissed-out faces wandered in.

"One of us will have to make an emergency pit stop at the restroom," Nick decided.

"Ugh. Can't you just fake an important phone call?"

"Strangers are willing to wait around while you take a call. They don't want to hover outside a bathroom door when they know a toilet is about to be violated," he explained.

"Valid."

A six-foot-tall dude with gray hair and one of those cool Vandyke beards strolled up. He was wearing a spa uniform. "Mr. and Mrs. West?" To Nick's ear, he sounded a hell of a lot like the cartoon cat Puss in Boots.

Nick didn't consider himself well-versed on what constituted an attractive man, but judging from the hungry looks every woman in the room was throwing his way, Silver Fox was hot. Even Riley was noticing.

Maybe he should forget about the Nick Charles mustache and go for the beard?

Nick clamped an arm around her waist. "That's us."

"I'm Hector. I'll be your guide today," he said with a smile that made crinkles next to his crystalline blue eyes appear.

Hector held out a hand to Nick. He reluctantly released Riley and shook. The guy had a grip like Sylvester Stallone in *Over the Top*. "That's a strong hand you've got there, Hector."

The man released him. "It comes from years of massaging sore muscles." His attention shifted to Riley. "A pleasure," Hector said, taking Riley's hand in both of his.

Her cheeks turned a distinct shade of pink. "Hi," she squeaked, forgetting her accent.

Hector released her hands and gestured toward the door. "Please, follow me."

Behind his back, Nick nudged Riley. *"Hi,"* he mouthed, pretending to toss his hair flirtatiously.

"He's so pretty," she mouthed back.

"I'm pretty too," he hissed in her ear.

She patted his cheek. "Of course you are, Mr. West."

———

"And this is what's known as the quiet room," Hector said, gesturing them through the open door. "It is where guests wait for their spa services."

The room had dark paneled walls and a fire crackling merrily in the massive fireplace. Spa goers decked out in robes and flip-flops lounged in chairs or browsed the small beverage and snack buffet.

"Mind if we sample some of the goods?" Nick asked.

"By all means," Hector said, opening his hands in invitation.

Nick grabbed a delicate coffee cup while Riley perused the snack selection. "Quarry spotted," he whispered in her ear.

She stiffened and glanced behind them.

"Be cool. She's in that alcove thing over there," he said and jerked his chin to the right of the fireplace.

"I didn't recognize her without makeup," she confessed.

"Tell Hector you have the runs and go pump her for information," he said.

She was already shaking her head. "Uh-uh. No way."

Nick put the cup under the first thermos he spotted and opened the spout. "You're just saying that because he's hot."

"First of all, I'm proud of you for finally recognizing another man's physical appeal without wanting to challenge him to a pissing contest."

"Usually it's a push-up contest. Pissing contests are too messy and hard to judge unless you both have a liquid measuring cup."

She ignored him. "Bella isn't going to talk to me. She's going to have no idea who I am, and I'll have to waste five full minutes reminding her we've already met a dozen times. You, she remembers."

He wasn't a fan of the points Riley was making, mainly because it meant he was going to have to leave his girl alone with Mr. Effortlessly Suave. But she was right, and they didn't have much time.

"Fine. But if that guy tries to get you in bed, I wanna know immediately."

"Deal. Now try to look like you're clenching your butt cheeks really hard," she teased.

He rolled his eyes before heading in Hector's direction. He was waiting patiently at the door. "Can you point me in the direction of the nearest restroom? That Taco Bell isn't sitting right," he said.

"Of course. Down the hall and on your right."

"Cool. Don't wait for me. I'll catch up with you two."

Nick ducked into the restroom and counted down from twenty. When he poked his head out the door, he saw Hector leading Riley in the opposite direction.

Riley held up a subtle thumbs-up behind her back.

Nick took his coffee cup of brown liquid and hurried back to the quiet room. Bella was still there with her face buried in a magazine that had Beth Weber on the cover announcing her comeback from cold case obscurity to being the country's newest reality TV star.

He took the seat next to her and stretched out his legs. "You've been avoiding my calls," he said.

A woman in a brown robe lowered her e-reader and shushed him.

Bella looked up, startled. "Oh, hi, Nick."

"Don't 'oh, hi, Nick' me. Your fiancé nearly got shot yesterday, and you're too busy getting body parts oiled up to care? Seems a little cold to me."

Bella lowered her magazine, her eyes looking slightly less cartoon puppy without the fake lashes and troweled-on makeup. "Do you have any idea how hard it is to book appointments here? I had to schedule this trip six months ago, and I already had to cancel my seaweed body wrap and sugar scrub this afternoon for our interview. I'm not canceling the rest of it just because Griffin didn't get hurt."

"What interview?"

"Didn't Griffin tell you? Channel 50 is doing a special interview with us about our harrowing experiences."

"Yeah, you look real harrowed." Nick took an irritated sip and nearly choked on the thick sweet liquid. "What the hell?" He scowled down at the cup.

"That's the hot cocoa. Isn't it divine?"

"Tell me why you shouldn't be my number one suspect right now," he said, then hazarded another taste of the cocoa. It was good. Really good.

"Because I love him and I would never ever want to hurt my Griffy Wiffy Bear."

"Errrr!" Nick made the buzzer sound.

"Shhhhh!" hissed the woman with the e-reader.

"Sorry. Sorry," he whispered. "Wrong answer."

"Fine. If you don't want to believe that Griffin and I are in love, believe this. He is worth more to me alive than dead. His family won't let him add me to his will or life insurance policy or bank accounts until the marriage is official. If something happens to him before we get married, I get zip-a-dee-doo-dah."

"There are other reasons besides money to hire someone to commit murder."

"Well, none of those reasons apply to me." She haughtily turned a page in her magazine with glossy pink nails. "I've worked hard to get where I am today. I'm not about to let someone with a grudge and a few hired guns ruin all my plans."

"Really? How is hiding away at a spa going to help keep your fiancé alive?"

"You're the one who's supposed to be keeping him alive. That's what rich people do. They hire not-rich people to solve their problems."

"I'd be more inclined to make sure he doesn't get his ass murdered if I knew he'd actually pay when this is all over."

"I can make sure that happens," Bella insisted earnestly.

"Yeah. Right. I'll believe that when I see it."

"Fine. What if I help you in another way?"

"If you even think about hitting on me right now, I'm dumping this cocoa on you and telling everyone you touched my no-no spot," he warned.

She rolled her eyes. "You want to be paid, and I want this wedding to happen. We're on the same side. I can give you information."

"What kind of information?" Nick asked.

"What do you want to know?"

"Griffin's medical leave. Tell me about it."

She hesitated before answering. "He was in a car accident, and then he couldn't work for almost three weeks."

"I'm not buying that you're as dumb as you pretend to be. And I'm sure as hell not as dumb as you think I am."

"I'm telling you the truth. There was an accident."

"When?"

She tapped a fingernail to her chin. "I remember it was May because I hadn't switched to my humidity tamer hairspray yet. He had to go away for some kind of special treatment. What does that have to do with someone trying to shoot him?"

"What kind of treatment? Did he leave the country?"

She shrugged. "I don't know. It was before we were engaged, and I didn't pay attention to things like that."

These two yahoos were going to make a mockery of the thing Nick had finally decided to take seriously: marriage. It annoyed him enough to self-soothe with the rest of his hot cocoa. He set the empty cup down with a snap.

"When did Chupacabra start working for you? Was it before or after Griffin got back from his 'special treatment'?"

Bella pursed her lips, then brightened. "After. Yes! That's right. She came on the show for the small business segment Griffin hosts, but it was one of his first days back on the show. He couldn't do the leg workout she had planned, so the producers had me stand in for him. She said I was pretty and offered me a discount on in-home workouts during the commercial break."

"How much of a discount?"

"Buy one workout, get three free every single week."

———

Nick poured himself another cup of hot cocoa on his way out and went in search of Riley and Hector. As much as it annoyed him to admit, Bella Goodshine didn't fit as primary suspect. Mainly because the only money she had was Griffin's. Unless of course she'd found a richer guy willing to help her clear the decks. But then why wouldn't she have just left Griffin?

He'd almost reached the end of the hallway when he heard a familiar moan.

"What the hell?" he demanded, stopping in the open doorway of the last room on the right.

Riley was facedown on a massage bed—fully clothed, thank freaking God—and Hector's hands were on her. "You have beautiful spinal flexibility," Hector told her.

"It's the yoga," she said on another sex-noise moan.

"I thought I told you not to let this guy talk you into bed," Nick complained.

"You've got to try this N–Matty," Riley slurred, sounding like she'd just stumbled out of one of Mrs. Penny's happy hours. "He's magic."

Hector helped Riley sit up, steadying her when she wobbled dreamily.

"Yeah, I'm not really into the whole stranger-rubbing-me-down-while-someone-plays-the-pan-flute thing," Nick confessed, glaring Hector down.

"You've never experienced a massage?" Hector asked. A single silver eyebrow arched gracefully.

"It's not really my jam. But clearly it is *my wife's* jam."

"Please. Allow me to show you," Hector said, gesturing toward the table.

Riley all but collapsed against Nick. "You have to."

"No."

She cupped his face in her hands. They smelled vaguely of chocolate. "I'm asking you to be brave and do this one nice thing for yourself."

"I'm brave. I'm fucking heroic. I got shot at and thwarted a robbery. I carry on conversations with your grandmother," he reminded her.

"Then you must try," Hector said, patting the massage bed.

"Fine. But I'm going to hate every second of it," Nick promised.

"I'm going to go get some tea," Riley said dreamily as she floated out of the room.

"Get the hot cocoa," Nick said, reluctantly putting his face in the squishy round cradle at the top of the bed. Every muscle in his body was as rigid as Home Depot's lumber section. The things he did for his woman.

He stiffened when Hector's hands skimmed over his shoulders.

"So much tension," Hector mused. "You must carry many responsibilities."

"Actually my life is pretty chill—oh God. Oh sweet baby Jesus," Nick moaned as Hector's fingers gripped his rigid shoulders.

"Relax into my touch," Hector said, his voice soothing.

Nick fought to cling to his comfort zone for another ten seconds before the war was lost. "I'm not really a guest here. I'm a PI and I didn't have the runs. I was questioning a suspect or a witness or whatever the hell she is," he blurted out.

"Interesting," Hector said as his hands moved down Nick's spine, pressing and stretching and rubbing as they went.

"I grew up in a competitive family and never learned how to have healthy relationships," Nick continued into the face cradle.

"That is very common and is nothing to be ashamed of," Hector assured him.

"Once when I was in junior high, I stole my dad's car, drove to his restaurant in the middle of the night, and deep-fried an entire bag of mozzarella sticks. I ate the whole thing, drove home, and threw up in my bed. The marinara sauce made it look like I was bleeding internally, and my parents took me to the emergency room. It cost them five grand."

He felt something strong and hard dig into the muscle just below his shoulder blade. An elbow? A knee? A goddamn crowbar? Nick didn't care.

"The truth releases with the muscle," Hector said wisely.

"Listen, Hector, I'm getting my shit together so I can propose to my girl. But if I weren't already in a committed relationship and straight, I'd ask you to marry me right now," he said.

"I've received many proposals in the spa," Hector said as his magic fingers released a knot Nick hadn't known existed but felt like it had been there for all of eternity.

"Oh God. Okay. What's a cool but romantic way to propose? Do I have to get down on one knee? And I don't like the whole asking for the dad's permission. Mainly because I don't like to ask for permission for anything. But also it feels kind of like seventeenth-century 'how many oxen is your daughter worth?'"

"I find something as important as a proposal should be a reflection of the couple as a whole."

"Gah! It hurts but it feels so fucking good."

"As does life," Hector advised.

Nick released a sound that wasn't even human as the man worked his way down to his lower back.

"You're so smart. And talented. Did you know my girlfriend is psychic? I think it's really cool. She's really cool," Nick said dreamily into the face cradle.

"Uhhhh…"

Nick managed to lift his head and smile at the stunned Riley in the doorway.

"It is all right," Hector promised. "He has confessed all."

"And Hector still loves us," Nick said, melting into the table.

"You both will return, and I will massage you," Hector predicted.

28

I'm already exhausted," Riley said on a yawn as Nick turned onto Front Street. The Susquehanna River looked gray under the cloudy autumn sky.

After leaving the spa, he had taken her back to the gun range and made her shoot her way through four targets and eight magazines of ammo. She still wasn't a great shot, but there was marginal improvement.

Afterward, Nick had announced he had half a dozen urgent errands to run.

She was fairly certain these "errands" were just a way to avoid being at home with her obnoxious ex-husband. But since she also had no desire to hang around Griffin, she was happy to be along for the ride.

They'd been all over both sides of the river, stocking up on groceries, eating lunch, buying office supplies, and even swinging by a hardware store for a dozen folding chairs, "Just in case we need them." She was too tired from the early-morning workout to question him. However, even in her state of physical exhaustion, it didn't escape her notice when Nick checked the rearview mirror for the fifteenth time.

She sat up out of her slump. "Are we being followed?"

"We are not being followed," he said.

"Then why do you keep looking behind us?"

"To make sure we're not being followed."

"Glad we cleared that up," she said as he swung the SUV into their driveway.

He pulled up to the mudroom door and turned off the engine. They both sat staring through the windshield.

"Remember the good ol' days when we could just walk into the house and have sex on the kitchen table?" Nick said.

Riley sighed. "Back before my ex-husband and our old roommates became our current roommates."

He reached over and squeezed her knee. "We could just drive to the airport, get on a plane, and have frozen drinks with umbrellas in hand by tonight."

She wrinkled her nose. "Much as I'd like to run away with you, we can't tonight. We're babysitting, remember."

Nick thumped his head against his seat. "Fine. But when this is over, we're planning a vacation."

There was a lot of "this" to overcome. Attempted murder, the roof collapse next door, getting the business back on its feet… But if there was a chance she could watch Nick Santiago take his shirt off on a beach and slather every inch of muscle and tattoos with sunscreen, she'd do whatever it took to make that happen.

"Count me in."

They reluctantly unloaded their errand haul and trooped inside.

The bag of sticky notes, pens, and file folders slipped out of Riley's grasp and hit the floor. Nick ran into her back.

"Are you seeing what I'm seeing?" she whispered.

Mrs. Penny, Josie, and Gabe were seated around Griffin at the kitchen table. Griffin wore a blindfold, and from what Riley could tell, he had his hands tied behind his back. Burt sat on the floor next to Mrs. Penny, raptly watching the occupants of the table.

"Why is our *client* bound and blindfolded at the kitchen table?" Riley asked.

"Shh! Don't distract him." With spritely fingers, Josie dipped a piece of celery into a shallow bowl in front of Griffin.

"Mouth," Mrs. Penny barked.

Griffin obediently opened his mouth, and Josie shoved the celery inside.

Everyone watched with rapt attention as Griffin chewed in tiny mincing bites.

"Even the way this guy chews makes me want to punch him in his fucking face," Nick muttered, dumping the bags of groceries on the island.

"Truffle mayo with"—Griffin pursed his thin lips—"soy sauce!"

Scattered applause and appreciative murmurs broke out around the table.

"We could have been at the airport by now," Nick complained as he opened the fridge and began shoveling groceries onto the shelves.

"Are you seriously taste testing mayo?" Riley asked, ignoring her boyfriend.

"We didn't believe Gentry could taste the difference between Bucket o' Mayo and his thirty-dollar-a-jar truffle brand," Mrs. Penny said, as if that explained anything.

"It's called a condiment palate, and very few people in the world have it. I'm very lucky," Griffin explained.

"He even tasted the pickle juice we slipped into his Hershey syrup," Josie said.

"But why are his hands tied?" Riley asked, looking to Nick for help.

"I don't care if they spoon-feed him Drano," he said, stealing a slice of Swiss cheese out of the deli pack.

"Mrs. Penny insisted it is part of official sanctioned taste tests," Gabe explained. "Is this not correct?"

The woman in question tapped her chin. "Maybe I got it mixed up with pie-eating contests."

Riley felt the relaxation Hector had bestowed upon her vanish and be replaced with rigid tension.

Nick stuffed a package of mini tacos into the freezer and closed the door. "Yo, Jos. Where's your husband?"

"In his office. Said he was too busy to play Feed Griffin a Bunch of Shit."

"Gabe, you're in charge," Nick said, putting his hands on Riley's shoulders and steering her out of the kitchen.

"Mouth," Mrs. Penny said.

Griffin opened his mouth, and Josie fed him another piece of celery. "Hmm, tastes like Tabasco annnnnd...Nesquik!"

They found Brian frowning at four of his six monitors in the skinny office he shared with Josie. He didn't bother looking away from what looked like pages of data, but he did remove his headphones. "What's up, coz?"

"Update time," Nick said, flopping down in Josie's chair and pulling Riley into his lap.

"Did they get to the Tabasco and Nesquik yet? That was my suggestion."

Nick's fingers found their way under the hem of Riley's shirt and stroked at the skin just above the waistband of her tights. "Not an update on that condiment-swilling idiot. What do you have on our encyclopedia-long list of suspects?"

"Oh, them," Brian said, swiveling to face them. "Good news is I found a lot of dirt. Bad news is I found a lot of dirt on everyone."

"For instance?" Nick growled.

Apparently his Hector-induced relaxation had worn off too.

Brian's fingers flew over his keyboard, and a picture of Claudia Mendoza appeared on the monitor closest to them. "Let's start here. Gentry got Mendoza fired a few years back. She recovered with a lateral move to Channel 49's morning show and has been there ever since."

Nick threw a fresh pad of sticky notes at his cousin. "We know this already," he complained.

Brian dodged the office supplies and called up another screen. "Ah, but did you *also* know that Claudia filed a wrongful termination lawsuit that was finally settled out of court last year? I haven't found my way into any sealed court documents, but I *did* find a few vague Facebook posts on her personal account from around that time about never settling for less than you're worth and how karma always wins in the end."

"I knew she was lying about finding peace. No one finds peace where Griffin is involved," Riley said.

"Did you *further* know that Claudia spent time with family last Christmas…in Colombia?" Brian pressed on.

Nick's hands tensed on Riley. "Hmm," he said.

"That's where the shooters were extradited to, right?" Riley asked. She hadn't bought the news anchor's new kombucha-and-kumbaya vibe. However, she still didn't see Claudia hiring a pair of dimwitted hit men to right a years-old wrong. She seemed more like the sneaky revenge type. Unless Griffin had done something to reignite the flame of vengeance, which was entirely plausible.

"Solid find, Bri," Nick said, lazily stroking circles over Riley's skin with his fingertips.

Brian pulled up another set of tabs on screen. "Moving on to everyone's second-favorite douchebag, Ingram Theodoric the Third. The first being the victim himself, of course."

Riley shivered, recalling their close call with the drunken, rifle-wielding man.

"He's got motive what with Griffin sleeping with his girlfriend. He's also got means. Not only is his compensation in the low seven figures, he also comes from family money thanks to his grandfather Ingram Theodoric the OG, who started a chain of roast beef shops, paid his workers below minimum wage, and spent his free time slaughtering zebras and gorillas all over the African continent."

"Inherited assholery," Nick remarked.

"Big time. Ingram the Second almost went to jail for assault and battery against his third wife, but the charges were dropped after the wife 'moved to Oklahoma.'"

"Why the air quotes?" Riley asked.

"Because the only people who claim to have had contact with her since then are Ingrams Two and Three, but I digress," Brian said. "The Third had his country club membership canceled recently after a dispute on the golf course got ugly. I didn't get many details, but rumor has it he went after a caddie with a three wood after his fourth gin and tonic. I dug up a couple of old girlfriends of the Third," Brian continued. "None of them were willing to talk about him, but one did mention an NDA. So he could be covering his tracks that way. Bottom line, he's a bad dude."

Riley agreed wholeheartedly.

Nick scrubbed a hand over his jaw. "Sounds like he's got a temper with private-plane-and-hit-man money to back it up."

"Next up is Kiki Knappenberger. Nice find, by the way, Ry," Brian said, rearranging more tabs.

She preened. "Thanks."

"Not only does our new pal Kiki have reason to hate Griffin, she also set off our resident psychic's alarm bells, and for good reason." He pulled up a spreadsheet. "I couldn't dig too deeply into her finances without raising suspicions, but I *did* discover that she has a recurring subscription of gummy dicks sent to Griffin's address every month for the last six months."

"Heh." Nick chuckled in approval.

"Thanks to these grainy-as-shit photos Willicott took with an actual film camera, we also know that she followed Griffin to lunch." Brian clicked through a series of photos that showed Mr. Willicott's confused face as he apparently tried to use the lens as the eyepiece. Over his shoulder, Kiki could be seen in oversize sunglasses and an honest-to-goodness trench coat, sneaking up to Griffin's car.

"Stalking is a step up from hilarious dick-shaped pranks," Nick noted.

Brian drum-rolled his hands on the counter that served as his desk. "Speaking of people who have reasons to want revenge on Griffin, that brings us to—pause for a moment of silence because Josie said we are absolutely not naming the baby—Chupacabra Jones."

"You've still got a couple months to wear her down," Nick said.

"We're not naming our baby Chupacabra," Josie bellowed from the opposite side of the house.

"Your wife scares me," Nick whispered.

"Join the club," Brian said cheerily.

"Back to Chupacabra. Did you find anything out about this mysterious Pete?" Riley prompted.

Brian triumphantly tapped at the keyboard. "Do you mean *this* Pete?" he asked with a flourish as a face appeared on the screen.

"I don't know. Maybe?"

"Peter Rodman, age thirty-three, former limo driver and second cousin to Chupacabra Jones, lost his job when the Escalade he was driving struck a woman outside the Harrisburg Airport when he was dropping off a client. The woman was fine thanks to her impressive array of luggage taking the brunt of the low-speed impact."

"What does this have to do with Griffin?" she asked.

"Patience, my psychic friend," he said. "According to the police report, the driver claimed it was the passenger who grabbed the wheel and turned into the woman because—and I quote—'he thought someone on the sidewalk recognized him and might want his autograph.'"

"Gee. I wonder who that could be?" Riley asked dryly.

Nick pinched the bridge of his nose. "New rule. No more working for someone I hate."

"No offense, but that would severely limit our income potential," Brian pointed out.

"So Pete got fired," Riley said, bringing them back to the topic at hand.

"Fired *and* sued, by the victim and—wait for it—his passenger, who claimed he was injured and lost weeks of income while recuperating on medical leave. Pete's insurance company settled the suits and then did what insurance companies do. They sued him for $150,000 to recoup their losses. Funny thing is Griffin didn't claim he was injured in the accident until a week later, when his lawyer pushed him into the police station all bandaged up in a wheelchair. Even funnier, Pete insists that when he jumped out of the car to see if the woman was all right, Griffin walked right into the airport and got on a plane."

"Did the cops interview Griffin at the scene?" Nick asked.

Brian shook his head. "Nope. In fact, there seemed to be some confusion about whether Pete actually had a passenger until Griffin showed up a week later, claiming to have been injured."

"So Griffin ruins the cousin's life, and Chupacabra installs herself as the couple's personal trainer to do what? What's her endgame?" Riley asked.

"Payback? Maybe she wants to drop a weight on his head?" Nick guessed.

"At this point, who doesn't?" Brian said, gesturing to his screens.

Nick blew out a breath. "Thorn, I need you to do something disgusting. Something horrible and potentially emotionally scarring."

"I already told you last night I'm fine with your Princess Leia fantasy."

"Not that. I mean, definitely also that. But I need you to poke around in Griffin's head while I interrogate the little fucker."

It was Riley's turn to sigh. "Fine. But can I be drunk when I do it?"

"If you can get drunk in the next thirty seconds," he said. "Gentry! Get in here."

Brian hit a button, and screen savers of his wedding day with Josie filled all six monitors. The bride wore black.

Riley slid off Nick's lap and perched on the counter in the corner.

Griffin appeared, carrying a spoon of what looked like

straight mayonnaise. He slurped it up like it was soup. Brian gagged.

"Okay, spirit guides. Don't let me get lost in there," Riley said in her head.

"Does someone want an autograph?" Griffin asked hopefully.

She felt herself drifting. Her body was still in Brian's office, but her mind was floating up, up, up into the clouds.

"Tell us about this accident you were in back in May," Nick ordered. He sounded like he was far away.

"What accident? I wasn't in an accident," Griffin insisted, licking the spoon.

Riley cast her mind forward, slipping around Brian, who seemed amused, and then Nick, who was a roiling mass of frustration, before landing on Griffin's unwrinkled brow.

Either her connection wasn't good or there wasn't much of anything going on in Griffin's brain. She had a feeling it was the latter.

"The one that required you to take a three-week medical leave of absence from the morning show," Nick prompted.

"Oh, *that*," Griffin said, catching sight of his reflection in one of the monitors and combing his shellacked hair to one side.

"Yeah. That," Nick repeated. "Tell us about the accident."

"Well, there I was, driving down Second Street, when the car in front of me stopped for a yellow light..."

Riley's nose twitched, and then she found herself following along with Griffin in his spiffy little sports car as he waved to people on the sidewalk with the audio of the morning show blaring from his speakers. But it wasn't a recording of the show, it was a compilation of everything Griffin had said on the show.

Spirit World Riley rolled her eyes.

Griffin leaned forward to check his teeth in the rearview mirror just as the light ahead changed from yellow to red.

Smack!

She found herself up close and personal with the license plate of the city bus Griffin had just rear-ended.

"Not that accident. The one where you sued the driver," Nick said through clenched teeth.

"You'll have to be more specific. I sue a lot of people," Griffin said amicably.

"The airport. When you hit a woman in the crosswalk."

She could feel Nick's molars gnashing together.

"Oh, *that* one," Griffin said, sounding to Riley like he was underwater.

She tried to navigate her way around conceited mental wonderings about whether his left profile or his right was the more perfect before landing in the back seat of an SUV as it approached the departures drop-off at the Harrisburg Airport.

"I didn't hit anyone. I wasn't driving," he explained.

She was treated to an image of Griffin holding up a hand mirror and admiring himself. Everything else seemed to be blurred.

Oh God. She was *in* Griffin's point of view.

"Who's the best boy in the whole wide world? It's me! I am!" Griffin winked at his own reflection a moment before he saw something shinier outside.

He lurched forward between the seats, saying something Riley couldn't make out.

"Dude! What the fuck?" the driver yelped.

Clonk.

She didn't get a clear vision of what had happened because Griffin had already hopped out of the back seat and clearly wasn't interested in what was going on at the front of the SUV.

"I'm Griffin Gentry. Bring my bag to the lounge," he said, pointing finger guns at an airport employee. The man's face was also blurred, but it was clear he was gaping at Griffin.

Whistling, the narcissistic fool strolled right through the automatic doors into the terminal, ignoring the shouts for help outside.

His cheerful tune was still echoing in her head when Riley slid back into the present moment.

It took her a moment to realize she was still in Griffin's head. *Me. Me. Me. Mine. Mine. Mine.* The words bounced around, echoing like a mantra.

"I'm going to ask you again. Have you ever been to Colombia, Gentry?" Nick's voice floated faintly through her mind.

Gentry sounded louder, crisper, and Riley felt Griffin's attention light up at his own name. "Columbia University?" he asked.

"Colombia, the South American country, jackass." Nick's snarl sounded so far away.

She caught a glimpse of verdant green hills, tall palms, and then they were gone, replaced by a distant pain down her legs, dulled by a pleasant wooziness.

"Nope. Never. Why? Do you think I have fans there?"

Brian's and Nick's faces were dim pixelated blurs as if they weren't just unimportant but an actual threat to Griffin's self-esteem. However, she was in sharp focus... Well, her boobs were. But the rest of her was pretty clear too.

Mine.

Riley watched herself blanch and dry heave once through Griffin's eyes.

It was a dizzying, nauseating journey to be ripped from her ex-husband's head only to reinhabit her own mind and body as Brian shoved a trash can under her face. Sparkles exploded before her eyes, chasing away the pain and vertigo, leaving behind a rush of euphoria.

Nick jumped up, the chair he vacated wheeling backward into Griffin.

"Owie!"

Nick took the trash can from Brian and cupped the back of her head. "You okay, baby?"

"Just peachy. This might be nothing, but Griffin was in the back seat of a black Escalade. I think I remember one stopping in front of our house after the shootout."

271

"Could be a coincidence," Nick pointed out.

"Or could be the limo driver guy just moved up the suspect list," Brian said, cheerfully clicking keys on his keyboard.

"Did you just have one of those vision things?" Griffin asked her.

"Maybe," Riley said, avoiding his gaze.

Griffin wrinkled his nose. "That's weird. You shouldn't do that anymore, or people will think there's something wrong with you. You definitely can't do it when we get back together. I have a reputation to uphold," he explained patiently.

Nick's growl brought Burt bounding into the room. Riley gripped his arm to hold him in place. Brian preemptively wheeled himself into his cousin's path and slapped a hand to his chest.

"Josie! Get in here before Nick kills Griffin!" he yelled.

"You can't kill me before the big interview. Speaking of, shouldn't we be leaving soon? I need at least an hour in hair and makeup."

"What interview?" Riley asked.

"Shit," Nick muttered.

29

Every once in a great while, Nick had a moment that caused him to question his life choices. Like maybe once every twenty years or so.

This was one of those moments.

He and Riley stood behind the camera crew in Griffin and Bella's formal library and watched two vapid narcissists try to out-narcissist each other. Channel 50's darlings, as the network's graphics advertising this special live shit show had dubbed them, were seated on Gentry's white couch, facing an empty chair.

Tyrell "the Terror" Tutley, a former professional football player and Channel 50's veteran sportscaster, was supposed to be occupying the chair, but he was too busy pacing in front of Nick and Riley.

"I usually only report on sports," Tyrell said to them as he dabbed at the sweat on his forehead. "Not murders and shootouts. But the network offered me an extra five hundred bucks to tape this interview, so here I am."

"You'll do fine," Riley assured him.

"It's just I kinda hate these two. But I love sports. And if I don't do a good job with this, I might get fired. Griffin fires a lot of people. Like *a lot*."

"Tyrell, buddy, pal." A guy Nick vaguely recognized from that summer's Channel 50 hostage situation and subsequent accidental bombing bustled up. He had multiple food stains on his shirt, and his hair stuck out in all directions over and around his headset. "We need you to take your seat because this is going to be live in"—he glanced at his watch—"two minutes."

"Don't nervous vomit. Don't nervous vomit," Tyrell chanted as he was led away.

"I don't think my cheekbones look sticky-outy enough," Griffin said, frowning into the hand mirror the makeup artist held for him.

"Is my hair big enough?" Bella asked no one in particular. "It doesn't feel big enough."

Tyrell took his seat and gripped his note cards hard enough to leave sweaty fingerprints behind. "Uh. Right, so I guess we'll start with me asking you about the uh…the body in your backyard. Then you can walk through the shootout and the arrest."

"Staff!" Griffin's high-pitched scream brought his assistant galloping into the room and had Nick reaching for his weapon. Henry dodged his way around a stepladder-wielding guy with a thick silver mustache and backward ball cap.

"Oh, there you are. How's the lighting? Am I tan enough?" Griffin demanded.

"I adjusted it myself to your specifications," Henry assured his boss, pointing toward the studio light above the couch.

Griffin sat back on the couch and emitted a rubbery fart-like sound. "Don't worry, everyone. It's just my butt doughnut for my injured tailbone," he assured the group.

"I want to pop that thing," Nick complained.

"Griffin or the cushion?" Riley asked.

There were too many people in the room, all of them looking vaguely annoyed at having to spend their Sunday afternoon with Griffin. Every single one of them could be a suspect.

"Hey, you with the ladder," Food Stain called as he popped

an antacid in his mouth. "Close that air return up there? We're getting feedback on the boom mic. And, Shirley and Erin, triple-check the teleprompter script. We don't need a repeat of last week's 'Over to you, Smella Goodshine.'"

The aforementioned Shirley and Erin shared a smug look.

"Are your spidey senses tingling?" Nick asked Riley.

"Uh, yeah. Only all of them. I'm starting to think everyone in this room could be our murderer even though I doubt any of them have private-plane money," she said, nose twitching dramatically as she scanned the crew.

"No more taking jobs from ex-husbands."

"Agreed," Riley said on a sigh.

"How about her? Do you recognize her?" He pointed to a woman in a sharp-looking purple suit planted between the two cameras with a direct line of sight to Griffin. She had dark skin and expert eye makeup and had her thick black hair pinned at the nape of her neck in a bun. She was frowning down at the stack of note cards in her hand.

"Live in one minute, people!" Food Stain Guy bellowed.

"I don't recognize her," Riley said. "She could be with the network."

"Only one way to find out," Nick said and headed for the woman in question. "Who are you?" Nick asked her without preamble.

She looked up coolly from her note cards, which looked as though they had a series of emojis on them.

"I'm Rebecca Maylen. Mr. Gentry's attorney. And you are?"

"The guy who's reluctantly trying to keep your client alive. You must sue a lot of people."

She gave him a sharp smile. "My beach house in the Outer Banks is named Gentry Windfall."

Nick rubbed a hand over his stubbly jaw. "Question from one professional to another. How do you get him to pay up?"

"I'm apparently smarter than you, because I followed the money. Griffin's father pays me an embarrassingly large annual retainer to keep his son out of legal trouble. Now if you'll excuse me, I need to make sure my client doesn't make himself look like more of an idiot than usual."

"Good luck with that," Nick said.

Food Stain Guy called for quiet and counted down for the live broadcast, and Nick sidled back over to Riley. He gave her a nudge and mouthed *"lawyer."*

Riley glanced over and frowned, her nose giving a little twitch. "She hates him but loves the money. She'd be annoyed if her meal ticket dropped dead."

"Hello, central Pennsylvania. I'm Tyrell Tutley coming to you live from the home of Channel 50's own darlings, morning news anchor Griffin Gentry and sunshiny weather girl Bella Goodshine, who recently had to go on defense on their home field."

"You know what?" Nick whispered in Riley's ear.

"What?"

"Let's just quit. We'll let Griffin get murdered, sell the house, and move to a beach somewhere. You can wear bikinis all day, and I'll fish for our supper."

Riley snorted, earning a dirty look and a *shush* from a production assistant.

"You've had to step up your defense due to recent happenings off the field," Tyrell continued on set. "Care to break down the play-by-play for our viewers and tell everyone what's been happening?"

"Well, Tyrell," Bella began in her breathy for-the-cameras voice. "It all started on a dreary fall day. It was a high of forty-eight degrees with precipitation."

"We were watching *The Price Is Right* and agreeing that I would be a much better host," Griffin said, glancing toward his lawyer.

Off camera, Rebecca waved her arms and held up a note card with a heart on it. Griffin frowned and cocked his head like a golden retriever with a fur coat full of hair product. The lawyer pointed frantically at Bella. Griffin brightened and reached for Bella's hand. The lawyer held up a smiley face sign.

Nick shot Riley a look. She rolled her eyes ceilingward.

He rolled onto the balls of his feet and took another gander around the room as Griffin and Bella took turns babbling at each other about the body in the backyard. Most of the crew was clumped together at their stations, looking both bored and pissed off.

"I was very brave," Griffin said directly to the camera.

Nick gritted his teeth. *What a fucking asshole.*

Riley elbowed Nick in the gut.

"Ow. What was that for?" he whispered.

"For what you were about to say audibly on live TV. Oh shit—"

"Oh shit what?" he demanded.

Her nose twitched, and she gripped his forearm.

"What have you got?" he asked under his breath.

Her brown eyes took on a glassy sheen as she stared straight ahead. Nick held on to her while he scanned the room again for threats. No one appeared to be making any suspicious moves. There were no menacing gunmen in the windows. The lawyer was holding up a frowny face sign. The producer was inhaling more Tums. One of the camera people was covertly flipping Griffin the bird.

Riley came back in a gasp. "The light!"

It was all she said before launching forward, knocking the producer out of his chair and into one of the camera operators. Nick was on her heels as she lunged onto set. He saw it then as if it were happening in slow motion.

The support wire on the overhead studio light snapped.

Riley dove for the couch and its occupants. Nick reactivated his high school football muscle memory and threw himself after her.

"Keep rolling!" the producer screeched from the floor.

They were both airborne; then the couch was tipping backward as they made contact. Nick heard the surprised cries and felt the whistle of air as the heavy light smashed to the floor, just missing his arm. His body landed on two soft female forms just as glass shattered in an explosive arc, peppering the exposed bottom of the couch with shrapnel.

"Are they dead?" one of the crew asked.

"You guys are supposed to stay *off* camera," Griffin whined from under Riley. "This is my moment to shine. Remember?"

"Are you okay?" Nick demanded.

"No! I think you smeared my makeup," Griffin complained.

"Not you, you idiot. Riley, are you okay?" Nick repeated into the pile of limbs.

"Crushing. Me," she wheezed.

"Me. Too," Bella said in a voice even breathier than usual.

Nick managed to climb off them and helped Riley to her feet. She had a cut on her forehead and a long orange smear of Griffin's makeup down her arm.

"I'm good. I'm fine," she insisted, pulling Bella to her feet.

"Someone tell me we're still rolling," the producer shrieked.

"Still rolling," one of the camera people confirmed, sounding much more excited about the broadcast.

Tyrell was standing on top of his chair, looking like he didn't know whether he should tackle something or run.

Nick and Riley hauled Griffin off the floor. "My suit is all wrinkled, and look what you did to my couch."

"Riley just saved your life, you diminutive fuck," Nick snarled, scanning the room. There were multiple someone's missing, including one of the teleprompter ladies and Griffin's assistant.

"Bleep that in the delay," the producer shouted.

"Bleeping!" someone answered.

Griffin and Bella gaped at the studio light that lay where they'd been seated only seconds before.

Bella let out a low keening wail and started flapping her hands.

"Do *not* start that again," Nick ordered, snatching a box of tissues off the end table that had miraculously remained upright. He pressed a wad of them to Riley's forehead.

The weather girl obligingly clamped one hand over her

mouth and continued to flap the other hand like a baby bird learning to fly.

"You saved my life," Griffin said, looking wide-eyed at Riley. He grabbed her and turned her to face the camera. "Don't worry, America! I'm okay thanks to Riley Thorn and this other guy. They're my bodyguards, and they just saved my life!"

"Griffin, you just faced down death again. Tell me what you were thinking when you were scrambling out of the pocket," Tyrell said, still standing on his chair.

"This interview is over," Nick said, grabbing Griffin by the lapel and drawing his gun. "Let's go."

30

Riley walked into Nick's office with Burt on her heels. She found her boyfriend irritably rearranging suspect photos on his whiteboard. "I told you. He's a raving narcissist who's built an entire interior world where other people don't matter. He's not trying to piss you off. He just legitimately doesn't realize you exist as anything other than a servant," she said, continuing the conversation they'd begun upstairs after the latest attempt on Griffin's life.

"None of that makes me feel any less murdery," Nick complained, glaring at the small bandage on her forehead. Burt snuffled over to the trash can and stuck his head inside.

"Yeah, well, I'm not too happy about it either," she promised, securing an earring to her lobe.

"How's your head?"

She shrugged. "It's fine. I'm just feeling lucky that Bella's nails didn't go lower. I could have lost an eye."

"Listen, Thorn. I've put a lot of thought into this. How about I just murder him?" he said.

Riley put her hands on her hips. "Then we won't get paid."

"But maybe the first murderer will pay us for doing their job for them?"

"I'm not sure that's the way this works," she said.

The desk phone rang shrilly. Burt popped his head up with a sticky note stuck to his muzzle and gave a *woof*.

Nick lifted the receiver, slammed it down, unplugged the phone, and threw it in a drawer. Since the live broadcast, their house and office phones had been ringing off the hook with media and relatives wanting exclusive interviews.

"We don't have to take the girls out," Riley reminded him as he yanked a blank piece of paper out of the printer tray. "They'd be just as happy here with almond butter sandwiches and extra screen time."

On the word *sandwiches,* Burt bolted out of the room and headed in the direction of the kitchen.

"No way," Nick said, scrawling a circle on the paper. "Your nieces already like Gabe better than me. Tonight's my chance to win back some ground."

"I can't believe I'm saying this, but shouldn't we be keeping a close eye on Griffin?"

"Josie has him, Bella, and the dog in a safe house. Weber checked in on them, and Josie's already demanded a raise twice. They're fine. We're going out," he said, slapping the paper to the top of the whiteboard.

"Is that a stick figure?" she asked peering at the drawing.

"No, it's a suspect."

He didn't sound very open to artistic criticism, so Riley wisely changed tactics. "Who is it?"

"Facial Hair Guy." He pointed to the jagged squiggle in the middle of the circle.

"Who?"

Nick sighed and reached for her. "You know what? Gentry has stolen enough time from us. We have the next few hours to be a normal hot couple."

"Well, you *do* look good in those jeans you found on the floor," Riley mused, looping her arms around his neck.

"And you look good in those clothes I'm going to take off you at the first possible opportunity."

The brush of his lips against her neck had her shivering in anticipation. "I like that you like taking clothes off me."

"I'm really good at it. Fast too. Maybe the girls will be late and I can lick—"

On cue, the doorbell rang, echoing through the house. Burt woofed a greeting.

"Hold that thought," Riley said, nipping Nick's lower lip before dancing out of his arms.

———

River, Rain, and Janet were carbon copies of their mother in progressively smaller sizes. They all shared the same dewy brown skin, the same thick natural hair, the same upturned button nose of Wander's biological dad.

The oldest, River, was most like Wander in character. She was calm and patient and, at eight, was already showing signs of her Basil psychic gifts.

Rain, six, had been a furniture-scaling, clothing-rejecting toddler hellion. Montessori school had helped channel some of the energy into an aggressive T-ball career.

Janet, four, was currently teaching herself to read and demanded scientific explanations for all life's mysteries. Her interrogation of the adults around the summer solstice table had successfully ruined Santa, the Easter Bunny, and the Tooth Fairy in one conversation.

"Ladies," Nick said, ushering them inside.

"Hi, Aunt Riley! I like your earrings," River chirped.

"Hi, Aunt Riley. Uncle Nick, can we go to that indoor skydiving place?" Rain demanded as she stormed inside in rain boots.

"Uhhh," Riley said.

"We'll see if we have time after," Nick said smoothly.

"After what?" Janet wanted to know.

Riley was curious herself.

"You'll see," he said with a conspiratorial wink that Riley wasn't sure she trusted.

With a shrug, Janet marched into the foyer after her sisters.

"What are you two up to on your date night?" Riley asked Wander and Gabe.

The happy couple shared a glowy look.

"We're going to the Bibsom Pharmaceuticals open house at their new headquarters," Wander explained.

"Really?" Riley asked. That seemed out of character for her excessively granola sister.

"We will be protesting their corporate practices in front of the building," Gabe explained, beaming proudly as he unrolled a bedsheet with the words *Stop Animal Testing Now* painted on it. "And then we are going for dessert."

"I want dessert," Rain announced from the foyer table she was standing on.

"All part of the plan," Nick promised, plucking her off the marble top.

"About this plan..." Riley ventured.

"I thought I smelled whippersnappers," Mrs. Penny said, exiting the kitchen with a bucket of fried chicken.

"That tofu smells funny," Janet said, frowning at the chicken.

"You know the rules," Wander said firmly to her girls.

"We eat when we're hungry and what we're hungry for, even if it's not something we usually eat at home," the girls chorused.

"Good. And?"

"We try to make the best choices possible, prioritizing health, safety, and fun," they responded.

"Your sister is a way cooler parent than my sister," Nick pointed out.

"We'll drop them off at your place in a few hours. After texting first, of course," Riley said with a smug look in Gabe's direction.

Wander's grin was almost sly. "That would be very much appreciated."

"Okay, ladies or however you choose to identify," Nick began.

River held up a finger and conferred with her sisters. There was a lot of whispering and nodding.

Rain stepped forward. "We have chosen to be identified as unicorn chipmunk skunks."

"I like skunks," Janet announced.

"Nice choice. Now we've got eight minutes to forage for supplies," he said, leading the way into the kitchen.

"What are you doing with the girls?" Wander asked, swapping minivan keys for SUV keys with Riley.

Riley shrugged. "I have no idea. Nick planned the whole evening."

"I can't wait to find out. We'll see you later." Wander linked her arm through Gabe's.

"Have fun chanting rhymes at Big Pharma," Riley said as she walked them to the door and opened it.

"Oh, it's you," said the woman on the front porch.

Nick's sister, Carmela, stood on the welcome mat, looking none too thrilled that Riley had answered the door. On the other hand, her husband, Andy—Riley's old college boyfriend—looked delighted.

"Hey, Riley! Great to see you again. You look good," Andy said. "Really good."

Carmela swiveled on her husband. "Excuse me. I worked my literal ass off to fit into a cocktail dress that cost as much as my first semester of college, and all you said was 'You look nice.'"

"You do look nice," Andy insisted, either unaware of the thin ice bearing his weight or not particularly concerned with it. "How's the psychic investigation thing going?" he asked, turning back to Riley.

"Uh, it's going well." Minus the whole working for her ex-husband and reminding herself what a terrible human being he was. "Is Nick expecting you?"

It was Andy's turn to swivel on his wife. "You didn't call your brother?"

"It slipped my mind. Excuse me for being busy running a commercial real estate empire and raising your child."

Carmela was a pretty, prickly cactus of a woman who was constantly on the lookout for something to be offended by.

Esmeralda, Nick's ten-year-old niece, appeared in the doorway. Her glasses were slipping down her nose, and she hugged a thick hardback to her chest like it was a teddy bear.

"So what was the plan? You were just going to throw Esmeralda out of the car and yell as you drove by?" Andy teased his wife.

"No, I was going to tell Nicky that it's his turn to do something for the family for once—"

"What are you guys doing here?" Nick demanded, leading Riley's three nieces out of the kitchen. Each had child-size tumblers with bendy straws and a personalized baggie of snacks.

"You're watching your niece tonight," Carmela announced, giving Esmeralda a gentle push across the threshold. "We have a thing with Mom and Dad."

Esmeralda looked up, up, up at Gabe as he looked down at her. He smiled and gave a finger-wiggling wave. She gave him a shy smile back and pushed her glasses up her nose.

"Please excuse my wife. She forgot her manners in her other nice cocktail dress," Andy said.

Nick ruffled Esmeralda's hair. "Hey, kid. Long time since we've hung out. Looks like it's ice cream for dinner for us again."

Carmela shoved a giant tote bag into Nick's hands. "There will be *no* ice cream for dinner. *No* learning to play poker. Dinner will consist of a lean protein and *two* vegetables. Esmeralda needs to practice the violin for thirty minutes, and you need to quiz her on her vocabulary words for Wednesday's test. We will be home at precisely nine p.m. You will meet us there, and our daughter will be intact and ready for bed without a stomachache or a sugar rush. I expect proof of life photos every thirty minutes."

"See? Buzzkill," Nick said to Wander and Gabe.

"I don't know if you two have met my sister, Wander, and my friend Gabe," Riley said, trying to recall if Carmela and Andy had shown up at Nick's surprise accidental-orgy birthday party.

"It's great to meet you," Andy said, enthusiastically shaking their hands. "I'm Andy, Riley's college boyfriend, and this is my wife, Carmela. She's Nick's grumpy sister."

"I don't know why I should expect a childless hobbyist to understand the importance of rules, boundaries, and schedules," Carmela said acidly, ignoring everyone.

Nick grinned. "Yet here you are, Carm. Begging a childless hobbyist to take care of *your* kid." He turned to Esmeralda. "No offense, kid. You know I'm pumped to hang with you. I just like giving your mom shit."

Esmeralda didn't quite manage to hide her tiny smile.

"I'm already regretting this," Carmela complained.

"Riley is great with kids. She's supersmart and funny," Andy began.

"Hey, man. You snooze, you lose," Nick warned him.

Carmela had had enough. "Ugh. Fine. Just keep my daughter alive."

Riley had a funny feeling tickling the pit of her stomach. "Where are you guys going?" she asked.

"My firm facilitated the build of the new Bibsom Pharmaceuticals. Mom is one of their guests of honor tonight for her work on Oblituspan."

"It's a new dermal filler that lasts longer than Botox but causes memory problems in sixty percent of the people who use it," Andy added helpfully.

"Didn't there used to be an after-school program for underprivileged kids there before you built a five-story office building and parking lot?" Nick asked his sister.

"What a coincidence! That's where we're going," Wander said. "Would you like to ride with us?"

Carmela skimmed Riley's sister from braids to recycled-tire sneakers. Then she looked at Gabe in his head-to-toe, body-hugging black. "Absolutely not."

"Then we'll see you there," Wander said with a smile.

"You really do look great, Ry," Andy said earnestly.

Nick slammed the door in his brother-in-law's face and tossed Esmeralda's tote bag to the floor. A violin case fell out.

The girls giggled.

Nick clapped his hands. "Okay, unicorn chipmunk skunks, this is my niece, Esmeralda. She's cool and smart. Es, this is River, Rain, and Janet. They're also cool and smart. And we're about to have the best night ever."

It turned out that the best night ever started at Pretty Paula's Nails, a small nail salon crammed into a strip mall between a pet store—their next stop to soothe the sting of not allowing Burt to accompany them—and a tax preparer.

They entered to the strum of a harp and took in the storefront. The interior reminded Riley of a 1980s neon Trapper Keeper.

"Nicky Santiago." The woman Riley presumed was Paula got up from behind the turquoise-tiled desk and opened her arms. Best guess put her in her late fifties. She was tall, even without the platform wedges, and all soft curves and big hair. She wore jewelry like she was a display case, and her nails were talons that looked like they'd render activities like basic hygiene impossible. "Long time no see."

"Heard you went straight. Had to see for myself," Nick said as he returned her hug.

"You kids know this guy?" Paula asked, chewing aggressively on her gum.

All four nieces nodded.

"He's one of the good ones, even if he did try to send me to jail."

"Paula, this is my girlfriend, Riley."

"Girlfriend?" Paula fluttered mile-long lashes and clapped a hand to her impressive chest. "Is Nicky Santiago settling down?"

"They live together too," Esmeralda piped up.

"But they don't have to get married if they don't want to," Rain announced from where she was spinning circles in the chair behind the desk.

"My mom says I can't get married until after my master's degree," Esmeralda said.

"I'm sure there's room for negotiation." Riley patted her sympathetically on the head.

"What are we doing here, Uncle Nick?" River asked, eyeing the bottles of polish with interest.

Nick gestured with a flourish toward a row of leather chairs, each with fancy-looking drinks already in the cupholders and stacks of kid-friendly magazines. "We're getting pedicures."

The gasps were genuine, making Riley grin.

"Are you getting a pedicure too, Uncle Nick?" Esmeralda asked hopefully.

"He sure is," Paula said, clamping her hands on Nick's shoulders, making several pieces of jewelry jingle. She steered him toward the chair in the middle that had a beer in the cupholder.

This news pleased the nieces even more than the initial pedicure announcement. "Yay, Uncle Nick!" all four girls chorused.

"Not cool, Paula. Not cool," Nick muttered under his breath.

"Paybacks, Nicky."

Riley grinned and helped the girls choose their chairs.

"I saw you two on the news today," Paula said. "Everyone's talking about the couch tackle. You're Harrisburg famous…again."

Riley winced. "Thanks?"

Paula clapped her hands, and several nail technicians in bright pink smocks appeared. "Who's ready to pick their color?"

Four little hands shot into the air.

———

"This isn't so bad," Nick said half an hour later as his nail technician applied a second coat of Pixie Dusty Pink to his toenails. The color had won in a unanimous female vote. Nick had his feet propped up on the rim of the tub and his chair massage heads going full speed.

Janet, next to him, did too. "Ahhhhhhhhhhhhh," she said as the chair vibrated her little body against the leather. Her tiny toes were a garish dark purple. Nick told her it looked like she had cute goblin feet, and Janet took that as a compliment.

Esmeralda had gone with a classic French pedicure while River had gone with Call Girl Red—a name Riley had decided not to explain. Rain had gotten a different color on each nail.

"The giggling during the exfoliation was definitely worth it," Riley agreed.

It turned out that Nick Santiago had very ticklish feet, news that had entertained their nieces to no end as he had screeched and cackled every time his nail tech reached for his feet.

"Manly guys can still be ticklish," he insisted, taking a slurp of beer through the purple bendy straw.

"This was really nice of you, Nick," she told him, nodding at their four nieces, who were carrying on several conversations at once.

"Damn right it is," he said, looking at the girls fondly.

The image of the dimpled bad boy holding the cherubic baby on his hip popped into her brain again. Was Ticklish Nick really fatherhood material?

"I think the unicorn chipmunk skunks are having a good time," she observed.

"I am too. I can't believe I've been missing out on stuff like massages and pedicures," he said as the massager kicked into high gear. "No wonder you and Jasmine do this all the time."

"You're welcome to come along next time," Riley offered. "You don't actually have to get color on your nails if you don't want to."

"It probably wouldn't be the worst thing ever to do this with you once in a while. Especially if we pay Hector a visit too," he mused.

Riley admired her own toes. River had insisted she go for Arctic Snowflake Sparkle. Its diamond flecks of glitter reminded Riley of her recent sparkly visions. But if jeweler

Wilfred Peabody wasn't the bad guy, what were her spirit guides trying to tell her?

"Any new leads from Brian and Kellen's background checks?" she asked, lowering her voice.

Nick shook his head. "The deeper we dig, the guiltier everyone looks. I might have to do something drastic."

"How drastic?"

His phone vibrated. He glanced at the screen, smirking before showing it to her.

Mom: Why is your girlfriend's sister protesting at my award night?

Riley groaned. "Your mother is never going to run out of reasons to hate me."

"It's what she does," he said, thumbs flying over the screen.

"What are you saying to her?"

"That you're sorry you couldn't be there with your own sign and you want to know how many beagle puppies her business built its empire on the back of."

"Nick!"

"I'm just kidding."

"Aunt Riley?" Janet piped up from Riley's elbow. "I'm hungry."

"Perfect timing, unicorn chipmunk skunks. Time for dinner," Nick said.

31

"Mom says I have to be exceptional in all things. Normal is for losers," Esmeralda announced from the back of Wander's minivan.

Riley smiled out the window. There had been a time in her own life when she would have sold internal organs for a shot at normal. But after Nick, well, the man had opened her eyes to the delights of an abnormal life.

"No offense, Es, but your mom is full of sh—crap," Nick said.

"Shcrap," Janet repeated gleefully from her booster seat.

"Our mom says we have a responsibility to find out what brings us joy and follow it through life," Rain said, kicking her feet in the air.

"You know what? This is one nieces' night out. Let's not try to undo a lifetime of parenting," Riley suggested.

"Aunt Riley, how many boys or girls have you kissed?" River asked.

Nick's gaze slid to her from behind the steering wheel.

"Why do you ask?"

"I'm considering having my first kiss, but I want to go to an expert for advice."

"Your aunt Riley is an expert kisser," Nick assured River.

Riley's expertise most likely paled in comparison to the legions of women that Nick had kissed. But she *was* pretty confident in her abilities.

"Good. How do you not smash noses?" River asked.

"Ah. Excellent question. You have to tilt your head to one side, and your kissing partner has to tilt their head to the opposite side," Riley explained.

Esmeralda was leaning forward, absorbing the information like it was periodic table flash cards.

River frowned. "How do you know which side to tilt to?"

"Uh…there are a couple of approaches, I guess. You can take charge and tilt first. Or you can wait until they tilt and then tilt the opposite way," Riley explained, wondering how her sister was going to feel about Aunt Riley's Kissing 101.

"Or you can take their chin in your hand and tilt it for them," Nick added.

Riley's cheeks flushed, recalling how he'd kissed her exactly like that…and then they'd gotten naked.

"Yeah, that's good too," she said, adjusting the vent so the air hit her heated face. "Oh, and don't forget to make sure the other person wants to kiss you."

"How do I do that?" River asked.

"You could say, 'You have a kissable face. Mind if I kiss it?'" Rain suggested, ending with several dramatic air kisses.

"Maybe stick with something classic like 'I'd like to kiss you now,'" Nick suggested. Beads of sweat were popping up on his forehead, and Riley could sense a rising panic in him.

"Oh. I was thinking about just running into him with my mouth," River explained.

"Christ," Nick muttered.

"I see where you're coming from, but you could accidentally bite him that way," Esmeralda pointed out. "And it bypasses the whole consent conversation, which is very important."

"Maybe you four unicorn chipmunk skunks should

consider not kissing or dating until college. Wait, no. College was worse," Nick said, swiping a hand over his face.

Riley reached over and put her hand on his leg. "I think that's enough advice for now."

"Thank you for your feedback, fellow unicorn chipmunk skunks," River said.

"Okay, who's hungry?" Nick sounded desperate. He took the turn into the parking lot just fast enough to make the tires chirp.

The car behind them did the same.

"Are you okay?" Riley whispered.

His knuckles whitened on the wheel. "I'm just envisioning them dating. Do you know how disgusting and awkward and stupid teenage boys can be?"

"Yes. Yes, I do. But hopefully today's boys are being raised by parents who prioritize showing them at least how not to be disgusting and stupid. I don't know if they can do anything about the awkward though."

"We must protect them at all costs," he said, looking at the girls in the rearview mirror.

"You know the best way to protect girls from choosing bad partners?" she prompted him.

"Eliminate all contact with men and boys of all ages?" he suggested hopefully.

"No. We show them what good partners and good relationships look like."

Nick nodded as he swiped an arm over his sweaty forehead. "Yeah. Okay. We've got this. We have a few years before River starts dating. I'll get her signed up for self-defense classes. She can have a black belt in something before her first date."

"Are we here?" Janet asked, peering out the window from her booster seat.

"Wow! I've never had Taco Bell before," Esmeralda said, gleefully pressing her face to the window. Her book was long forgotten in the back seat while she and River took selfies with funny Snapchat filters on Nick's phone.

"Are you sure you want to take three mostly vegan and one paleo kid through the Taco Bell menu?" Riley asked.

"It's time for this sacred canon event," he announced like he was the movie voiceover guy. "Besides, it's Wander's car, not ours."

And just like that, Nick Santiago had fully recovered from his parenting panic.

"This is the best night of my life," Esmeralda whispered.

"How do you say no to that?" Nick asked Riley, hooking a thumb at the girls behind them.

Riley responded by rifling through the glove box for vomit bags and fast-food napkins.

"Okay, unicorn chipmunk skunks," Nick called, "I don't have the patience to wait for all of you to figure out exactly what you want so I'm gonna go through the drive-thru, order one of everything, and we'll eat it all on the way to our next stop. Cool?"

"Cool!" they agreed.

"Please tell me the next stop is a living room with a TV next to a bathroom," Riley muttered.

"Everybody shut your mouth holes and let me order."

———

"What are these doughy thingies with the stuff in them?" Janet demanded in a high-pitched voice.

"That, my friend, is a Cinnabon Delight," Nick explained, eyes on the rearview mirror as he headed south on Route 15.

"I want to eat ten of them," Janet announced. "Also, I tooted."

"Me too," River confessed.

"Me three," Rain said.

"Me four," Nick announced.

Riley snickered.

"What? I did," he insisted to the delight of all four nieces. His gaze skated back to the side mirror.

Rain groaned. "I accidentally dropped part of a taco on the floor."

"That's okay. That's why we papered the entire van in napkins," Riley said as Nick took a surprise exit onto Capital City Mall Drive. He was frowning now, gaze glued to the mirror.

"Uh, everything okay?" she asked quietly.

"Remember when you asked me today if we were being followed?"

"Yeah. And we weren't."

"Guess what? Now we are."

She whirled around to see a pair of headlights in the dark behind them. "How long?"

"Since Taco Bell."

"Damn it." They had four kids and eighteen pounds of tacos in the car. This was not an ideal time for a high-speed chase. "What do we do?"

"Text Mrs. Penny."

"You think Mrs. Penny is going to ride to the rescue?"

"I do not. Text her the stupid code word."

It was possible that Nick was overreacting. It could absolutely be a coincidence that the car behind them was still there. But Riley wasn't about to take any chances. Not with their nieces in the car.

Riley: We have a Cold Burrito situation.
Mrs. Penny: I was born ready for Code Cold Burritos. See you at the drop site.

"What's the drop site?" Riley asked.

"The safe house," he said grimly.

A safe house was only safe if they didn't manage to lead the bad guys to it. Riley closed her eyes and somersaulted into Cotton Candy World. She didn't even bother asking the spirit guides for help before casting her mind to the car behind them.

Her nose twitched violently.

"Lesbians?" she said quietly.

"What?" he said.

She opened her eyes. "I don't know. Lesbian energy is all I got."

"My dentist is a lesbian," Janet chimed in.

"That's great, kid," Nick said, eyes on the rearview mirror. "Is Janet's dentist following us?"

"Doubtful. But something about them feels familiar."

"Yeah, like Griffin-Buttface-Gentry suspect list familiar," Nick said, whipping the minivan into a parking lot on their right. "Okay, kids, change of plans. Who likes jumping?"

All the female occupants under the age of ten screamed their assent as the tires squealed.

"What's the plan, Santiago?" Riley demanded while clinging to the handle. The sedan behind them slowed but continued on past the parking lot.

Nick brought the minivan to a screeching halt in front of the commercial building. "Everybody inside."

"Ohhhhh nooooo," Riley moaned as she read the sign. "They just ate Taco Bell, Nick! They can't go in there."

"No choice. Everybody out. You take them inside. I'll be right behind you." He punctuated the words by throwing his wallet at her and dialing his cousin. "Yo, Brian. Same sex couples of the female persuasion on the suspect list. Who've we got?"

Grimly, Riley took the wallet and the four girls, some of whom were still clutching taco wrappers, and guided them through the front door.

Bouncy Boo's was a childless adult's living nightmare.

After paying the astronomical admission, adults and children alike were unleashed into a huge space filled with inflatable obstacles and bounce houses. There was a snack bar, a foam pit, and not nearly enough hand sanitizer to ward off all the different strains of pink eye that were being smeared around.

"Whoa!" Esmeralda whispered in awe.

"Everyone stick together," Riley yelled over the noise of both joyful and tearful screams as she frantically swiped Nick's credit card. She kept her eyes on the door as the dead-eyed teenage attendant slapped wristbands on everyone.

"You look familiar," he said. "Aren't you the girl who tackled the news guy on TV today?"

"No, that was some other poor unfortunate soul," Riley lied.

She had all four girls by various limbs as they each struggled to get free when Nick strolled inside. Several nearby mothers looked up from their e-readers to admire the real-life book boyfriend.

"What are you doing?"

"Making sure no one kidnaps our nieces."

He grinned. "It's fine. Let them play. You and I are going to sit here on this unnaturally sticky bench and watch the front door."

"It's okay, Aunt Riley. I have a good feeling about this," River assured her, patting Riley's arm.

Nick's and River's confidence lowered her stress level enough to release the girls.

"Fine. Be safe. Stick together. Don't let anyone bite you!" she called as the four girls stampeded toward a bounce house shaped like a gigantic squid.

As soon as they disappeared, she smacked Nick on the muscly bicep. "What the hell? I thought we were in danger!"

"At the time, it was a possibility."

"'At the time' was less than three minutes ago," she pointed out. She huffed out a sigh of indignation and sat on the sticky bench. "Yuck."

He slid his arm around her shoulders. "Do you really think I would drive a minivan full of nieces to Bouncy Fucking Boo's if I thought assassins were on our tail?"

"Honestly, with you, it's hard to tell."

"I know who's following us, and the only thing we're in danger of is getting strep throat in this germ factory."

"And if you're wrong?"

"Pfft. I'm never wrong. And we're about to find out just

how not wrong I am." He nodded toward the front door as two women entered.

The first was on the short side with long blunt bangs that brushed the tops of her glasses. She had a peaches and cream complexion and was dressed like a Nirvana fan, with a flannel shirt tied around her waist and ripped gray jeans. The second woman was all long legs and sharp angles with bronze skin. She had a nose ring and an eyeliner cat eye, and wore high-waisted slacks with a David Bowie crop top.

Both of them were frowning. To be fair, most of the adults trapped in the building full of screaming children, spilled soda, and vacant-eyed employees were also frowning.

The moment the women spotted them, Riley felt a punch of recognition from them. "They're definitely here for us."

The women reluctantly paid the teenager at the cash register and accepted their wristbands before walking straight over to their bench.

"We're not attempted murderers," the shorter one announced.

"We're not baby seal clubbers," Nick said.

"Cut the crap," the taller one grumbled.

"Sorry. I thought we were trying out some kind of new small talk," he said.

"Chill out, Betty," the shorter one said, laying a hand on her partner's arm. "Look, we know you're looking at us for the Griffin Gentry attack."

"What makes you think that?" Nick asked.

Betty pulled out her phone and pushed a button.

A familiar voice came out of the speaker. "Yeah, this is Penny PI with Santiago Investigations. You two are suspects in an attempted homicide investigation and are legally required to be interrogated by me and my associates."

There was a fit of coughing.

"Jesus, Willicott. Chew your damn food. Don't inhale it! Anyway. As I was saying, call me back so I can come interrogate you and search your house. Okay. Bye."

Nick sat poker-faced while Riley covered her eyes with one hand.

"Tyra and I wanted to talk to you on neutral ground," Betty said, eyeing the chaos of bouncing children behind them. "And tell you that we had nothing to do with what happened to Gentry."

"So you can call off your geriatric watch dog," Tyra said.

Nick slapped his palms against his thighs. "I don't know about you ladies, but I could go for an Icee. Who wants? I'm buying."

They hit the snack bar and moved from the sticky bench to a stickier table with a view of the foam pit and the inflatable cross-eyed-lizard obstacle course.

"How did you know we were following you? We watched a couple of YouTube tutorials on surveillance. I thought we were doing pretty well," Tyra said as she spooned up a bite of fruit punch Icee.

"You made one rookie mistake. You parked in the Taco Bell lot while we went through the drive-thru, and then you followed us on our way out. Nobody pulls into Taco Bell and doesn't at least get a burrito. You would have been less suspicious if you'd gone through behind us."

"That's what I told you," Betty said, sighing into her piña colada calamity Icee.

"Yeah, but you know what happens to me after I eat too many chalupas," Tyra reminded her.

"Can we rewind for a minute and talk about why you two are on the suspect list in the first place?" Riley asked, setting aside her berry belly blast.

"Gentry told us you had a merchandising dispute," Nick said before slurping up some of his root beer rocket.

Riley saw Rain pause halfway up the inflatable climbing wall to hang by one hand so she could take a bite of the chipotle chicken roll-up she'd squirreled away in her pocket.

The way-too-young-to-be-responsible-for-children's-lives attendant blew his whistle. "No outside food or drink!"

"*Merchandising?*" Betty repeated as if Nick had just said, "Selling kidneys on the dark web."

"Oh my God. I'm gonna kill him. Figuratively, of course," Tyra said quickly.

"Griffin's recollection has historically been a little skewed," Riley said sympathetically.

The couple shared a look. Betty sighed. "We knew Griffin from a few golf tournaments. We played a few rounds with him, had dinner a couple of times. He seemed like a nice, good-looking guy."

"So we asked him for his sperm," Tyra said, cutting to the chase.

Nick choked on his drink.

"It was more like we floated the idea," Betty explained. "We wanted to have kids, and we didn't want to go through a sperm bank, so we had a list of men we knew who seemed somewhat normal."

"He said yes. Immediately," Tyra said, picking up the story. "We were ecstatic."

"I bought a frigging onesie," Betty put in.

"And a crib," Tyra added.

"Yeah, but I'm trying to make myself sound more stable. You were so grateful you built that lean-to thing in his backyard over that god-awful naked statue that he never paid you for."

Tyra blew out a breath. "Fine. We were both unstably grateful. About a month after he said yes, we get this letter in the mail from his lawyer stating that our 'transaction' fell under Griffin's trademarked branding and that we could license his sperm for $500,000."

Riley's spoon slipped from her fingers and hit the floor. "Half a million dollars for his *sperm*?"

"What's sperm, Daddy?" asked a little boy who was being dragged away from the claw machine by an aggrieved man in flannel.

"Ask your mother."

"The agreement also included clauses about allowing him

to borrow the offspring for public appearances if said offspring was deemed attractive enough," Betty said. "We'd told our family and friends. We'd spent a butt-ton of money on baby stuff. We'd picked out names. One of them was even Griffin."

Tyra rubbed her temples. "I just can't believe we even considered him to be baby daddy material. I mean, what a fucking dumbass."

"The baby would have been born with a mirror in one hand and a selfie stick in the other," Betty agreed.

"One second," Nick said, getting to his feet. "Esmeralda! Let the kid out of the headlock. He didn't push you. He tripped."

"That's awful. I'm so sorry that happened to you," Riley said.

Nick sat back down. "Sorry about the yelling and the Gentry-being-an-opportunistic-sphincter thing."

"Look, do we have a reason to hate Griffin?" Betty asked.

"Absolutely," Tyra said.

"But we didn't hire some contract killer to take him out." Betty said.

"We don't have the budget for that. I work for a general contractor, and Betty is a fourth-grade teacher. We do okay, but not pay-for-murder okay, and day care is crazy expensive."

"We know this because we have two kids in it," Tyra said, smiling for the first time.

Betty linked fingers with her wife. "A year after Griffin tried to license his sperm to us, we adopted a brother and sister out of foster care. The minute we saw them, we knew it all happened for a reason. Those kids were meant to be ours."

"We're thrilled to be parents to our babies. But I would like to reiterate that we legit do not have the money to pay for a hit man. And even if we did, if I wanted to ruin Griffin's life, I wouldn't kill him. I'd kidnap him and do laser hair removal on his scalp and eyebrows," Tyra said wistfully.

"You're muddying the *we're innocent* waters, babe," Betty warned her.

Tyra winced. "Sorry."

"Okay. So there you have it. You can subpoena our finances and our phone records, but that's just going to be a waste of your time and ours, and the hassle will just piss us off more than having to waste our one date night a month on tracking you guys down," Betty said.

"I appreciate you talking to us. And my apologies for my elderly business partner," Nick said.

"She gets a little aggressively overzealous," Riley explained.

Betty waved away the apology. "Believe me. We understand. We have Mrs. Sapperstein next door. She's eighty-six and tried to open a marijuana dispensary in her garage."

Nick leaned across the table. "Listen to me very carefully. Whatever you do, do *not* let her move in with you."

"Aunt Riley! Esmeralda just threw up in the foam pit!" Janet yelled.

―――――

"You didn't call Brian until after we pulled into the parking lot," Riley said, breaking the silence in the vehicle and broaching the subject that had bothered her since before Esmeralda had spewed her dinner everywhere.

They had dropped off their little vomit queen eight minutes late and had to listen to Nick's sister's rant about timeliness and responsibility, which made them half an hour late dropping off Wander's daughters.

"That was a big risk," she continued.

"It was a minimal risk," he countered. "I pulled in *after* your vision."

She looked at him and frowned. "You made a potentially life-threatening decision based entirely on my blurry psychic vision?"

"You're good at what you do. I trust your visions like I trust Brian's backdoor research, Josie's knife-throwing skills, and my right cross. If we were in real danger, you would have felt it, and you would have told me."

Riley felt a little glow in her belly that had nothing to do with the Cheesy Gordita Crunch. "You don't think it's weird… or that I'm weird?"

"You're the most powerful psychic in a long line of psychics. What kind of guy would I be if I didn't respect that?"

Griffin Gentry, Riley realized. That was what kind.

"Six tacos," she said, changing the subject. "I thought your sister was going to set you on fire when you told her Esmeralda had thrown up six tacos in the foam pit."

"Heh. Kid's definitely got the Santiago appetite." Nick's half smile was illuminated in the glow of the dashboard.

"We were doing really well up until that point," she mused.

"Are you kidding? We kicked ass tonight. I got high fives *and* hugs from all three of your nieces," Nick pointed out. "They barely said a word to—what's that big shiny dome at Epcot called?"

"Spaceship Earth?" Riley supplied.

"That's the one. They barely said a word to Spaceship Earth when we dropped them off."

"To be fair and accurate, two of the three of them were asleep. Do you believe we are in a competition for the affection of children?" Gabe asked from the back seat of Nick's SUV.

"Of course not," Riley said.

"Yes," Nick countered.

"Besides your wonderful girlfriend, your life must be very meaningless," Gabe observed.

"Anyway, as I was saying before Spaceship Earth Loser of Children's Affection interrupted, I think we did great. All four kids are still alive, and they all said it was the best night ever."

"Six tacos. A medium-speed chase with potential suspects. A foam pit full of vomit."

"That cleaning fee is definitely going on Gentry's tab."

Riley was about to argue when she realized they were heading in the wrong direction.

"Why are we crossing the river?" she asked with a sinking feeling.

"It's because of the Code Cold Burrito," Nick said as if that explained everything.

"What does a cold burrito have to do with crossing the river, Nick?"

She knew it before he made the turn up the hill she was hoping he wouldn't. "Nooooo. Nick! I've had a really long day. I don't have the energy to pretend to be nice when someone is aggressively passive-aggressive to my face."

32

Hello, Riley. So nice of you to move your family tree of progressively weirder guests into my home without giving me a choice," Dr. Marie Santiago said coolly when she opened the front door of her home.

Riley didn't think it would go over well if she pointed out that she wasn't actually related to any of them.

"What's the matter, Ma? Wasn't your trophy big enough tonight?" Nick asked, pressing a perfunctory kiss to his mother's cheek as he walked past her into the house.

"It wasn't a trophy, Nicholas. It was a crystal award."

"You did say it was kinda small," Nick's dad, Miguel, piped up from behind Marie's shoulder.

Marie sent her husband a withering look that he seemed completely immune to. "I'm not someone fazed by the size of my award—"

"Yes, you are," Nick and Miguel said together.

"What *does* bother me is the half dozen protesters chanting nonsense at the attendees from outside and then coming home to discover my *son* told a battalion of strangers where we keep the spare key and invited them to move in with us."

"You had already said yes to Gentry. I figured what's a

couple more bodies? Besides, it's just for one night. Four tops," Nick called over his shoulder as he dragged Riley inside.

"Oh God," Riley muttered. She didn't think she could survive one night under this roof, let alone four. She'd have to take matters into her own hands and murder Griffin herself just so it would all be over.

"Hello, Gabriel. It's nice to see you without your accusatory bed linens," Marie said crisply.

Gabe either didn't get the sarcasm or had graduated to the level of pretending not to get the sarcasm. "Thank you for inviting me into your home, Dr. Santiago," he said, taking her hand in both of his. "It is lovely to see you outside the yoga studio."

Riley decided she needed to take a page out of Gabe's book and become immune to Marie's caustic wit.

"What'd he say?" Miguel demanded in a half shout.

"Ugh. I can't even with you right now, Miguel," Marie said. "And you!" She turned back to Nick.

"What did I do?" he asked, feigning innocence.

"Why couldn't you date Claireabell Stewart's daughter. She's an ophthalmologist. I have her number, and unlike *some others*, I doubt that she would ever need to use your parents' home *as a safe house*," Marie screeched, looking directly at Riley.

Riley pointed at herself. "Me?"

"First of all, Ma, Claireabell Stewart's daughter isn't an ophthalmologist anymore. I served her the papers in the lawsuit that took away her license for trying to make meth in her practice's break room."

"An ex-doctor is still better than a current psychic."

"Second," Nick continued, ignoring his mother, "I'm in love with Riley Freaking Thorn, and if you can't deal with that, you and me are going to have a big problem."

"Remember when your parents didn't want you dating me, Marie?" Miguel said, wading into the conversation again.

"That was entirely different. My parents were uptight

snobs who were more concerned about appearances than their child's happiness."

Nick looked at Riley and gave her a palms-up shrug. "I mean, she opened the door. I can't *not* walk through it."

"You really can. I believe in you," Riley insisted. Her head hurt and not just from her heroic head wound.

"Quick question, Ma. Are your parents the pot or the kettle in that scenario?" Nick asked his mother.

"Excuse me," a familiar voice piped up. "Can someone get me a sparkling water, a refrigerated eye mask, and an aloe plant? I prefer my aloe straight from the source."

"I wish I had a foam pit to vomit in," Riley said as a silk-pajamaed Griffin came into view.

"And I sleep better with the temperature set to sixty-five degrees. That's American, not Canadian degrees," Bella said, appearing next to him. She was wearing a pale purple negligee with fur at the bodice and hem and holding her dog…which had on a matching outfit.

"Are those real rabbit tails?" Nick wondered out loud.

Marie's demeanor underwent an abrupt change. "Of course, Griffin. Right this way. I keep an aloe plant in my home office."

"I'm Bella," Bella said, curtsying in her nightgown.

"Yes, dear. I know. I'm Dr. Santiago. We met an hour ago and then again when I showed you to your room."

"Oh, silly me! I thought that was the housekeeper."

Marie paused to study the lingerie-clad weather girl. "You're not by chance getting Oblituspan injections, are you?"

Bella blinked. "I don't remember."

Marie slipped her arms through Griffin's and Bella's. "Let's go get that aloe and take a peek at your prescriptions."

"I don't suppose you provide dermal filler injections in bed for special VIP guests, do you?" Griffin asked as they headed down the hall.

"I'm a chemical engineer and executive, so no," Marie said.

"Your mother gave them the guest room and forbade me from giving you the second guest room. She made me take the mattress off the frame and put it in the garage," Miguel told them. "So you two have to sleep in the basement."

"That sounds about right," Nick said. "We'll be back up for booze and snacks, Dad."

"The blintzes will be ready in ten minutes. Don't tell your mother," Miguel said loud enough that most of the neighborhood knew about the blintzes.

Nick led Riley and Gabe to the basement door and ushered them through.

"Nick?"

"Riley."

"Why are we here?" she hissed as they descended the carpeted stairs.

"Because someone out there is still trying to whack Gentry."

"Someone has been trying to whack him for days. Why do we have to sleep in your parents' basement?"

"Because that human bucket of hair products made sure the entire viewing area knows we're investigating, which officially makes us targets too. If our new LGBTQ-plus friends found us that easily tonight, imagine how fast another professional killer will do the same."

Riley came to an abrupt stop on the last step. Nick barreled into her, almost knocking her down, but Riley barely noticed.

The Santiagos' basement lounge was buried under elderly people in sleeping bags.

"Welcome to the sleepover," Fred said, adjusting his bedtime toupee, which was attached to a striped night cap. He was stretched out at the foot of the fold-out couch.

"This is stupid, and I hate it," Josie said, arms crossed on the couch.

Mrs. Penny, in an extra-large Ludacris T-shirt and plaid pajama pants, was wedged between Josie and Brian with headphones on and a game controller in her hand. She and Brian appeared to be battling against snot-slinging trolls on screen.

Lily popped up into a seated position from her Hello Kitty

sleeping bag on an air mattress near the patio doors. She had curlers in her hair, and this time it was a blue mask on her face. "I saved you a spot right next to me, Nick," she said with a wink.

"I am delighted to be part of this sleepover," Gabe announced.

"We sewed two sleeping bags together for you. But we couldn't find your jammies, so I guess you'll just have to sleep au naturel," Lily said to him, batting her eyelashes coquettishly.

"I'm going to sleep in the car," Riley decided. But Nick's hand on her shoulder held her in place.

"Sorry, Thorn. No one goes out by themselves."

"I'll sleep with your girlfriend in a car far away from here," Josie volunteered.

"Can it, Chan. We're sticking together...and taking shifts upstairs to make sure no one breaks in and finishes the job on Griffin," Nick added. "My mother will kill me if henchmen get blood on the carpet."

Riley covered her face with her hands. "This is the worst night ever."

He pulled her in for a hug. "Look at it this way. It's either this or air mattresses in your parents' backyard."

"Yes. I'd rather do that. I don't even need an air mattress. I'll sleep on the cold, damp, chicken-infested ground."

"Come on, baby. How bad could it be?"

———

"Oh my God. *Seriously?* Was that an air mattress or another fart?" Nick demanded, punching his pillow into submission.

"Does it even matter at this point?" Riley asked wearily through the blanket she had pulled up over her nose and mouth.

It was four in the morning. Josie had just relieved Nick in the guarding of Griffin's bedroom door, and Riley hadn't gotten a wink of sleep yet.

The only basement resident who seemed to be sleeping soundly was Burt. The dog had wriggled his way up between

Nick and Riley, turning himself into a canine wedge. His cold wet nose was nuzzled against Riley's chin.

"Just try to get some sleep," she told Nick. "You're grumpier than usual on no sleep."

"I'm never grumpy. I'm a fucking ray of goddamn sunshine."

The door at the top of the stairs opened, and she heard the scamper of feet. Griffin appeared, hugging a pillow to his chest.

"Can I sleep with you guys?" he asked. "Bella snores."

"You've got to be shitting me," Nick groaned into his own pillow.

Mr. Willicott popped up from his air mattress. "Someone say *waffles?*"

"No one said *waffles!*"

"Stop yelling, Nick," Riley yelled.

Fred sat up. His toupee was askew across his forehead and one eye. "What's all the ruckus? Did the murderer get in yet?"

"No. But I might decide to do them a solid and finish the job myself," Nick said.

"How did you get past Josie?" Riley asked her ex-husband.

"She was in the kitchen eating peanut butter and growling like a bear," Griffin explained. Apparently tired of waiting for an invitation, he stepped on Riley, Burt, Nick, and Mr. Willicott to get to the couch. "This is nice," Griffin said, settling himself under the covers next to Brian, who had worn his gamer headphones to bed.

The basement went silent again. Nick punched his pillow again. Burt grumbled happily in his sleep.

"My night nanny used to sing lullabies to me. Do any of you know any Polish lullabies?"

"That's. It." Nick sprang to his feet.

Ferp went the air mattress.

"Oh my. Did someone stinker?" Lily asked with a giggle.

"It was the *air mattress*," Nick barked.

Burt woke and added his own half-hearted bark to the conversation directly into Riley's ear.

"Would you people please keep it down? My pregnant wife

is trying to—" Brian ripped off his headphones and eye mask, then screamed.

"Hi, bed buddy," Griffin said, wiggling his fingers in a friendly wave.

"Where's my wife, and why am I in bed with a man?" Brian asked.

"She's upstairs foraging through my parents' pantry, and don't act like this is the first time you woke up next to a dude."

"It's the first time since college," Brian insisted.

The patio door slid open, and everyone screamed. Nick pulled his gun out from under his pillow and pointed it.

"What's all the racket?" Mrs. Penny strolled inside from the lower patio. She held two pizza boxes and a greasy paper bag.

"Where the hell were you?" Nick demanded. "What part of 'Nobody leaves this house' didn't you understand?"

"Relax, Screamy McYelly Guy. I ordered DoorDash and met them in the driveway. I didn't see any murderers."

"Someone say *waffles*?" Mr. Willicott asked again.

"No, but I got two heartburn-lover pizzas and twenty-two jalapeño poppers," Mrs. Penny said.

"Brian," Nick said through clenched teeth.

"Yeah?" Brian yawned.

"I need you to get in your chair and get ready to go."

"Go where? Those poppers sound pretty good."

"We're gonna catch a murderer."

———

"You can't leave me here," Riley said, following Nick outside into the dark as he wheeled Brian onto the basement patio. Burt jogged off to the closest flower bed and relieved himself on a bush.

"Relax. No one is going to try to murder Griffin at my parents' house. And if they do, Josie will murder them first," Nick insisted.

"No. Not that. You can't leave me here with your parents. Specifically your mother."

He turned around in the dark and cupped her face. "You've been chased. You've been shot. You've been abducted. You almost drowned in a fountain *and* got blown up in a news studio. You can handle my mother."

She was already shaking her head. "See, that's where you're wrong. I can't handle your mother. She reminds me of my grandmother, only my grandmother has to love me. Your mother is still trying to set you up with other women *in front of me.*"

"And I am trusting you to deal with her in whatever capacity you want while I go catch a murderer so we can get some fucking sleep in our own house."

"But why can't I go with you? You know I hate missing out on cool PI stuff." Riley kicked at the patio tile with her socked foot.

"Because you are the smartest, most reasonable, most responsible adult in this entire house. And I need you to make sure that Griffin and Bella and all the other pains in my ass stay on lockdown until I tell you it's safe."

She'd been wanting more responsibility, but she definitely hadn't anticipated it involving more quality time with Marie Santiago.

"You'd tell me if you were just avoiding everyone inside this house by pretending to track down a killer, right?" she asked.

"One hundred percent. And for the sake of honesty, that's exactly what I would be doing if I didn't actually have a plan."

"It would be nice if you'd let me in on this plan of yours."

"It's more like a hunch than a plan. But if it pays off, you're going to be so impressed with me, you'll institute Naked Tuesdays."

The man was confident. She'd give him that.

"I need you to say, 'Yes, Nick,'" he insisted.

"Fine. Yes, Nick. I won't let anyone leave, and I'll try not to let them maim or kill each other," she said.

"That's my girl." He grabbed her by the front of her shirt

and yanked her in for a hard kiss before pulling back. "I promise you by tonight, everything will be good."

"Tonight? That's more than twelve hours from now!"

But Nick was already pushing Brian through the yard and around the side of the house. "Naked Tuesdays, Thorn!"

"Tell my wife I was kidnapped by my cousin," Brian called over his shoulder.

33

Riley passed Josie in the hallway of the Santiago home. She was holding a long sharp knife and a mixing bowl of chicken salad in one hand. Riley was armed with a stun gun and pepper spray. They exchanged curt nods and no words.

They'd been on high alert since Nick and Brian had left early that morning. High alert and high annoyance.

"I hate this house. I hate this chicken salad. I hate these shoes. This isn't even my favorite knife."

Riley sighed at Josie's internal hate list.

Part of being on high alert meant she'd lowered her shields to make sure she caught even the slightest whiff of incoming danger. Unfortunately, this also meant she had a front row seat to everyone's inner monologues. If she had to hear Lily compare Griffin's and Gabe's butts one more time, she was going lock the woman in Marie's linen closet.

"Driveway is clear," Mrs. Penny said, peering through the blinds with Miguel's bird-watching binoculars from her perch on the writing desk under the living room window. All the items that had previously called the desk home were in a broken tangle on the floor.

Thankfully, Miguel and Marie had both gone off to work

that morning to maintain the illusion of normalcy in case anyone happened to be watching their house. It was unlikely given the fact that they lived in a gated community with its own overzealous security team. But Riley wasn't about to point that out if it meant that Nick's mom would stay to continue her merciless siege on Riley's already fragile self-esteem.

Griffin and Bella had called into work sick and spent the morning critiquing their Channel 50 substitutes on the news.

A deep baritone "*Ohmmmmmmmmmmmm*" blasted her, and her gaze automatically found Gabe.

He and Griffin were sitting on the couch in the living room. Griffin was verbally issuing a timeline of all the awards he'd won in his lifetime. Gabe, to his spiritual guide credit, was staring blankly and apparently chanting loudly enough internally so as not to listen.

Bella was sitting on the floor having a conversation with her dog and Burt while she painted their nails. Burt gave Riley the side-eye when she passed the doorway. She gave her dog a sympathetic shrug before moving on.

"Another golf cart!" Mr. Willicott barked from the dining room window that overlooked the backyard.

"It's the same golf cart. It's neighborhood security," Josie explained grumpily for the third time.

On cue, Riley's phone signaled a text.

Neighborhood Security: Perimeter is clear. See you in 15.

The gated neighborhood's golf cart–driving full-time security officer had little to do besides enforce HOA ordinances and had embraced Nick's request for frequent drive-bys.

She stepped into the dining room, making a note to find the glass cleaner and remove all of Mr. Willicott's face smudges from the windows. "Did Brian tell you anything about what he and Nick are up to?" Riley asked Josie desperately.

"Nope. Which means either they're busy doing whatever

it is they're doing, or he fell asleep. In which case I will put fire ants in his boxers."

Pregnant Josie was even more bloodthirsty than regular Josie.

Lily and Fred marched into the room and saluted Riley. "Per your orders, the lunch dishes are cleaned up as is the accidental olive oil spill in the basement," Fred reported.

"Great," Riley said dryly.

"Also two of the four toilets in the house are clogged, but no bad guys have breached the perimeter yet," Lily added.

Riley pinched the bridge of her nose. "Fabulous. See what you two can do about the toilets. Oh, and can you clean Mr. Willicott's face prints off the windows?"

They saluted again. "Aye, aye, captain," Fred barked.

Griffin scuttled past the doorway with his phone to his ear. "My credit card number? Okay. Hang on. Let me find my wallet."

Riley abandoned the Bogdanovich twins and followed Griffin into the guest room. He and Bella had packed five suitcases of clothing and beauty supplies.

"What are you doing?" she demanded, stepping over a bag full of hair products.

Griffin beamed at her. "I won a special award for Best White Teeth on Morning TV. They need my credit card number so they can ship my trophy."

Riley snatched the phone out of his hand. "Hello?"

But the caller had disconnected.

"How exactly did you find out you won this award?" she asked with what little remaining patience she had.

"I got a message on a dating app," Griffin said.

She counted backward from ten slowly. "Okay. First of all, why are you on a dating app? You're engaged."

"Oh. It's an old profile from this summer," he said with a dismissive wave.

"You were engaged this summer."

He smiled coyly. "I was? Oopsie."

"Whatever. Moving on. Why would a legitimate organization be contacting you through a *dating app* instead of your work email or your agent or your lawyer to tell you that you won an industry award?"

Griffin patted her arm like she was a child. "Business is done on the apps these days. It's not like it was ten years ago when you were in your prime."

"How have you not been murdered yet?" Riley wondered out loud.

"Just lucky I guess."

"Show me the message," she said, handing his phone back.

She rolled her eyes over Griffin's shoulder as he scrolled through a full inbox of DMs from "sexy singles" before opening a message. "Here it is. Completely legitimate," he said.

Riley ran her tongue over her teeth. "This message is signed by Mimi Mappenberger."

He nodded vigorously. "Uh-huh. She's the award lady."

"Her username is PaybaxRHail."

"Mine is FamousTallnRich," he said proudly.

"Griffin, Mimi Mappenberger—the woman you were going to give your credit card information to—is Kiki Knappenberger. You cheated on her five years ago."

He pursed his lips and tried to furrow his brow. "Hmm. Doesn't ring any bells. You'll have to be more specific."

"You cheated on her, and she started the Griffin Gentry Sucks Support Group, which meets once a month to discuss all the ways you've screwed people over."

He gasped. "Griffin Gentry Sucks? Why would anyone say something so mean?"

"Why would a grown man go through life selfishly taking what he wants from people and then discarding them?"

"Are you saying I'm not getting a trophy for my teeth?"

"No, Griffin. You're not getting a trophy for your teeth."

Riley's phone vibrated, and she yanked it out of her pocket. It was a call from Nick.

She pointed at Griffin. "Do not answer any calls, texts, or messages until I say it's okay."

He grinned and tried to slide an arm around her waist. "You just want me all to yourself, don't you?"

She knocked the wind out of him with a swift elbow to the gut, then answered her phone.

"Please tell me you caught the bad guy and I can leave these people to destroy your parents' home," Riley said by way of a greeting.

"Almost, babe. I need you to do something for me."

"Anything."

"It's probably dangerous," he cautioned.

"As long as it's dangerous outside this house, count me in."

———

"Yay! My house," Griffin said, bouncing in the back seat when Riley parked Nick's SUV in front of his place. "I love my house. I can take a shower with my expensive shower gel and style my hair with my expensive sculpting mousse. Then I'm going to put on an expensive fresh suit and eat something yummy for lunch that someone else makes for me."

"Why are there so many cars here?" Josie frowned. The driveway and most of the cul-de-sac were lined with vehicles.

"Maybe they're throwing a surprise party for me," Griffin suggested hopefully.

"Who's *they*?" Riley asked as they got out of the vehicle.

"I don't know. The worker people who do stuff for me? Maybe they were worried about me after I almost heroically died yesterday."

"I doubt that," Josie muttered not far enough under her breath.

The front door opened, and Nick sauntered outside.

"What's going on, Nick?" Riley asked.

"You'll see," he said with the patented Nick Santiago charm.

"No. You'll tell us before we walk in there, because we've spent the last thirteen hours suffering mental and emotional torture," Josie said, stepping up until her nose nearly brushed Nick's sternum.

"Okay. Geez. I'm Thin Manning the case."

Josie looked at Riley.

Riley looked at Nick. "You didn't…"

His smug grin delivered both dimples. "Oh, but I did. Come in and see for yourself," he said, gesturing them inside.

"What's Thin Manning?" Josie asked as they headed toward the back of the house, where a disgruntled ruckus was in full swing.

"I'm scared to guess because if it's what I think it is…" They turned the corner and entered Griffin and Bella's library. "Oh, hell."

It was what Riley thought it was going to be.

All their top suspects and a few of their unlikely ones were seated in neat rows on the folding chairs Nick had insisted on buying.

Josie whirled around to face Nick, who was grinning. "Did you seriously put every suspect we have in the same room and then have us deliver the guy at least one of them is trying to murder?"

"Pretty much. Yeah."

Josie nodded. "Cool. I like it." She waved to Brian, who was across the room next to the patio doors with his laptop plugged into Griffin's TV.

Griffin strutted into the room. "Surprise for me! Thank you, everyone, for throwing me this special party."

The crowd went silent, and then someone started booing. In less than five seconds, the entire room was booing Griffin.

"Um, Nick?" Riley said.

Nick stopped booing. "Yeah?"

"I'm not sure this was a good idea."

"It's a great idea. Trust me." He glanced around the room. "But, uh, just in case things go slightly south, I want you to stick close to me. And if things go really far south, hit the floor and crawl out the front."

"I never should have gotten you those movies," she said.

Nick cupped his hands. "Everybody shut up," he shouted over the booing.

"Are they saying *woo* or *boo*?" Griffin asked with a frown.

The booing continued until Nick climbed up on the coffee table. "Listen, people! The sooner you shut up, the sooner we can all get out of here."

Josie and Riley exchanged looks and took a step in front of Griffin.

"You might start with why you gathered us all here," Griffin's next-door neighbor Belinda said. She had a margarita in hand.

Claudia Mendoza, Channel 50's ex–news anchor, leaned in. "Where did you get the booze?"

"I brought it from home."

"Smart," Claudia said.

"You're all here because someone is trying to kill Griffin Gentry," Nick announced.

The room finally went quiet as the suspects started giving one another sidelong glances.

"Kiki Knappenberger," Nick said, pointing at the GGS founder, who was casually going through Griffin's desk drawers.

Everyone gasped.

"What?" Kiki asked. Dressed in tight jeans and a designer top, she didn't look the least bit concerned about being named a suspect.

"Five years ago, Gentry cheated on you. And you never got over it," Nick said.

"I wouldn't say *that*."

"You started a Griffin Gentry Sucks Support Group and have been stalking him and pranking him for years," he pointed out.

"She just tried catfishing him for his credit card number less than an hour ago," Riley added.

"Great. She's the almost murderer. Can the rest of us go home now?" Chupacabra asked. She was wearing a violet workout set and doing squats next to the last row of chairs.

"Ah, Chupacabra Jones," Nick said.

"Damn, that's a great name," someone whispered.

"You just so happened to sign on as Bella Goodshine's personal trainer mere weeks after your second cousin lost his limo driving job thanks to Griffin Gentry."

Chupacabra paused in the bottom of the squat. "It's a coincidence."

"Yeah. I don't believe in them," Nick said. "Especially not when you and your cousin have been meeting with Bret Michaels."

The crowd gasped.

"Not the Poison one. The lawyer one," Nick said. He pointed to his cousin. "Brian, fire it up."

The TV turned on to reveal a photo of the personal trainer entering a building.

"I believe this is you, Chupacabra Jones, and your cousin with a substantially less cool name walking into the law offices of Bret Michaels. You took this job to get access so you could gather evidence for your cousin's countersuit against Gentry," Nick said.

Chupacabra stood up and crossed her arms, making her biceps bulge. "So what? The dude committed insurance fraud. I'm just evening the score."

"Good for you," Kiki said, flashing her a double thumbs-up.

"But what are the odds that your family's pockets can outlast Griffin's legal budget?" Nick asked. "Maybe your lawyer bills were adding up, and you were still no closer to bringing your nemesis to justice. So you decided to bring him to justice on your own."

Another gasp rose up from the gathered suspects.

"Just a side note. You guys might want to hold the gasps for the end, or you're gonna hyperventilate," Nick suggested.

Chupacabra's nostrils flared. "Bull. Shit. You better watch what you're accusing me of, Santiago."

Griffin poked his head over Riley's and Josie's shoulders. "I don't like this surprise party. Where are the balloons and the ice cream cake?"

"Oh my God. Here," Josie said, fishing a handful of gummy dick packets out of her pocket. "Eat these and shut up."

"Oooh! Trophy candy!"

"Who's next?" Nick asked, scanning the crowd.

Wilfred Peabody, the jeweler, shifted uncomfortably on an overstuffed ottoman and avoided eye contact. Betty and Tyra, the adoptive moms, were next to him.

"I don't know about the rest of you, but *I* don't have time for this," Claudia announced, hitching her purse up her shoulder. "I've got real news to cover at Channel 49."

"Claudia Mendoza, ladies and gentlemen. Claudia was originally a morning news anchor for Channel 50 until Gentry's father gave her the ax and put his son in her chair. Isn't that right, Claudia?"

She snorted. "That's old news. I've moved on. I don't even think about Griffin anymore."

Nick winced theatrically. "I wish I could believe you. I really do. But then how do you explain this?" He pointed to the TV screen, where a blurry photo of Claudia sitting behind the wheel of a vehicle in a parking lot appeared.

Riley recognized Mr. Willicott's artistry in the blurriness and crooked composition.

"You've got me. It's true. I drive my own car," she said acidly.

"I guess you also do your own vandalism?" Nick asked.

A series of slightly less blurry photos appeared on the screen. Griffin pulling into a handicapped parking space in the same parking lot. Griffin and Bella exiting the car. Claudia, now wearing sunglasses and a ball cap, approaching their empty vehicle. And finally Claudia scraping her keys down the driver's-side door of the shiny red sports car.

The suspect in question shrugged carelessly. "He parked in a handicapped spot. He's an asshole and deserved to have his car keyed."

"Very true," Nick agreed. "Where did you spend Christmas last year?"

She frowned at the change in questioning. "With family in Colombia. Why?"

"This tidbit hasn't been released to the public yet, but these two men who chased Gentry down and shot at him?" He pointed at the new picture on the screen. "They were contract killers extradited to Colombia after their arrests on charges of murder."

"That's like saying, 'Gee, I know you went to kindergarten in Texas. You must know my third cousin Fred in San Antonio,'" Claudia said in a mock baritone. She crossed her arms and drummed her fingernails on her biceps. "If you're seriously suggesting all Colombians know each other or that I had anything to do with this, you're as dumb as your client."

"What I'm suggesting is you have as good a motive as anyone else in this room."

"Then you're a dumbass," she muttered.

"We'll see about that," he said before turning away from her.

"Is it smart for a small business to piss off local media?" Josie wondered.

"I guess we'll find out," Riley whispered back.

"Henry Wu," Nick called.

"Who?" Josie asked.

"Him," Riley said, pointing at Griffin's assistant, who was trying to blend in with a large potted palm.

"Uh. Present. I guess," Henry said.

"As Gentry's personal assistant, you have access to the house. In fact, you're the one who let all of us in. Isn't that true?"

"Yeah. I guess."

"And as Gentry's personal assistant, how much money do you earn?"

Henry looked around as if searching for an escape. "Well, nothing so far. I'm an intern. My parents think internships are character building."

"Even though you're on call twenty-four seven? Even though you missed your grandmother's seventy-fifth birthday party to capture a spider that turned out to be a set of fake eyelashes on Gentry's bathroom floor? Even though you had to cancel the date you finally landed with the hot guy from the gym because your boss needed you to mop up the barbecue sauce he spilled all over the kitchen floor on a Saturday night?"

Tyra and Betty shook their heads and tut-tutted. "You're a monster," Betty said to Griffin.

Riley was in agreement.

Griffin's mouth was too full of gummy candy dicks to respond.

"You got payback though, didn't you? Starting with the chest waxing," Nick said, pointing at the TV.

A photo of Griffin's hot-pink G appeared.

Titters of laughter rose up. Henry looked down at his feet and shoved a hand through his hair.

"But pranks weren't enough, were they? You personally adjusted the studio light that fell during Gentry's interview, didn't you?" Nick pointed at Brian.

The image on the TV shifted to time-stamped video footage of Henry setting up a ladder on set and climbing it about an hour before Griffin and Bella's interview. Only his legs were in view, but when he climbed back down, he was smiling.

"I swear, I didn't sabotage the light. I mean, I did. But not how you think. I double-checked that the filter on the light had a green base tone to mess up Griffin's tan on screen. I always do that because it makes Griffin mad, and then he gets another spray tan, which just turns him more orange."

"Henry, Henry, Henry, you expect us to believe that you didn't cut through that mounting cable after everything Gentry has put you through?" Nick asked.

"Honestly, none of us would blame you," Belinda told him sympathetically.

"It wasn't me! I swear," Henry insisted, sweat coursing down his face. "Maybe it was the lighting guy? I saw him adjusting it after me and thought maybe he saw what I'd done. I swear I didn't cut the cable. I didn't want to kill him. I just wanted him to look bad!"

Henry looked more than a little green around the gills, and the suspects sitting in front of him took notice and spread out.

"A likely story," Nick scoffed.

"Aw. My candy's gone," Griffin said, holding up the empty baggie before throwing it on the ground. "What's everybody talking about?"

"You being a pencil-dicked moron who deserves to be tortured and publicly executed so I can piss all over your corpse." Ingram Theodoric III rose from his seat in the front row, face ruddy with rage.

"Oh, hi, Gingham! Haven't seen you on the pickleball court in a while," Griffin said cheerily.

"It's Ingram and you know it, you trust-fund fungi!" Ingram started toward Griffin, which meant he was actually starting toward Riley and Josie since they were standing between him and the man who had stolen his girlfriend.

Nick jumped off the coffee table and put himself in Ingram's path. "And there's the man of the hour. Mr. Ingram Theodoric the Third, everyone."

"I thought I was the man of the hour?" Griffin complained.

Josie turned and shoved her hands into the news anchor's hair. She ruffled them back and forth. "Go fix your hair, you dumb little idiot."

The messy-haired Griffin headed toward the powder room down the hall.

"Step aside and let me finish this," Ingram snarled.

"Looks like the boss caught his killer," Josie mused.

But Riley frowned as Nick slapped a hand to Ingram's chest. Something didn't feel right.

"I'd love to, man. But you see, I can't. Because I was hired by this tangerine pain in my ass to find out who is trying to kill him. And if I let you get your gin-soaked hands on him, I won't get paid," Nick said.

Twin veins in Ingram's neck pulsed dangerously. "Fine! Then I'll go through you."

Riley heard a faint thump upstairs, but no one else seemed to take note. They were all watching Nick and Ingram's standoff.

"Let's talk about why you've been at the top of the list from day one," Nick said.

Riley's nose twitched, and she surrendered to the vision, willing the chaos around her to disappear.

The clouds enveloped her in warm blues and pinks before breaking open before her.

"*Did Griffin get taller?*" A bodiless voice echoed around her.

There was something flying toward her. A thin silver object rotating end over end. The light from Cotton Candy World caught it and glinted off the razor-sharp tip.

"*He looks taller,*" another voice noted, floating through the ether.

The object was still coming at her in slow motion. Riley put her hand up and caught it.

It was a knife. But not just any knife.

She snapped out of the spirit world. "Wait! Griffin, stop!" He turned around, hands in his hair.

"Now what? I need to fix my award-winning hair."

"You said the first threat was stabbed into your pillow in your bedroom, right?" Riley asked.

"That's right. It was very scary because that pillowcase had my face screen-printed on it."

"What kind of knife was it?"

"Where are you going with this, Riley?" Josie asked out of the corner of her mouth.

"I don't know. One of those surgical knives doctors use," Griffin said.

"A scalpel?" Riley asked.

"You're stepping on my big reveal, Thorn," Nick warned.

"It wasn't Ingram," she said. "I mean, I know it looks like it should be him since he's a drunk, and he stole his ex's dogs, and he shoots antique rifles at his neighbors and is generally a scary human being."

"I'll show you scary after I'm done with Gentry…and this guy," Ingram snarled, gesturing toward Nick.

"Talk to my girlfriend like that again, and I'll remove your face and give you a colonoscopy with it," Nick warned.

Riley ignored them. "Griffin, when you were on medical leave, was it from the accident at the airport, or was it because you had some kind of plastic surgery?"

"Aw, man," Nick grumbled.

"Plastic surgery?" Griffin's laugh was laced with anxiety. "I would never. I was born handsome. I'll have you know I would have won Cutest Baby in Dauphin County if it weren't for the Kraker twins." With another nervous giggle, he backed toward the powder room door.

"Griffin," Riley began.

"Gentry," Nick said at the same time.

"Bye!" Griffin said and slammed the door. They all heard the snick of the lock.

"I'm going to destroy Griffin Gentry," Ingram growled.

"Not if I get to him first," a new voice from the back of the room announced.

"Now you can gasp, people," Nick said as he edged his way between Riley, Josie, and the newcomer holding the gun.

34

"D r. Dilbert, I presume," Nick said after the gasps and screams had died down.

The man was sporting a dark tan and had distinguished gray hair swept back from his face. He was dressed in black joggers and a fitted long-sleeve shirt that accented lean muscle. He had accessorized with a Kimber Stainless LW pointed at Nick and Ingram.

It wasn't ideal, but it was better than it being pointed at most of the other reasonably innocent people in the room, Nick thought.

"Get in line, buddy. I think I've earned the right to murder the world's smallest colossal prick," Ingram said, drawing the newcomer's attention.

Riley eased up behind Nick. "Hey, quick question. Is this part of your plan?"

"Eh, not exactly. I think we're just going to have to roll with it."

"Should we start panicking?" she wondered.

"Not yet," he assured her.

"I'm bored. Can I start throwing knives?" Josie asked.

"Maybe. Gimme a minute," Nick said before turning his

attention back to the new guy. "You look pretty good without fake facial hair."

Riley snapped her fingers in excitement. "You're Stick Figure Guy!"

"A.k.a. Dr. Byron Dilbert, missing and presumed dead New York plastic surgeon to the mob," Nick announced, giving his girlfriend a smug half smile.

The gunman scoffed at him. "You're not actually humble-bragging about seeing through my disguises when I'm the one who got the drop on you, are you?"

"You'd be amazed what I can brag about," Nick offered.

"I can assure you, your time to boast is ticking down. Once I'm done disposing of Mr. Gentry, it's your turn, Mr. Santiago."

A fresh round of whimpers and murmurs went around the room.

Chupacabra half rose from her chair, hand raised. "Before you start murdering people, I gotta ask. What do you bench?"

"Three reps at two hundred twenty-five pounds, but most of my workouts are agility. I compete in a parkour league on the weekends," Byron said modestly. "It's how I was able to scale the wall and climb in through a second-floor window."

"Well, you look great," Chupacabra said, giving him a thumbs-up. "Also please don't kill me. I have a big title fight this weekend."

"And we have babies at home," Tyra added, pointing between her and her wife.

"And I have a very high-maintenance new jewelry client who could single-handedly save the business Griffin Gentry almost bankrupted," Wilfred said, peeking out from behind Chupacabra's broad shoulders.

Ingram drew himself up to his full height. "You're certainly not murdering me. I'm very rich and important."

"You sound just like Griffin," Josie pointed out.

"Relax. I'm only here to kill Misters Gentry and Santiago… and anyone else who gets in my way," the not-so-good doctor explained. "Now, if one of you would be so kind as to direct me to the former."

"You know, I always get former and latter confused," Nick said, stalling for time. *Take my gun*, he shouted in his head, praying his psychic girlfriend was listening. Immediately, he felt her hands at the small of his back. *You're so hot*, he added.

She gave him a warning pinch on the ass.

"This is ridiculous. I'm putting an end to all our misery," Ingram announced. "You'll find Gentry in the—"

Nick swung hard, landing a perfectly placed jab to Ingram's jaw. The man crumpled to the floor. Kiki started a slow clap that no one else was brave enough to follow.

The gun swung back to Nick. "Now that wasn't very nice," complained the doctor.

"Trust me, you would have ended up doing it and messing up those nice surgeon hands of yours," he said.

"So, Nicky," Brian called from the back of the room. "Maybe now's a good time to officially introduce us to your friend?"

"Great idea, Bri. Ladies and gentlemen, meet our wannabe murderer, the late Dr. Byron Dilbert." Nick snapped his fingers and pointed to the screen, where a news article with a large photo of the man in question appeared.

"A slide deck? Are you serious? You promised us justice, not a second chance to sit through junior high," Kiki complained.

Nick ignored the murmured agreement. "Dr. Dilbert had quite the career as the Buffalo-based cosmetic surgeon for the mob. Until he messed up Jimmy the Nose's tummy tuck."

"That's definitely not good," Betty whispered to Tyra.

"I warned him there was a chance of blood clots if he kept smoking after the surgery. But mobsters never listen," Byron complained.

"They never do," Nick agreed. "You disappeared shortly thereafter—rumor has it a butt load of mob money went missing around the same time—and everyone assumed your employers had put you in cement shoes." He pointed to the TV where an obituary for the doctor appeared.

"They hardly ever do that anymore. Most of them own crematoriums. It's more convenient and lucrative," Byron explained.

"Interesting," Claudia mused. "I don't suppose you'd have time to sit down with me for an exclusive interview after you're done shooting Griffin?"

"Please hold your interview requests for the end," Nick said, turning around to face his audience.

Riley had the gun hidden behind her back and looked more than a little nervous. Josie was holding two blades, one in each hand, and grinning. He gave them a reassuring wink, then nodded at Brian in the corner.

"But you were *ready to run* and took advantage of an *open door*," he continued pointedly as if he were addressing a class. "So you faked your own death and ran off to South America, where you eventually got bored drinking banana daiquiris on the beach and decided to get back in business under the assumed identity. Thanks to the stolen mob start-up fund, Dr. Dil quickly became one of Colombia's top private cosmetic surgeons."

The slide on the TV dissolved. Dr. Dil's website homepage spiraled onto the screen, showcasing beautiful smiling people with thin thighs and large breasts.

Brian inched his wheelchair closer to the patio doors. The other still-conscious former suspects exchanged nervous glances.

"It was a good gig," Nick continued. "You were making more money than ever, enough to buy yourself a private plane. You had a mansion on the beach and two Ferraris. You'd even devised a way to ensure that every single one of your clients paid."

"Yes, well, you'd be amazed to know just how often the hedge fund manager from Boca is going to try to fly home and stick you with the bill for his liposuction," Byron explained to the audience.

Nick turned back to face his quarry. "You took out life insurance policies on each of your clients with you as the beneficiary. That way, if you thought one of your newly pretty patients was *getting ready to run* out on the bill, you made sure they didn't live long enough to enjoy their fancy new body parts."

"Who can blame me? The audacity of these people. I'm an artist. And they think they can take up my time and talent and then not pay me what I'm worth?" Byron was gesturing the gun at himself now. "People like Griffin Gentry are entitled little pricks."

"Ah, but he wasn't such a 'little' prick when you were done with his calf extensions."

The crowd gasped.

"Ohhh. That explains *a lot*," Riley said.

"You had hit men on your payroll who took care of problems like Griffin Gentry for you," Nick said, gauging the distance between them.

"Hit men *and* women. I'm an equal opportunity employer of international professional killers. I would have sent my number one, Svetlana, but she was on her honeymoon."

"So you accompanied the B team to the U.S. to babysit them and then had to stand by while they killed the wrong guy and got themselves caught," Nick filled in.

Byron shrugged affably. "You know the old saying. If your best assassin is on her honeymoon and you want the job done right, you've got to do it yourself. Now, let's see about getting on with it."

"But I'm not finished yet. For future reference, in case you do get lucky and manage to escape this room, you should rent a less conspicuous getaway vehicle next time. Everyone's going to remember a shiny black Escalade leaving the scene of a crime," Nick said, pointing to the screen where a grainy traffic cam photo of the SUV cruising down Front Street appeared. Next to it was another shot, this one from a doorbell cam. It was of the same Escalade parked on Griffin's cul-de-sac.

"I'll take that into consideration next time," Byron snapped irritably. "Now tell me where Gentry is. I've got a hip bone reduction tomorrow at four and parkour club at seven."

"But I'm just getting started. You tried to take Griffin out by making it look like an accident," Nick said, stalling for time.

Byron rolled his eyes. "Life insurance tends to pay out faster with an accident than with a suspicious death."

"You disguised yourself as a crew member from the studio and sliced through the support cable on the studio light that just missed crushing Gentry." He pointed at the TV where footage showed a goateed Byron climbing the ladder on set before the interview with wire cutters in hand.

"I told you it wasn't me!" Henry said, pumping his fist into the air in a short-lived victory. Byron swung the gun at him, and the assistant hit the floor. "Sorry. I got excited for a second. Forget I'm here."

The doctor turned his attention back to Nick, and Brian used the opportunity to unlock the sliding door to the patio.

"The real criminal here is you, Mr. Santiago, and that interfering girlfriend of yours. I would have gotten away with it if it weren't for you two imbeciles bumbling into my path."

Josie leaned in and murmured, "Can someone say Scooby-Doo villain?"

"This is all your fault. My men would have solved my problem with that shove down the stairs at the gala if you hadn't gotten everyone's attention. They tried to rectify the situation by staging a road rage incident, but once again, you were there to foil my plans. The light wouldn't have missed Griffin if it not for you and your girlfriend playing tackle football on live television," Byron snarled. He pointed to the ridiculous oil painting of Griffin hanging on the wall. "You're the reason this man is still walking around and enjoying the extra inch of height I gave him."

"Hey, there's no need to rub it in," Nick said, rolling to the balls of his feet and imperceptibly beginning to lower his hands. The doctor was cracking. It was now or never. Nick just needed a small distraction…

The powder room door flew open behind Byron, and a newly moussed Griffin appeared in the doorway. "I need someone to make me a snack," Gentry announced.

Byron's eyes lit with a vengeful fire as he turned toward his quarry.

It was as good a distraction as Nick was going to get. He sprang into action, grabbing Griffin's portrait off the wall and swinging as hard as he could just as Byron raised his gun.

"Now!" Nick yelled as the portrait smashed down over Byron's head at the exact second the gun went off. A knife whistled past his head. Four more gunshots rang out, raining down chunks of drywall from the ceiling.

People screamed and bolted through the open patio door.

"Dr. Dil? What are you doing on my floor? Is it time for my follow-up already?" Griffin asked, oblivious to the chaos.

Nick dove for the doctor, who, despite the knife through his right hand and the portrait around his neck like a collar, was crawling for the exit.

Glass shattered all over the house, and Nick heard a loud *whump* that sounded a lot like the front door falling off its hinges. "Police! Nobody move!" someone shouted as eight cops, armed to the teeth, stormed into the room.

"You couldn't have come in, like, a minute earlier?" Nick complained to Weber as he wrestled the surgeon's hands behind his back.

Weber, in full tactical gear, slapped the cuffs on Byron. "We lost sight of him when he went around the side of the house. We thought we'd have him in the backyard, but the son of a bitch shimmied up a drainpipe to the second floor, and your wire kept cutting out."

"Parkour," Byron groaned into the carpet.

"I can't believe you missed my whodunit PowerPoint," Nick said, sitting back on his haunches and looking for Riley.

He spotted her in Gentry's kitchen, dumping ice into a food storage bag. She had his gun tucked into the waistband of her jeans, the bandage still on her forehead, and drywall dust mixed with sweat in her hair. He'd never seen anything more beautiful in his life. His heart kicked up another notch as he headed for her.

"Thorn."

She looked up at him, her pretty brown eyes relieved and maybe even a little amused. "Santiago."

He had so much he wanted to say to her, but all the words just got tangled up in his throat. "What's the ice for?"

"Your hand."

He looked down at his already bruising knuckles, then back at Ingram, who was still unconscious on the floor.

"Thanks," he said as she wrapped the bag in a dish towel with Griffin's face on it. "We need to talk."

"If this is about the damage to your parents' plumbing, I already called your cousin," Riley said.

He shook his head. "Not about plumbing."

"Santiago," Weber called.

"In a minute," Nick said without looking away from Riley.

"Everybody freeze! Santiago Investigations is taking over this crime scene," Mrs. Penny bellowed through her bullhorn as she tromped into the room with Gabe and Bella behind her.

"I thought you hid that from her?" Riley said as Nick hooked a finger through her belt loop and tugged her closer.

"I'll get a better hiding place. Pay attention to me."

"Oh no! Griffy! Why is that man wearing your portrait?" Bella crooned behind them.

"Marry me," Nick said to Riley.

The bag of ice fell to the floor. She looked up at him with wide-eyed shock. "I'm sorry. My ears are ringing from all the gunfire and screaming. Could you repeat that?"

"Marry me," he repeated earnestly.

"Did you get hit in the head when I shot up the ceiling?"

"I don't have head trauma, and I'm not overreacting to yet another criminal fiasco. I want you as my wife. My partner. You're it for me. And I know I should have found a better way to do this, like with champagne and flowers and maybe a fucking violin. But this is us. Messy. Complicated. Slightly injured. Standing in the middle of yet another crime scene together after saving the day. So say yes. Marry me."

She stood motionless, barely breathing, and Nick started to sweat.

Then he remembered the deal-sealer. He shoved his hand into his pocket and pulled out the ring. Riley gaped at him as if he'd just produced a mackerel from his jeans. But instead of a live fish, it was a sparkly-as-fuck cushion-cut diamond surrounded by other smaller but equally shiny diamonds.

She blew out a breath and put a hand to her heart. "That's an engagement ring, and we're broke."

"Wilfred is a big fan of mine, what with saving his business and thwarting an armed robbery," Nick explained. "Plus Penny raised our rates on this case we just solved."

"You've been busy."

"You're stalling, Thorn. Say it."

She bit her lip and looked up at him, eyes sparkling with a mixture of tears and happiness. "You managed to surprise a psychic. That's impressive."

"I had a little help from a friend," Nick said, glancing in Gabe's direction. The man was clutching a box of tissues to his massive chest and watching them from the breakfast nook with teary eyes.

"I'm telling Gabe you called him your friend."

"If you do that, my first act as your fiancé will be to call you a dirty liar. Now say it so we can run away together and start a new life under assumed identities."

"Yes."

"Yes?" he confirmed.

She nodded. "Yes, I'll marry you. I'm not sure about the running away part. But yes to the marriage thing."

Nick didn't give her a chance to say anything else or change her mind. He slid the ring onto her finger, bent her backward, and kissed the hell out of his fiancée.

Dimly, in the back of his mind, the celebratory whoops

and applause registered. But all that mattered was the woman in his arms.

———

The red tape and departmental bullshit took an unnecessarily long time, as usual.

Nick was just getting ready to tell the officer who was taking his statement in the kitchen where he could shove his notebook when Weber strolled up.

"I think we're done here. If we have any more questions, we know where to find you," Weber said.

"About damn time," Nick complained, stripping off the faulty wire he wore and slapping it into Weber's hand. Griffin and Bella were in conversation with Griffin's lawyer, Rebecca, who was drinking straight vodka and looked like she was making a list of all the people she planned to sue.

"I see she said yes," Weber said, nodding toward Riley through one of the few unbroken windows in the room. She was showing off her ring to Brian, Josie, and Gabe on the patio. Gabe looked up and gave Nick a toothy grin and a thumbs-up.

"I didn't give her a chance to come up with another answer. Now I just have to keep her busy from now until the wedding so she doesn't have time to come to her senses."

Weber gripped Nick's shoulder. "I'm happy for you. Really. Try not to fuck it up."

"Thanks." Nick's throat started to tighten again. "Oh, and thanks for showing up late and endangering the lives of a bunch of mostly innocent people."

"Fuck you," Weber said without any real heat behind the words. "I told you, if you had given me more of a heads-up, I would have had more officers on scene. And what did I say about the wire?"

"'Don't fucking move around because the wires are loose,'" they said together.

Nick smirked. "How was I supposed to know *don't move*

around much means *stop breathing and turn to stone or else the cops won't know when the bad guy slips past them*?"

"Get out of here, Nicky. Your face is annoying me."

"I'm going. Beer tomorrow?"

"Yeah. Okay."

"Hey, Henry," Nick said, spotting Griffin's assistant sitting glumly on a kitchen barstool. "Got a minute?"

———

Nick joined his team on Gentry's patio. Dusk had fallen, and someone had thought to ward off the autumn chill by starting a fire in the firepit. It looked as though the fuel for the blaze was a large stack of Griffin's signed headshots.

"Congratulations, coz," Brian said. "Dibs on planning the bachelor party."

"I am very pleased for you both," Gabe said.

Nick wrapped his arms around Riley from behind. "Thanks, guys. And thank you for helping me keep it a surprise," he said to Gabe.

"How did you manage that with a psychic girlfriend?" Josie asked.

"I just followed Gabe's advice and didn't plan anything. The spirit guides weren't going to blow the surprise if *I* didn't know I was proposing," he said with pride.

Riley snickered against him. "You know that's not how it works, right?"

"Seriously?" Nick looked at Gabe, who returned his glare with a grin.

"There is no real way to predict what messages the spirit world chooses to pass along. But it seemed like something you wanted very much, so I gave you incorrect advice."

"Remind me to ruin your life later, Undertaker."

Josie and Brian frowned. Gabe cocked his head. Riley tilted hers back to look up at him.

"You know, the Undertaker wrestler from WWE. Big tall scary guy?" Nick prompted.

Brian shook his head.

"Weak," Josie decided.

"You try coming up with dozens of size-related insults," Nick complained.

"You make it look effortless," Gabe said.

"He's being sarcastic again, isn't he?"

"Oh yeah," Riley agreed.

Nick gave her a squeeze. "Did you know?"

"Have I been having visions of happy sparkles? Yes. Did I think you were going to demand that I marry you in the middle of a crime scene at my ex-husband's house after you saved the day? No," she admitted.

Nick lifted her hand to admire the ring he'd put on it. "This was a damn good day," he said with satisfaction.

"By the way, thank you for doing this at Griffin's house and not ours," Riley said.

"It was a pain in the ass moving all the chairs, but I figured the potential property damage would make it worthwhile."

"Speaking of potential property damage..." Josie said, nodding as Griffin, Bella, and their attorney stepped outside.

"Hey, Griffin buddy. Case is closed. We'll take that check now," Nick called.

"Gosh. I don't think I have my checkbook with me," Griffin said, patting his pockets.

"I had a feeling you'd say that," Nick said. "Henry!"

Griffin's assistant appeared in the doorway. "Yes, boss? Did you want some coffee or a goat cheese omelet? Maybe I should schedule a massage for you?"

"No," Nick said with a sly grin. "I mean, maybe on the goat-cheese-omelet thing and definitely on the massage. I need you to get me on Hector's calendar at the Hershey Spa. But first I need your ex-boss's checkbook."

"I thought your name was Staff. And what do you mean ex-boss?" Griffin demanded, looking wounded.

"I'm interning for Santiago Investigations now," Henry said, whipping out a leather checkbook cover embossed with what looked like Griffin's profile. "If I'm going to work for free, I'd rather work for someone who doesn't suck."

"Hey, wait a minute," Griffin said.

"There's your checkbook and your itemized bill," Nick said, slapping a printout into the man's tiny hands.

"Well, I can't sign a check without my favorite pen—"

Henry produced a fancy-looking pen with a gold cap and lacquered body from his back pocket.

"This kid's good," Nick said to Riley.

"I don't understand," Griffin whined. "People don't make me pay for things. I *say* I'll pay for them, but then they let me not pay for them because I'm so likable."

"My client has been traumatized enough by today's happenings. He will review your baseless claims at a later date," Rebecca the lawyer said in a clipped, professional tone.

"Hold your horses," Mrs. Penny said into her bullhorn from the open doorway.

Everyone winced at the electronic screech as the eighty-year-old all but skipped toward them.

"Case is closed, right? We caught the bad guy, didn't we?" she asked Griffin.

"Well, yes. But I don't think I should have to pay for that. I'm famous."

"Are you refusing to pay the cashola owed?" Mrs. Penny demanded.

"It's not so much as a refusal as I'm just not going to do it," Griffin clarified with a winning smile.

Mrs. Penny smugly reached behind her back and pulled a stack of papers from the elastic waistband of her slacks. "I think your lawyer lady will find our engagement contract quite enlightening."

The lawyer snatched the contract away from Mrs. Penny and began a haughty skimming of the document. She only got a few paragraphs in before her expression changed. She flipped to the last page and grimaced. "What did I tell you about signing documents without me reading them first?" she demanded.

Griffin frowned in concentration. "I wanna say you told me to always do that?"

"Never. I said *never* do that."

Mrs. Penny held up a stopwatch. "Time's a tickin'."

"What are you up to, Penny?" Nick asked.

The woman smirked. "I had a feeling this weasel would try to dine and dash, so I had my creepy smart great-nephew lawyer Billy make a few changes to our standard client contract. You've got twenty-two seconds left to write that check, Gentry, or you'll be writing an even bigger one."

Rebecca cleared her throat. "It appears that you agreed to an accelerated balloon payment clause."

"What are accelerated balloon payment clowns?" Griffin squeaked.

"Once payment is requested and refused, the client has one minute to make payment for the amount due plus $10,000 for annoyance. If the client does not provide valid payment in that minute, the cost goes up by $10,000 every minute."

"Oops. Minute's up," Mrs. Penny said, holding up the stopwatch in triumph. "You owe us forty thousand smackeronis. If you don't wanna make it fifty, I'd get busy writing that check if I were you."

"Fix it, lawyer lady!" Griffin wailed.

The attorney pursed her red lips. "While I would love to be billing you for the hours and hours that would absolutely earn me that ski chalet in Lake Tahoe, this is a legally binding document that you willingly signed."

"Look at that. There's another minute. Time sure flies when you're refusing payment," Mrs. Penny announced.

With a panicked yelp, Griffin grabbed his checkbook, then stared blankly at it. "Someone tell me how to write a check!"

"How does someone so stupid survive for so long?" Nick asked.

"Pretty people are protected by the less-pretty people. It's science," Bella explained patiently.

"Question. Do we still have to be nice to them now that they're no longer clients?" Josie asked Nick.

"Hell no."

"In that case," Josie said, turning back to Bella, "I'm going to science your face if you don't get out of mine."

"Okey-dokey. Bye!" Unconcerned with being threatened, Bella waved and wandered back into the house.

"Damn, that felt good," Josie said. "I need a snack."

"I too would like a snack," Gabe admitted.

Mrs. Penny poked Nick with her cane. "Happy hour debriefing?"

"For fifty grand? You deserve happy-hour-steak-night-debriefing," he said, giving his business partner a one-armed hug.

35

R iley was happily buzzed on cocktails and steak. She had her dog's head in her lap, a gorgeous diamond ring on her finger, and some of her favorite people gathered around the dining room table with her. It was amazing the difference a few hours, a good meal, and an engagement could make in a woman's outlook.

Mrs. Penny pushed her chair back with an earsplitting screech and stood up. "Imma make a toast," she slurred, raising her glass. "To fifty Gs." The woman had mixed celebratory drinks strong enough to intoxicate an entire platoon on shore leave…or lay waste to a private investigation practice.

"Hear, hear!" Nick said, squeezing Riley's hand. "And to Mrs. Penny for being a diabolical genius and getting us paid."

"To Nick and Riley on their engagement," Gabe toasted as he listed hard into Weber.

"To me being a bridesmaid," added Lily.

"To getting older but not wiser," Fred said.

"To taking another criminal off the street," Weber said, doing his best to remain upright under Gabe's weight. Due to his recent hangover from hell, the detective had wisely decided to stick with water.

"You're so law-abiding it's annoying," Nick complained.

Mr. Willicott stood on shaky legs and raised his glass. "Anyone seen my Old Spice?"

"I don't think he knows how this toast thing works," Fred whispered at full volume.

All eyes came to Riley. She sighed and raised her glass. "To us. I won't say it was a pleasure going through the last few days with all of you, but I *will* say that it means a lot to me that you were all there to suffer with. I love you guys."

There was a chorus of "aw."

"Oh, and thank you for helping me take back some of my ex-husband's money, because that was *really* satisfying," she added.

"Woo-hoo!" Lily cheered.

"We're the coolest," Fred hooted.

"I stabbed a guy today," Josie said.

"Okay, Nicky. Story time. How did you make the connection from Griffin to some cosmetic surgeon in Colombia?" Brian demanded as he pushed his empty plate away.

"Wait. He didn't let you in on it either?" Riley asked.

Brian shook his head. "He wanted to impress you. Although I doubt getting a bunch of semi-innocent people maimed or murdered would have had the desired effect."

"That wasn't my fault. Weber was supposed to get the asshole as he was breaking in," Nick pointed out. "You think I would have invited the nice suspects if I'd thought there'd be trouble?"

"I don't know. Maybe? It depends on your mood," Josie said.

"How about you just tell us how smart you are?" Riley suggested.

"Easy," Nick said. "We knew the shooters had worked in Colombia prior to this job since they were being extradited back to face murder charges. And when I went through Griffin's shit to steal back the cuff links—"

"I should not be listening to this," Weber complained.

"I found his passport with a stamp from Colombia. That trip lined up with Chupacabra's cousin's accident at the airport and Griffin's suspicious medical leave. And why does the little shrimp leave the country?"

"To get cheaper cosmetic surgery," Riley said, shooting her handsome fiancé an approving look. He was going to get so lucky later.

"Okay. But how did you figure out it was Dr. Dil...er, Dilbert? Colombia has to have thousands of plastic surgeons," Brian pressed.

Nick smirked over his glass. "But only one that offers calf and hamstring extension surgery. Everyone kept saying the little troll looked taller. I connected the dots. And every cop in the tristate area followed the story of Dilbert's disappearance, so I recognized his headshot when I saw his website."

"I seriously can't believe that's a surgery you can get," Josie said.

"Oh, it is," Nick assured her. "And for the bargain price of $250,000, a shithead like Griffin Gentry can gain up to an inch in height."

"A quarter of a million? For an *inch*?" Weber repeated.

Mrs. Penny shook her head. "And not even on the penis. What a waste."

"How did you know the doctor would show up to finish the job himself?" Riley asked.

"I figured if we used Gentry as bait, we'd either catch another hit man who might talk or we'd get the big boss himself. Unfortunately, the cops were supposed to nab him in the yard before he started shooting the place up."

"Definitely my bad," Weber said, putting a hand over his heart. "We don't have the budget for wires that work one hundred percent of the time."

"Look at us. A coupla diabolical geniuses." Mrs. Penny gestured with her glass and sloshed liquor all over herself and the table.

"And Thorn almost stepped on my big reveal with her perfectly timed vision." Nick pressed a kiss to her temple.

Riley grimaced. "I thought I was saving you from embarrassing yourself and blaming Theodoric."

"I was trying to get a rise out of Ingram so the cops would have a reason to search him."

"Why?" Josie asked.

"A few years back, he was quietly arrested for assault with a deadly weapon and isn't allowed to own or carry any firearms," Nick said.

"Such a shame when the Harrisburg PD finds a weapon in an ankle holster on such an upstanding member of the community." Weber sounded not at all sorry. "We had to send a squad car to his house and confiscate every weapon he had."

"That is sarcasm," Gabe announced, pleased with himself.

"You're damn right it is, buddy," Nick said.

"So when are you two getting married?" Lily asked Riley. "And how many times do you plan to have sex on the honeymoon?"

"On that note, I'm leaving," Weber said, throwing his napkin on the table.

The doorbell rang, and Nick dropped his napkin on the table. "Let's go, Thorn."

"Me? I don't think I can handle another surprise."

"How many surprises didn't you like today?" he asked, drawing her to her feet and pulling her out of the room.

"Just the one with the murdery surgeon pointing a gun at the guy I'm going to marry," Riley admitted.

"This is better than a murdery surgeon," Nick promised as he led her to the foyer.

He threw open the door, and Riley's best friend barreled inside.

"You're getting married!" Jasmine threw herself at Riley and folded her into a very aggressive hug.

"I know. I FaceTimed you about thirty seconds after it happened," Riley wheezed.

"Well, I know your mom is planning a vegan celebration dinner—"

Riley groaned.

"But I wanted to give you your engagement present now," Jasmine said. She reached into her stylish tote and pulled out a folder. "This is for you from me."

Nick snatched the folder away. "Don't steal my thunder, Patel."

"Don't ask for free legal work, Santiago."

"I believe I was promised a present," Riley said.

Nick handed over the folder. "I meant what I said."

"About what? Killing Griffin now that he paid up?" she asked, pulling out the documents inside.

"About being partners."

She skimmed the papers until her eyes got too misty to see the words. "This is a partnership agreement."

"That's right, Thorn. I'm giving you half my shares in the business."

"Nick. This is…amazing. And not necessary."

"I want us to be all in together on everything. Marriage, business, keeping Mrs. Penny out of prison," he said earnestly.

"That's very sweet of you, but—"

"No *but*s. If I had done this from the start, we wouldn't have been broke enough to take the job from Gentry. I'm not making that mistake again. So we're both in this with equal say. If you see me being a dumbass in our personal lives or our business lives, you get to call me on it."

"Really?" Riley asked, hugging the papers to her chest.

"Oh. It's you," Weber said, sauntering into the foyer.

Jasmine flipped her hair over her shoulder. "Ugh. Why are you in front of me again?"

"Why are all my friends so mean to each other?" Riley asked.

"I know you're my fiancée and all, but ever think that maybe you're the common denominator?" Nick suggested to her.

"I was the one invited to dinner. You're the party crasher," Weber said to Jasmine.

"I was invited, Detective Dick. But I was too busy drawing up these legal documents for my friends here," Jasmine countered. "They probably only invited you out of pity."

"Why don't you two take your foreplay outside?" Nick suggested, ushering Jasmine and Weber toward the door. "I need to call a partners meeting and then have sex with my fiancée."

"I'll come by tomorrow after work with all the bridal magazines I can find. We can start comparing venues and dress shops," Jasmine said to Riley over Nick's shoulder.

"I love you," Riley called after her.

"Congratulations again, you guys," Weber said before following Jasmine out onto the porch.

"I can't tell if they're going to fight to the death or start making out," Riley said.

Mrs. Penny jogged into the foyer, her fresh drink splattering all over the marble floor. "Somebody say *partners meeting*?"

"Yeah. Penny, meet our new partner," Nick said, gesturing toward Riley.

Mrs. Penny gave a brisk nod and took a slurp of her drink. "'Bout time you brought on someone responsible."

"First order of business. We're not getting $50,000 from Gentry."

Mrs. Penny took another deliberate sip, then sprayed a fine mist of liquor into Nick's face. "What? Why? You didn't have enough time to gamble it away yet."

He used the hem of his T-shirt to mop his face. "I didn't gamble it away. I shared it. Or I plan to if my partners are open to it. I figured we weren't the only ones inconvenienced by his existence. So Peabody the jeweler, Tyra and Betty, and Chupacabra's cousin are all getting a piece of the action. And maybe, if I'm feeling generous, I'll buy a wire that actually works and donate it to the police department."

"That's very sweet of you," Riley said. The man was definitely getting laid tonight.

Mrs. Penny rolled her eyes. "All right. Fine. But don't make it a habit of thinking with your squishy feelings. We're running a business here, not a charity foundation."

"Agreed," Nick said.

"It almost makes me not want to give you your engagement present," she grumbled.

"Another present? I like this engagement thing," Riley said.

Mrs. Penny reached behind her and produced a remote control from her pants. "Here," she said, handing it to Nick.

"What's this?"

"It's a remote, dummy. It's for the new TV I had installed in your room. I also cornered that tall lesbian suspect who works for the contractor. She's sending a crew out tomorrow to give us a quote on the roof next door. They only employ women, so Lily won't be as aggressive with her sexual harassment."

Nick launched himself at the elderly woman and wrapped her in a bear hug. "I'm sorry for every mean thing I've ever said about you."

Mrs. Penny reluctantly patted him on the back. "No, you're not."

"I'm really not. But this is nice," he whispered into her purple hair.

"You're weirding me out, and I need another drink." Mrs. Penny gave Riley a high five and left them alone.

Riley glanced at the remote in Nick's hand. "You're going to—"

"Sanitize this? Absolutely." He drew her in.

She looped her arms around his neck. "Good. Maybe we should go upstairs and—"

The doorbell rang again.

On several four-letter words, Nick yanked it open. "I thought I told you two to—"

But it wasn't Weber and Jasmine. It was Bella Goodshine and her dog, dressed in coordinating sweats. Burt bounded over and eagerly sniffed his canine friend.

"If you've come to beg for your boyfriend's money back, no givesies backsies," Nick warned.

"Actually, I got you two an engagement present," Bella said, handing over a small envelope.

"How did you know we were getting engaged?" Riley asked.

Bella let out a silvery peal of laughter that Riley found charming despite her best efforts. "I've been proposed to eight times. Believe me, I know when a man is thinking about popping the question."

"Well, uh, thank you," Riley said awkwardly.

"Don't be silly, Riley. It's the least I can do for encouraging your husband to cheat on you with me!"

Nick leaned in. "I say this with absolute sincerity. You and Griffin are perfect together."

"Aw! Thank you! That's so sweet of you to say."

"Hang on. You called me Riley," Riley said, blinking in surprise.

Bella batted her fringe of lashes. "That's your name, isn't it, silly?"

"It is. But you don't ever recognize me."

"That was before that nice doctor housekeeper lady adjusted my medication dose."

"Is she talking about my mother?" Nick wondered.

"Now I can have no wrinkles *and* recognize female faces. Anyway, La La and I have to go. Somebody needs her special wecial hair treatment, doesn't she?" she crooned to the dog. With a toss of glorious blond locks and a wave of La La's paw, Bella departed.

"I have no idea which one of them was getting the special wecial hair treatment," Nick confessed.

"I'm telling your mom the weather girl still thinks she's a housekeeper," Riley said, opening the envelope. "Wow. It's a gift card to the Hershey Spa."

Nick snatched it out of her hands. "I'm calling Hector! We're gonna get massages and pedicures and plan the coolest wedding ever while we wear those weird bathrobes and drink hot cocoa by the gallon."

"That sounds…blissfully normal," Riley admitted.

"Trust me, Thorn. Our days of gunfights and bad guys are behind us. From here on out, it's nothing but run-of-the-mill cases and high-paying, low-stakes clients," Nick insisted, slinging an arm around her shoulders and guiding her toward the stairs.

Riley's nose twitched definitively, and she tensed. There was something waiting for her in those pastel clouds.

"I'm gonna pretend I didn't see that," Nick said.

"I'm good with pretending I didn't feel it. Besides, you know what today is, don't you?" she asked.

"Monday?"

"Naked Tuesday Eve."

If you love Lucy Score's Riley Thorn series, you'll be over the moon for Blue Moon Bend. Read on for an excerpt from Lucy's

NO MORE SECRETS

1

Summer Lentz hefted her suitcase and laptop bag into the trunk of her snappy little rental car. She paused to catch her breath, grateful for the parking space she had snagged just half a block down from her Murray Hill building.

Every once in a while, her body inconveniently reminded her that recovery was a very long journey.

She took a deep breath of late spring air and resisted the urge to walk back to her apartment to verify that the door that she checked twice before leaving was indeed locked and the stove—that she never used—was off.

It was a week upstate. She'd be back to civilization before she knew it. Besides, maybe a few days without the bustle of Manhattan would allow her to recharge her batteries. Or—she grimaced at the thought—she'd completely disappear from the consciousness of everyone at work. At *Indulgence*, if you weren't there eleven hours a day, you weren't there. The sleek Midtown West headquarters were as glossy as the pages of its magazine. And more cutthroat than a season of reality TV.

Summer had carved out a place for herself at *Indulgence* without selling too many pieces of her soul. Nine months into her promotion to associate editor, things were finally falling into place.

She had upgraded her shoebox studio to a slightly roomier one-bedroom. Her wardrobe had seen a gradual and tasteful edit. The blog that she was so proud of had grown exponentially. On the outside, her social life was a whirlwind of parties, openings, and meetups. Though at times, it was hard to tell where work stopped and life began.

If she could hold herself on this trajectory without any other major crises, she could almost taste a senior editor position in her future.

The phone in her cream-colored Dooney & Bourke signaled an incoming call.

Summer slid behind the wheel and swiped to answer.

"Are you farm-bound yet?" The deep, smooth voice of her best friend warmed her ear.

"Well, if it isn't the famous Nikolai Vulkov. What's the Wolf doing today?"

Niko was second-generation American, but after too much vodka, one could begin to detect the slightest hint of Russia in his bedroom tone. He had a reputation as both a talented photographer and a ladies' man, hence the nickname.

When Summer hadn't instantly fallen under the Wolf's spell at the magazine, they had become fast friends instead.

"You sound out of breath. Are you pushing yourself too hard?"

Summer wrinkled her nose. "What are you, my dad?"

"Do not spend this assignment hauling hay bales and tipping cows. You understand me?" he warned.

"Is tipping cows even a thing? I think that's an urban myth."

"Way to dance around the issue, brat."

"I promise to take care of myself. I'll probably be in bed every night by eight." She flipped the sun visor down to check her eye makeup. "I doubt there's any midnight martini special in town."

"Well, while you're there, text me a couple of pics of Old MacDonald and his organic farm so I can start planning for the shoot in July."

"Will do. And while I'm gone, try not to fall desperately in love with any models."

"I can't promise anything. So don't stay away too long. I may need you to vet a Brazilian beauty."

"Never change, Niko," Summer sighed. "I'll see you in a week."

She hung up and plugged the address into the GPS. Just three hours to Blue Moon Bend.

Author's Note

Dear Reader,

I had the best time writing this book. I had just come off ten months spent writing books 2 and 3 in the Knockemout series, so to be able to spend time with Riley, Nick, Burt, and Mrs. Penny again was like a hilarious vacation for my writer brain.

I hope you found something on the page to make you laugh out loud! You know what they say, romantic comedies about psychics and grumpy PIs are the best medicine...or something along those lines.

If you're looking for more laughs while you wait for the next Riley Thorn book, check out my Blue Moon series. Or just subscribe to my newsletter so you can read about my hot-mess real-life antics. I'll see you on the page...or the screen...or in your earhole if you're an audiobook listener.

Xoxo,
Lucy

Acknowledgments

First and foremost, to my readers for being the loveliest, most supportive mob of love muffins in the world.

The Thin Man books and movies for providing entertainment and inspiration.

Flavia and Meire from Bookcase Literary Agency for agenting your butt off, playing tour guide, and not letting me get lost in Europe.

The Bloom Books team for selling the heck out of my paperbacks and keeping me out of trouble (mostly) on tour. Shout-outs to Pam for mom-ing me when I got sick on tour and Katie for feeding me all the chicken nuggets.

LEO PR and Attorney Eric for preventing me from saying or doing too many well-intentioned but completely dumb things.

Jess for her eagle eyeballs on these pages.

Taylor Swift and The Eras Tour for being absolutely amazing (and for bringing back friendship bracelets).

Mr. Lucy, the man, the myth, the legend.

Team Lucy, especially Joyce, Tammy, and Dan for being so good at everything I'm not!

About the Author

Lucy Score is a #1 *New York Times, USA Today,* and *Wall Street Journal* bestselling author. She grew up in a literary family who insisted that the dinner table was for reading and earned a degree in journalism. She writes full-time from the Pennsylvania home she and Mr. Lucy share with their obnoxious cat, Cleo. When not spending hours crafting heartbreaker heroes and kick-ass heroines, Lucy can be found on the couch, in the kitchen, or at the gym. She hopes to someday write from a sailboat, ocean-front condo, or tropical island with reliable Wi-Fi.

Sign up for her newsletter by scanning the QR code below and stay up on all the latest Lucy book news. You can also follow her here:

Website: lucyscore.net
Facebook: lucyscorewrites
Instagram: scorelucy
TikTok: @lucyferscore
Binge Books: bingebooks.com/author/lucy_score
Readers Group: facebook.com/groups/BingeReaders Anonymous
Newsletter signup: